Praise for *Seven Lies*

"A dark, gripping story with one of the most interesting and compelling narrators I've ever encountered. Highly recommended!"
—Shari Lapena, *New York Times* bestselling author
of *The Couple Next Door*

"An electrifying psychological thriller. . . . Even readers who suspect where the story is heading should brace themselves for a wild and surprising ride. Kay . . . is off to an impressive start."
—*Publishers Weekly* (starred review)

"Scalpel-sharp writing and a killer concept—dark, clever, compelling, and utterly assured."
—Lucy Foley, *New York Times* bestselling author
of *The Guest List*, a Reese's Book Club pick

"*Seven Lies* is a relentless, chilling story of what happens when friendship becomes obsession. Keep the lights on—you'll be turning pages deep into the night with this one."
—Harlan Coben, #1 *New York Times* bestselling author of *Run Away*

"Wicked entertainment." —*Kirkus Reviews*

"Shockingly intimate and scarily insidious. *Seven Lies* explores the explosive truths behind obsession, love, and a seemingly perfect friendship." —Lisa Gardner, #1 *New York Times* bestselling author
of *Before She Disappeared*

"A tense nerve-shredder that wrong-footed me again and again, leaving the hairs on the back of my neck standing up."
—Val McDermid, international bestselling author of *Still Life*

"I loved it from the first page: spellbinding, urgent, creepy, and impossible to put down. *Seven Lies* is a hugely satisfying novel of deeply disturbed psychological suspense."
—Chris Pavone, *New York Times* bestselling author
of *The Paris Diversion*

"*Seven Lies* is brilliant."
—Clare Mackintosh, *New York Times* bestselling author
of *The Donor*

"Dark, vivid, and engrossing. You won't want to put this one down!"
—Cara Hunter, bestselling author of *The Whole Truth*

PENGUIN BOOKS

SEVEN LIES

Elizabeth Kay works in the publishing industry under a different name. She lives in London and has a first-class degree in English literature.

Seven Lies

Elizabeth Kay

PENGUIN BOOKS

PENGUIN BOOKS

An imprint of Penguin Random House LLC
penguinrandomhouse.com

First published in Great Britain by Sphere, an imprint of Little,
Brown Book Group Limited, a division of Hachette UK Limited, 2020
First published in the United States of America by Pamela Dorman Books/Viking,
an imprint of Penguin Random House LLC, 2020
Published in Penguin Books 2021

A Pamela Dorman/Penguin Book

ISBN 9781984879738 (paperback)

THE LIBRARY OF CONGRESS HAS CATALOGED THE HARDCOVER EDITION AS FOLLOWS:
Names: Kay, Elizabeth (Novelist), author.
Title: Seven lies / Elizabeth Kay.
Description: [New York] : Pamela Dorman Books/Viking, [2020]
Identifiers: LCCN 2019047737 (print) | LCCN 2019047738 (ebook) |
ISBN 9781984879714 (hardcover) | ISBN 9781984879721 (ebook)
Subjects: GSAFD: Suspense fiction.
Classification: LCC PR6111.A898 S48 2020 (print) |
LCC PR6111.A898 (ebook) | DDC 823/.92—dc23
LC record available at https://lccn.loc.gov/2019047737
LC ebook record available at https://lccn.loc.gov/2019047738

Printed in the United States of America
1st Printing

Designed by Cassandra Garruzzo

For Anne and Bob Goudsmit
or as I have always known them,
Mum and Dad

CONTENTS

Seven Lies

The
First Lie

Chapter One

And that's how I won her heart," he said, smiling. He leaned back in his chair, lifting his hands behind his head, expanding his chest. He was always so smug.

He looked at me, and then at the idiot sitting beside me, and then turned back again to me. He was waiting for us to respond. He wanted to see the smiles stretch across our faces, to feel our admiration, our awe.

I hated him. I hated him in an all-encompassing, burning, biblical way. I hated that he repeated this story every time I came to dinner, every Friday evening. It didn't matter who I brought with me. It didn't matter which degenerate I was dating at the time.

He always told them this story.

Because this story, you see, was his ultimate trophy. For a man like Charles—successful, wealthy, charming—a beautiful, bright, sparkling woman like Marnie was the final medal in his collection. And because he was fueled by the respect and admiration of others, and perhaps because he received neither from me, he wrenched them instead from his other guests.

What I wanted to say in response, and what I never said, was that Marnie's heart was never his to win. A heart, if we're being honest, which I finally am, can never be won. It can only be given, only received. You cannot persuade, entice, change, still, steal, steel, take a heart. And you certainly cannot win a heart.

"Cream?" Marnie asked.

She was standing beside the dining table holding a white ceramic jug. Her hair was pinned neatly at the top of her neck, loose curls around her cheeks, and her necklace was twisted, the clasp beside the pendant, hanging together against her breastbone.

I shook my head. "No, thanks," I said.

"Not you," she replied, and she smiled. "I know not you."

I want to tell you something now, before we begin. Marnie Gregory is the most impressive, inspiring, astonishing woman I know. She has been my best friend for more than eighteen years—our relationship is legally an adult; able to drink, marry, gamble—ever since we met at secondary school.

It was our first day and we were queuing in a long, thin corridor, a line of eleven-year-olds worming their way toward a table at the other end of the hall. There were groups huddled at intervals, like mice in a snake, bulging from the orderly, single-file line.

I was anxious, aware that I knew no one, psychologically preparing myself for being alone and lonely for the best part of a decade. I stared at those groups and tried to convince myself that I didn't want to be part of one anyway.

I stepped forward too fast, too far, and stood on the heel of the girl in front. She spun around. I panicked; I was sure that I was about to be humiliated, shouted at, belittled in front of my peers. But that fear dissipated the moment I saw her. It sounds ridiculous, I know, but Marnie Gregory is like the sun. I thought it then; I often think it now. Her skin is shockingly fair, a porcelain cream tempered only occasionally—after exercise, for example, or when she is overwhelmingly content—by rosy pink cheeks. Her hair is a deep auburn, twisted into spirals of red and gold, and her eyes are a pale, near-white blue.

"Sorry," I said, stepping back and looking down at my shiny new shoes.

"My name's Marnie," she said. "What's yours?"

That first encounter is symbolic of our entire relationship. Marnie has an openness, a tone that invites warmth and love. She is unassumingly confident, unafraid and unaware of any presumptions you might bring to the conversation. Whereas I am intensely aware. I am afraid of any potential animosity and am always waiting for what I know will come eventually. I am always waiting to be ridiculed. Then, I feared judgment for the pimples across my forehead, my mousy hair, my too-big uniform. Now, my tone of voice, the way it shakes, my clothing, comfortable and rarely flattering, my hair, my trainers, my chewed fingernails.

She is light where I am dark.

I knew it then. Now you'll know it, too.

"Name?" barked the blue-bloused teacher standing behind a desk at the front of the line.

"Marnie Gregory," she said, so firm and self-assured.

"E . . . F . . . G . . . Gregory. Marnie. You're in that classroom there, the one with the 'C' on the door. And you," she continued. "Who are you?"

"Jane," I replied.

The teacher looked up from the sheet of paper in front of her and rolled her eyes.

"Oh," I said. "Sorry. It's Baxter. Jane Baxter."

She consulted her list. "With her. Over there. Door with the 'C.'"

Some might argue that it was a friendship of convenience and that I would have accepted any offer of kindness, of affection, of love. And maybe that's true. In which case, I might counter that we were destined to be together, that our friendship was inked in the stars, because further down our path she'd need me, too.

That sounds like nonsense, I know. It probably is. But sometimes I could swear to it.

Yes, please," said Stanley. "I'll have some cream."

Stanley was two years my junior and a lawyer with a number of degrees. He had white blond hair that flopped over his eyes and he grinned constantly, often for no discernible reason. He could speak to women, unlike most of his peers: the result, I guess, of a childhood surrounded by sisters. But he was fundamentally dull.

Unsurprisingly, Charles seemed to be enjoying his company. Which made me dislike Stanley even more.

Marnie passed the jug across the table, pressing her blouse to her stomach. She didn't want the fabric—silk, I think—to skate the top of the fruit bowl.

"Anything else?" she asked, looking at Stanley, and then at me, and then to Charles. He was wearing a blue-and-white-striped shirt and he'd undone the top buttons so that a triangle of dark hairs sprouted from between the fringes of the fabric. Her eyes hovered there for a moment. He shook his head and his tie—undone and loose around his neck— slipped farther to the left.

"Perfect," she said, sitting down and picking up her dessert spoon.

The conversation was—as always—dominated by Charles. Stanley could keep up, interjecting successes of his own wherever possible, but I was bored and I think that Marnie was, too. We were both leaning back into our chairs, sipping the last of our wine and absorbed instead in the imagined conversations playing out within our own minds.

At half past ten, Marnie stood, as she always did at half past ten, and said, "Right."

"Right," I repeated. I stood, too.

She lifted our four bowls from the table and stacked them in the curve of her left arm. A small bead of pink juice from a raspberry still sitting in one of the dishes bled into the white of her shirt. I picked up the now empty fruit bowl—she'd made it herself at a pottery class a few years earlier—and the jug of cream and followed her into the kitchen at the back of the flat.

This flat—their flat—was a testament to their relationship. Charles had paid the hefty deposit, as Charles paid for most things, but at Marnie's insistence. She had known instantly that the flat was meant for them, and it won't surprise you to know that persuasion has always come very naturally to Marnie.

When they moved in, it was little more than a hovel: small, dark, filthy, damp, spread over two floors and desperately unloved. But Marnie has always been a visionary; she sees things where others cannot. She finds hope in the darkest of places—laughably, in me—and trusts herself to deliver something exceptional. I have always envied that self-confidence. It comes, for Marnie, from a place of stubbornness. She has no fear of failure, not because she has never failed, but because failure has only ever been a detour, a small diversion, on a journey that has ultimately led to success.

She worked tirelessly—evenings, weekends, using all of her annual leave—to build something beautiful. With her small hands, she tore wallpaper, sanded doors, painted cupboards, smoothed carpet, laid floorboards, sewed blinds: everything. Until these rooms emitted the same warmth that she does; a quiet confidence, a recognizable yet indefinable sense of home.

Marnie loaded the bowls into the dishwasher, leaving a space between each.

"They clean better this way," she said.

"I know," I replied, because she said the same thing every week, because I made the same noise—a tiny grunt—every week, because it seemed such a waste of water to me.

"Things are going well with Charles," she said.

A prickle climbed my spine, pulling me straight, forcing air into my lungs.

We had only talked about their relationship once before then and it had been a conversation fraught with the long, twisted history of a very old friendship. Ever since, we had spoken only in practical terms: their plans for the weekend; the house they might someday buy far beyond the outer limits of London; his mother riddled with cancer, living in Scotland and dying a very slow, painful, lonely death.

We had not, for example, discussed the fact that they had been together for three years and that several months earlier I had found unexpectedly—and I know I shouldn't have been looking—a diamond engagement ring hidden in the depths of Charles's bedside table. Nor had we discussed the fact that, even without that ring, they were careering toward a permanent commitment that would bind them eternally, in a way that—even after almost twenty years—Marnie and I had never been bound.

We had not discussed the fact that I hated him.

"Yes," I replied, because I was afraid that a full sentence, perhaps even a two-syllable word, would send our friendship hurtling into chaos.

"Don't you think?" she said. "Don't you think that things are looking good for us?"

I nodded and poured the remaining cream from the jug back into its plastic supermarket container.

"You think we're right for each other, don't you?" she asked.

I opened the fridge door and hid behind it, slowly—very slowly— returning the cream to the top shelf.

"Jane?" she asked.

"Yes," I replied. "I do."

That was the first lie I told Marnie.

I wonder now—most days, in fact—if I hadn't told that first lie, would I have told the others? I like to tell myself that the first lie was the least significant of them all. But that, ironically, is a lie. If I had been honest that Friday evening, everything might have been—would have been—different.

I want you to know this now. I thought I was doing the right thing. Old friendships are like knotted rope, worn in some parts and thick and bulbous in others. I feared that this thread of our love was too thin, too frayed, to bear the weight of my truth. Because surely the truth—that I had never hated anyone the way I hated him—would have destroyed our friendship.

If I had been honest—if I had sacrificed our love for theirs—then Charles would almost certainly still be alive.

The
Second Lie

Chapter Two

This, then, is my truth. I don't mean to sound so dramatic, but I think you deserve to know this story. I guess I think that you need to know this story. It is as much yours as it is mine.

Charles is dead, yes, but that was never my intention. In truth, it never occurred to me that he would ever be anything other than painfully, permanently present. He was one of those overpowering, dominant people: the loudest voice, the grandest gestures, taller and broader and stronger and better than anyone else in any room. You might have said that he was larger than life, which now, of course, feels rather ironic. That said, the simple fact of his being seemed evidence enough that he would always be.

For the first years of my life—and, I suppose, this is true for the first years of most lives—my family formed a framework. The big choices, those that defined my everyday—where I lived, who I spent time with, even what I called myself—were not mine at all. My parents were the puppeteers dictating the shape of my life.

Eventually, I was expected to make my own choices: what to play and with whom and where and when. My family had been everything, the only thing, until they became but the foundations from which I built an identity of my own. It was refreshing to discover that I was, in fact, my own entity and yet it was a little overwhelming, too.

But I was lucky. I found a companion.

Marnie and I soon became inseparable. We looked nothing alike but our teachers regularly called us by the other's name. Because we were never one without the other. We sat side by side in every lesson and walked between classrooms together and traveled home on the same bus at the end of the day.

I hope that one day you experience a similar friendship. You can tie yourself into a teenage love in a way that feels eternal, bonded by new experiences and a newfound sense of freedom. There is something so enchanting about a first best friend at twelve. It is intoxicating to be so needed, to crave someone so acutely, and to have that feeling of being so completely entwined. But these early bonds are unsustainable. And someday you will choose to extricate yourself from this friendship in the pursuit, instead, of lovers. You will extract yourself limb by limb, bone by bone, memory from memory, until you can exist independently, until you are again one person where once you were two.

We were still two, Marnie and me, when—after university—we moved into the flat in Vauxhall. It was modern, in a new build erected less than a decade earlier, surrounded by other similar buildings with other similar flats, all off corridors with blue carpet and behind identical pine doors. It had plastic wood-effect flooring, sleek white kitchen units, and soulless magnolia walls. There were spotlights in every room—the bedrooms, too—and peach tiles on the bathroom floor. It felt cold somehow, wintry, and yet it was always too warm. But it was our haven from the fiercely bright lights and the never-ending noise of a cosmopolitan city in which neither of us, at that time, felt entirely comfortable.

Things were different then. We discussed our diaries over cereal and delegated responsibilities for the day: a new bottle of shampoo, batteries for the remote, something for dinner. We walked side by side to the tube station. We boarded the same carriage. It would have made sense for me to board at the other end, so that my exit was in front of me when I disembarked, but our lives were so intricately woven that traveling separately would have seemed ludicrous.

We rushed home from work to cement the gaps that had opened over the course of a single day. We boiled the kettle and turned on the oven and laughed at ridiculous colleagues and sobbed over terrible meetings. We were intimate, cohabiting in a way that bonded us: shared pints of milk in the fridge, shoes in a pile behind the front door, books mingled on shelves, framed photographs perching on windowsills. We were so thoroughly embedded in each other's lives that a crack, however small, seemed impossible.

We had little money and little time and yet every few weeks we ventured out to a new corner of this new world, to visit a restaurant or a bar and to explore a new part of this new city. Marnie was freelancing alongside her job and was always looking for something to write about. She dreamed about being the first to recognize a restaurant that was later granted a Michelin star. She had worked in the marketing team for a chain of pubs since graduating but, just a few months in, had decided that she wanted to do something more creative, more rewarding, more intimate, too. She had started writing a blog about food: collating information and restaurant reviews and eventually writing her own recipes as well.

That was the beginning of it, the most exciting part probably. Soon, her audience began to expand rapidly. At the request of her online followers, she started recording her own cookery videos. She accepted sponsorship from a high-end kitchenware company, who filled our flat with cast-iron pans and pastel ramekins and more utensils than two people could ever possibly need. She was offered a regular column in a newspaper. But at first it was just us, flicking through the free maga-zines to find the latest new places to visit.

I think you can tell a lot about a relationship by the way two people dine together in public. Marnie and I loved to watch as couples entered hand in hand, groups of men in tailored suits grew louder and louder, expanding to fill the available space, the illicit affair, the anniversary meal, the very first date. We liked to read the room, to guess the pasts and predict the futures of the other patrons, telling stories of their lives that we hoped might be true.

If you had been one of those other customers, sitting at one of those other tables, playing that same game and watching us instead, you would have seen two young women, one tall and fair, one shrunken and dark, entirely comfortable in each other's company. I think you might have known that we enjoyed a friendship with strong branches and coiled roots. You would have seen Marnie—without thinking, without asking, without needing to—reach over to take the tomatoes from my plate. You might have seen me, in response, take the slithers of pickle or slices of cucumber from hers.

But Marnie and I haven't dined alone in three years, not since she moved in with Charles. We are never so at ease now as we were back then. Our worlds are no longer entwined. I am now an intermittent guest in the story of her life. Our friendship is no longer its own in-dependent thing, but a skin tag, a protrusion that subsists within an-other love.

I did not think then—and I do not think now—that Marnie and Charles had a love greater than ours. And yet I understood implicitly that their love—a romantic love—would and must subsume ours. Even though our love—one that flourished strolling shoulder to shoulder down school corridors, on buses to day-trip destinations, on sleepovers—seemed so much more deserving of a lifetime together.

Every Friday, at around eleven in the evening when I left their flat, I found myself saying goodbye to a love that had shaped me, defined me, decided me. It always felt so cruel to be both within it and without it all at once.

And a truth that I knew then—and one that I still cannot fully comprehend—is that, crueler still, it was a situation entirely of my own making. I am wholly responsible for that first detached limb, for that first broken bone, for that first forgotten memory.

Chapter Three

Three months after I met Jonathan, I moved to live with him in his maisonette in Islington. We were young, yes, but we were completely, utterly, entirely in love. It was unexpectedly easy, in a way that something new rarely is. It was lively and exciting, in a way that my simple life rarely was. I had loved living with Marnie—I had been happy—and yet eventually I began to crave something more, something other.

I had spent most of my childhood in a home that seemed loving from the outside but consistently failed to deliver on that promise. My parents were twenty-five years married before they divorced. But they should have separated much sooner, because their squabbling and bickering made our family home intolerable.

The short version is that my father was a philanderer. He had a twenty-year affair with his secretary, and there were many other women who danced in and out of his affections over the course of my parents' marriage. My sister was four years younger, and so I did what I could to protect her from the noise and the drama and the tension. I took her out and turned the music up and was forever distracting her with promises of something interesting somewhere else. But I suppose that's another story for another time. What I mean to say is that I—perhaps more than most—was susceptible to the ideals of a romantic love. I adored Marnie. But this new love consumed me completely.

Jonathan and I met on Oxford Street when we were both twenty-two years old. It was six in the evening and we were heading to our respective homes at opposite poles of the city. The station entrances were gated, as they so often are, due to overcrowding on the platforms. The sky was dark, threatening rain, and thick gray clouds passed quickly over our heads.

Jonathan and I—unbeknownst to each other—were both enmeshed in the crowd queuing to enter the ticket hall. The throng felt like its own person, with its own consciousness, an impatient desire to be anywhere else emanating from us as one. I could feel other bodies invading my own: arms squeezed against mine, thigh on thigh in a way that seemed far too familiar, someone's chest forced against the back of my head. We were pressed together so tightly that I couldn't see beyond the back of the man standing in front of me.

Eventually there was a clanging, metal on metal, somewhere up ahead as the gates were opened from the inside. The crowd began to vibrate, everyone readying themselves. The man in front of me—blocking my view—leaned forward and then, as I stepped into his empty space, he staggered back. He bumped into me and I into the person behind. The two sides of the crowd shuffled forward steadily as we, there in the center, sent a surge, a rolling wave, pushing the middle in the wrong direction.

"What the . . . ?" I said, regaining my balance.

"You . . ." he said, turning to face me.

I knew. As I had with Marnie. Immediately, I knew. It sounds so stupid, so naive, I know. People have levied that criticism against me hundreds of times—when I moved in with him, when I agreed to marry him, even on the eve of our wedding. And all I could say in response to them then and all I can say to you now is that I hope one day you know, too.

I suppose that it was different with Marnie. We were both looking for someone. The next seven years at that school were stretching out in front of us and neither one of us wanted to live that alone. The joy we felt at finding each other was heightened by an overwhelming sense of relief.

Whereas with Jonathan . . . I don't know. I had never felt like the sort of woman who would fall in love in that way. And so there was no want, no empty space, no something that needed substantiating. I simply saw him and I knew instinctively that I needed to know him better. I could tell you how it felt with words that over the decades have become synonymous with great love, but those truisms were never true for me. The world didn't fall away beneath my feet; instead I felt solid and substantial in a way that I never had before. There were no trembling hands, no quivering hearts, no faces flushed with pink. There were no butterflies. There was simply the sense that he felt, for me, like the home I'd always needed but never really known.

"You . . ." I said, straightening the lapels of my coat. His eyes were olive green, and as he stared at me, bewildered, I felt this inappropriate urge to lift my palm to his cheek. "You just—"

"My scarf," he said, gesturing toward the floor. "You stood on my scarf."

"I did no such—" I looked down. I was still standing on the tassels of his navy scarf. "Oh," I said, quickly stepping aside. "Sorry."

"You want to fucking get on with it," came a voice from behind us, loud and gruff, the voice of the crowd.

"Yes, right," he said, turning around. "Sorry."

He began to shuffle forward and I followed, smiling in an inane, vacuous way, my face still pressed tightly between his shoulder blades. We stayed like that, forced together, through the ticket hall, down the escalator, and toward the platforms. At some point we began talking. And I couldn't tell you now what it was that we said, but when it was time to separate, he to go north and I to go south, we were squabbling both about the scarf and about a pub that he said didn't exist.

"You don't know what you're talking about," I said. "I've been there dozens of times. I could take you there right now."

"Okay," he replied.

People were rushing around, filtering into two streams, one on either side of us, and dispersing onto the platforms.

"What?" I asked.

"Let's go," he replied.

The pub did exist, as I'd said it would: a traditional wood-paneled, almost medieval hideaway with low ceilings and an open fire. It was—and still is, although I haven't been there in years—called The Windsor Castle. It's ten minutes from Oxford Circus and tucked down a narrow cobbled street, a welcome nod to an older version of the city that stood long before the towering flagship stores and coffee shops that repeat every hundred yards.

We stayed there for hours, until the landlady rang her bell for last orders, when we trundled back to the ticket hall, now almost empty, and said our goodbyes with kisses—which were entirely out of character—and promises of next time. I felt something shift inside me when he lifted his hands from my hips. As I watched him walk away from me, his dark green coat flapping at his thighs, I knew that I loved him already.

That love was the foundation on which I would have—could have—built a life. There is a version of this world in which Jonathan and I are still together, still smitten. We promised each other an unyielding love, a life that celebrated laughter and a bond that would never for a moment waver. It is sometimes impossible to believe that we failed to deliver on something that once seemed so certain.

He asked me to marry him a year later—to the day—in that very same pub. He knelt awkwardly on one knee and told me that he'd planned a speech, he'd learned it by heart, but that he couldn't remember a single word he'd wanted to say. But he'd love me for as long as he lived, he said, if that was enough for now.

I thought it was more than enough for me.

We were married that autumn in a registry office. We had no guests and we celebrated with the most expensive champagne that the nearest off-license stocked. We went to The Windsor Castle for our wedding breakfast. It felt only right that it should be the headquarters for all the major milestones of our relationship. I placed our order at the bar, carefully enunciating as I declared that *my husband* would like a burger. The bartender rolled her eyes but smiled, vaguely amused by this young bride in a pale blue dress and her groom in a green tie. Our desserts— brownies accompanied by vanilla ice cream—were served with *Congratulations* written in chocolate icing around the rim of each plate.

We wheeled our bags to Waterloo and caught the train down to the south coast to stay in a small bed-and-breakfast in a seaside town called Beer. We arrived late that evening and checked in, announcing in the way that only newlyweds do that the room was booked for Mr. and Mrs. Black.

"For Jane?" said the elderly woman managing the front desk. It was nearly ten o'clock and she was clearly keen that we recognize the inconvenience.

"Yes," I replied. "For Jane Black." She could say whatever she liked, do whatever she wanted, and none of it could even begin to scratch at the edges of my happiness.

"Upstairs, end of the corridor, on the right." She held out a small gold key attached by a thin gold chain to a thick wooden slab engraved with the word *four.* "Anything else?"

We shook our heads.

Jonathan carried our bags upstairs, down the hallway, and into our room. The floorboards were dark wood and the bedspread embroidered with small pastel flowers. The curtains—the color of rust—had been drawn closed and a small pink lampshade shone softly in the corner. A miniature bottle of champagne had been left in an ice bucket on an old-fashioned mahogany desk. He popped the cork and poured two glasses, and we toasted our wedding a second time.

We woke the following morning as the sun rose and speckled our bed-spread yellow and orange. I remember the warmth of his chest against my back as he bent himself around me, the soft skin of his palm smooth-ing my stomach and his lips against my shoulder blade. I remember how it felt to be enveloped by him, to be wrapped so safely inside someone else, and the way his hands would turn me toward him, his kisses would shift and solidify, when he wanted something more.

It was only later, when there was a knock at the door and a woman apologetically handed over the towels that should have been left in the bathroom, that we scrambled from the bed and made a plan for the day. I pulled back the curtains and looked out at the sea. It was flattened across the horizon and bordered on either side by white cliffs topped with thick green grass. It was October and yet the sky was bright, cloudless, welcoming.

We pulled on our walking boots and our thick woolen jumpers.

Outside, the beach was pebbled. I started along the path toward it, toward the sea, toward the waves that rolled inward, collapsing against the shore.

"This way," called Jonathan, pointing upward instead at the cliffs above. "I think we should go this way."

And so we climbed the road, marching along the pavement, past parked cars and curtained windows, until we reached a grassy verge with signs about hours and bank holidays and a small ticket machine.

"Let's keep going," said Jonathan, weaving through the few parked vans and across the grass.

From then, we walked in silence, sometimes hand in hand, some-times he was in front and I behind, getting distracted by something and then rushing to catch up.

He was always so focused, particularly outdoors, always there with his camera, wanting to see what was farther on, around a corner, what might be waiting for him ahead. For me, it was simply wonderful to be so isolated, nothing to hear but the sea crashing against the rocks beneath and the squawk of gulls overhead.

After an hour or so, we approached another seaside village, smaller than Beer, it seemed, but with a car park, a tiny building that housed a few public toilets, and a café with a thatched roof.

"Perhaps it's open," said Jonathan, and because Jonathan was with me, it was.

He ordered a mug of coffee for himself and, for me, a glass of cold orange juice. We sat outside on the picnic benches and watched the sea as we waited for our bacon sandwiches. Fishermen were huddled together, protecting one another from the wind. I imagined them discussing their catch, the price of cod, their plans for the rest of the day.

After breakfast, we wandered along the beach, the waves swimming in and out, licking at the crevices in each stone and at the soles of our boots. Jonathan spotted a small cutaway in the overgrowth at the foot of the cliff and insisted that we explore further. We pierced the dense shrubs, stepping away from the coast into a forest and zigzagging through thorn bushes and nettles on a narrow mud-pressed path. We climbed higher and higher and still the cliffs were towering above us.

After ten, maybe fifteen minutes, we reached a fork in the trail; the left had steps carved into the slope, the right had a thin path on the very edge of an overhang.

"Let's try this," said Jonathan, pointing up and to our right.

"I don't think so," I replied.

He had spent his childhood in the countryside, been raised in mud and hay and knee-high grass. But I wasn't comfortable in that world. I was mesmerized by the views and the sounds and the endless space, but I felt like an interloper, uneasy and unwelcome.

"This looks safer," I said, gesturing left.

"Come on," he said, and he smiled. "You'll be fine."

I hesitated. But I was tempted, encouraged by his faith in me, his certainty. I found it so difficult to deny him whatever it was that he wanted. Truthfully? I'd have done almost anything he asked.

I unfurled my fists, stretched out my fingers, and stepped one foot toward him, onto the small lip that jutted out from the rocks.

He stepped backward—so easily, so agile—like a funambulist balancing on a tightrope.

"There you go," he said. "You're doing great."

The shelf was narrow, less than a foot in width. It was impossible to stand with two feet side by side.

"Take another step," he said.

I heard our future in that moment: Jonathan talking to a child, encouraging him, too. The memory of it, something that hadn't yet happened, settled within me and it made me feel bolder.

"What are you waiting for? Keep going," he insisted. "I've got you."

I lifted my back leg and slowly swung it forward, over the sea below. Finally, my foot found purchase on the ledge and I exhaled.

"What now?" I asked. I had twisted, somehow facing the cliff, my chest pressed against it, the backs of my heels resting only on air. "How are you doing this?"

"You can walk normally," he said. "Or just shuffle along. Try not to overthink it."

I looked up at him just a few steps ahead. He grinned at me, the beginnings of wrinkles creasing around his eyes and dimples pressing into his cheeks. His hand was stretched out toward me reassuringly, the ring on his finger glinting in the sun. His other hand was holding on to a ridge above us, and I could see a strip of his hip where his T-shirt had lifted from his trousers.

I leaned toward him. But then my back foot slipped and I remember the feeling of dipping, my weight falling down to one side. I remember the air sucked into my lungs, my fingers skimming the rock face, the panic that streamed through me. I felt his hand slam into my back as he pushed me firmly against the rocks and my chin grazed the sharp surface of cliff.

"You're fine," he said. "You're okay."

"No," I said. "This isn't safe. We shouldn't be here."

My face was stinging and my knees aching from the impact.

"You're fine," he said. "I promise. You're okay."

I shook my head vigorously.

"Okay," he said. "Okay. Don't get upset. Just edge that way."

I shuffled a few inches to my left, back onto the grassed pathway.

"There you go," he said. "Okay?"

I nodded. I held my hand to my chin; I thought it was bleeding, but my fingers came away clean.

"Okay," he said. "I'll meet you at the top."

I nodded and he darted upward.

I said, I know, that I'd have followed Jonathan anywhere and that was true. But there was something about his fearlessness that was so at odds with my innate fearfulness. And, try as I might and try as I did, sometimes fear won out. I opted for the safer route and our paths crossed again a few minutes later, back at the top of the cliffs.

If I had known then that we had just a few months ahead of us, I'd have found the courage to spend those few minutes with him.

There is a tragic irony that—with hindsight—has embedded itself in every fiber of my relationship with Jonathan. We met in a small corner of the city and that place became a fundamental part of how we lived and loved and existed together. Until it became the place where our relationship ended. Jonathan and I fell in love on a corner of Oxford Street and—fatefully—that was where he died.

I can tell you far more about that day than I can about the day we met. I rolled through that dark slideshow, the sequence that led to his death, nonstop for weeks. Sometimes I still do.

Jonathan was running, for the first time, in the London marathon. We were expecting rain and sleet, insistent winds. But he was excited. He had been training since the autumn; he was used to running in the rain and so he wasn't concerned.

He was uncontainable that morning, fidgeting and waffling on about something and nothing, his anticipation contagious. We were so ordinary. Our morning was set against a backdrop of alarm clocks and coffee and breakfast and showering and looking for the house keys and almost running late but not quite and the steady, reassuring rhythm of the everyday.

I wanted to share his victory and so I went straight to the Mall. I stood there by the metal barrier waiting for hours and barely noticed the time slipping past. The atmosphere was electric, excitement and nervousness and encouragement sweating from the crowd around me. The elite racers flashed by first—they made it look easy—followed soon after by a few men, and then some women, and then a couple dripping profusely from their faces, their bodies encased within dinosaur costumes.

Jonathan was determined to complete the race in under three hours, and I didn't doubt that he would do just that. I watched him speed past after two hours and fifty-one minutes and he crossed the finish line just three minutes later.

I have never been destined for great success. I have always worked hard, but never excelled. I have always participated; I've never won. But Jonathan did; Jonathan won. He surpassed even his own bold goals.

I was therefore not at all surprised when he was announced as the millionth marathon runner to pass the finish line since the inaugural London marathon of 1981 and interviewed for a recorded segment to be aired that evening on the BBC News. He had always been behind the camera at sporting events, filming for news channels or sports broadcasters, but he was so charming and modest with his answers that day. I remember wondering if he should consider a career in front of the camera rather than behind it.

After his interview, we headed to The Windsor Castle for a quick drink, just one, to celebrate his success.

We never arrived.

As we threaded our way from the tube station at Oxford Circus toward the narrow cobbled street, a drunk driver burst across a pedestrian crossing, mowing my husband down.

I can remember him lying there on his back on the sidewalk. His knee was twisted at a jaunty angle. His eyes were closed, peaceful almost, his chin resting snug against his chest. He was still wearing his black shorts and his tight yellow T-shirt. His rucksack was a yard or two away and the thin foil wrap he'd been given peeped from between the zippers. His bottle of water was rolling—so slowly, it seemed, inching like tar—toward the curb.

A crowd formed, cyclists and pedestrians, but not the driver of the taxi, who remained frozen in his seat.

Jonathan was frozen, too, strangely still, too rigid and yet somehow too serene to be asleep. A puddle of blood began to form beneath his cheek, to pool beneath his body.

I remember the ambulance arriving, pulling up beside us, its siren screaming. It was quickly muted; I recall the sudden absence of noise where before it had been deafening, but the flashing continued, red and blue and red and blue. Paramedics jumped from the van, two of them, both dressed in green, and they marched toward us, shouting over the hood of the ambulance. Everything was unfolding in half time: she snapped on white latex gloves, her right hand first, and then her left, pulling at each fingertip. A bag was swung over his shoulder. There was a policewoman wearing a hat and I can still see her now, gesturing at the crowd to please take a step back, move along now, please, nothing at all to see here.

The paramedics fussed around us, taking Jonathan's pulse, spreading their hands over his body, cutting off his T-shirt, shining a bright white light into his eyes.

"If you could just—" the woman said, and I sat back on my heels and out of their way. Their arms stretched around me, the reflective strips of their uniforms redirecting the van's headlights into my eyes. I squinted and I realized that they were wet.

They slid him onto a stretcher, a strange plastic slab, and lifted him into the back of the ambulance. We crawled through the streets of London and south to St. George's Hospital. The police car followed and the policewoman—still in her hat—reached for my elbow as I stepped down from the back of the ambulance, and she sat with me in the waiting room. She told me to keep breathing: in through my nose for six, and hold for six, and then out through my mouth for six. And then she left and then I was all alone, still waiting. It was dark outside when a doctor called me into a side room to tell me what I already knew, to confirm that Jonathan had died.

He offered to call someone for me, and I don't remember if I answered his question. I left and hailed a cab and recited the address for the flat in Vauxhall. When I arrived, there were three young men in shorts and T-shirts sitting around a picnic table at a pub on the river, gold marathon medals hanging around their necks. I pictured Jonathan sitting there with them, his shorts and his T-shirt, his medal, celebrating his victory and a bubble burst within my chest. I felt bile rising in my throat and I swallowed it because it wasn't time, this wasn't real, and yet I couldn't remember what I ought to be doing or how to be me in that moment.

I sat down against the entrance to the building. I pictured him standing up, rubbing at his elbow, brushing his hands down his chest to release small specks of pavement. I imagined him shocked, and sort of angry, and a small cut beneath his right eye where he'd landed, but otherwise fine: walking, talking, moving, alive. I closed my eyes and saw his hair, too long, his arms crossed over his chest, and his chin slightly pointed, freckles scattered on the bridge of his nose, from all those afternoons running for hours in the sunshine.

I retched because it wasn't real—there was no small cut beneath his eye, no hair too long, no freckles, no more hours of running—and I would never see him again and he would never again be seen and that was simply too big, too impossible, to be a thing.

Chapter Four

For a time, I was winning. And I mean that in the simplest sense of the word. If life is a competition, something that can be lost—and I am certain that it can be lost—then it must also be something that can be won.

Marnie was going on dates with a never-ending barrage of unsuitable men who drank too much and got stoned in children's playgrounds on the weekends and snorted coke off toilet tanks, and I was falling in love with a brilliant man. While her university friends were spending their Friday nights in horrible clubs with loud music and neon lights and sticky floors, I was planning a honeymoon. While they grew despondent, lamenting the failure of yet another dead-end relationship, drowning their heartbreak in gin and feeding it takeout, I was married. I had a husband. And—even better than that—I really, truly loved him. They were arguing over small bedrooms and split bills and spilt milk, tackling the buildup of pubic hair in the drain, the shower overflowing, the piles of dirty dishes sitting just above the dishwasher. Whereas I was living in a lovely maisonette with high ceilings and big windows. I had paint samples in patches on the walls and framed prints propped against the fireplace, waiting to be hung.

Marnie had handed in her notice. Others were being made redundant and sometimes fired and bitching about their bosses and the menial tasks that made up their day-to-day: fetching coffees and booking taxis and ordering reams of paper for the printer. I was being promoted. I had started in an administrative role for an online retailer—they sold everything: books, toys, electronics—and they offered me a position in a new team sourcing furniture. I was in a role that I liked, in a job that I felt had a future, in a growing company.

I was better than all of them. I was happier than all of them.

I suppose I liked that I had found love first. I feel uncomfortable saying that now, because it sounds so stupid, so childish, but it's the truth and that's what I've promised you.

Marnie was the first of us to find a boyfriend. We were thirteen and Richard was a year older. His parents were divorced and he lived with his mother. He had bright orange hair and his cheeks were speckled with freckles. He and Marnie went to the cinema and their fingers touched in a box of popcorn halfway through and they held hands for the rest of the film. She went to his house for their second date and his mum cooked them chicken nuggets. But Richard broke up with Marnie the following day. He had decided that he had feelings for another girl in our year—I think her name was Jessica—whose hair was similarly orange and who was consequently much more compatible.

I was determined that I, too, needed a first boyfriend and so, in the midst of Marnie's heartbreak, I negotiated a date with a boy called Tim. We didn't go to the cinema but instead on a walk, and he bought me an ice cream and I was quite sure that I had found my soul mate. It helped that he was, by quite some margin, more attractive than any of the boys that my classmates had dated. He increased my popularity dramatically and suddenly I was very much the go-to for everyone's dating conundrums. Unfortunately, I wasn't having quite such a positive influence on his reputation, so he called things off after a week and a half.

Marnie and I grieved together, determined never to fall in love again and to become lesbians instead.

Which in itself is sort of curious, don't you think? Already we were very aware that a simple friendship wouldn't suffice into adulthood, that it wouldn't be enough. We knew—from our early teenage years— that romantic love would always become the most important.

I couldn't tell you quite when everything changed. For years—over a decade—we were at the epicenter of each other's lives. We told each other everything, and that included boys and then men, and dating and then sex, and relationships and then love. And then, at some point, a chasm opened between us and our romantic lives became something that existed outside of our friendship: something we filtered in conversation, pulling out highlights or updates, rather than living through it together.

I suppose this, too, was a situation of my own making. Did I tell her how it felt to fall in love with Jonathan? Did I tell her how it felt that first night? I don't think that I did.

Instead, I abandoned her. I had been to visit Jonathan after work, and he had cooked me dinner, and commented on all the spare storage in that flat, the empty shelves, the half-filled drawers, and he'd asked if I'd like to fill them. The promise of a home like that—a home with him—was simply too enticing.

"I'm moving out," I said to Marnie when I returned that evening.

"Oh, right?" she said, distracted. She was sitting on our blue and white sofa, her slippered feet on the coffee table, drumming her fingers against the keys of her new laptop. She had recorded her first video the previous evening: her recipe for carbonara, which had always been my favorite. "This is just impossible," she said. "How do I—" She picked up her phone and began stabbing her thumbs furiously into the screen.

"With Jonathan," I said.

"When's that?" she replied.

"Tomorrow," I said.

She looked up. "What?" Her forehead was creased with confusion. "Tomorrow? But you've only just met him."

"It's been three months," I replied.

"But that's nothing!"

I shrugged. "It's something to me."

"Oh," she said quietly. "And you're sure?" She folded the screen of her laptop. "It has to be tomorrow?"

I nodded.

It would be easy to look back now and to judge myself for moving too fast, for being too eager, but the truth is that I wouldn't change a thing.

She helped me to pack my bags and she gave me a set of sharp knives, a casserole dish the size of a cauldron, and a red dinnerware set. "Because you're going to have to learn to cook," she said. "You can't live off beans and toast."

"I'll be back at mealtimes," I joked.

"I hope you will," she said. "I'll have no one to cook for without you here."

I wondered at the time if she was indulging me, if she thought I'd return in a couple of weeks. But I don't know now that she was. I think she understood that this was my next step, the start of something new.

I watched as she wrapped an old *Evening Standard* around a set of red ramekins that I knew I'd never use. She set them down on the side and sighed. "You're sure about this?" she asked. "Because you know I think he's great, and I promise I'm asking this for you and not for me, but this is quick, and are you sure—are you definitely sure?"

"I am," I said, and I was.

"I'll miss you," she said.

"I know," I replied. "Me, too."

A bubble of tears rose in my throat as I thought of all the things I'd miss: her brightly colored socks drying on the radiator, plastic-wrapped leftovers waiting for me in the fridge, smiley faces drawn in the mist on the bathroom mirror. I swallowed it and I smiled, and she took my hands in hers and squeezed them tightly.

The first weeks felt a little frantic as I tried to be everything to both of them. I didn't want Marnie to feel that I loved her any less—because I didn't—and yet I so wanted Jonathan to know that I was his completely. When Marnie's grandmother died, just a few weeks later, she called me in tears in the middle of the night. I got dressed and fumbled my way onto the street and into a taxi, and I was at the old flat in less than thirty minutes. I think, after that, she knew that she only ever had to ask, that I'd always be there, just as I'd always been before.

Marnie and Jonathan became good friends. She had never been taught to cycle as a child, and he took it upon himself to show her how. He gave her one of his old bikes and she liked that it was built for a man. She taught him how to cook carbonara. She had tried to teach me, she said, but it was too thankless a task, and so she was going to share her culinary secrets with him instead.

We worked perfectly as a trio. Jonathan had so many hobbies—cycling and camping and climbing—and I had only Marnie. So when he spent the weekend in the countryside in a tent that flapped in the wind with spiders in his sleeping bag and shoes damp from the rain, I stayed in the old flat, cozy and warm with my very best friend. Those few years were the greatest of my life. It was such a joy to discover that I was worthy—and capable, too—of two great loves.

When Jonathan died, I thought that our friendship would snap back into the thing that it had been before. It didn't quite. I don't know if it was his absence, but everything in my life felt emptier.

I missed so many things while I was with him. I hadn't seen a cloud for over two years; I was always blinded by blue. I'd found joy in stupid places: in children walking slowly, and dogs barking in the park, and the light of the moon through my blinds late at night. I thought that his eyes were green like olives. And yet I haven't found an olive as beautiful since. Each laugh is hard won. Each smile is fleeting. Every ache feels eternal. My ability to take the good and the bad of this world and to balance them has disappeared completely. I am uncalibrated.

I thought that I would find myself again with Marnie. I thought that I could reset myself. But things had moved on while I'd been looking elsewhere.

Chapter Five

Stanley and I were silent as the elevator descended to the lobby. We were silent as we exited from the front doors of Marnie and Charles's building. We were silent as we walked down the pebbled pathway that led out to the street. We were side by side and yet I felt very much alone.

"That was nice, wasn't it?" said Stanley eventually. He secured the buttons on his coat and lifted the collar up toward his ears. "Did you have a good evening?"

I looped my scarf around my neck a second time. It was September and I tend to think that September is still summer but it never is. It is always a little sharper, a little cooler, despite the bright evenings.

I didn't answer the question. "What do you think of Charles?" I asked instead.

Charles had regaled the table with the story of his and Marnie's first meeting. It had been in a bar in the city. He had sent Marnie and her colleagues bottle after bottle of champagne until finally she acquiesced and joined him at his table. He thought it showed the strength of his love. She thought it demonstrated charm and commitment. I thought it made him seem desperate.

"Great guy, right?" Stanley replied, turning toward me and grinning. "Really great guy."

I didn't look at him; I stared forward and down the road ahead. I always hoped that, one day, I would ask that question and someone would turn to me and smile and say instead, "Absolute wanker, right?"

Because that was entirely true of the man that I knew. He was simply unbearable.

"But do you really think that, Jane?" Charles would say to me, whenever I expressed an opinion that in any way contradicted his own. "Because I really think that we're on the same page here," he would continue, "and what you meant to say was—"

And then he'd launch into a lecture on the housing crisis, or understaffing in hospitals, or the economics of inheritance tax, as though he was an authority on the subject. And then later, when we had nearly moved on, when the conversation was almost forgotten, he would say, "I'm really glad we're in agreement on that, Jane." Even though my position hadn't been altered at all but simply silenced by his volume and his posturing and his overweening confidence.

He would tap twice and in quick succession on the thin rim of his wineglass when it wanted refilling, but only when the bottle was at my end of the table, because I was seemingly unworthy of actual words. He would sometimes pick up my hand and unfurl my fingers and say, "You should really stop biting these, Jane." And then later, toward the end of the evening, when everyone's eyes were shot with blood and alcohol and slipping shut with tiredness, he would say these things, vulgar things—always aimed elsewhere but always meant for me—like, "Probably time for you to be getting Jane home, isn't it?" and then he'd wink and say, "If you get my drift. Do you get my drift?" And we all did, and so we smiled and laughed. And yet every time something would sink lower within me. Because I hadn't slept with anyone in three years, not since Jonathan, and the thought of another man's hands on my skin made me bristle and wince.

You see, the version of Charles that talked to everyone else, that charmed them, that laughed at their jokes? He was simply a disguise, a costume worn to conceal the truth. And he deceived them all: the men, in particular, but most of the women, too, who thought him handsome and carefree and charismatic.

"So," said Stanley, as we arrived at the bus stop. I stepped away from him and pretended to read the bus times printed against the concrete post. "So," he repeated. "The plans?"

I looked pointedly at my watch—it had been a present from Marnie—and still I said nothing.

"We're probably nearer yours, don't you think?" he said.

"Are we?" I replied. I ran my finger along the time sheet, the numbers printed black on white paper, fixed between two panels of plastic. I tried to look relaxed and natural, as though this was something people often did and not a bygone act from a previous decade.

"I reckon so," he said. "Not much in it, but a bit closer to yours."

I continued pretending to read.

I heard his footsteps against the concrete paving slabs, the weight of him approaching. His breathing was loud behind me, thick and steaming and scorched with alcohol, and I knew he was about to touch me.

"Jane?" he said. He took another step toward me until he was standing right behind me, and then he snaked his arms around my waist. He kissed the back of my head, wet and noisy, and I solidified myself, drilling my heels into the ground beneath me, fixing my breath and holding my body firm so that I didn't flinch. He squeezed me—not particularly forcefully—but still I felt that my entire body was being strangled, that I was suffocating.

"How are—" He cleared his throat. "Your place?" He stroked his right palm up and down over my stomach, the upward brushes climbing higher and higher with each movement until I could feel his fingers skimming the stiff wire at the base of my bra, until I could feel them reaching the smooth fabric above. "Jane, you and me . . ." He breathed into my ear, his words slurred and warm and moist.

"Stanley," I said, and I moved sideways, away from him, away from the concrete post. "Stanley, I'm afraid I'm not sure that there really is a you and me."

"Oh," he replied, slightly affronted but more confused than anything else. "But I—"

"It's not you," I said.

He nodded solemnly. "Is this about your late husband?" he asked. He was confident again, sure that he had found the answer to some unasked question, sure that he knew the very ointment to ease this wound. "Marnie said—"

She would have warned him to be gentle, to be careful.

"No, Stanley," I said. "This isn't about Jonathan." Which was true. "And it's not about you." Which was also true, I suppose. "This really is just about me."

A red double-decker rounded the corner, its lights bright against the night sky and, for once, entirely on schedule.

"Do you think that maybe what you're feeling is—"

"This has been lovely," I interrupted, although I don't know why I bothered because it was very clearly not even the slightest bit true. "And do feel free to keep in touch with Charles if that makes you happy. But I think this is probably it for now. In terms of a you and me. Sorry," I said. "And goodbye."

I put out my left hand and the bus slowed, stopping beside me. I climbed aboard and, as the doors juddered shut, I offered Stanley an unnecessarily enthusiastic wave. He was still frowning as we pulled away.

I have dated too many men in the years since Jonathan. I didn't speak to another man for over a year. But everyone started to fret, to worry that I was being overwhelmed by my grief, and it felt important to reassure them that I was still an active participant in my own life. Because—and this is something else that we all learn eventually—everyone knows that a single woman who is not at the very least in pursuit of romantic love is almost certainly entirely miserable.

That's a joke. You could smile.

The truth is that I wasn't looking for another love; it was too much to expect to find another great love in my otherwise underachieving life. I'd had Jonathan, and I couldn't begin to imagine that another love could ever come close to that one. And I had Marnie. And it made her happy to think that I was still looking, that I had faith, that I believed in the goodness of the world.

And yet I tried not to date any man for too long, hence my swift departure. Partly because I found them all—and that's the truth: every single one—suffocatingly smug and wholly insufferable.

And also because a very small part of me worried that they might actually start to like me.

Does that sound conceited? It isn't meant to. Before Jonathan, I didn't think that it was possible for someone to feel that way about me. I couldn't believe that anyone would find that sort of love in someone so cheerless and so insecure. But Jonathan found things to like, things to love. He admired my competitive nature. He was impressed that I'd never lost a pub quiz. He thought it right that I was always early. He was amazed when I read a novel in a day. He loved that I was meticulous, a perfectionist, that I wanted to hang our pictures myself. And, eventually, I began to love those things, too.

I didn't want these men to fall in love with me because I knew that I could never fall in love with them. And I knew then—I still know—that rejection is a blister beneath the skin, a small hurt that can swell into something far more significant.

Is that an exaggeration?

I don't think it is.

But this isn't the time.

I wish I could tell you that this would be an easy story to hear, but I don't for a moment think that it will. There will be a lot of death this evening and I wish it were any other way, but I have promised the truth and this, finally, is a promise on which I can deliver.

I am still unsure where this story really started—and I have no idea where it will end—but how to begin?

A couple of years ago, Marnie and Charles were living together in their flat and I was dating men who were not my husband and my family life was complicated but manageable. Those are the foundations on which this story started. This is the story of how he died.

Chapter Six

Most women in their late twenties and early thirties like variety, spontaneity, the chance to meet new people and do new things. That was never me. I have always been that eleven-year-old girl cowering in a school corridor and anticipating rejection. I have never actively looked for friendships, and so I find myself with very few, but those that I do have really do matter.

Because, you see, I had a friend. And none of the others—the pretty blondes in tight denim shorts that cut above the creases of their bums, the guys in loose jeans and hoodies nestled together around a spliff, the sports stars in their tracksuits and trainers, the library girls in their glasses and blouses, the posh boys in their chinos and jackets—none of them compared. I didn't need them and so I didn't pursue them.

I knew what I liked. I liked routine and repetition. I still do.

And so the morning after I axed Stanley from my life, I went to visit my mother. She was living in a residential home in the suburbs and it always took at least an hour to get there. And, because I liked to arrive no later than nine o'clock, so that I could be there for the beginning of visiting hours, I would set an alarm before I went to sleep and then leave home early to catch one of the first trains of the day.

The carriages were always quiet on a Saturday morning. There was normally a man in a suit, hungover from a Friday night that had rolled unexpectedly into a Saturday morning. There was often a woman with a pram, a new mother trying to fill the hours between wake and sleep and sleep and wake, hours that hadn't existed a few months earlier. There were sometimes security guards, cleaners, nurses, all traveling home from night shifts. And there was always me.

I saw Marnie every Friday evening and I went to visit my mother every Saturday morning.

The dayroom was at the front of the building and I passed it on my way to my mother's room. I tried not to peer inside, to focus only on her door at the end of the corridor, but it always pulled my gaze. It had an otherworldliness that was strangely magnetic. It was full of old people in armchairs, some in wheelchairs, all with blankets draped over their legs. The carpet was every color, ornate and fiercely patterned. It reminded me of the carpets in fancy hotels, where the managers were afraid of food stains and mud and makeup.

Here, the patterns were similarly effective. They disguised dirt and vomit and, yes, food stains, but not from raucous three-course meals with laughter and gossip and wine, but from sticky, thick mashed potato flung deliberately onto the floor.

Other than the multicolored carpet, the room itself was rather bland: empty beige walls, no photographs or pictures, no paintings or posters, and dark leather armchairs, easy to wipe clean. I suppose the decor itself was really rather unimportant. This room was compelling not because of its specifics, but because of its inhabitants. It served as a backdrop for a scene that depicted life and death and the thin periphery that existed between the two. Those people were half in and half out. Their hearts were beating and blood was trickling through their veins, but their souls were slipping, their minds melting, their bodies crumpled and broken. It was an eerie, uncanny place, a room full of people who were barely still people, of life that was almost not life, of death that was not quite death. My mother never wanted to spend time in there and the nurses had long given up insisting.

She was in her room instead and was sitting upright in bed when I arrived.

I stood in the doorway and watched her, just briefly, as she fiddled with the bobbles sewn onto the blue woolen blanket draped over her duvet. She pulled the bedding up toward her chin and knotted her hands together and they bulged beneath the covers. The window was wide open and a cool breeze lifted the fabric of the curtains so that they fluttered and cast a shadow against the wall.

At sixty-two, my mother suffered from early-onset dementia. The doctors at her facility—when they visited, once a week; we rarely overlapped—had pointed out that she was at the older end of early onset, as though that was a revelation that should provide some comfort. What they meant, of course, was that others had it far worse. I understood. But broken arms didn't ease my splinters.

I knocked, then stepped inside. She looked up and I smiled, hoping that she would remember me. Her face was static, creases etched deep into her forehead and her lips permanently pinched. I could see her hands moving beneath the duvet and I knew that she was using the index finger of one hand to pick at the dry, ragged skin around the nail beds of the other.

Sometimes it took her a few minutes to recognize me. She was staring and I knew that she was flicking through the box files buried deep in the alcoves of her mind, trying to process my entrance, to place my face, my outfit, desperate to decipher this new arrival.

Looking back now, it's hard to believe that she had been living there for eighteen months. It always felt temporary, a sort of limbo. I didn't think it then, although it sounds impossible now, that of course nursing homes are temporary. They are the midpoint, not between two moments in this life, but at the fringe of life itself.

She had been diagnosed at sixty but, by then, she'd been living alone for a year, her divorce finalized, and my father long gone. I had known for several months that there was something wrong; I thought at the time that she might be depressed. She was short-tempered in a way she'd never been before, sniping at me for little inconveniences—too much milk in her tea, mud on the soles of my shoes.

She started swearing. In the first twenty-five years of my life, she had never once—certainly not in front of me—said "shit" or "fuck." She opted instead for "sugar" or "fudge," muttered very quietly beneath her breath. And yet suddenly the most flamboyant profanities were part of her everyday language. *All I wanted was a pinch of shitting milk. You're getting fucking mud fucking everywhere.*

Sometimes she'd forget when I was due to visit, despite my steadfast routine. I would ring the doorbell early on a Saturday morning. I would hear her slippers padding against the carpet as she approached the front door. I would hear a tinkling as she secured the chain. She would pull the door back, just a couple of inches, and poke her nose through the small gap. She would scan me, sliding her eyes up to my face and down to my feet, and say, "Oh. Is it today?"

I wondered if she was drinking too much. I took her to see a doctor. He nodded while I explained the situation and I felt sure that he understood. I felt sure that he knew exactly the cause of this shift in her personality, that he knew the answers I'd failed to find online, the medication or therapy or advice that would put an end to this.

"Menopause," he said, when I'd finished describing my mother's symptoms. He nodded solemnly. "Definitely the menopause."

The following morning my mother fell down the stairs. I received a call from her neighbor. He'd heard a strange noise and, thankfully, had let himself in with a spare key. My father had given it to him years earlier, to water the plants and feed the fish while we were all in Cornwall.

By the time I arrived, my mother was sitting on the sofa, her dressing gown secured tightly around her waist, clutching a cold cup of tea and arguing with her neighbor, who was really rather keen that she go to the hospital, just for a quick once-over, purely to be on the safe side.

"Oh, not you, too," she said when she saw me. "I missed the step. I wasn't concentrating. I'd have righted myself in a minute or two, but this busybody couldn't keep himself to himself, could he, letting himself in as though he lives here, too, the bloody cheek of it."

He was a kind man—far too nice and far more patient than I'd have been in the presence of such a rude and ungrateful neighbor— and he promised that he would keep an eye on things. He worked from home, he said, so he was always nearby. The walls were thin, he said, so he'd keep his music turned down, just in case she ever needed help again.

I wondered how many arguments he'd heard over the years.

She fell again two weeks later. He heard the crash and called an ambulance. She had a cut on her forehead where she'd ricocheted off the banister. She said it was fine, not too deep, just a graze, but he insisted that she go to the hospital. It was still bleeding when I met her there nearly two hours later.

We were seen by a doctor, a woman not much older than me, who frowned when I knowingly nodded and said confidently, "Menopause."

"Do you think it's the menopause, Mrs. Baxter?" asked the doctor, and my mother scowled. "I'm not saying it isn't the menopause," the doctor continued, "but is that what *you* think this is?"

My mother raised her nonbloodied eyebrow in response and then sighed and shook her head.

"In that case I'd like to run a few more tests. Would that be okay?"

My mother nodded.

She was diagnosed with suspected dementia that afternoon. She lived alone at home for a little longer, getting progressively worse. But when her diagnosis was confirmed six months later, she moved into the residential home, with the support and the nursing and the care that, even living with her, I wouldn't have been able to provide.

I sat down in the armchair, laying my coat across my lap. I opened my mouth to speak, but my mother shook her head. She wanted to find the right file; she didn't want my help.

"You're late," she said eventually.

"Only a few minutes," I replied, twisting to see the clock hanging above my head.

"The train?" she asked.

I nodded.

She was there. Her eyes were focused and warm. Sometimes I feared that she'd given up, that she was willing the dementia to sprawl across her brain like a fungus, to seep in and destroy the final shreds of her humanity. But, on days like that one, I felt sure that she was still fighting, pushing back in her own small ways, refusing to be indoctrinated by the emptiness any sooner than was absolutely necessary.

"Did you end it with that boy?" she asked. Stanley and I had been on two previous dates, one of which hadn't been awful, and I'd told her about it—the picnic in the park, the drinks in the pub—when I'd visited the previous week. But I'd also told her that he was a lawyer, that he was boring at his best, that his only saving grace was his very soft hair.

I could see that she was proud to have remembered our previous conversation. Often she could remember the tone of a discussion—if she was angry with me or pleased or if she simply enjoyed the company— but sometimes she remembered small details. I remember wondering then if she wrote them down when I left, prompts for the following week, ways to stay connected when her mind was trying so very hard to disengage.

"Stanley?" I asked.

"Maybe." She shrugged. "I don't have enough space in here"—she tapped her forehead—"to remember all the names."

"Then, yes," I said. "I did it last night."

"Good," she said. "He didn't sound much like a Jonathan to me."

My mother's dementia had—somewhat conveniently—erased her memories of my relationship with Jonathan. Her recollection was simply that I fell in love and then he died. Which wasn't what had happened at all.

It wasn't that my parents disliked Jonathan. In fact, I think they quite liked him: he was magnetic and funny and always very polite. But I think they liked him in the way that parents like an early boyfriend. He was fine. He would do. But he wasn't what they envisaged when they imagined me married.

They were livid when I told them we were engaged. Having failed to agree on a single thing for the previous decade, they were both adamant that I was making an irreversible mistake. They argued that we were too different. He loved space and fresh air; I loved the coziness of my own home. He loved people and noise; I loved familiarity and silence. I think they felt that he wasn't good enough, wasn't smart enough, didn't earn enough as a cameraman. I didn't care.

In the weeks after we'd gotten engaged, my mother would call me repeatedly, sometimes multiple times in a single day, to insist that I was ruining my life. She ranted relentlessly, zealously, telling me that love wasn't easy and that it was far too complex, too multifaceted for me to possibly understand and that marriage was for another time, another decade, another life. She claimed that we were too young, too naive, too set on something beyond our comprehension. In the background, I could hear the air whistling past the mouthpiece as she paced the hallway at home, the sharp turns at either end of the corridor, the wild sighs between sentences. She didn't quite say it, not in these words, but I think she was trying to protect me from her mistake, from a marriage that had narrowed every part of who she once was into a few wilting words: into "wife," into "mother," into "heartbreak."

She told me that I had to make a choice; I chose Jonathan.

Perhaps it should have been a difficult decision. But it wasn't.

When Jonathan and I were alone, we were both entirely ourselves. That was my greatest joy, having found someone with whom I could be myself and who, in turn, was his truest self for me. When we were with others, my parents in particular, we were both a little better—that little bit funnier, that little bit nicer, that little bit more in love. We amplified ourselves in order to be the sort of couple that made others comfortable. He made jokes at my expense, lighthearted gibes that elicited laughter from the other men, from my father, and I was politer, bringing him drinks and asking if he wanted anything more and encouraging him to just shout if he needed something from the kitchen. And we touched in a way that sometimes felt contrived, his arm around my waist, my head against his shoulder. When we were alone, our bodies bled into one, limbs entangled, skin stretched against skin.

It was an easy choice.

I suppose I thought that my mother would surrender in time, that she'd decide that she could live with my marriage. It didn't seem fair that this should be the moment when she reinstated her motherly love.

When I was nearly four years old, my sister, Emma, was born seven weeks early in a wave of chaos. She was rushed to intensive care and deposited in an incubator as my mother was wheeled into surgery to stem some unstoppable bleeding. They both returned home several weeks later but, in just that one month, everything had changed. From then on, my mother became more and more obsessive, fretting increasingly over her younger daughter: asking always is she cold, and is she hungry, and is she breathing. I became closer to my father as a result—he could do nothing right in those first few months—but my mother was there for me only in body. She wasn't interested in bedtime stories, or first school photographs, or the intricacies of what went on during a child's day. She hasn't really been interested in me since and so I couldn't believe that she felt me worthy of her attention in adulthood.

Shortly after my wedding, my father asked my mother for a divorce and moved out. Judy, his secretary and long-term mistress, had been widowed a year earlier. She'd threatened to leave my father if he didn't commit to her fully. My mother's threats had always felt unconvincing, but evidently Judy's were not. It was no surprise to any of us that my father chose her.

I thought my mother might need me more in the aftermath of that loss. I guess I should have known better.

There was a year when we didn't speak to each other at all. I remember expecting a phone call on my birthday—because surely mothers and daughters are bound by birth, if nothing else—but it never came. I didn't hear from her when Jonathan died. I wondered if she would attend the funeral. She didn't. I hadn't given her the details, but I suppose I thought—maybe I even hoped—that she might have asked for them from somebody else.

But then, unexpectedly, just a month or so later, she started sending me emails, one or two a week, nothing significant, just updates on her life, things that made her think of me: a new furniture shop on the high street, an article in a magazine, a trailer she'd seen for a film that she thought I might enjoy.

I replied eventually—I'd seen the film and I thought it tedious—and somehow we settled into an uncomfortable dialogue. I was angry with her at the time, really angry, because there was so much still unsaid. I found myself inserting those small truths, those small angers, into my messages and into our conversations, concealed in sharp asides and abrupt sign-offs and sometimes in long delays between responses. It was far easier to pick at those scars than address the mighty grief swelling within me.

I hated her. I really did. And then, one day, I didn't. She, too, had lost the man she loved. And then she lost so much more: her mind, her memories. Our lives were in very different places and yet we were both broken, and we found something familiar in each other's jagged edges. After more than twenty years of failing to understand each other, we finally had something in common.

Eventually I found that I, too, could erase my memories of the drama; they weren't the actions of this woman, of this mother, but of some other person, now lost to the pleats of history and time.

"No," I said eventually. "Stanley wasn't at all like Jonathan."

"Then you're well rid," she said. "Don't you think?"

"I'd say so," I replied.

I turned on the television and we watched the news together. A teenager had been stabbed; his assailant was disguised in a grainy photograph, an image frozen from CCTV. A disgraced politician spoke to the press, explaining without apology, justifying his actions. A young mother sobbed; her benefits had been revoked and she was unable to afford childcare in order to work or to work in order to fund childcare. We were shocked and unsurprised and then sad, our expressions twisting in unison.

The newsreader eventually bid us farewell and I gathered my coat and my handbag and snuck back into the hallway, leaving my mother asleep and the television murmuring the opening credits for a new quiz show.

I'm telling you about my mother because it's important that you understand her role in this story. I did hate her, but I also forgave her. Remember that.

Chapter Seven

I didn't have a date to bring to Marnie and Charles's the following Friday, but I regularly visited alone, and I was very much looking forward to it. Until Marnie called me at midday to say that I couldn't come for dinner that evening because Charles had organized a surprise weekend in the Cotswolds. She rang from the car and I could hear the hiss of other vehicles rushing past on the motorway. I wondered how long she had known she was going away. She must have been told at least a few hours earlier. Because she'd had time to pack and drive out of the city with its tight streets, small and cramped, bordered by parked cars and with red lights every few hundred yards. She could have called earlier.

"Whereabouts are you going?" I asked, although I don't know why: I wasn't particularly interested in the answer.

"Some hotel," she said. I heard the crackle of her phone against her cheek and I imagined her turning toward Charles, who would have been sitting next to her, in the driver's seat as always, dictating their path. "What's it called?" she asked.

I heard him speaking, not individual, isolated words but a murmuring, the timbre of his voice echoing against the metal innards of the car.

"He can't remember," said Marnie. "But it's . . ."—that crackle again—"Google says we'll be there in two hours."

I pictured them sitting side by side: Marnie's shoes lying abandoned in the footwell, her feet curled up on the seat against her thighs; Charles in a smart shirt and warm jumper, ever aware of the autumn chill, the sort of man who liked to drive with the window down and his elbow perched on the open ledge.

"Jane!" I heard him shout. And then more quietly, tenderly even, "Can she hear me?"

"I can hear him," I said.

"Go on," Marnie replied, but not to me. "She says she can."

"Jane!" he shouted again. "Can I get a favor? I'd like this beautiful woman to myself for the weekend. What do you reckon?" he continued. I pressed my thumb to the earpiece to smother the sound. "Can you do that? Just forty-eight hours. You'll be all right."

Marnie laughed, a girlish titter, and so I laughed, too, and I shouted, "Sure thing. She's all yours." Because what else was I to do? What else could I have said? I knew what this meant.

"But we'll see you next week?" said Marnie. "Same time as normal?"

"Yes," I said. "Same time as normal."

"Let me know if Stanley's coming," she said.

"He won't be," I replied.

"Oh," she said. "Really? That's such a shame." She was surprised in the way that optimists so often are by facts that betray the fantasy. She always hopes, always assumes, that the next man will be the right man, which is foolish because the evidence suggests otherwise. She has never met any of my suitors, as she calls them, more than a couple of times. "Well, let me know if you want to bring anyone else," she said.

Marnie ended the call and I listened to the silence where her voice had been seconds before. I knew what was coming and I knew, too, that I was afraid. I took a deep breath, inhaling noisily, because my chest was tight, my ribs sort of shivering, and because air kept catching in my throat.

You know already that there was an engagement ring. I had assumed that it was still in Charles's bedside table; I'd had no reason to believe otherwise. But, in that moment, I was quite sure that it was on the road, slipped inside a jacket pocket or in the front pouch of a suitcase or in the glove box of that shiny white car.

As I lay in bed that evening, I pictured it in their hotel room, tucked in the drawer of a new bedside table, lying in wait until the perfect moment. I could see it housed in its red velvet box, a gold band with three bright white diamonds.

I hated the thought of it. I hated the thought that she might marry him.

As a child, Marnie's relationship with her parents had been strained: more like coworkers than relatives. Her mother and father were both doctors and very successful in their respective fields. They had always traveled, and so Marnie and her older brother, Eric, had been left at home for weeks at a time ever since they were old enough to get themselves to school and to cook their own meals. Her parents turned up on the good days—the parents' evenings, the school plays—but they weren't particularly present. She had no one there on the bad days, the normal days, the everydays that make up a life.

Until me. That was my role. I loved her completely, unconditionally, without question.

Charles thought that he could fill that space, too. But he was wrong. Because a bottle of champagne sent across the bar isn't selfless but showy. An expensive flat isn't generous. It's desperate and excessive. And an extravagant ring isn't a symbol of commitment but of blind confidence, the sort of arrogance deemed acceptable only in a man like Charles.

I had discovered the ring a few months earlier.

Marnie and Charles were about to go on holiday for a week. They were going to the Seychelles, I think—perhaps it was Mauritius—and we were due to have a heat wave in London. Marnie had been fretting about the plants on her balcony, if they would survive seven days with strong sunshine and no rain. And Charles was saying that she was ridiculous, because they were just plants and she could always buy some more.

I ate my dinner listening to their bickering and keeping very deliberately quiet. I'd be lying if I said that I received no satisfaction from the squabble—I enjoyed seeing Charles fail to understand Marnie—but I knew that there was nothing to be gained by my intervention. Even so, I wanted to tell Charles not to be such an arsehole, to say that if the plants mattered to Marnie then they should matter to him, too. But I didn't.

The following morning Charles called me and asked if I would mind watering the plants while they were away.

I didn't have a car; I couldn't drive. It normally took about half an hour to get from my flat to theirs on the tube and so I knew immediately that it wasn't going to be particularly convenient.

I wondered if they had other friends who lived nearer—colleagues of Charles's perhaps, who could also afford extravagant apartments in old mansion houses. They did; they must have. And yet Charles had asked me.

Perhaps, I thought, I am their closest friend.

I knew, of course, that it wasn't true.

They had asked me simply because they knew that I'd say yes. Marnie had plenty of other friends—so did Charles—but I was efficient, reliable.

Charles explained that he would leave their spare key with the concierge and that if I could just pop in after work from Monday through to Friday, and actually once on Saturday would be great, too, then that would be brilliant.

On the Monday, I left work at half past six, exhausted from a day sitting behind a desk and in front of a screen, trying to explain to restless shoppers why their packages hadn't arrived at the time they'd elected. I had taken almost ten weeks off when Jonathan died, and when I'd returned, I'd discovered that we were no longer selling furniture and that I'd been moved into the customer service team to answer calls. They were adamant that there'd be opportunities to contribute to the company in a significant way, but it felt like a demotion to me.

The help line was closed on the weekends and so the beginning of the week was always the worst. By Monday, those whose packages had failed to arrive on Saturday were so irate, so totally beside themselves with frustration—no garden furniture for their barbecue, no presents for their son's birthday, no outfits for the fancy dress do—that they were entirely unable to contain their rage. They instead spent the best part of an hour hissing and spitting and swearing and shouting into their phones. And I spent an hour soothing and reassuring and promising to correct the error and topping up their accounts with small sums of compensation.

I arrived at Marnie and Charles's flat just after seven.

"And can I see some ID?" the concierge said when I asked for the key.

"I don't have any," I replied. "But, Jeremy," I said—he was wearing a name badge—"you've seen me here once a week for years. You know who I am. And look, I can see the envelope with the key right there on your desk. Jane Black. You know that's my name."

"No ID?" he repeated.

"I'm afraid not," I replied.

I offered him my sweetest smile and was frankly astounded when he slid the key across the desk conspiratorially and said, "You didn't get this from me."

I took the elevator to their floor and, as the doors parted and I stepped out, the lights in the hallway flickered on. Marnie and I had spent a year stepping out of elevators onto blue carpet and the building I lived in now offered much the same experience (the carpet was taupe, but just as muddied and worn). This building, however, was noticeably different and never failed to make me feel somewhat inferior. The walls were lined with framed artwork, painted signatures adorning the bottom right corners of each piece, and lights hung from the ceiling in neat pendants. The parquet flooring was thickly varnished, glinting under the lights, and the only evidence that any other shoes had ever walked those hallways was a very slight fading, a few small scuffs, at the doors to the two elevators.

I let myself into their flat and was—stupidly—surprised to find it dark. On Friday evenings I would ring the bell and Marnie would rush to answer, pulling open the door and smiling, and then darting back into the kitchen to stir or to season or to shake. Normally the camera would be set up on the countertop, filming her preparing her latest concoction. Her brief departure—my arrival—featured regularly in her articles, her recipes, and her videos, too.

I always wanted to go out for dinner. I wanted it to be just the two of us again. But she needed to be in the kitchen, she said; it was how she paid her half of the mortgage. Charles was desperate to have a little woman, a little wife, someone he could own. But I knew she didn't want that for herself, and I didn't want it for her, either.

From the hallway I would overhear her saying, "And that was exactly the moment I was hoping that Jane would arrive."

I'd close the door behind me, quietly, and pause to listen.

"Because I could dart off for just a second and I knew nothing would overflow or burn and that I wouldn't come back to scorched pans and stodgy sauces."

I would hear her tinkering in the kitchen for a moment or two—a spoon circling a pot, or the crackle of oil in a frying pan, or an ensemble piece with drawers and cupboards opening and closing—and then, eventually, she would say the line that I was listening for, waiting to hear. It was always something like this:

"But you remember what I always say, don't you? Jane is basically family to me. So I know that she's out there now hanging up her coat or taking off her shoes or whatever and she's fine to fetch herself a drink or open a bottle—*mi casa es su casa* and all that. If your guests are more demanding, then I would suggest scheduling their arrival for the end of the next stage when you can take a proper break and really be the hostess with the mostess."

I was alone in the hallway in those moments, yes, but it felt so very different. There were lights on, lights everywhere, bulbs hanging overhead and side lamps shining in corners. There were scented candles running along the radiator covers, the mantelpiece, the coffee table, flickering on every surface. I could always hear Marnie, chattering to herself, to her audience, to her ever-growing following. There was the hum of the oven and the French doors would always be open, leading onto the balcony, and I would hear the whistle of the wind and the purring of cars and drivers sounding their horns on the street below.

But that night it was lightless, scentless, silent.

I liked it, the sense that the flat was unencumbered by any other presence; it felt unowned and sort of hollow.

It took me a while to find the watering can (beneath the bathroom sink) and the key to the balcony (in the drawer beside the teaspoons). It was nearly dark by the time I made it outside but I could see spiderwebs threaded between the leaves of the plants, stretching from the stems to the metal railings, glistening in the evening light. There was one visible spider, small and brown, centered in a web. I lifted the spout above it and watched as the wall of water sent everything—it and its web, too—tumbling toward the patio.

By the time I arrived home it was nearly nine o'clock.

The following morning, I packed a small suitcase with enough clothing and toiletries to last until the end of the week. I even brought my own bedding. They had asked for a visitor, a guest, someone who would show up intermittently, half an hour each day, simply to water their plants. Instead, I became a lodger of sorts.

I didn't think they'd mind particularly, but I wasn't going to tell them.

I let myself into their flat that evening and stood again in the dark hallway. This would be my home now—just for the week—but my home nonetheless. I turned on all the lights—exactly how Marnie liked it—and made up their bed with my own sheets and pillowcases. I unpacked my food into their fridge, into their cupboards, turned on their radio, looked through their bookcases. It was easy to work out which titles belonged to Marnie and which to Charles; most of his had dark spines, bold gold titles, whereas hers were in pastel tones, pinks and yellows primarily, and with intricate handwritten type.

I returned from work each evening and embedded myself in the folds of their cushions, the thin layer of grime crawling up their shower tiles, the lip balm stains tarnishing their glasses.

There is something very odd and also rather comfortable about being alone in someone else's home. I recall feeling distinctly aware of their presence, even though they were hours away—continents, even—on the other side of the world. I felt like I was seeing them—the real version of them as a couple—for the very first time. I found myself rifling through their cabinets, keen to discover their favorite herbs and those with the foil lid still stuck in place. I went through their drawers and was astonished to discover that Marnie had become the sort of woman who bothered with matching underwear. I looked through their medicine cabinet—an endless array of painkillers and cough drops and Band-Aids and a thermometer still in its blister pack—and felt that I knew them a little better afterward than I had before.

Marnie's bedside table housed an array of knickknacks, nothing significant: packs of tissues, samples from beauty counters, inkless pens, old birthday cards, empty pill packets, a pair of old sunglasses, a string bracelet from a trip we'd taken to Greece while at university. I discovered, in Charles's, three magazines, two bookmarks, four flash drives, some Polaroid photos from a friend's wedding—one with Marnie in a blue silk dress that I'd helped her to choose—and, wrapped in a brown paper bag at the very back, a red velvet box.

So I knew what was coming; I'd had time to prepare.

It was Sunday afternoon and I was still lying in bed when I received a second phone call from Marnie. I held my phone above my face and looked at her name written in block capitals on my screen, the photograph taken in her kitchen, apron strings knotted around her waist, red hair scraped away from her face, when I'd upgraded to a smartphone two years earlier.

I took a deep breath and I answered.

"Jane?" she shouted. "Jane. Can you hear me?" She was giddy, wild with excitement.

"Of course," I said. "What is it? What's the matter?"

And I knew what it was and that nothing was the matter and yet we plodded through the charade regardless.

"Charles proposed," she squealed. "He's asked me to marry him." She was entirely unable to control the volume or the speed of her words. "I'm sending you a photo of the ring," she said. I heard her fingertips tapping against the handset. She lifted the phone back to her cheek. "Has it arrived?" she asked.

My phone vibrated against my ear. I already knew, of course, what this image would show. I didn't feel ready to see that ring snug on her finger, nestled against her fair skin, binding her to a very specific future.

"Not yet," I replied. "I'm sure it'll come through shortly."

I was going to look at it, but later. I was planning to put a bottle of wine in the fridge and tidy the flat and go for a walk and then, hours later, when it was quiet and dark outside, I would open the message and I would look at it then.

"And you'll be there, won't you?" she asked. "Of course you will. At the wedding? We might do it abroad, maybe, we'll see, we're not sure. And you'll help me decide what to wear?"

"Of course," I replied. I wasn't convinced that I sounded quite enthusiastic enough. "Of course," I said again, hoping that mindless repetitions would create the illusion of excitement when in fact I felt rather nauseated.

"And you'll be my maid of honor," she said. "You will, won't you?"

"Yes," I replied. "Of course I will."

"Okay, then, I have to go—we're heading home now, and I need to make a few more phone calls and, oh, Jane, isn't this just the most exciting thing? I really can't believe it; I really can't. Will you let me know when the photo arrives? Or I can send it again. It's really something, really special. You'll like it, I think. Or at least say you do. But I'm sure you will really as well. Okay, I'm blathering and Charles is rolling his eyes—yes, yes, I'm coming—so let's talk later and I'll see you on Friday if not before and—yes, okay—love you!"

She hung up.

Chapter Eight

I went to bed early that night. I sat there propped against my pillows, sweating in flannel pajamas, staring at the photo on the screen of my phone. It showed her hand, the gold band neatly circling her ring finger. It was a very beautiful ring, but I couldn't help envisaging it made of rope, as a noose that could suffocate, the end of something rather than a beginning. The hand—while obviously Marnie's, with her slender, elegant fingers and neat, painted nails—felt somehow other, like its own individual being, quite separate from her as a whole.

I woke abruptly—ten past two in the morning—drenched in sweat and shivering and with the absolute certainty that I'd forgotten to do something of incredible importance. It was then that I realized that Marnie had called me from the car again—not only the first phone call, but the second one, too. There had been that same sound of traffic and the reverberation of shuddery wheels at speed. And she'd said, hadn't she, that they were traveling, that they were on their way home.

I was entirely sure that Charles would not have—would never have—proposed in a car. That wasn't his style at all. He'd have wanted flowers and champagne and violinists and probably moonlight, too. I felt a little surprised that she hadn't called me earlier.

When Marnie was sixteen years old, she fell in love with a boy called Thomas. He was seventeen and six foot four and played rugby for the county. She loved his chiseled jaw and firm abs and broad shoulders and strong arms. I couldn't stop staring at his bizarrely large forehead. But he was utterly charming and I say that as someone not easily softened by good manners and charisma and a slightly crooked smile.

I didn't hate him, but I should have. I didn't kill him, but I wish that I had.

Stop it. Don't look at me like that.

Stop being so judgmental and listen to the story.

I liked the way that their relationship worked. He was hoping to be offered a sports scholarship at a top university and so much of his time was spent training or competing. Most evenings, in fact, and always a match on weekends. They saw little of each other and their romance thrived instead on notes passed in corridors and threads of texts and winks across the cafeteria.

The summer arrived with its eager mornings and long, humid afternoons. I didn't notice that Marnie was still wearing sweatshirts until she absentmindedly rolled up her sleeves one lunchtime and I spotted four equal bruises crowded above her elbow. She saw me staring and garbled some nonsense about a bump against a bed frame.

I don't know how I'd missed it. She was secretive with her phone, where once she'd read her messages aloud and together we'd crafted replies. She was quick to anger, quick to bite, restless and skittish and I hadn't noticed any of it.

I knew what was happening. And I knew that I could stop it.

There was a trellis tangled with wisteria that scrambled up from the backyard of her parents' house to her bedroom window. I climbed it. I opened her wardrobe. I stepped inside and I sat cross-legged, cushioned by a mound of clothing.

I waited.

I knew that he was playing rugby that afternoon. She was watching the match and I knew that they would return to her room afterward because her parents were at her brother's music recital and, at that time in our lives, an empty house was too tantalizing to ignore.

I heard the key in the lock, their voices on the front step, the tap running in the kitchen, a cupboard opening, a glass clinking against the marble worktop. I heard their feet on the stairs, the bedroom door smoothing the carpet, the springs of the bed.

I took my phone from my pocket and I turned on the microphone and I held it at the gap between the two doors where the light seeped in. I still have the recording:

"Can we maybe . . ." she says. "Maybe just not today?"

"Ah, come on," he replies.

"No," she says. "I'm being serious. Can you just . . ."

"But you said," he says. "You said today. And what? You've changed your mind?"

"Next time," she says. "I promise. But my parents. They'll be back any minute."

"You're doing it with someone else, aren't you?" he says, unprovoked.

"I'm not," she replies. "I promise, I'm not."

"You're a fucking slut, that's what you are."

"I'm not! I promise I'm not," she says. "There's no one else. I promise."

"You know that if I wanted to, I could, right? You know that, yeah?"

"Please, Tom. Let's not—"

"I can do whatever I want. You know that."

"Stop it," she says. "Come on, now. Don't threaten me."

"You think that's a threat? It's a fucking promise."

She starts to cry.

"My parents are away next weekend," he says, and he stands up—the creak of the mattress—and he opens the door—the bristle of the weight of the wood on the carpet—and then he leaves.

I stopped recording but I stayed crouched inside the wardrobe.

Marnie went to the bathroom a few minutes later and I crept back out of the window and down the trellis. I sent the recording to his rugby coach with an accompanying email from an anonymous address and Thomas was quietly dismissed from the team. He sent some abusive messages to Marnie, but we read them together and she never saw him again after that. She invited me to take some self-defense classes with her, some sort of martial arts medley, and it was—it still is—rewarding to know that my actions have made us stronger, tougher, less vulnerable.

I think that she knew it was me who recorded him and sent that email. But she never said anything. And I think that if she thought I'd overstepped, she would have done. Still, in the months that followed she would occasionally turn to me, as though about to speak, and then change her mind and close her mouth.

Now, I suppose, I hope that she knew. I hope that, in that moment, she realized that our roots were so tightly locked together—the thicker, barkier skin so eroded at the tightest junctures, flesh on flesh—that we were entirely inseparable. I hope that she knew that we were both all in, at all costs, for always and forever.

The wedding was due to take place eight months after Charles's proposal, on the first Saturday in August. I had wondered if their engagement would change things, but thankfully the steady rhythm of our everyday seemed unaffected. The intervening months passed without issue. Marnie and I still talked to each other regularly, sometimes several times a week. We still had dinner together every Friday evening and while, admittedly, our conversations often turned to floral arrangements, I had expected far worse. And so I had been relieved to discover that we were still very much the same people we had always been.

At the beginning of her last unmarried weekend, on that Friday evening, Marnie and I were sitting together on the floor of her flat, stringing silver name tags to small boxes of sugared almonds. The many lists of things to do had dwindled over the previous weeks until there were just these few final details, the last of the legwork that needed completing.

"When's Charles's mother arriving?" I asked. "Is she staying here?" It was a struggle to negotiate the thin silver thread through the small paper hole, and that kind of meticulous, detailed work had never been my strength.

"Eileen?" said Marnie. "Oh. I don't know. I don't think so. But then . . . I don't know where else she'd be staying. Hang on." She went into the kitchen and returned with her laptop. She sat down on the sofa and lifted the screen. "I don't know," she said again. "I hope she isn't staying here. I'd have to make up the bed and everything."

"I can help you," I said. And then we moved on to the menus, all of which needed hole punching at the top and ribbon looping through the punctures to be tied in a bow.

Charles arrived home an hour or so later. It must have been nearly nine o'clock. We knew that he was in a foul mood from the slam of the door behind him, the crack of his briefcase on the wooden floor, the grunt as he hung his jacket over the banister.

"I'll check on him," whispered Marnie.

I heard her voice in the hallway, a soft buoyant murmuring, with its own tune, almost a song. And his replies, short and sharp and snapped. And initially it was just the unpacking of a day, the unraveling of a rage, but then her voice began to shift, too, undulating, and instead of her calming him, he was riling her.

"I've literally just walked through the door," he said, and his voice was loud now, carrying in that way that a proud man's can. "And you're asking me about wedding things. And I don't have a clue, Marnie. I couldn't tell you anything about anything to do with the wedding."

"I asked about your mother," she said. "She's your mother."

"It's in hand."

"She's on the table plan."

"Well, why is she on the table plan?" he replied.

"Because she's your mother," insisted Marnie. And then quieter, kinder: "Isn't she coming? We haven't seen her in ages and—"

"I'm going to have a shower," he said, and he marched up the stairs and she groaned and walked into the kitchen.

I heard the tap running and the clicking of the hob and her speaking into the camera, melodic again. I continued cutting, threading, tying ribbon, and piling the finished menus into boxes.

Charles came into the living room about ten minutes later, wearing jeans now, his hair damp, and he slumped onto the sofa beside me. He was so big, so tall, over six foot and with broad shoulders and the sort of physique that men hone simply because they want to seem strong.

"You didn't invite her," I said as I measured lengths of ribbon between my fingers.

"What?" he said.

"You're lying," I said. "You didn't invite her."

I don't think he wanted to confide in me—if he'd had a choice he'd have chosen not to—but his pause revealed the truth. "I don't want her there, okay?" he said.

"I get it," I said, and I did. "I didn't invite my parents to my wedding."

"Exactly," he said.

And I think that he misunderstood, that he thought that our parents were the same, that we were the same and we weren't at all.

"Because she's sick," he continued. "And I don't know that I can deal with that on my wedding day, you know. If she's there, it becomes all about her. You wouldn't believe it, the way people are around sickness. I'm out with her and they want to talk, all of them, about her bloody wig and her ongoing nausea and about diets that eradicate cancer. It's absurd. I think she likes it: the attention. I think it gives her a purpose, gives the sickness a purpose. Anyway, it's much easier to not invite her."

"But she's your mother," I replied.

"What?" He had already pulled his phone from his pocket and was distracted by someone different somewhere else.

"You can't not invite her because she's sick," I said. "Does she know that it's happening?"

"Maybe," he said, and he didn't seem embarrassed at all. "I guess my sister might have said something at some point."

"But isn't she devastated?"

"I don't know," he said. "I haven't asked. We aren't close."

"It's cruel," I said.

He put his phone down on the side table and ran his fingers through his wet hair. "I don't think you have any right to say that," he said, and then wiped his hand dry on a cushion. "When you didn't invite your parents, either. And it's my wedding, so it's my decision. And I don't like sick people."

"You don't like what?" said Marnie, catching only part of his sentence as she entered the room with blue and white ceramic plates and silver cutlery piled in her arms. She lowered them onto the table.

"I haven't invited my mother," he said.

"Because she's sick," I said.

"What?" asked Marnie, as she arranged first the knives and then the forks. "Because she's sick? Surely that's a reason *to* invite her?"

"Exactly," I said.

"No," he said. He wasn't angry, not like he'd been before, not like in the hallway, but he was firm and determined. "It's my choice," he said. "And I don't want her there. I don't like sick people."

"What if I get sick?" asked Marnie as she placed the plates in their positions on the table.

"That'll be different," he said.

She looked at me and she raised an eyebrow and a conversation passed unsaid between us, one that acknowledged that it really wasn't that different at all. And yet, while I was horrified by the sentiment, I think Marnie was mostly frustrated. The table plan would need re-drafting.

"As long as that's true, then I'm just going to pretend that this conversation never happened," she said nonchalantly. "I think that's probably the best thing." And then she went back into the kitchen and Charles turned on the television and I finished the menus and then we sat down for dinner as though it genuinely hadn't happened.

But it stayed with me, this strange exchange. Because it confirmed that he wasn't good enough for Marnie and that he never would be, never could be. I had a concrete moment that I could return to in which he had vociferously reassured me that he wasn't right for the woman he was about to marry.

I felt smug.

Is that bad?

Because it was confirmation that he really was detestable, that my hatred wasn't unfounded or undeserved but justifiable and fair. And more than that, because it proved something that I hadn't felt confident articulating before then: that I really was better than him. I took care of those who needed me: I understood that it was part of the contract of love, of duty, of family.

I could see then that he wasn't all in—not at all costs; not at all.

Chapter Nine

The day eventually arrived, the first Saturday in August, and despite an unpromising forecast, the weather was unexpectedly warm, the sky unexpectedly bright. There were hundreds of guests, from every avenue of their lives—school, university, work—and some they had never before met: partners of cousins, friends of their parents, and new infants squalling and then giggling, seemingly without reason. Guests had traveled to Windsor from all over the world: Charles's sister and her husband arrived from New York early that morning, his aunt and uncle interrupted their yearlong sabbatical to join us from South Africa, and Marnie's brother, Eric, jetted back from his high-flying job in New Zealand to be there for the celebrations.

You will think that I am lying when I say this, but I promised you the whole truth and this is that: it really was one of the best days of my life. Marnie and I spent the morning together at her parents' house and we ate toast layered with jam in our pajamas and she had a bath and I sat on the floor beside her and stretched out across the tiles and we talked about how we met in that long, thin queue and the various strings that had been pulled and released and that had led to that very moment.

I watched her marry a man whom I hated but whom she loved and it wasn't as horrible as I thought it would be. I watched her exclusively—absorbed in the way her red hair was curled into a bun at the back of her head; the diamond necklace; the full white skirt; the long lace veil—and I enjoyed her joy. I felt so proud to be part of such an important moment in her life. I ate too much and I drank too much and I danced until my feet were blistered and sore, and yet I felt wonderful.

His speech was quite charming, really. I'd expected it to be nauseating—I thought that he'd talk about the unparalleled force of his love, the strength of his attachment, the way that marriage would bolster their bond—but he didn't and it wasn't. He said that he'd never met anyone so determined, so creative, so unafraid. He said that he'd known immediately, the moment he'd seen her, that she was somehow different, special, unlike anyone else. He said things about her that I knew to be true, and I found myself nodding in spite of myself.

I didn't sit down until after midnight, when most of the guests had left and the band was packing up their instruments and the two bridesmaids were pressing the too-drunk guests into their taxis home. The caterer was organizing the leftover bottles of wine and beer back into their boxes and the manager of the venue was stacking chairs in the dining room. The doors of the conservatory were open, and the air was still warm and fresh with pollen. The fairy lights twinkled overhead, and I knew that I was a little drunk because the brightness was fuzzy, as though the light had been smeared beyond the glass baubles, yellow bleeding into the darkness.

Charles sat down beside me, and he thanked me for my contribution—those were the words he used—and I almost felt like he was being sincere. His waistcoat was undone, slipping from his shoulders, and he'd abandoned his navy bow tie. We watched Marnie floating across the dance floor. Her dress was almost black at the bottom, the grime and dirt of the day sullying the white silk. Her cheeks were pink and some of her ringlets had fallen from their clips, hanging around her face and damp with sweat.

"Quite something, isn't she?" said Charles.

I nodded.

I'm not now sure—the passing of time has blurred the edges of my memory—if what happened next really happened. It may have been simply a figment of my hatred, an illusion, the result of too much champagne and too much anger. But I don't think so.

Charles sat back, leaning against the glass wall of the conservatory, his hands reaching up behind his head, and then he sighed.

"Really quite something," he said again.

He lowered his arms and one fell behind my head, slithering down the back of my neck. He pulled me toward him and he kissed my forehead. His lips were wet, glazed with saliva, and the moisture burned cold on my skin when he withdrew.

"We're a lucky pair," he said.

He was slurring. I'd drunk too much, certainly, but he was definitely too far gone, different somehow, sloppier than I'd seen him before. His left hand crawled over my shoulder, toward my collarbone, sweeping past my armpit. I held my breath. I fixed my ribs. I didn't want to inhale, to expand, to force my chest toward his palm. His hand swung there, inches from my breast, shackling me to the bench. I couldn't move without moving into him, making him touch me, molesting myself against him.

He laughed, a coarse and ugly chuckle.

He said, "Oh, Jane," and then his fingertips grazed my nipple through the yellow silk of my bridesmaid dress. I lowered my chin, choked by the compulsion to look down at my chest. He pressed his palm into me, and as he withdrew, he quickly pressed my nipple between his thumb and index finger.

I wish I could tell you that I did something or said something. I wish I'd challenged him. Perhaps he'd have been shocked—I might have recognized genuine astonishment—and I would have known then that what I thought might be happening wasn't happening at all.

But I did nothing, so there's no way to know now.

"I can't believe it's nearly over," said Marnie, sitting down beside us and resting her head on his shoulder. "What a day," she said. "It's been, just hasn't it been, just the best?"

Charles slowly pulled his arm away. I felt it slipping across the back of my neck, my shoulders, retreating carefully, until we were no longer touching. I felt the space between us, that sliver of fresh air, cold and welcome, like a fault line splitting enemy states. My nipple ached, a shadow pain.

"Is everything okay?" she asked, smiling. "What's happening here?"

Charles looked at me and if you believe that I was sober enough to read a look right then, know this: it was a look that demanded silence.

"Nothing's happening," I said, sliding a few inches farther away, farther down the bench, a little bit farther from them and their love. "Nothing at all."

That was the second lie I told Marnie.

You see, don't you, that I didn't have a choice? What could I have said? If I had been honest, she might have felt forced to choose. And, anyway, I was all in, at all costs. And, back then, I thought that meant maneuvering the truth in order to make her happy, to keep her happy, to protect our roots.

Here is an absolute truth. That day didn't change my feelings toward Charles. I had hated him for years and that day changed nothing.

Is it cruel to say that their love was the most offensive, unrelenting, repulsive love I have ever known? It is, I know. But their love disgusted me. I hated his face, the smirk that lurked at the tip of his lips, the exaggerated expansion of his chest as he inhaled, the way he drummed his fingers against the table as if to say, *You bore me.* I hated feeling his hands on my skin through that flimsy fabric, but no more than I hated every other facet of his existence.

I would have liked to erase him from my life. I need to be careful saying that now, I know, because it sounds like *intent.* What I mean is that I wish our stories shared no chapters, that the ink of his life wasn't there on the pages of mine, that our lives had existed concurrently, yes, but had never overlapped.

But do I regret his death? No. I don't.

I'm not sorry at all.

The
Third Lie

Chapter Ten

—————

I told her that it was nothing, that nothing had happened.

And today, more than ever, that feels relevant, an important part of the story, an important part of your story. I'm not talking about a motive—please don't try to misinterpret what I'm saying—but when something happens, something unexpected, something frightening, the steps that led to that moment are cast in a different die.

There was one other person, one other and now you, who knew that something had happened that evening. I told her the day afterward, long before I was afraid to say that there had ever been anything other than "nothing" between Charles and me.

The morning after the wedding, I was lying in bed, pretending that I didn't have a headache, that I wasn't desperate for a glass of water, that I didn't urgently need the bathroom, that I was fine, when my doorbell rang.

My blinds were down but the sun was leaching in around the edges, thin white lines of light speckled by flecks of dust. I ought to vacuum, perhaps mop the floor, I thought, but I knew that I'd do neither. The place was untidy—littered with books and magazines—but I was too hungover, too tired to care. My wardrobe doors hung open and clothes fell from between them and onto the floor, endless pairs of jeans and shorts and sweaters. A rickety wooden chair stood by the window stacked high with piles of clean clothing and bedding and, there on the top, my corseted nude knickers from the night before. My bridesmaid dress was hanging on the back of my bedroom door, dark patches staining the underarms, a few lighter splotches—champagne, perhaps— discoloring the skirt. The air in the room was thick and musty, heavy with the stench of sleep and sweat. It ought to have been disgusting, insufferable, and yet it felt like a familiar space, a familiar mess, a familiar smell.

I stayed still, as though the noise of rustling sheets might leak through my bedroom door, down the small hallway, and into the corridor beyond my flat.

The bell rang again.

There was a thumping—three times—and the door flinched within its frame, shaking on its hinges.

"Jane?"

I recognized the voice immediately. It was Emma, my sister, younger by a few years and even more my reverse than Marnie. If I am very much dark and Marnie is very much light, then Emma was very much both. She not only had the fairest skin and the darkest hair, but she was also the highest of highs and the lowest of lows, the most vulnerable and yet invincible, afraid and still brave, broken in so many ways but unyielding at the same time.

The doorbell rang a third time. She depressed the buzzer for several seconds so that the drilling darted through the entire flat.

"I know you're in there!" she shouted.

I stayed tucked beneath my quilt, refusing to move.

"I have breakfast," she called.

Her voice lifted at the end of the sentence and she sang the word "breakfast." She knew that she was playing her best hand, her ace of spades, and she knew that I knew it, too.

On weekdays, my breakfast of choice was a bowl of cereal. I tended to opt for oaty flakes that looked and tasted like recycled cardboard floating in thick full-fat milk with the consistency of cream. Curiously, it was less sugary than the semi-skimmed alternative. I had first tried it a few years earlier, just after my husband's death, when I was on a no-sugar diet, trying to become very thin, as small as humanly possible. Which had been a mistake. Because no small decisions made in the aftermath of an almighty loss are good decisions. And so the other compromises—brown rice, and no fruit juice, and brownies made from beetroots—were quickly forgotten.

On weekends, I always wanted something sweeter.

"Can you smell the croissants?" Emma called. "From the bakery less than ten minutes ago. Yum-mee."

She paused, listening for my footsteps. I pictured her standing on the worn taupe carpet, under the bright yellow lights, shifting her weight between her feet, impatient as ever, frustrated at being ignored.

"Come on, Jane!" she shouted. "I haven't got all day."

I sat up and flung my feet over the side of the mattress and into my slippers. I loved her—I really did—but there were never any boundaries. She didn't think it was at all abnormal to stand at my door in the morning, without warning, and to hound me with her knocking and her banging and her shouting. Because our lives had always flooded to-gether: the challenges, the struggles, the minutiae of the day-to-day.

Although that isn't quite right. It is more accurate to say that her life streamed constantly into mine. I was the vessel for her anxiety. I was the ear into which she confessed, the shoulder on which she felt sup-ported, the hand for her to hold. She bled her burdens into me until she felt a little better. And then I would carry and nurture her fears instead.

It had always been that way. I was loved too little and she was loved too much, and it might surprise you to know that both are equally un-bearable. She was often seeking space, suffocated by being the favorite. I became her ally, her safe place.

She needed me. I didn't know then that I needed her, too.

"Get a move on, will you?" she shouted. "It's not like I'm going to eat them."

I heard her laugh. Her humor was wicked. It still had the power to shock me, even when my mind was filled with her thoughts, her wit, her traumas.

I pulled on my dressing gown and secured the belt around my waist. It was dark purple and worn, the fibers clumping together along the sleeves where something had once been spilled. It had belonged to Jonathan and was far too big for me. The shoulder seams sat inches down my upper arms and the hem hung below my knees, almost touching my ankles. He'd worn it whenever he'd woken early on weekends to prepare a cooked breakfast.

I opened the front door. She was wearing a thick navy jumper and loose jeans cropped above her ankles. Her white socks looked like those we'd worn in primary school, thick with elasticated bands at the top and fabric bobbles along the fringes of white trainers. Her hair had been trimmed, cut short to mirror her jawline, sliding into a pointed chin.

"About bloody time," Emma said. "You look like shit."

I turned to look at myself in the small round mirror that hung from a nail on the wall in the hallway. I hadn't removed my makeup the night before. My eyes were surrounded by smudges of black and my lipstick had bled into the folds around my mouth.

I shrugged. "It was a good night."

"Good?" she asked. "Your best friend's wedding and all you can say is *good*? Is that it?"

She handed me a brown paper bag filled with pastries. I peered inside: a plain butter croissant, a *pain au chocolat*.

"For you," she said.

She headed toward the sofa and curled herself into the cushions, her feet coiled beneath her, sinking into my furniture, very much at home. I poured myself a glass of orange juice from the fridge.

"It was great," I said instead. "A really great night. That better?"

"Urgh, that's even worse," she groaned. "You're rubbish at this. Tell me something interesting. Were there any arguments? Any fights? Who got to sleep with the maid of honor?"

"No one got to sleep with the maid of honor," I replied. "And no fights, as far as I'm aware."

"Charles on his best behavior, then?" she asked. "Not too much of a cunt?"

"Not too bad," I said. "Although there was this one thing right at the end of the evening."

My flat is surrounded by other flats on all sides but one and is always that little bit too warm. So whenever I have guests—which, frankly, isn't very often—I watch them gradually undress throughout the course of their visit. At first, it's just their coats and sweaters, then it's their shoes and cardigans, and eventually they are sitting sockless in camisoles.

Emma was no different. But I was frightened by what I saw that day.

She lifted her jumper over her head. Her shoulder bones were sitting high above the flesh of her shoulders. Her collarbone protruded, pressing against her skin and stretching it, so that it looked too thin, almost translucent. Her upper arms were scrawny, like the wings of a bird, all skin and bone and no fat at all.

I took a sharp breath, a sigh in reverse, and Emma looked up with her eyes wide and wary.

"Don't," she said, reading the concern written in the crease at the center of my forehead and between my eyebrows. "I'm not interested."

"Em . . ." I said, but then she looked at me, fierce and unblinking, and I knew that there was nothing more to say.

Emma was twelve when she first fell between the gaps in our concentration. I don't remember the early days of her illness. I was so busy revising, so focused on things that would never matter to me—quadratic equations, the formula for respiration, river landscapes—that I failed to recognize the deterioration of the thing that mattered most of all.

It was July, I think. Emma and I had both finished school for the summer—if I remember rightly Marnie was in the South of France—and our parents were busy, as ever, hacking away at their marriage with pickaxes disguised in insults and eye rolls. It was hot, too hot for England, the temperature over eighty-five degrees. We went to the open-air pool and I squeezed our towels in between the hundreds of others, the families with five children dipping and diving and running dripping across the grass, the women with their curves, the older couples sitting on folding chairs with their newspapers. I was wearing a swimsuit and I was sweating in the sun, moisture trickling between my breasts, droplets simmering on my top lip. Emma was wearing knee-length shorts and a woolen jumper, and she was shivering. I wanted her to go in the pool with me, but she wouldn't: she said something about valuables, but we had none, just towels and clothing and one book each. I nagged, of course, because I'm an older sister and that is my right, and eventually she relented. I remember her easing her jumper over her head, and her shoulders and collarbone were so much worse then, desperate to escape her body, pushing at her thin, fair skin. She slipped her shorts over her thighs and her legs were shapeless, straight lines of bone with so little flesh, so little depth. She stared at me, challenging me to respond to her frail, frightful body, and I said nothing.

Over the next few months I forced food onto her plate and sometimes she ate it and sometimes she didn't. And then she was better, briefly. And then she was worse again. And the next couple of years continued in this pattern, never in the best of health, never in the worst, until I left for university when she was just fourteen. And then there were very few peaks and so many troughs. Until eventually even my parents could no longer deny the situation sitting there at their dining table and she was hospitalized and then released and then eventually hospitalized again.

I know that this casts her as a very particular character in a very particular story. But, if you'd met Emma—I wish that you had; you'd have liked her, I think—you'd know that she wasn't that person at all. Emma was never a victim. She was sick, yes, and for a very long time, but that was such a small part of her narrative.

Her sickness existed somewhere within her, a strange plague that she couldn't control, there in her mind and in her bones and in the very tissue of her being. It was a significant part of her life, but think of it as a path that she didn't choose, didn't want, but that she learned to travel in her own way. She eventually chose not to be treated anymore and I did my very best to respect that decision.

"Stop looking at me like that," she said, curling up on my sofa, shielding herself, hiding behind her jumper. "Like you've seen a ghost."

I raised an eyebrow; I couldn't help it.

For years—for almost my entire time at university—I had nightmares about Emma's corpse. I would be dreaming of something else when, in the middle of whatever I was envisaging—holidays, lecture halls, Marnie—I would discover Emma's dead body, her limbs stiff and blue, eyes clouded and open wide. I would wake gasping for air, sweating and shaking in cold, damp sheets.

"Fuck's sake," she said eventually, pulling her jumper back over her head. "It's fine. I'm fine."

And I had no choice but to let it go. There was nothing to be gained in an argument and everything to be lost.

"Charles," she said, patting the space beside her on the sofa. "You were saying."

I sat down and recalled the events of the previous evening. I told her about his slurring, the endless bottles of champagne, the relentless top-ups. I talked about his arm draped over my shoulder, the coarse fabric of his starchy white shirt at the back of my neck. I closed my eyes; I knew that I was blushing as I described his palm falling over my breast, his fingertips over my nipple. I explained the space that expanded between us, the bright white of Marnie's dress as she approached and sat beside us, and that sense of something being sucked back into its box.

Emma was wide-eyed, openmouthed. "And what did she say?" Emma whispered.

"Nothing," I replied. "She didn't say anything. She didn't *see* anything."

"She didn't see anything at all?" Emma looked down at the cushion clutched to her chest.

"Are you quite sure?" she asked. "Definitely sure? This definitely happened exactly like that? He wasn't just drunk and loose-limbed and a little bit handsy without really meaning to be?"

I shrugged. "Maybe," I replied.

"Although it's not very Charles to be anything other than exactly what he means to be really, is it? That's not really him at all."

I smiled. Emma had never met Charles. So the only version of him that she knew was mine.

Here, then, is something that I've thought about regularly over the last few months. Emma didn't know Charles. She had no reason to doubt my experience, no reason not to believe that he really was a depraved pervert who would grope the maid of honor at his own wedding and in front of his beautiful wife. And yet Emma's instinctive response was to question not Charles's character but my version of events. What does that say about me? About my capacity for truth? About my ability to accurately read a situation?

Does it, in fact, suggest that Charles was innocent of all wrongdoing that evening? That the error of judgment was mine and mine alone? I don't think so, but it's worth your consideration. This is my truth, after all. And that is not the same as *the* truth.

"Are you going to tell Marnie?" she asked. "That her new husband groped you? Because I really think that would be a bad idea."

I shook my head.

"Still creepy, though," she continued. "Definitely odd." She rotated the cushion in front of her chest, pinching it at the corners, spinning it like a wheel. "Were you scared?" she asked.

"Of Charles?"

"Yeah," she said. "Like, did it frighten you?"

"No," I said instinctively. "No. Not really."

And as soon as I'd said the words, I realized that they weren't true. I had been scared. Not terrified. It wasn't like that. But unnerved and uneasy and suddenly very aware of myself as something much smaller stuck in the presence of something much bigger. And it was more than the small fear that I often feel in situations that I cannot predict. It was more than the walk home from the tube station late at night and a man's footsteps behind me, and more than someone standing too close at a pedestrian crossing, and more than a group huddled up ahead in the tunnel beneath the railway tracks. Because this was calculated. It had purpose, an objective—and if it was to make me feel frightened, then it had succeeded.

"How was Mum?" I asked.

Emma looked down at the floor and fiddled with a strand of wool hanging loose from her jumper. "I didn't go," she replied. "I just . . . I couldn't."

I exhaled slowly, trying very hard not to sigh. I had explained several times to my mother—I'd even written it on her calendar—that I wouldn't be coming that Saturday, because of the wedding, but that Emma would be there instead.

"Don't tell me off," said Emma. "Please don't. I called. I told the receptionist. I just couldn't do it. Okay? I just couldn't."

When we were younger, still children, my mother and my sister were incredibly close. It looked quite disgusting to me, to be fused so snugly to somebody else. And yet while Emma sometimes struggled with feeling so stifled—and would briefly escape to spend time with me elsewhere in the house—she needed my mother in a myriad of ways: emotionally, practically, for comfort and company. She was a worrier, like my mother, even then, and was uncomfortable and uneasy around new people. She hid behind my mother's legs in strange places, peering between her thighs. At home, she followed my mother between rooms, wanting to help in the kitchen, with the cleaning, with whatever it was that our mother was doing. In the evenings, she liked to be cuddled and read to and bathed. Emma needed my mother and my mother needed to be needed.

But when Emma really needed my mother—when she really needed support and love and strength—she received nothing. Her anchor slipped away, embarrassed at the very nature of the need. I look back now, and I know that my mother was simply frightened. She was never idealistic, and she must have known what was happening and how difficult—impossible, perhaps—it would be to untangle. So she ignored it, pretending that her daughter was fine and scraping food into the bin without question and washing up cutlery that hadn't been used.

Emma's need grew and grew and my mother's avoidance intensified, until Emma was so angry and isolated and my mother so afraid for her future that there was really no path to recovery. Emma never truly forgave her. She moved out as soon as she was well enough.

I thought that she blamed our mother for her illness: not for how it began, but for how it survived. I thought that their bond had been dismantled, that they were held together, in the end, not by love but by blood, a single filament stretching between them that could never be snapped. I was wrong. There were other threads, thicker threads, ones that held them together and that I simply couldn't see.

"Jane, please," said Emma. "Come on now. I really did try."

I didn't reply. I wanted to ask her to think about how her actions affected other people, to explain that her decision made me feel guilty for not attending myself, that our mother likely felt incredibly lonely. But Emma had so many feelings that she found it almost impossible to negotiate the world from anyone's hill but her own.

Instead, I asked her about her volunteer projects and her flat and a book I'd recommended about a dysfunctional family, which it turned out she still hadn't read. I had a shower and put on a clean pair of pajamas and we spent the day on the sofa, watching DVDs that had once belonged to our father—action films with male heroes and laughably incompetent women—and which I'd taken as my own when he left. We had watched them together, and he had pulled me onto his lap and let me curl against him and fall asleep with my head to his chest, while my mother was fretting elsewhere.

Emma took a few with her when she went home that evening. She said that they'd always been hers and I knew that it wasn't true, but I didn't really mind. There were so many things that we couldn't talk about, never said, and so this felt like a comparatively minor transgression. I watched as she left with them tucked in her rucksack, and I tried to focus only on the sharp cut of her hair just above the bag, and not on her matchstick legs poking from beneath it.

Chapter Eleven

Marnie and Charles were leaving on the Monday after their wedding to spend two and a half weeks honeymooning in Italy. Charles had planned everything: outlining their course across the country, booking their flights, reserving the most luxurious rooms in the most extravagant hotels. He wanted it to be a surprise, he'd said, and so he had harassed me with every minute detail and with his eagerness in the preceding months. He'd rented a car in her favorite color, a classic convertible. He'd opted for hotels adorned with plush velvets and ornate chandeliers, rather than the sparse monotone palette that he'd have preferred. He'd tracked a route through culinary favorites, places he thought she'd enjoy.

"How would she feel about a cooking class?" he'd asked, earlier in the year.

"What do you think of this?" he'd said as he scrolled through the website of a swish new restaurant. "Do you think she'd like this sort of food? And what about the view?"

"What about Rome?" he'd quickly whispered one evening while she was still in the kitchen. "Has she been there before?"

She hadn't, and I said so, and as a result of these incessant exchanges, I became well acquainted with their itinerary. And so, that morning, I pictured them arriving at the airport, in the departure lounge, sitting side by side on their flight, and then waiting at the carousel for their luggage. I could see them laughing together as they bundled their things into the tiny boot of their car, the way his hand would sit on her thigh throughout the drive. I could see the entrance to their first hotel, the purple sofa in their suite, the infinity pool surrounded by hammocks and overlooking vineyards. I knew every step that they'd take and I had an ache in my stomach for the duration and I knew that I was jealous. I loved her and I wanted her to be enjoying the most wonderful honeymoon and yet I wished that I could be part of it, too.

We had traveled together, once or twice, visiting trashy beach destinations where we had overindulged in garishly bright cocktails with sugar sediment in each sip, and I had bronzed in the sun and she had grown paler by comparison. We had shared a bed at night and thought nothing of it, and held hands on turbulent flights, and negotiated passport control together. But it was more than that. We had laughed and gossiped and confessed our secrets. We had enmeshed ourselves into one, with private jokes and joint suitcases and tacky threadbare bracelets that cost nothing but meant something.

But we hadn't traveled together since she had met Charles.

All of those things she now shared with him: a bed, a suitcase, her secrets.

I thought of them over those two weeks, intermittently, but always with a tight dread across my chest. I felt that our roots were loosening and that seemed shocking and unacceptable simply because before then I hadn't thought that it was possible.

Marnie called me late in the evening, just after she'd arrived home from her honeymoon, when I was already almost asleep. She wanted to hear my thoughts about her wedding day, the things that stood out most, the things that I remembered. I told her about Ella, her six-year-old niece, who was wearing only socks and underwear by the end of the first dance and had beads of sweat glistening on her forehead as she jumped and twirled. I told her about her brother, who napped drunk beneath a table during the speeches. I told her about the registrar, who was caught in traffic and running late and sending panicked text messages ahead of the ceremony.

She laughed when I told her that the cheese tower had collapsed moments after it was cut. She sighed, and I could hear that she was smiling, when I told her that her parents were still dancing, her mother's head turned sideways against her father's shoulder, long after the band had finished, as the staff cleared the room around them.

"It's so lovely to hear these things," she said. "I feel like I missed so much on the day. I planned everything so perfectly, but then I could only be in one place. I'm waiting for the rest of the photographs. We've got a few already. Only a dozen or so, some of the favorites, but there are some lovely ones of you. Are you coming on Friday? I'll show you them then."

"Will you send them over?" I asked.

We had been angled around a floral archway, the two of them, and then all of us together, and then smaller groups—parents, siblings, friends. We were ushered into position, told to pose, then pushed quickly out of frame. I didn't know if there was a photograph of the two of us alone, but I hoped so.

"Sure," she replied. "I'll forward you the email. You'll laugh at the one of my parents."

"They were good, I thought, on the day," I said.

"I know," she replied. "I thought that, too. Although—and this is just typical—it turns out that they were in Florence at the same time we were. Mum had a conference, something about allergies, and Dad went along, too. But did they tell me? Nope. Did they want to meet? To have lunch or dinner with us? Nope."

She always saw the worst in them, looked for the things that proved their indifference.

"I don't know if that's so bad," I said. "Perhaps they didn't want to encroach?"

"Well, that's a nice way of thinking about it," she said. "But I don't think so."

I yawned, which I hoped might signal the end of the conversation, but Marnie continued regardless.

"You know something?" she said. "I feel different now. Can I say wiser without sounding like a twat? Or maybe not? I'm not that sure I can."

"No," I said. "I'm not sure that you can."

"I feel more like an adult," she said. And then she paused. "No, that's not quite right. I feel like I've just taken part in a very public display of adulthood. Like I'm pretending. Does that make sense?"

"Not really," I replied.

"Anyway," she continued, "that's sort of why I called. We've decided to sell the flat. You know. Being adults and all that."

She paused, and I said nothing.

"We talked about it while we were away, and we think it feels right."

She paused again.

She was testing each step, placing one foot at a time on the brittle wood to see if it buckled. I knew that she was wondering—asking in a silent sort of way—whether this would be upsetting for me, if the change in routine would be a problem. They had been saying for ages that one day they would move beyond the limits of the city, to a house with a garden and a driveway and bedrooms that overlooked fields. I wasn't sure if she was saying this with her silence, too.

She was careful not to mention money. Charles was very successful, by which I really mean very wealthy, working in a private equity firm where he bought companies and sold them in parts for a profit. And Marnie was working harder than ever, writing about food and talking about food. She had recently taken on a new sponsor, a company selling only knives and each at a ridiculous price. Apparently, they'd seen a significant uplift in sales since she'd started featuring them in her videos and so she'd successfully negotiated a better rate.

I, by contrast, had never felt less engaged by my job, where it seemed my primary objective was to handle customer complaints and pay as little compensation for our failings as possible. I could barely afford my rent. And she was sensitive to that, never wanting me to feel inferior.

Oh.

Yes.

No. You're right.

I'm trying very hard to be honest. Unsurprisingly, it doesn't come very naturally to me. I've slightly misrepresented my situation.

I had money—I still have money—but saved somewhere else.

Jonathan—as a cameraman, freelancing, with no company benefits whatsoever, and because he was so endlessly efficient—had taken out a life insurance policy. I was his next of kin and so the payment had come to me.

But I couldn't—I still can't—spend it. He wanted me to have it, but I cannot stand the thought that his life has been assigned a value. Because no amount of money can compensate for that loss. It doesn't even come close. How can you quantify the light still on in the hallway when you come home after dark? How can you price a recognizable smile waiting late at the bus stop to walk you back to bed? What does it cost to replace someone whose hand so perfectly fit your own, whose warmth was reassurance, whose laughter was excitement, someone who had willingly woven his life into yours?

If you were to try, to use their algorithm to assign numbers to loved ones, you'd discover that a man like Charles was worth far more than a man like Jonathan. Which further proves my point.

Emma thought that I was being ridiculous. She thought I should invest the money. She sent me dozens of links to properties: modern flats in the center of the city, two-bedroom terraces in the suburbs, even a sea-view apartment on the south coast. She set me up on a date with a friend of hers—a man she volunteered with at the food bank who'd inherited a small fortune from his late wife—so that we could discuss returns on investments and the property market and a whole world in which I had no interest whatsoever. I said that I didn't want a date, and she said that it was a banking date, and I said that wasn't a thing and refused. And then she said the words "silver lining" and we never spoke about or acknowledged that the money existed again.

It's still there in that bank account.

"I think it's because now that we're husband and wife we just feel like a flat probably isn't the right sort of home for us anymore, you know?" Marnie continued. "We just feel like a house would be more appropriate. I love that flat, but there's an argument, isn't there, that this is the time to start thinking about the next steps in life. Room to grow and all that. Maybe in September. I think that's meant to be a good time to sell."

"You should do what you want to do," I said. "Whatever feels right."

"You sound just like Charles," she replied. "You're both so sensible. He keeps saying that we're only just married, that we have all the time in the world to do these things, that there's no pressure whatsoever. But I think he wants to do it, too, you know, just that he doesn't want to be pushy. I think he likes the idea of more space. I could get him a dog—you know the one he wants; is it a husky? But then, as he says, there's always more time, and dogs are so much work, aren't they?"

I didn't respond.

"Jane?"

I turned off my bedside lamp and closed my eyes.

"Shit," she said. "I'm so sorry. Was that insensitive? There isn't always more time. I know that. It's why I think this way, I think, because of Jonathan. I know that sometimes life shifts unexpectedly, that the choices get taken away. Shit. Jane, I'm sorry. I was just . . . Jane?"

"It's fine," I replied. "Really."

I wanted to go to sleep. I didn't want to have this conversation.

I could see that her life was expanding as mine was shrinking. I had once had the conversations that she was now having—asked myself those very same questions—and looked ahead toward a life that offered answers.

Jonathan had always wanted to move away from the city, to live in the countryside: he'd wanted to keep chickens, and have more bedrooms than children, and build a treehouse at the bottom of the yard.

"You know the smog outside the flat? Well, there'd be none of that," he'd say, trying to persuade me.

"Did you hear that?" he'd whisper, in the middle of the night, in response to bottles being broken or tires screeching on the street outside. "You don't get that in the countryside."

He'd go to the supermarket and, as he unpacked the vegetables, each clinically wrapped in plastic, he would say, "I could have grown this myself."

I knew that eventually I would say: "Yes. Okay. Let's do it."

But that moment never came.

Chapter Twelve

Here's the thing. When something starts to slip away, it becomes almost impossible to think about anything other than how it was at its best. I tried to fall asleep, but I couldn't. I could only work backward through our friendship and try to find moments that felt equally fragile.

We had one row at school, only one. It was about something and nothing, as arguments so often are. She always pressed snooze on her alarm clock, half a dozen times at least, until she was frantic and rushing and falling into the classroom. We were partnered in every lesson, and drama was first on a Thursday. Almost every activity required a pair; a one on its own simply wasn't enough. She rarely apologized for being so late. And eventually I lost my temper. It was selfish of her not to think of me, to forget that her behavior affected others. I said that I wasn't sure that I wanted to be her partner anymore. She said fine, if that was how I felt, and she stormed off with her scarf trailing behind her and her homework still clasped in her fist.

This friction lasted an entire day. We didn't sit together and we walked separately between classes. The hostility was unprecedented. We were normally the harmonious anomaly in among endless teenage conflict. Our teacher was so shocked by the situation that she sat us down after our last class and unraveled the issue—with words like "responsibility" and "compassion"—and insisted that we stop being so immature and learn to address our problems in an adult manner.

And that was it. The only argument. We forgave each other, but we didn't forget it. Instead, we carried it like a trophy, because just one argument in the course of an entire friendship seemed something worth celebrating.

There hadn't been another blip since. We'd moved to separate cities to study at eighteen but it felt like we were barely apart, because there was always a reason to call, a story to share, something only she'd understand. We snapped back together three years later. And then we were better than we'd ever been, a concrete team against a world that seemed confounding.

It was in that first year in the Vauxhall flat—perhaps only a month or two before I met Jonathan—that Marnie first tried to quit her job. She'd written a letter of resignation, but her boss, Steven, had refused to accept it. She'd returned to the flat that evening perplexed and rather despondent but determined to find a solution. She hated the work and the people and her boss in particular, who thought he was irresistible to younger women, which was very much not the case. I'd met him a few times before—at her various work events—and it was clear that he still thought himself as handsome as he'd been thirty years earlier.

Marnie tried to resign again the following week. She cornered her boss and confronted him with her letter in front of their managing director.

"As discussed," she'd said firmly, "my resignation."

"Oh, I'm so sorry to hear that," Abi had said. "You must be disappointed, Steven."

"Very," he'd replied as he reluctantly accepted the envelope.

"I hope you're moving on to exciting new things," Abi had said, and she'd smiled. She had been appointed a few months earlier. She was six foot one and fiercely ambitious. The younger women in the company were impressed by her; the older men less so.

And so Steven wasn't going to make things easy; he was determined to make Marnie suffer for the simple crime of suggesting that she might not be entirely content in his presence. He pulled Marnie aside later that day and informed her that she had a six-month notice period and would be expected to serve the full duration. Marnie argued that it was ridiculous—that she hadn't known what she was signing and that it was a disproportionate term of notice for an assistant—but he was insistent.

That evening she threw herself onto the sofa and buried her head beneath the cushions and seethed because it wasn't fair, simply wasn't going to happen, because she couldn't do it, wouldn't do it, couldn't be expected to work for such an odious man for another six months.

"Help me," she pleaded, peeking at me from between two pillows. "I will die if I spend another month with that man. I can smell his breath on my clothes," she said, "and I can hear his nasal laugh grating in my head all the time, even when we aren't together, even on week-ends. Help me, Jane."

So we devised a plan. I had done this before, of course, without her, to retaliate against her seemingly charming but fundamentally volatile first boyfriend, but it was so different, so invigorating to be sharing the anticipation. Their company's annual summer party was the following weekend. It was a big event designed to charm their suppliers and investors and to thank the employees and to entertain their partners. It was held on the river in the garden of the company's largest pub and the attention to detail was inspiring. It was themed—they always were—and this year the spotlight was on the circus.

We arrived early. Giant gates sprayed in gold paint had been erected in the car park and we were ushered in by two clowns and directed through to the circus itself. There was a big top tent in stretched blue plastic and a man on stilts strolled past in bright red flares, looking straight ahead, as though entirely unaware of the world playing out around his feet, the smaller lives scrabbling at ground level.

Marnie took my hand and together we weaved through the masses.

She was wearing a black leotard and sheer black tights and she looked elegant, confident, as though her body was the very thing that she wanted it to be. I was wearing a long floral skirt and a small crystal ball on a chain around my neck. I had wanted to wear my jeans.

Marnie paused in front of the bar and pointed at a very tall woman dressed in a red leather jacket with striped gold cuffs and black leather lapels. A small red top hat was perched on her head and a bull whip was clasped in her fist.

"There," she said. "That's her; that's Abi."

I nodded. "And where will I find you?" I asked.

Marnie pointed at a wooden caravan just beyond the popcorn stand. It was painted lime green and had bright yellow stripes down the sides. "Behind that," she said. "In fifteen minutes."

I approached Abi. I interrupted her conversation. I introduced myself as Pippa Davies.

She recognized the name immediately. Pippa Davies was the daughter of one of their principal suppliers. Pippa had called Marnie the previous week and said that she was no longer able to attend, and Marnie had chosen not to amend the guest list.

Abi was delighted to see me. She led me through the circus—she wanted to show me their site, their flagship pub, the scale of their operation—and she was pitch-perfect as she sold me their success and their ambition. I followed her willingly and slowly, subtly, focused on maneuvering us past the popcorn stand and toward the green caravan.

"This is very elegant," I said, and I started to circle it.

"Sure," said Abi, a little surprised by the unexpected detour. "I expect your father has mentioned the parties we host for the customers, too: Saint Patrick's Day, Halloween, New Year's Eve."

I stopped and I stared. It had worked. I could see that they were squabbling and so I cleared my throat. Marnie looked up and then her posture softened slightly, her weight shifting to one side, her hip jutting out, and she stepped toward him and put her hand on his shoulder. It looked illicit, flirtatious, and I felt both repulsed and delighted.

"We feel that attention to detail is paramount and, for me, this is one of the many things that separates us from our competitors and—"

Abi looked up and made a tiny noise, a tiny gasp, and her hands flew up to cover her lips, her whip falling to the ground beside her.

"Steven," she said. "What on earth . . . ? What is this?"

He furrowed his eyebrows—it was rather endearing, really—and he glanced among the three of us, bewildered and unable to process what exactly was happening and why his boss was looking so shocked, so horrified. And then he understood. He looked at Marnie and he raised his eyebrows and he turned his head to one side as though about to shout, and then he recognized that there was a more important concern, someone else who he ought to address.

"Abi," he said, and he stepped backward away from Marnie. "This is not what it looks like. This is absolutely—"

"Don't," said Marnie, and she held her hand up and out. "Please. Let's just be honest. We can't keep this a secret, not now, not anymore."

She was not a great actress, probably not even a good one, and her words were stilted and sharp, her actions unnatural. But he was playing his part so perfectly. His wide eyes were scanning the garden either side of us, presumably looking for his wife. His mouth was opening and closing, unsure what to say, unsure where to start.

"I'm sorry. We should have told you," continued Marnie. "But for obvious reasons we've been trying to keep this quiet. But you should know, I think, that Stevie and I . . . we're in a relationship."

"A relationship?" said Abi.

"A what?" said Steven.

"And I know—I've checked the policy—that one of us needs to resign. I understand and you know already that I've been thinking about my next steps and—"

"Effective immediately?" asked Abi, clearly keen to find the least disruptive solution and to minimize her own embarrassment.

"Of course," said Marnie. "I'll collect my things on Monday."

"Fine," said Abi. She turned to me and put her hands on my upper arms and apologized profusely for the behavior of her staff and promised to address it immediately and asked if I'd please excuse her so that she could have a quick word with her colleague. And then she walked up to Steven and marched him into the pub.

Marnie ran up to me and she squealed and she threw her arms around my neck and we were laughing because the whole moment was so ridiculous, and because we couldn't believe that it had worked but it had, and because we felt powerful and galvanized, and because we thought then that we were agents of our own lives rather than simply two young women. We were united. It bonded us in a way that felt exciting: a secret shared, a collective triumph, the sense that together we were unstoppable.

We went to a bar on the way home and commandeered two velvet armchairs tucked into a corner. It was still early in the evening and there were few other customers, but the band was warming up at the back and the bar staff were lighting candles and cleaning glasses. I ordered a bottle of champagne, because although my salary was low and hers now nonexistent, we had something to celebrate.

We walked home later that evening, her arm looped through mine, and we recounted the madness of our day. She clapped her hands together excitedly when I reminded her that there was no work anymore, that she was free from the nine-to-five of office life. She breathed hot air onto the mirrored wall of the elevator and drew a smiling face with her finger. She jumped on our sofa and insisted that I jump, too. It was silly. It was fun. She held my hands as we bounced. I remember that we were laughing and that it felt so ordinary to laugh noisily together. But now? I struggle to recall what it really felt like to be that way with her, to lose myself in her, to be so effortlessly us.

Chapter Thirteen

I visited Marnie and Charles the following Friday—just after they'd returned from their honeymoon—and we were sitting, the three of us, on their sofa. The chandelier overhead was switched off and the wall lamps cast a golden shadow against the walls. There were candles everywhere, flames flickering around their wicks. The balcony was hidden behind thick red curtains hanging in waves.

It had turned into the wettest August on record and—everyone had agreed: the postman, the weather forecaster, my colleagues—the most miserable in living memory. Every day that week had been obscured by dense, heavy rain, fat droplets that bounced when they hit the sidewalk or the hood of a car.

"The rain!" said Marnie. "We'd not seen anything like it for weeks, not a drop. Everyone had said that summer in Italy was madness, that we'd roast right through, and they were right. So we weren't dressed for it at all when we landed back here. We were drenched by the time we got the bags out of the cab and into the lobby. Weren't we, Charles? Weren't we drenched?"

He nodded with the rhythm of her words. "Oh, absolutely," he replied. "Soaked right through."

They said that they had ventured out only once in the last two days, a hasty trip to the supermarket to restock the cupboards, and kept the curtains closed and the windows locked and the rain as far away as possible. Rebecca and James—I recognized the names—had come for lunch the day before.

"They've taken shared parental leave," said Charles. "They're both off work. It's the strangest thing."

"Did I tell you they had a baby?" asked Marnie. "She's four months now. I've genuinely never seen a cuter child. She's adorable. These big, bright eyes, piercingly blue—"

Charles pointed at my empty wineglass. "Top up?" he asked, and I nodded.

"He was so good with her," whispered Marnie, as he went into the kitchen. "Honestly, there is nothing sexier than an attractive man with a baby. He does this swaggery, confident thing, I know, but he's soppy as anything, really. He wanted to hold her the whole time. He barely let me have a go at all."

I smiled and nodded, although I couldn't imagine it.

"Did you fill mine?" asked Marnie as Charles returned with the bottle.

"Of course," he replied. "It's on the side."

"Thank you," she said, standing to kiss him. "I better check on dinner."

He filled up my glass and then connected his phone to the fancy new television, bought, he said, with gift vouchers from the wedding.

"I'll show you some of the photos," he said, and then explained the intricate details of this specific model—the display, something about pixels, the strength of the processor, and several different acronyms that meant nothing to me. I nodded and smiled and tried to look impressed. I was struck more than anything by the size of it; it was stretched across the entire fireplace.

I reached for the remote control, which was standing upright in a small wicker basket on the side table. Charles was in front of the screen, facing it, blocking my view, and yet he must have heard my movement because without turning around he said, "Put it down."

"Don't you need—" I began.

"The control? No. If I need it, I'll get it. If that's okay with you, Jane."

He twisted, peering over his shoulder, inspecting me, staring at the remote still clasped in my fist. I placed it on the sofa cushion.

He smiled. "Trust me," he said. "You'll be amazed at what this thing can do."

He pressed a few buttons and began scrolling through their honeymoon photographs. Somewhat unexpectedly I found myself intrigued by the different locations, the beautiful scenery, that sense of the unfamiliar. I wasn't so keen on his ongoing commentary—"and that was where we . . ." and "when we visited that beach . . ." and "that was the bathroom of the second hotel"—but the images themselves were quite something. I responded to his questions, to his descriptions, to his endless twaddle—"Oh, what glorious fields," I said, and, "Sorry, where was that again?"—but I wasn't really listening.

Instead I imagined myself on their trip: posing beside Marnie on the Spanish Steps, smiling on a bike at the top of a hill, surrounded by a dozen wineglasses in a vineyard. It was surprisingly easy to erase Charles from each image, to blur his entire being, so that he barely existed. I could unsee his broad shoulders, his tight T-shirts, his white teeth embedded in a perfect smirk. I could unsee his hair, slicked back and thick with gel, and his muscular calves and his golden tan.

I could hear Marnie in the kitchen, and I amplified her noise to overwhelm his. She was talking into her camera, filming herself as she prepared dinner, describing each step that she was taking, every ingredient added, every slice and stir and shake.

"I always wash my hands after breaking eggs, particularly when I'm separating out the yolks, and I've been doing this quite a while, but it still gets everywhere."

"Should you throw spaghetti at the wall to see if it sticks? I mean, it's entirely up to you, but I firmly believe that it's the most accurate way to test whether or not your pasta is cooked, and oh"—a yelp—"looks like it is!"

"Should you put tomatoes in a green salad? Absolutely not.

"Two minutes," she called. And then, a little quieter, "When someone's cooking for me, I'm always grateful to have a little bit of notice before I'm due to sit down to eat because—and maybe this is just me; let me know in the comments if you get this, too—I always need to go to the bathroom before a meal. I don't know what it is, but I just do!"

Charles looked over and rolled his eyes—gently, lovingly—and I smiled in response.

"Right-oh," he said. "Let's whiz through the last few before dinner. You're not bored, are you?"

I shook my head and he flicked through the photographs at speed—beautiful sunsets, orange and yellow and pink and purple, the rolling hills, rippling in every shade of green, the poppy fields, a canvas of red peppered by small black seeds. Bowls of pasta, platters of cured meats and cheeses, pizzas the size of dustbin lids. Charles on a train, his eyes closed, a crossword half finished on the table in front of him. (You might like to know that crosswords were the only thing that Charles and I could discuss, could do together, without the air thickening around us.)

He continued to jab at his phone, but the television had frozen and one image remained static and unblinking on the screen. It was a photograph of Marnie, sitting up on a sun lounger, her legs either side of the wooden frame, smiling as she rubbed sunblock onto her arms. Her straw hat hung jauntily over her forehead and her bikini had lifted slightly, revealing the even fairer skin on the underside of her breast. She was smiling, laughing, I think, and I can picture her scolding Charles, like a mother might scold her son, telling him not to take a photo, not then, only when she was ready.

But I would have taken that photograph, too. Because entirely unaware of the camera she was far more herself, far less stretched and posed and pouting, and far more the woman we both recognized and perhaps loved.

"That was the last hotel," said Charles, turning off the television so that the screen snapped back to black. "It had the most incredible restaurant. It had a Michelin star. We did the tasting menu, which was quite expensive but totally worth it, just delicious."

I wondered if perhaps I would one day go on a second honeymoon. I thought it unlikely then and I think it even less likely now.

Marnie called us to the table.

"I've made carbonara," she said. She looked at me as she pulled out her seat. "But not the normal one, not the one we used to make at the flat." She turned to Charles. "It's an homage to our honeymoon," she said. "With the recipe from that hilltop place. Do you remember the one? Did you show Jane the pictures from the top? The food there was just—" She held her fingers to her lips and kissed them: a loud, wet *mwah*. "I had to beg for the recipe—a family classic, apparently—but it's particularly good, I think. Better than the one we did in the flat. I'll stop rambling. I'll let you try it."

She scooped a large serving into my bowl and a ridiculous portion onto Charles's plate. He didn't like to eat from bowls. He didn't like it when the different constituents of a meal mixed together. He didn't want to have spaghetti and salad in the same mouthful.

I twisted my fork against the lip of my bowl, and I could see straightaway that the texture was different. The eggs had formed a silky coating around each strand of spaghetti. Our carbonara—and don't get me wrong; I liked it, and I still think it's my favorite—was clumpy with lumps of scrambled egg.

"Delicious," said Charles. "Honestly, this tastes exactly the same."

Marnie clapped her hands together. "That's what I wanted you to say. And, Jane? Do you like it?"

"Well," I said, "I'm not going to say that I prefer it to *our* carbonara, because that would be disloyal, but it is delicious."

Marnie smiled. "I knew you'd love it." She refilled my wineglass. "We brought this bottle home," she said. "I thought it was a bit mad— you know it's never going to taste as good—but actually it's traveled rather better than I thought it would. Don't you think?" she asked.

Charles nodded. "Definitely," he replied. "Great pasta, wonderful wine. If it weren't for the rain, I could almost believe we were still there."

This might sound strange—and perhaps you won't believe me—but until that moment I'd never once felt like an unwelcome guest in their relationship. I'd been very aware of the two competing relationships. But I'd assumed that they could coexist, sort of side by side. And yet I was becoming more and more conscious that my friendship with Marnie felt like a paragraph in their story, that there was no space for anything other than that one love.

The first few months after Jonathan died are shadowy; I can't remember much of what I did or where I went or who I spoke to. But I eventually went back to work and Marnie invited me for dinner at the end of that first week. Charles worked late—often until after eleven, sometimes not returning to their apartment until the early hours of the morning—but he was determined never to work late on a Friday evening. He said that his weekends were sacred. It was all about balance, he said. But he was always exhausted by the time he returned home at eight, maybe nine o'clock at the end of the week. He never wanted to go out, or to see friends, or to do anything much. He just wanted to be at home. And so my weekly visits became a recurring thing, a pattern that continued and was rarely interrupted.

But I felt that their marriage might mean the natural end of that routine. It had been one way for years, but I knew, better than most, that everything ends eventually.

At half past ten, Marnie stood, and said, "Right."

I remained seated. She lifted our three dessert bowls from the table, stacking them in the corner of her arm, balanced against her inner elbow. She picked up the now empty fruit bowl, the jug of cream, and disappeared into the kitchen. We heard her switch on the radio, the sound of stringed instruments purring together, and the clink of ceramic dishes against one another. We listened to her footsteps, her socks padding against the floor as she moved from one side of the kitchen to the other, opening and closing the fridge, the dishwasher, the cupboards.

I should have followed her, but I didn't.

"The wedding," I said, and I don't know why because I knew instinctively that it was a bad idea but once I had started I didn't know how to stop.

"Such a good day," said Charles, yawning, stretching his hands above his head, just like he had done that evening, the exact same movement, his shirt once again straining against his belt. "Just the best."

"The end, though," I said.

"The end?" he repeated. "What about it?"

He seemed genuinely bewildered.

Now, very quickly, just one thing before I go on. And perhaps this should have been explained to you earlier. It is easy to forget since you have told very few lies in your lifetime. Whereas I have told a great many. So perhaps you can learn a little something from my experience.

The first thing you must consider is that a lie is just a story. It is made up, a fiction. The second thing is that even the strangest fiction, the most ludicrous lies, can feel entirely true, entirely possible. We want to believe the story. The third is that believable lies are therefore no great feat. But the most important thing of all, something you must never forget, is that we are not immune to our own lies. We revise our stories, altering the emphasis, increasing the tension, exaggerating the drama. And eventually—after we have told this modified story a few times, improving it with each recital—we begin to believe it, too. Because we are revising not only our stories but also our memories. Our fictions—moments that we created, that we imagined—begin to feel real. You can see the situation unfolding, the revision as it might have happened, and you begin to question where the truth ends and the lie begins.

"The end," I repeated, and he shrugged his shoulders and furrowed his eyebrows. "The end of the evening. The end with you and me."

"You and me?" he asked. "Jane. Come on, really. What is this?"

It was too late, you see. He had been granted the time to revise his recollection, to deliberately misremember that moment. There was no longer a single, solid truth. Had he replayed that story again and again? Had he altered his actions each time? Had he grown to believe his revised narrative, so that his incredulity, his confusion, would now seem authentic?

I felt stupid, as though I was talking nonsense, and then I saw something, a shadow sliding down Charles's face. His forehead wrinkled and then again was taut. His left eyebrow twitched, just once. His cheeks flushed pink, perhaps with embarrassment, perhaps with rage. He licked his lips, and then pressed them together between his teeth so that the edges faded to white. He made a brief, unintentional noise and bit at the corner of his lip.

I was no longer sure of anything.

"You know what I'm talking about," I said.

"I don't think I do," he replied. He placed both palms flat on the table, spreading his fingers.

"You do," I said. And I didn't know if he did, but I really thought that he might.

"I'm sorry, Jane," he said, and his face was stone, his features solid, entirely untouched. "I'm afraid I'm not sure what you mean."

"You don't?" I asked, hoping still that he might make a mistake and expose a truth.

"What *do* you mean?" he asked, and he tilted his head to the left slightly, as though he really was curious, as though he really was bewildered by my question.

"I think—" But I didn't know what I thought. "You touched me," I said instead. "Do you remember that? You were drunk but . . . you touched me."

He contorted his face into a portrait of shock. It felt false. His brows were too high on his forehead, his eyes too wide, his jaw dropping his lips into a sham little O.

"Jane," he said. "What do you mean, touched? You're not suggesting—"

"You remember," I said. "I know that you do."

He softened his face, adopting a strange look of concern.

"Jane, I'm sorry, and I really don't want to be rude, but I don't know what you're talking about at all. I want to help . . . and I'd hate for you to think— Why don't you start at the beginning?" he said. "Tell me what it is that you think has happened."

"At the end," I said. "When we were sitting down."

Something felt different; something felt wrong.

"Go on," he said.

"You put your arm around my shoulder," I said.

I could tell that it was dark outside because the red curtains looked black against the pale walls. The candles were fading, flickering on metal seats.

"I mean, if I'm being completely up-front with you," he began, "then I have to say that I don't remember that. But I suppose, yes, I'm not surprised by it. I think I hugged almost everyone there at some point throughout the day. It was a party, a celebration. And I . . . Is that it, Jane? My arm around you? Is that what's made you so uncomfortable? Because I wouldn't have thought . . . But if it did . . . I really didn't mean to cause any offense."

"No," I said. "No, that's not it, not at all. Not your arm around my shoulder. That's not what I'm talking about. Your hand," I said. "You were touching me."

And then I noticed that he wasn't quite looking at me anymore. He was instead looking over my head, beyond where I was sitting, to something—someone—behind me. And I realized that the radio wasn't on and that I couldn't hear Marnie's feet padding against the kitchen floor or the clinking of china or the seal of the fridge unsticking and then sucking itself closed. All I could hear was the quiet hum of the dishwasher.

I had no way to know how long Marnie had been standing there listening to our conversation; I didn't know how much she had heard. But I was absolutely sure that Charles had been manipulating the interaction for her benefit, performing a version of it that he wanted her to see, rather than the equivalent, the truth, that might have played out had it been just him and me.

He shrugged—he didn't need to use words to convey his meaning: *I have no idea what the hell she's talking about*—and I looked at her over my shoulder.

She was still wearing her apron. It was gray with white detailing and white rope tied around her waist and around her neck. She had a dishcloth in her hand, damp, ready to wipe the place mats. Her head was tilted to the left and her eyes were pinched, squinting at me over the dining table.

"What's going on?" she asked. She was looking right at me.

But before I could reply, she turned to Charles. "Are you all right?" she asked.

He shrugged.

"Jane?" she said. "What is this?"

It was too late.

"He touched you. That's what you said, isn't it? When exactly did he touch you?"

I knew that she was angry, but I was too stupid to realize that she wasn't angry on my behalf. My heart was thundering in my chest. I know that if I looked down I would see it trembling beneath my clothing and my skin. My palms were clenched, clammy.

I wanted to say, *Oh, nothing*, but Charles had puppeteered me into a corner and it was too late to pretend that I had said anything other than what it was that I had actually said. He was smart. And he was a very good liar. Perhaps he was so good that he believed his own nonsense or maybe he was just incredibly convincing, but either way he was cunning enough to trap me in my own truth.

He'd maneuvered me into the edge of the web and I couldn't escape with a lie.

"What exactly are you accusing my husband of?"

I had hoped that the truth might be greeted with some semblance of compassion, that she might choose to trust me, to fix this problem with me. But I knew then where her favor lay and I knew that it wasn't with me. And—frankly—I had been ridiculous to hope otherwise. Emma had found the space in which to doubt me. And so of course Marnie would, too. Maybe you will as well.

Her fingers quivered as she lowered the cloth to the table. Her pale face was flushed. Red blotches were flowering on her neck and mushrooming toward her chest.

"Well?" she insisted.

"He assaulted me," I said. "At your wedding. I'm really sorry, Marnie, but—"

"Assaulted?" she said, and her voice was steady, deeper than normal. Her eyes darted between us.

I looked at Charles and he was flawless, so clever and so much better prepared than I was. His face was the perfect blend of apprehension—his eyes said, *She needs help*—and frustration—his tight jaw insisting, *You can't possibly believe this nonsense, can you?*—and his posture screaming, *I haven't got a fucking clue what the hell is going on.*

"Yes," I said, and I looked down at my hands clasped in my lap. "Assaulted."

"An arm around your shoulder? That's what this is. A shoulder?"

She was shouting by then, the pitch of her voice unsteady, as though she might cry. "Seriously, Jane. Is that what you're on about? Is that all this is? Because, seriously, then you need to—"

"No," I interrupted. "Not just that. Not at all. He groped me," I said. The words felt uncomfortable in my mouth. "He put his hand over my top, the top of my dress. And I didn't say anything then; it didn't seem right, not on your wedding day. But I had to say something. Can't you see that I had to say something?"

She tilted her head and looked at Charles and raised her eyebrow, asking a quiet question. I couldn't interpret it and so I just continued.

"I think he would have gone further," I said, "if you hadn't come over. I think he was . . . What were you thinking?" I turned to Charles. "If I'd encouraged you. Would you? Or was it just to make me feel small? It's always that, isn't it? Because you like to feel bigger and better than everyone else."

"Jane . . ." he said. "I'm not sure . . . I don't know what's happening here, but I wasn't looking for anything."

He stood up and went to stand beside Marnie, slipping his arm around her waist, coiling his hand into the rope waistband of her apron and rubbing the fabric between his fingers. I felt like a child, caught in a row on the other side of my parents, they towering above me, dictating the facts, I withering in the face of confrontation.

And then his tone changed and he was angry.

"Jesus, Jane!" he shouted. Marnie flinched. "It was my wedding day. And you're my wife's best friend. I don't know what you think happened, but . . . for fuck's sake. My God. No."

Marnie nodded slowly and it didn't really matter if he believed his own story because she certainly did. Her face was thunderous, her eyes lit like candles on a birthday cake, flickering with rage.

He thought he had trapped me, but there is always another lie, a better lie.

One day, at some point in your future, someone will tell you that *lies breed lies* and they will be right, but they will say it as though it is a problem when in fact it is the solution.

"He said that he wanted me, that he'd always liked talking to me; he asked if I felt the same way," I said. "His hand was touching me through my dress, and he was fiddling with the edge of the fabric, fingering it, the seams of it. When it was only his hand on me, touching me, I couldn't be sure, you know. It might have just been too much to drink, not thinking, not noticing what he was doing. But when he started talking, then I knew," I said. "I knew it was intentional."

And she was unsure again.

And was that a lie? Really? Because I truly think that another two minutes and that's exactly what would have happened; he'd have said something just like that—I know he would have—because that was the man Charles was. He knew how to use words to manipulate, to construct a story. And the words gave credence to an action that on its own was deemed insubstantial, unimportant, in no way noteworthy.

But, yes, okay. It was a lie. That was the third lie I told Marnie.

It would be the last lie I'd tell her while Charles was alive.

Chapter Fourteen

Marnie asked me to leave. After everything had been said and not said, she stood up straight and said, "I think you should go now."

I sat shocked and didn't move.

"You can leave," she repeated. "Now. Please."

Charles and I looked at each other and I could tell that we were thinking the same thing, that neither of us could confidently read Marnie's expression. We could see that she wasn't happy, not at all, but the anger had dissipated, replaced instead by something less clear. I didn't recognize the sharpness of her eyes, her pinched lips, rosy as ever but pressed tightly together. Her skin was sallow and heavy, the weight of it sinking into her jaw.

I saw him tighten his grip around her waist, a gentle squeeze.

She didn't respond. She was frozen, her hands fixed against her hips. I stood up.

"Okay, I'll go," I said. "But only if you're sure that's what you want."

Did I think she might reconsider? I certainly hoped so. But she didn't.

"I'm sure," she replied.

I walked into the hallway and plucked my raincoat from the row of pegs. My umbrella had been propped against the radiator and had left a puddle of water sliding across the wooden floor. I put my hand on the doorknob and then turned back to look at them. They were standing exactly as they had been before, side by side, his arm around her waist, but they were now peering over their shoulders and staring at me as though to make sure that, after all of that, I really did leave.

I let myself out and walked home. It took hours and the rain was relentless, but it was exactly what I needed in that moment. I needed to feel the water soaking through my shoes and my socks and my feet wrinkling within. I needed to feel the wind pulling at my umbrella, to have something to fight against. I needed to march, to stamp, to feel the water splash at my ankles and my elbows grazing my hip bones.

I stood outside my flat and rifled through my bag for my key, and by the time I had found it and let myself in, so much water had dripped onto the carpet that a patch of the taupe fabric was damp, a murky brown. I had a hot shower and turned up the heating and I lay in bed and I couldn't sleep. I needed to be somewhere else. London was too big and too busy, the people too fraught and stretched, the air too dense and angry.

I set my alarm and I was still awake when it echoed around my bedroom several hours later. The sun was finally shining and I went to visit my mother—briefly, she didn't recognize me and I didn't have the patience for her relentless questions and generic nonsense—and then caught another train, not back toward the city, but farther away, following in the footsteps of a younger version of myself.

I arrived at Beer in the early afternoon. I had only a small rucksack. I went straight to our hotel, barely recognizing that my legs were propelling me in that direction. Our room was available, just for the one night, on the first floor at the end of the corridor and with the window overlooking the beach.

I left my bag on the bed and walked outside, toward the coast.

I stood and stared and watched as the waves rolled in; the sun was out and yet they were angry, smacking against the pebble beach.

"This way," I heard him say. "Let's go this way."

I turned toward the cliffs, retracing the path I had walked four years earlier. The beachfront was busy, a draw for young families on a summer holiday and couples in love in their twenties or eighties or anywhere in between. There were very few young women alone, although I can't have been the first to bring her heartbreak to the beach. There were parasols and sand castles and children shivering in striped towels. There were badminton rackets and windbreakers and plastic shovels in reds and yellows and blues.

I walked away from it all. I climbed the road, trudged along the pavement. The gulls were still there, squawking and flapping their wings overhead, and I wondered if they remembered me as I remembered them.

I felt closer to Jonathan than I had in months. I hadn't been near our maisonette since the morning of the marathon; I never returned. It was packed up and sold without my involvement. And I never visit the places we loved. I haven't been to The Windsor Castle since that evening and I very rarely pass through Oxford Circus. But somehow there, in a place that felt familiar, the ache sort of seemed to ease.

I reached the café in the next village and I sat on the same picnic bench and I watched the sea from the same spot, and I was frightened by how much my life had changed. And how much I disliked it. I so wanted to be the other me, the one who sat there with her husband at the beginning of a life together. She was optimistic—uncharacteristically so—looking ahead to future anniversaries and new homes and children and a lifetime of laughter and love. I didn't want to be the newer version, the bitter, cold one who felt permanently unanchored from the life she was meant to lead.

I wish I could tell you that I have found a way to move past that version of myself. Wouldn't it be lovely if I could say now that I have let go of the sadness and the anger, that I have found something grounding and stable and secure? But I didn't. I haven't.

There were no fishermen; they must have been there earlier in the day, when I was lying in bed waiting for my alarm, more than a hundred miles away, in a world filled with car horns and smog. I walked along the shore again, underneath the cliffs, the pebbles crunching beneath my soles, still damp from the tide that morning.

I noticed the cutaway in the overgrowth at the foot of the cliffs. The thornbushes were dense and the gap was barely visible, but I think I was looking for it, trying to find ways to be near to him. I remembered him marching ahead, zigzagging with the path, clambering over the nettles, so focused on the climb.

I took my time.

It had rained and the track was still slippery, mud resting against the rocks and in the hollows where the path dipped. The trail was over-shadowed by tall branches with thick bushes on either side and I wondered how long it took for the sun to dry out this small thread of a path. I couldn't see the sea, but I could hear it. I couldn't see the gulls, but I could hear them, too. I was very much alone, but I knew that the world was still out there, mere minutes away.

I reached the steps carved into the pathway, heading left and toward the bank above. That was the route I'd chosen the first time. It took me away from Jonathan, although admittedly only for a minute or two. But there is nothing I wouldn't give now—no sacrifice too extreme—for just a minute or two together.

I decided to turn right. There were no steps, just the muddy path, drier now that I was higher, but still slimy and unstable. I imagined where his feet had landed and I placed my boots in their long-gone tread. I pressed myself against the cliff edge and I wondered if his body was once here, hugging these very same rocks. I remembered the feel of his hand against my back. His heart would have been beating calm and steady, though mine was floundering in my chest.

There were nettles ahead, but I felt confident that everything would be all right this time. The sky above me was a glorious blue, not a cloud in sight, and although I have never been a spiritual person—not at all—I knew that he was there with me. I turned, my back against the rock face, and looked out at the sea, at the waves crashing beneath. I felt giddy, as though I was drunk, almost light-headed with the adrenaline.

I thought I could do it. I thought that I could be as fearless as he once was.

I was wrong.

I continued to climb, my palms gripping the cliffs to my left and my feet moving forward, one in front of the other, a straight line, as close to the rocks as I could possibly be. I stepped carefully over the nettles and I kept my eyes up, looking ahead.

"I will meet you at the top," I whispered, mainly to myself but also to the space above the sea. "One day," I said, "I will find you and I will meet you at the top."

I noticed that my hands were trembling slightly and found somewhat unexpectedly that I was crying. *Breathe*, I thought, but I couldn't. The air kept catching in my throat, and I found that I was inhaling, gasping, over and over again. My breaths kept spilling from my lungs and congealing in my mouth, rushing so fast and so hard that I was shaking, like my bones were separating.

I tried to balance my trembling body on the edge of that cliff, to keep my feet fixed in place, but I couldn't. I shrank, sitting, trying to be as small as possible, hoping not to fall, and stayed crumpled there until eventually I was almost still but for the breaths softly shaking in my chest, hiccuping again and again and again.

At last, I stood and retraced my steps, back toward the fork in the path, sliding my hand along the rocky edge, not thinking, not feeling, trying very hard not to hurt. I took the other route—the steps on the left, the path from the first time—and clambered to the top.

I had failed. Again.

I climbed higher up the grassy plinth. I sat down with my legs straight in front of me and facing out toward the sea.

And then I cried.

There have been just a few loves in my life, but I think it's fair to say that the greatest love of all will have been forged in death. I was madly in love with Jonathan when he died. We hadn't been injured by the crashing waves and blunt traumas of a long and well-lived life. We weren't threadbare from a lifetime of ordinary love. We were still obsessed by each other, and the things I loved most—his pedantry, his efficiency, his unique way of folding his socks, his tousled hair in the mornings—hadn't yet become mundane or irritating.

If I'm being completely honest, I don't truly believe that they ever would have. He was always the very best. When he poured two glasses of orange juice in the morning and gave me the first and kept the second for himself, because he knew I didn't like the thicker, bittier juice at the bottom of the carton. When he let me wear his gloves, because my hands were cold even though his must have been, too. When he drove the long distances, because I refused to learn to drive, because I hated the thought of sitting still for that long. When I came home from work to the smell of bleach and furniture polish and knew that he'd cleaned the entire place so that I wouldn't have to, while I had been out with Marnie, having fun, being happy. When he turned out the lights every night when we went to bed, so that I would never have to climb the stairs in the dark. He loved me in a million little ways. He believed in a love that proved itself, again and again, that was present and generous and never unimportant. That love is forever frozen as it was when he left.

Marnie is my second greatest love. And yet I felt that I had lost her, too. It was a very different loss. Jonathan disappeared all at once. Whereas Marnie was slipping away. I was the sand: solid and static and stuck in one spot. And she was the sea: being sucked from me, siphoned away by a force greater than either of us.

There had been a moment in which she might have chosen me. She could have asked him to leave instead. She could have stepped away from his arm around her waist. But she didn't. Because she believed what he was saying, that he was innocent, that the lies were mine.

There are some natural disasters so devastating that it is almost impossible to recover all that has been lost.

I stood and walked along the grassy verge and back toward the hotel. I contemplated settling the bill and heading straight back to London. But I had committed to paying for the room already and so I unpacked my small rucksack and ran a bath so hot that the steam clouded the metal taps and the mirror and filled the room. I undressed and slid beneath the water, feeling it pull at my hair as my face broke back through the surface. The sun was low in the sky, decorating the tiles in shadow. I heard voices floating up from the road underneath my window, a young girl squealing delightedly and the resonating laugh of a much older man.

I stood up in the bath, the water lapping at my calves, and I peered out through the mottled glass, pressing my body against the wall to shield it from sight. She was very young, maybe seven or eight, and wearing only a swimsuit. Her father was wearing swim shorts, still wet, the water seeping into the hem of his T-shirt, and I remembered when my father walked around like that, on beach holidays in Cornwall, after a day spent nestled in sand. A woman—her mother—was behind them, two towels flung over her shoulder and a big woven basket swinging by her ankles. The girl started laughing again and bent in the middle, literally doubled over, unable to continue walking because the movement within her was just so much. Her father was laughing, too—at her, at her joy, at her fearless, noisy laughter. I wanted so much to be part of that family.

I pulled on my dressing gown, grabbed the hair dryer from beneath the sink, and went back into the bedroom. I plugged it in. I would dry my hair. I would put on my clothes. And I would be part of that family.

I don't mean literally. I wouldn't *literally* be part of that family.

But I was determined to be part of something more than myself.

I walked back along the corridor and through the reception area. I stepped out of the doors and onto a narrow road, bookended on either side by two small streams. There were lights everywhere: in the pubs, in the restaurants, in other hotels. I walked toward the sea, along a path with a steep slope down to the pebbled beach. There were children, naked but for the towels wrapped around their shoulders, skipping up and down, running to the top and then back to meet their parents, who were climbing more slowly, tired after a long day of sand and sea and games. There were two men carrying parasols and windbreakers and with sunglasses propped on their foreheads. And two women with their hair pulled back in tight ponytails, damp bikini triangles imprinted on their linen shirts.

I tried to imagine myself in the shoes of one of those women, rucksack on my back, my children circling, sand embedded in the creases of my elbows, and I couldn't help but imagine Jonathan there at my side, a brightly colored parasol slung over his shoulder.

Even then, I couldn't envisage a version of my future without him in it. Which was ridiculous. Because, by then, he had been dead for longer than we'd known one another.

Somehow it felt like no time at all.

Before he died, I had never given much thought to widowhood. Although I suppose if you had asked for my thoughts on it, I'd have offered a confident, considered response. I had lost grandparents and I knew the weight of that familiar ache. Those losses had been substantial— the culmination of long, well-lived lives—and yet their passing felt insignificant, too. Those deaths were not tragedies. They did not become ghosts.

Whereas Jonathan did. I still carry him into every conversation. I bring him to every table. I am the young woman whose husband died. His ghost sits beside me at weddings—*do you know that she was married, yes, she was, her husband died*—and at funerals—*she buried her husband a few years ago, did you know, yes, her husband died.*

He is there in every future, in every hope, in every dream.

He haunts me, always.

Chapter Fifteen

———

I visited Emma on my way home. She was living in a studio flat south of the river. It was a twenty-minute walk from the nearest tube station and the closest bus stop was almost ten minutes away and across an unlit car park. I didn't have much to spare, but even with my small contribution and the odd payment from my mother's account, it was all that she could afford.

We'd become even closer since she'd moved out of our parents' house. Away from my mother—who'd always insisted on being part of whatever we did together—we discovered that we really quite liked each other. She was refreshingly honest, as only a sister can be. And I think—and I hope that this doesn't sound petty—that being needed by her was fulfilling for me.

She didn't work regularly anymore. She had been a freelance editor and, for a while, she was incredibly busy, with manuscripts stacked on the linoleum tiles, working through the night in order to meet her deadlines, always in demand. She'd been so diligent and focused, never afraid to interrogate a problem, to ask the difficult questions. But her concentration dwindled, and she started to pore over every text, too indecisive, afraid that she might upset a rhythm, taking so long that eventually everyone stopped sending her new projects. She then spent much of her time working with local charities. But it was all voluntary.

I stood on the balcony in front of her flat and banged on the bright red door. There was a doorbell nailed to the frame, but it had never worked.

"I'm coming!" she yelled as I banged a second time. "Learn some fucking manners.

"Oh," she said when she opened the door. "I wasn't expecting you."

"Clearly," I said. "Is that how you greet everyone?"

The front door opened straight into the only room: the lounge, the kitchen, the dining room, and the bedroom all combined in one small space. The kitchen was at one end; the white units were relatively new but the floor tiles were speckled orange. The blinds were made of plastic and held together with thin white string. There was a coffee table, a sofa, a small television, a wardrobe, and a few bookshelves. And beside the door that led to the small bathroom, framed above the radiator, there was a large sketch of a very thin woman. It wasn't much, but Emma had never needed very much.

"No one visits," she said. "It's only ever someone trying to sell me something." She stepped back to let me in. "Why are you here?" she asked.

"Charming," I replied.

"I don't mean it like that," she said.

"I've been to Beer," I said.

"To Beer?" she asked. "In Devon?"

"Where Jonathan and I went. Do you remember?"

"Why'd you go there?" she asked.

"Marnie and I argued."

"You told her."

I nodded.

She gestured toward the sofa.

"I told you not to say anything," she said.

"I had to," I replied.

"You bloody didn't," she said, taking three dark chocolate digestive biscuits from a packet and placing them onto a napkin for me. "Watch the crumbs."

I nodded and sat down at one end of the gray sofa. She unrolled it into a bed each evening.

"You could have just pretended that everything was normal," she said. "Like I told you to. Then you wouldn't be in this situation."

"But she needed to know the truth about her husband. Wouldn't you want to know the truth about your husband?" It seemed obvious to me that if something couldn't be said and yet still needed saying, then it had to be said.

Emma sat on the sofa beside me. Her trouser leg lifted slightly so that I could see the bones that made up her ankle. She clutched a mug of warm tea between her hands. I bit into one of the biscuits and it was softer than I'd expected, almost damp inside.

She was quiet, thinking.

"No," she said. "I don't think I would."

"If your husband was a pervert?" I said. "You wouldn't want to know? And imagine that I knew he was a pervert. Put yourself in Marnie's position. You wouldn't want me to say something?"

"I wouldn't believe you," she said.

I sat up and several crumbs shook themselves loose from the napkin and fell onto Emma's sofa. She leaned over to brush them away.

"What do you mean?" I asked. "Why not?"

"Because," she said, and then she paused. "Oh, don't be so naive," she said eventually. "If I told you that Jonathan had hit on me, you wouldn't have believed me, not for a second."

"I'd have listened to what you had to say and then—"

"And then you'd have taken his side. You know what they say, and it's what everyone always says, to never give up your friends for a man, but it doesn't matter because everyone does. Friendships are one thing, but a true love, a romantic love? That trumps everything. Always has.

Always will. You might like to think otherwise, but you'd have hated me."

"It's different," I said. "Jonathan was . . . He would never—"

"Ah," she interrupted. "That's what everyone thinks. That's why you can't blame her for choosing him." She sighed. "They don't know they're thinking it, but it's always there, whenever anything bad happens to somebody else. A little voice that says, *But it wouldn't happen to me.*"

I laughed and more crumbs fell from my T-shirt. "What a luxury," I said.

Emma smiled. We both knew how it felt to be the people to whom bad things happened. It wasn't that way for most of our childhoods, but something changed in our adolescence. My father's relationship with his mistress became common knowledge and we became that family, those girls, the daughters of that man. Emma fell first; she became that girl, the thin girl, the girl who didn't eat. My husband died. Our father left. Our mother was diagnosed. Maybe once you start—once you become one of those people—you can never stop being one.

Emma and I are united by a history of stares and secrets and whispers. Perhaps that is why we both choose to live anonymous lives in a city so big it swallows you.

"Do you think she'll forgive me?" I asked.

"I don't know," Emma replied.

"I think she will," I say. "I think I can make her."

"You going to record him and send it to her?" Emma smirked. She loved that story.

"You said you wouldn't mention that again," I replied. She was always teasing, always trying to ease the tension within me. "And, no."

"You would if you could," she insisted. "I know you. It's still your style. Skulking in when the place is quiet, clambering into a wardrobe. *Detective Black. Delighted to make your acquaintance.* All those martial arts classes. Do you have a black Lycra jumpsuit?"

"He's too smart," I said. "He wouldn't say anything incriminating."

"Oh bloody fuck," she said, and she laughed. "You've really thought about it."

"Only just now because you brought it up." It was so typical of her. It was her idea but she was blaming me.

"Chill," she said. "You're getting crumbs all over the place."

"But you do think it'll be okay, don't you?" I asked.

"Probably. She'll see sense eventually."

"What do you mean?"

"Well, it's not going to last, is it? The marriage?"

"What makes you say that?"

Emma laughed. "You! Everything you've said. All the things he's done? The arrogance and entitlement, the pretentious affectations, those irritating phrases that are so bloody offensive and he doesn't see it at all. My favorite," she said, "was that one at the bar when he needed to squeeze past that woman and so he didn't say 'excuse me' like a normal person but put his hands on her hips to steer her aside—do you remember telling me this?—and she turned around and said, 'What was that? That you just did?' and got all huffy and in his face and he panicked and called her stupid so she told him to fuck off. Maybe you should tell him to fuck off more often."

"Sure," I said. "Marnie will definitely forgive me then."

"Good point," she said. "And anyway, if other people keep telling him to fuck off, then sooner or later she'll get the message. Just relax. It'll unravel itself."

What do you think? Whose side would you have chosen? Would it have been him or me?

I'm going to assume that you'd have chosen me and, frankly, you'd be stupid to say otherwise, because he's already dead.

I think that if you'd known him, if you'd had the space in which to form your own opinions, you would have listened to me, agreed with me, trusted me. I think you'd have found him overbearing and vindictive. We would have sat down together and listed his many wrongdoings and we'd have laughed at them. I would have been your ally.

But that will never happen. Because you will never know him. Which is why it's so important that you hear this story. I will tell it only once, and it has to be now.

This is how he died.

Pay attention.

The
Fourth Lie

Chapter Sixteen

I finished work early the day Charles died. I remember it so clearly, every part of it, from my alarm ringing that morning and the discovery that there was no milk for my cereal, to arriving home later that night after it had all happened. I can reel through the images like a film and I'd like to say that they move me in some way, to regret or to horror or to shame, but they don't. It was in so many ways an entirely unremarkable day.

Is that true? I am trying so hard to be honest. But sometimes it's difficult to know what you truly think about any one thing. For example, I wonder if I'm telling you that it was dull simply because I would rather not tell you about that day at all. It doesn't much matter either way; I promised that I would tell you the truth and the facts themselves are indisputable.

Work had been expectedly quiet for a couple of weeks. The summer months had been wet and overcast, but September was set to be bright and warm. We were receiving ten percent fewer calls than we had in the same period the previous year. I assumed that people were being drawn away from their homes and out to parks and pub gardens.

It was a Friday and I decided to leave early, thirty minutes before the phone lines had officially closed for the weekend. I simply picked up my handbag and, in a very nonchalant way, walked out of the office. I wondered if anyone would notice, but I don't think that they did and I wouldn't have cared if they had.

The sidewalks were quiet. The evening exodus had yet to begin. I contemplated heading toward my normal tube station and the line that took me home, but I decided against it. It was a Friday, after all. And I didn't go home on Fridays. I went to Marnie and Charles's.

I headed toward a different station: it was a longer walk, but I wouldn't need to change tubes halfway through the journey. I waited only a couple of minutes and picked a seat near the middle, where I was less likely to be disturbed by pensioners with their walking sticks and pregnant women with their protruding bumps. A young couple was sitting across from me, dressed casually, he in tracksuit bottoms and a matching sweater, and she in leggings and a navy blue hoodie. They were about sixteen—I wondered if they ought to have been at school— and utterly exquisite. They were so self-contained, so smitten. His hand rested on her thigh, higher than was really appropriate, and yet it felt endearing rather than vulgar. Her head was anchored to his chest; I expect she could hear his heartbeat. He dipped his chin and pressed his lips to her forehead repeatedly, not so much kissing, just touching. They seemed entirely unaware of everyone watching, everyone wishing that they, too, could be so oblivious, so in love, so naive.

I was so distracted by the young couple that it wasn't until they stood up and got off that I began to wonder about the reception I'd re- ceive from Marnie and Charles. Would they let me into the flat? Would they even answer the door? I used to carry around a collection of wor- ries just like these. All of them now seem wholly insignificant: the state of my nails, the gossip lost in office politics, the things my mother had and hadn't said. Jonathan taught me to unravel my anxieties by giving them context: my nails mattered to no one but me, even the very worst rumors could only lose me my job, my mother's words were beyond my control. I tried to apply that logic to this new concern, but it didn't dial down my panic but simply amplified it. Because within a broader context, this wasn't about whether the door was opened and whether they were cruel to me. It was about the trajectory of one of my most important relationships. I couldn't step back the way I had with my mother and simply accept that she was in a terrible place. I couldn't pretend that the very worst outcome would affect just a small corner of my life. Because there are only so many small corners that can be emptied before the room begins to look barren.

Marnie and I hadn't spoken in a week. I know that doesn't sound like a substantial period, but for us it was unusual. At school, we were always together: laughing too loudly on the bus, side by side behind two desks, eating lunch in the cafeteria. And, at university, we spoke every day because there were so many things that happened, so many moments, when we thought, *She'd find that funny*, or *interesting*, or *pertinent* somehow. And, even as adults, we communicated at least once a day, not always a phone call, sometimes a text or an email or just a photograph, but—like children with paper cups and a ball of string stretching between their bedroom windows—there was a channel that connected us always.

I hadn't known how to reinitiate a conversation. Whenever I thought about it, I felt a surge of panic swelling within me. I didn't want to acknowledge that she had been forced to choose and that she hadn't chosen me. I didn't want to acknowledge that she had, for the very first time, demanded that I leave her apartment. I couldn't begin to think that this might be unfixable. I wanted to send her a photograph of my beans-on-toast dinner, or the sun setting over the sea, or the strange curl in my hair that day.

I considered getting off the tube and heading home instead. I would have been fine at home, I think. I would have ordered takeout and watched a film. But I didn't. I wanted to see Marnie. I needed to see her.

I flickered between pretending that I was entirely comfortable— this was a familiar tube station, a familiar walk, a familiar building— and sudden floods of abject fear. I knew, I was sure, that she wouldn't sacrifice our friendship completely. And yet I wonder now if I was really as sure as I thought I was.

If I had been that sure, so categorically sure, would I have done what I did?

"Afternoon, miss," said the doorman as I entered the lobby.

"Evening, Jeremy," I replied, smiling. He didn't stand and walk toward me and declare that I was no longer allowed in this building and demand that I leave immediately, so I felt the beginnings of relief as I stood and waited for the elevator.

I hoped that Charles might still be at work and that I could talk to Marnie alone, to explain the situation as I saw it. I knew I could make her understand.

The elevator was empty, and I watched my face in the mirrored walls as it ascended. I think I always knew that Marnie was destined for that sort of life, with parquet floors and chandeliers and doormen and mirrored elevators in which the glass was always clean, never a fingerprint or a smudge.

I approached their door and rang the bell, but there was no response. The bulb overhead had blown, and I was shrouded in shadow, standing in a puddle of gray, with a gold haze on either side from the lights above the neighboring doors. It was quite beautiful, the dark between the light, and a little unnerving, too. I hovered there and waited what felt like an appropriate length of time before ringing the bell again, depressing the buzzer for longer this time.

Again, there was no answer.

I pressed my ear against the door. I was listening for Marnie's voice or the radio or the rush of cars passing beneath their balcony. I could only hear the sound of my own skin scratching against the thick wood of their door. I stood back and looked from side to side. There was no one around; no residents or visitors at any of the apartments on this stretch of corridor.

I rooted through my handbag: I knew that it was still in there. I hadn't used it in a very long time—I hadn't needed to—but I thought it might be useful, so I'd kept it. I found the key at the bottom of the little pouch sewn into the inner lining of my bag, the hidden compartment where I kept painkillers and tampons and sticks of lip balm.

I paused again, listening, and then inserted the key into the lock. I pulled my hand away and looked around, checking once more for neighbors. But I was still alone.

I want you to know that I wasn't planning anything sinister. I didn't know then what was going to happen next; there was no way to know. I suppose I really wasn't thinking that far ahead, not when I remembered that I had the key and not moments later when I found it.

I'd like to say that I wanted to drop off some flowers, to maybe leave a nice card. I'd like it even more were I able to say that I planned to cook them a meal, something special.

But those would all be lies—the kind that I've already warned you about, those that are so appealing that you, too, are tempted to believe them.

I had no reason to think that Charles would be dead less than ten minutes later.

I let myself inside. I suppose I was planning—and it is important that you know this now, that you understand my intentions—to quickly look downstairs and then upstairs and then I'd have gone back into the hallway to wait for one of them to arrive home. I wasn't going to move anything or take anything or overstay my welcome.

I certainly wasn't planning to kill him.

I had been planning to check the kitchen. I wanted to look in the fridge. I would have known then if I was welcome. If she had strawberries stored in the salad drawer, then she was expecting me. And if she had an unopened tub of ice cream in the freezer, then she was definitely on my side. She would only have bought ice cream for me. I would have known then that it wasn't over, that our friendship hadn't disintegrated entirely, that she wasn't willing to let me go.

There were photographs of us together on the mantelpiece in the living room and a new one, from the wedding, in a silver frame on a ledge at the foot of the stairs. If they had been gone, then I'd have known to worry. There were things I had bought her over the years: a purple umbrella that was always propped against the understair cupboard, a pink pom-pom lamp by her writing desk, and a cuckoo clock in the downstairs bathroom.

I guess I hoped that there might be evidence of some change in their relationship over the previous seven days. It would have been nice, for example, to find Charles's wardrobe empty, his clothes and shoes and suits all gone, and the magazines and bookmarks and flash drives missing from his bedside table.

I could imagine Marnie coming home and I, by then, would have been back in the hallway waiting for her. I would have pretended that I didn't yet know, that I had no reason to believe she would choose me over him. And she would have been overcome by sobbing, confiding in me, and saying that it had never felt right with him, that he had always been just a little too controlling and sometimes too distant and thank goodness I had found the strength to be honest with her.

But I didn't go upstairs and I didn't look in Charles's wardrobe. I didn't go into the kitchen and I didn't look in the freezer. I didn't look at the mantelpiece, either. I never made it that far.

Chapter Seventeen

In time, there would be pieces in newspapers that would argue otherwise. They would insinuate that I had manipulated the situation very carefully, suggesting that I had committed a perfect murder. But that isn't what happened.

I opened the door, but only very slightly, wanting to make as little noise as possible. I stepped into the apartment, turning to scan the corridor one final time. I didn't want the neighbors to see me and then mention, casually, at some point over the next few weeks, the young woman who popped by and let herself in. Thankfully, I was still alone. I shut the door quickly and I put on the chain. This, perhaps, was a little calculated. If they had returned, I would have rushed to grab the watering can from beneath the bathroom sink and pretended that I was looking after the plants. Or perhaps I would have rushed to the kitchen to boil the kettle or started folding the laundry—something helpful and almost acceptable—so that they didn't discover me rooting through their drawers.

The lights in the apartment were switched off. It took my eyes a couple of seconds to adjust to the darkness. I didn't see him straightaway. I didn't notice him there at the foot of the stairs.

I jumped and my back slammed into the door, my lower ribs catching on the handle. I instinctively bent forward and my handbag slipped from my shoulder, the metal clasp clattering against the floor. I watched as my things tumbled and rolled across the wood—a tube of lipstick, my purse, my keys, so loud as they landed.

I wondered if he might be dead. I felt a strange sort of joy—a little excited—as though that wouldn't have been the worst thing in the world.

When I looked up again, his eyes were open. He was lying on his back, but his left ankle was twisted and his shoulder was bent at an awkward angle. There was a patch of dried blood on his temple and a small burgundy stain on the wooden floor. He was wearing pajama bottoms, flannel with blue stripes, and a university sweater. I had never seen him dressed so casually.

He groaned.

I felt momentarily disappointed that he wasn't in fact dead. And then that disappointment was overwhelmed by anger.

Wasn't it typical of Charles to still be alive? A fall like that might have killed someone else, but, no, not Charles. He was just too persistent, always there, never anywhere else, always so very present.

He coughed.

"Jane," he croaked.

He cleared his throat and he winced as the movement in his chest sent vibrations through his shoulder.

"Oh, Jane," he said. "Thank God."

I turned on the light and he blinked a couple of times in quick succession.

"I fell," he said. "I don't know when . . . I was . . . What time is it? My shoulder. It's dislocated. And . . . I couldn't get up. My ankle. I think my back . . . Oh, you're here. I'm so glad you're here. My phone. An ambulance."

He furrowed his brow. He was confused. Perhaps because I was standing still, my back pressed against the door and the contents of my handbag pooled at my feet and doing none of the things that a normal person might be doing in this situation.

I remember seeing Jonathan fly. The taxi stole his feet from beneath him and the force of it propelled him forward and onto the sidewalk a few yards ahead. I didn't think about how to respond; I instinctively ran to be by his side and crumpled down beside him, touching him, trying to quell the bleeding, find the breaks, as though I had the capacity to save him. I wanted to climb into his body. I wanted to fix him from within. I was shouting at him—all manner of nonsense, the things you see in films—to stay with me, to keep his eyes open, not to worry, everything would be fine if he could just stay with me, stay with me.

But I was not rushing toward Charles. I was not asking him questions, one after the other, about what went wrong and where was he hurting and what could I do. I was not picking my phone up from the floor or crossing to collect his, which was lying just a few yards out of his reach.

I was doing nothing at all.

"Jane," he said. His forehead was creased, his eyes wide and frightened, and he was bleeding again where he'd lifted his head slightly from the floor and unsealed the wound.

"Charles," I replied.

"Jane, I need help," he said. "Can you call someone? Call an ambulance. Or just . . . pass me my phone, will you? It's just there. If you just . . ."

I should have been calling an ambulance. I know it now and I knew it at the time. There was a man lying on the floor, bones bent, body twisted, blood on his forehead, and it was very clear that he needed immediate medical attention. And yet I did nothing. It was instinctive. It was exactly the same involuntary response that I'd experienced with Jonathan, but it drove me in an entirely different direction. Then, I'd spontaneously tried to do everything. On this occasion, I did nothing.

"Jane," he said. "Please. I really need you to—"

"What happened after I left?" I interrupted. "Last week. When I left. What happened?"

This seems strange, I know, but it does make sense. That was why I was there, after all. That was why I'd let myself into their flat. I wanted an answer. I wanted to understand what had happened. I needed to know that things were going to be okay, that Marnie and I were still friends and that everything was going to continue as normal.

"Come on, Jane," he said. "I need help." He grimaced. "Can you . . . If you just pass me my phone. Please, Jane."

I walked toward it and I kicked it away from him. I didn't know I was going to do it until I'd already done it. It wasn't part of a plan. I felt like a character in a film, meeting her nemesis at his weakest moment, and it felt like the right thing to do. So I did it.

"I asked a question," I said. "Can you answer it, please?"

"Nothing," he replied. "Nothing happened. Jane. Come on, now . . . This is madness. I think I'm concussed. What time is it? Jane. I don't know how long I've been here." He coughed and his body contracted and he gritted his teeth. "I keep waking up and then— Oh, for fuck's sake, Jane. Yes, fine. Marnie was fuming, all right? She didn't know what to believe and she still doesn't, and I've explained my side of the story over and over again, but she's still going on about your nonsense."

I smiled. I felt sort of vindicated. I had slightly exaggerated what had happened between us and it seemed that I'd been right to do so.

"Go on," I said.

"That's it!" he shouted, and then winced again. "There's nothing more to it. She's been hot and cold with me all week, and I can't say we were expecting you this evening although I think I'm glad you're here . . . but I don't know. She was fucking angry, yes. With both of us. But she doesn't think anything happened—because it didn't happen, Jane, it didn't happen—and she keeps bringing it up, yes, but I think it's going to be okay, all right, for both of us, but if you could just . . . We can talk about this another time. I promise. We can talk about it. But please . . ."

He started to shiver. I wondered if he might be in shock. I didn't really know what that meant, but the paramedics and the doctors and the nurses had suggested it when I was waiting in the hospital for Jonathan to be pronounced dead.

I crouched down. The wooden floor was cold beneath my hands. The flat felt different without Marnie. I had liked it the last time: the lightlessness, the scentless silence. I had liked that it was hollow and empty.

But Charles was ruining everything. With him, the darkness felt suffocating. There was just the bright light above us, a harsh lamp glowing a dirty lemon yellow. There were no scented candles burning, no warm orange illuminating the room. It wasn't empty. And yet Charles wasn't enough to fill it.

"We haven't spent much time alone before," I said. "Not without Marnie."

"Maybe that's something we can do some other time," he said.

"Maybe," I replied.

I could see that the pain was getting worse. He was trying not to move but sometimes he shifted involuntarily, when he spoke or when his temper piqued, and then his face contorted for a second or two.

"How come you're home so early?" I asked.

"I really need your help," he said. "Please, Jane."

"Didn't you go to work?"

"I had a migraine. I think that's why I fell. That was all, Jane."

"Do you get them often?" I asked. "Migraines?"

"Sometimes," he said. "Every few months. Now—"

"I don't think I've ever had one," I replied. I couldn't hear the cars below. "You didn't open the doors," I said, "to the balcony."

"I've been in bed."

"You didn't have the radio on?"

"I've been asleep, Jane. Marnie went to the library to write up an interview and I stayed in bed. Jane, I really don't feel good at all. I don't know why you're—"

"When will she be back?"

"Soon," he said. "I think. What time is it? I reckon she'll be home soon."

"I'm not sure of the time," I said. "I'm early."

"Why don't you call her?" he suggested. "Ask her. Let her know that I'm here and ask when she's back. She's probably on her way. You want to see her, don't you? Use my phone. In my favorites. Ring her. Now. Put her on speaker so I can hear her, too. Go on, Jane. Or your phone. It's just behind you . . ."

I held my finger to my lips and he fell silent.

I needed to think.

I remember panic bubbling in my stomach, just simmering, the beginning of something that I knew I ought to be feeling. I remember taking a few deep breaths—as the policewoman had told me to in the hospital—in through my nose for six, and then hold for six, and then out through my mouth for six.

It must have silenced my anxiety fairly quickly. Because I didn't feel it again after that. I crawled across the floor, just a couple of feet, until I was beside him, close enough to touch him. I watched his Adam's apple bouncing in his neck as he mumbled and pleaded with me.

He started whimpering and I thought he might cry.

But then he got angry.

Chapter Eighteen

———

Jane," he said. "This is crazy. Are you going to help me or what?"

I shrugged. I didn't know yet. I wasn't planning not to help him, but I also wasn't planning to help.

"You're just going to leave me lying here in pain? Or—fucking hell, worse still—you're just going to sit there and stare at me? All because you think I groped you? Well, let's work this back, then, shall we?"

I don't think I nodded. I don't think I consented to the barrage of abuse that followed.

"Did I do it? Did I grope you?"

I could see that his vehemence, his animated rage, was causing him pain, and yet he didn't slow down, not at all, not for a second.

"Well, let me tell you this, then. I wouldn't touch you if you were the last woman in the world. I can't think of anything worse. The thought of it actually makes me feel a little bit nauseated." He paused and panted. "Or I mean that could be the result of my fucking head wound, but it doesn't look like we're doing anything about that yet, now, does it?"

He winced. He closed his eyes and took a deep breath. I thought he might be finished, but he wasn't.

"Did I say that I wanted you? Not a fucking chance. But how adorable. That you think someone might. That's nice, that is. That's nice, right? To have that self-assurance." He roared with the pain and then blew the last of the air from his lungs in a brief burst before continuing. "Well, let me tell you something else. You're going to need it. Because you want to know what happens next? I'm going to the hospital and my wife will be right there by my side. And she's not going to like hearing about this. You are on borrowed time, Jane, so borrowed." He made a high-pitched squeaking noise, but it still wasn't enough to stall him. "So this is fine," he continued. "Let's wait this out. Because we both know who wins here and it isn't you."

"That's not true," I replied. I felt sort of angry, but mainly agitated. I wanted him to stop.

"Well, let's just wait and see. Because I know what happens next, Jane. It's not even about you. It's about me. This is my time."

I reached out to rest my fingers against his neck. He flinched away from my hand and then groaned, a sort of agonized growl, overwhelmed by the pain. His cheek was so swollen, the skin stretched and shiny like a balloon, his eye blackening and bloodshot.

I tried again and this time he didn't move; he stayed perfectly still.

"Come on now, Jane," he said. "What are you doing? Come on. That's enough now. Please."

He was speaking through his teeth, deliberately holding his face static, trying to minimize the pain. I could feel him vibrating beneath my fingers.

"What are you doing, Jane? I need help. Can you just—" He flinched again. "Can you just take your hand off me? Take it off. Right now. Come on."

It felt sort of wonderful.

I look back on that moment and I don't recognize the woman sitting there on the floor with her fingers against the neck of an injured man. I don't recognize her smile. I don't recognize her eyes. She feels like an entirely different person.

I stroked his neck with my index finger and then with my entire palm. He was silent then and there was no more movement. I could feel stubble sprouting across his chin, see the five-o'clock shadow cast across his face, the result of not shaving for a day or two. He closed his eyes. I could see his chest rising and falling, hear the breaths as he sucked them in and threw them out. I ran my palm up toward his cheek.

I wondered if Marnie's palm had been there, too, on mornings together in bed or during their first kiss. I placed my other palm on the opposite side of his face and held his head steady. I inched my fingers into his hair, feeling the film of grease at the roots.

"Please, Jane," he whispered. "That's enough. I'm sorry. I didn't mean the things I said. Let's just— We can forget all of this. I promise."

"I can't help you," I replied. "I'm sorry," I said. "But I just can't."

"Then go," he insisted. "Just get out. I've had enough. Go."

I felt a sudden surge of anger. Was I really—seriously—being thrown out of that flat for the second week in a row? No. I was not. I was absolutely not. Because I was the one in control and I was the one who was going to make the decisions. No one was going to tell me where to go or what to do or if I was allowed to be there anymore. And certainly not Charles. He'd said his bit and now it was my turn. This was my moment.

I took a deep breath.

"I'm not going, Charles," I said, very calmly. I didn't want him to know that I was angry. I didn't want him to feel any more afraid than he already did. "I want to stay," I said. "I'm going to stay."

I guess I must have known by this point what it was I was going to do. I didn't want to alleviate his sense of fear because of some undue sense of compassion or empathy. I wanted him to feel less afraid so that his final burst of horror was all the more intense.

"Fine," he said. "Stay, then. It's not as if there's anything I can do to stop you."

"No," I replied. "There's nothing you can do at all."

He closed his eyes.

This was not my finest hour. I don't need to tell you that, I know.

And there's not an awful lot that I can say in my defense. I simply enjoyed watching him suffer. I liked that his shoulder was dislocated, that his right arm was completely useless, and that it was causing him pain. I liked the sight of the blood on his forehead, the thought of him lying there unconscious for hours, the idea of him concussed. I liked his broken ankle and his swollen cheek and his bloodshot eye. I liked him so much better than I'd ever liked him before.

I held his head firmly between my hands, my palms flat against his skin. There were tears seeping from the corners of his eyes.

You have never hated anyone the way I hated Charles, so I know that you can't understand how satisfying this moment was for me. I had that giddy feeling, that drunk, wild happiness. It was something I had never expected to experience around him.

I moved my hands a little and he groaned.

"Sorry," I whispered.

"Jane," he croaked.

I shifted onto my knees so that my weight was above him and then repositioned my hands. He knew, I think. It was then that he knew.

I took a deep breath. In for six, hold for six, out for six. I looked away and up the stairs, at the carpet runner, cream bordered by blue, and at the wooden banister varnished a mahogany brown. And then in one swift movement, I rotated my hands and I heard a loud crack and his neck fractured beneath me.

When I looked down, his eyes were closed and he looked peaceful, his jaw relaxed, his forehead uncreased; the pain was gone.

It had worked. I hadn't been sure that it would.

Chapter Nineteen

I swiveled around and scooped my things—my phone, my house keys—back into my handbag. I picked up the small gold key, the one that had allowed me into this apartment whenever I'd wanted, and I placed it quietly—I didn't know why I was being so quiet; it just felt appropriate—into the little bowl on the side filled with a dozen other keys.

I turned off the light. I stroked my top over the switch. I knew that it was highly likely that my fingerprints were everywhere in this apartment already, but it felt right to be cautious. I unchained the door and rubbed the metal carefully, pushing the fabric of my cardigan into the grooves of the chain. I opened the door, wiped the inside handle, and then let myself out.

I stepped into the hallway, into that puddle of darkness, and I pulled the door shut behind me, listening for the quiet click of the lock. And then, finally, I exhaled.

I moved a few feet down the corridor, toward the door to their neighbor's apartment, and sat on the floor, my back against the wall and my knees bent in front of me. It was brighter there; it didn't feel quite so frightening.

I took a book from my handbag and I opened it against my thighs. I wasn't reading—my bookmark was positioned several chapters forward—but it was reassuring to be pretending to do something. I could hear the soft ticking of the hands of my watch as the seconds slid slowly past. Marnie wasn't expecting me, and so maybe she was taking her time; perhaps she'd gone for a drink with a friend or was picking up dinner on the way home or walking instead, making the most of the sunshine. There was no way for me to know and so I simply sat and waited.

Even so, I was desperately aware that Charles's body was a couple of yards away, lying dead behind their door. I could picture him—exactly as I knew he was—sprawled with his ankle twisted, his neck twisted, entirely dead. I struggled to make sense of my feelings. I didn't feel sadness, none at all. I didn't feel satisfaction, either. I didn't feel very much of anything.

I focused very hard on pretending that I didn't know that he was there. I was telling myself that I hadn't been into their flat—I didn't have a key, did I, so I couldn't have entered even if I'd wanted to—and that, as far as I knew, he was still as painfully, permanently present as ever. I convinced myself of things I knew were false. I hadn't heard any noises from the flat: I rang the bell twice, but there was no answer and, as far as I knew, Marnie and Charles were both still out, he at work, she elsewhere: the supermarket, the florist, maybe even the library. I hadn't seen anything: I had simply been sitting here, reading, knowing nothing.

No. Don't smile. Stop it. Now.

It's not like I don't know why you're smiling. But if you want me to continue with this story, then you're going to have to try to see these things from my perspective. It was a rash decision, barely even a decision at all. I didn't choose to do what I did. I simply did it. So don't go dwelling on things like motive and intent, because there was neither one nor the other. It was instinctive.

The question that you should be asking—and if you were paying proper attention, you would be—is whether, in that moment, I had any regrets.

Well, I'm not answering that yet.

If you'd have asked it, I might have told you the truth. But you're too busy judging me.

Anyway. Where were we?

I was absolving myself—in a subconscious sort of way—of all responsibility, rehearsing my lie and pretending that the incident itself had never happened.

I scanned the open page of my book, running my eyes over the lines of black ink, absorbing none of the words, none of the meaning, as I skipped between paragraphs. I turned the pages and studied the shape of the letters: their curves, their bones, their breaks. I couldn't tell you how long I was sitting there, filling the time with empty sentences and stroking the lines of text.

Marnie eventually appeared at the end of the corridor. She was wearing a raincoat, buttoned up to her chin with a hood pulled over her hair and shopping bags hanging from her wrists. She was sifting through her pockets—she pulled out a tissue and then an orange train ticket—and then she looked up and saw me.

"Oh," she said. "It's you." She stopped a few feet from her door.

I stood up but stayed rooted in the glow. "Is it raining?" I asked.

"It's just started up," she said. She buried the tissue and ticket back into her pocket. "I wasn't expecting you. Have you been waiting long?"

I shook my head and then remembered greeting the doorman much earlier in the evening. "Just an hour or so," I said. "I finished work early and I had my book."

"Are you . . . are you expecting dinner?" she asked.

She approached her door and reached into her handbag to find the key to the flat.

I had been very calm, my breathing measured and my pulse consistently slow. But I could feel my heart beginning to throb in my chest and sweat bleeding onto my upper lip.

It's important to say that I was not at all afraid of being caught, not at this point anyway. I was aware of it as a vague possibility, but I was also arrogant, confident that I had done everything possible to make that impossible. Instead, I was afraid of her reaction. Terrified, if I'm honest, of what might come next.

"I don't need dinner," I said. "But I . . . I just wanted to talk."

I was still holding my book and it was swinging awkwardly from my hand and bouncing against my thigh.

Marnie sighed. "I love that book," she said. "Have you reached the part where—"

"Spoilers!" I shouted, and it was a relief to make a loud noise, to expel some of the chaos burning within me.

Marnie jolted backward, shocked.

"Jesus," she said. "Calm down."

I took a deep breath—in, hold, out. This was not the time to lose my shit. I laughed and it sounded strange, sort of insincere.

"Look," she said. "I'm not sure if I'm ready to talk. But you can come in and we can try. But Charles is ill and in bed and he's been sleeping all day and I absolutely do not want to disturb him. It's one of those migraines and loud noises are the worst, so if you . . . if I ask you to leave, you leave, okay?"

I nodded.

Marnie turned back to the door and lifted her key into the lock. I heard it scratching there, finding its way into the hollows, the grooves.

"It is nice to see you," she said. "I am glad you came. I just—"

"It's fine," I said. "I understand. It's complicated."

"Yes," she said, and she looked at me and smiled. "That's exactly it. It's complicated."

She pushed the door open, just an inch or two. "And you're welcome to have some dinner—of course you are. I want everything to be normal again. You're my best friend." She grinned. "So, yes. I'll pour us some wine and I'll put on some pasta and we can talk."

"Perfect," I said, and I smiled, too, ignoring the burn of acid at the back of my throat. "Thank you," I said. "I'm really glad to be here. I want it to be normal again, too."

She pushed against the door again and I closed my eyes.

Isn't that cowardly? I squeezed them shut as soon as her back was turned, entirely involuntarily, because I was gutless. I was petrified of her reaction. I knew exactly what she was about to experience—I know how it feels to see your husband lying dead on the ground in front of you—and I know what that sort of shock could do to a person. I know how it builds within you, relentlessly, until you have no choice but to believe it. I know how it evolves into grief, the incessant, terminal nature of the thing. I knew that her heart would break.

"Charles?" she said. "Charles!" she screamed.

I heard her footsteps as she darted across the wood, the crash of her shopping as it fell, her knees slamming against the floor.

I opened my eyes. I followed her in; I paused briefly in the doorway.

He was most definitely dead. His skin had changed. It was no longer pink and peachy, but sort of yellow, gray. She was hunched over his body, her hands against his shoulders, shaking him. If he had still been alive, he would have been in agony, her grabbing him like that, what with his dislocated shoulder. But he was dead, so I guessed it didn't really matter anymore.

"What the . . ." I cried. I spotted a hairpin lying beneath their radiator—I recognized it as one of my own—and so I emptied my handbag onto the floor, my things rolling everywhere, my book landing with a thud, my phone beside it. I reached down for my phone, dialed the emergency services, pressed it against my ear. "Ambulance!" I yelled, as soon as I heard a voice on the other end, before they'd had a chance to say anything at all. "I need an ambulance."

"Where to, please?"

I reeled off the address. "Quickly," I added at the end. "You need to come quickly."

Marnie was sobbing, her head buried against Charles's chest. "He's dead!" she screamed. "Jane! He's dead."

"We think he's dead," I cried to the person on the other end of the phone line, because I had no idea what else to say or what to do and I was becoming more authentically hysterical with each of Marnie's screams.

"And what makes you think that? Give me as much information as you can. The paramedics are on their way."

"Marnie, how do you— He's a funny color," I said. "Yellow and his body's twisted. He's fallen down the stairs."

Marnie screamed again and then looked straight at me, her eyes wild and unfocused, and then she shouted, "Tell them we can get him back," and she lifted herself above him, placed her hands at the center of his chest and began pumping.

"We're doing CPR," I said. "There's a doorman—Jeremy—he can— there's an elevator—they'll need to get the elevator."

"They're on their way now. They'll be with you very soon."

"Keep going, Marn," I said. "Are you . . . If you get tired, I can . . . I can do it, too." I was panting and adrenaline was pouring through me, flooding my body.

"Is he breathing?" the operator asked. "Can you tell me if he's breathing?"

"Is he breathing?" I shouted. "No," I said. "No, I don't think so."

"They're on their way."

"They need to come quicker!" I shouted, and I really believed it. I really wanted them to hurry, to drive fast, to be here, even though I knew that there was nothing they could do, even though I knew that it was already too late.

"They'll be with you very soon," said the voice at the end of the phone. "Just keep doing what you're doing. You're doing great."

We heard the sirens screaming and Marnie was sobbing, sweating in her raincoat, and I was standing, the phone still held against my ear, listening to empty platitudes and frantically pacing.

"They're here," I said to her. "That's them. They're nearly here."

Marnie stopped driving her hands into Charles's chest and collapsed on top of him, wailing into him. She knew, I think, that he was gone. She had known since she opened the door and saw him lying there, his ankle twisted, and his shoulder dislocated, and his neck snapped.

I crouched down and rubbed her back—small circular motions that I hoped would convey that I was here for her, here for her always, whatever she needed—until finally we heard the lift clanking up to this floor and the doors scraping open.

I jumped up and leaned out the door. "We're here," I called. "Over here."

Three paramedics ran toward me. An older man, overweight with no neck whatsoever. A younger man, faster and fitter and quickly in front of me. And a young woman, who hung back, nervous, new perhaps, and said nothing at all and never entered the flat.

"Can you tell us his name?" shouted the younger man.

"He's my husband," said Marnie, crawling away from Charles's dead body so that the paramedics could reach him. "Charles," she said. "His name's Charles. He's thirty-three. He has a migraine."

We laughed about that a few weeks later. "I still can't believe I said that," she said. "That he had a migraine. I mean, Jesus. A migraine."

Here is something you learn as you get older, as you start to live alongside death in its many guises, as it becomes an ever-present part of your world. Death becomes softer in the months and years that follow. It loses its sharp edges; they don't cut quite so deep and make you bleed in quite the same way. Sometimes you are laughing at something that made you cry just a few days before. But soft edges are still edges, and they are sharpened unexpectedly, by an ill-considered comment or an anniversary, or are filed to a point at the memory of a happy moment. There is no logic to grief, no well-worn path that we all must follow; there are simply the times when it is bearable and the times when it is not.

I heard her say those words—"a migraine"—and I saw the humor in them even then. I knew that it was so much worse than a migraine and yet they were the words that broke me. I had seen her see him, watched her desperately trying to revive him, heard her screaming, and felt only a strange—again, giddy—excitement. I had been caught somewhere between panic and hysteria, only ever a second away from doubling over and laughing like that little girl at the beach.

But those words changed everything.

Suddenly it wasn't about Charles anymore. It wasn't about his rigid body lying concertinaed on the floor. It wasn't about his behavior or my hatred or the tension that had lived between us. It wasn't about the fact that he was dead or the fact of his dying. It wasn't about Charles at all.

It was all about Marnie.

I had done to her what the world had done to me.

You were meant to ask me if I regretted it. This was the moment I first felt any kind of regret.

The fruit from the shopping bag had rolled down the corridor, toward the kitchen, and the chicken, still wrapped in plastic, was sweltering on the wooden floor, my hairpin glittering beneath the radiator. But none of that mattered. All I could think about was Marnie. The paramedics were working in my peripheral vision, doing something that was probably nothing. And we all knew that soon they would stand up and step back and clear their throats.

Marnie was curled up on the bottom step of the stairs. Her raincoat had fallen from her shoulders and it hung around her waist, strapped around her arms. She wasn't crying anymore. But she was trembling, shivering, almost violently, like there was something within her that needed to escape. Her jaw was slack and her eyes were swollen and red and she kept making these terrible little noises, tiny retching sounds, like an infant choking. She was small, her knees bent up against her shoulders and enveloped in her own arms.

I had broken her. I knew then that I had broken her.

And don't start now with any nonsensical platitudes. Those people, the ones who say they understand when they don't, are the worst. And you are not one of them.

I knew then that it was all my fault. I had driven her to this moment. It was my words, my lies. And, to you, I cannot deny that I was the one who turned his head, who snapped his neck.

The remorse was unexpected. And perhaps it would have been so intense as to make me regret my actions had it not been tempered by a seed of hope. Marnie and I had been separated by romantic love. Those openings were now empty, cracks that could be refilled and repaired, until it might seem that they had never existed. I had created that opportunity. I felt sadness for her suffering and for what she would go on to experience. But I didn't feel guilt. I mainly felt relief.

Things have changed substantially since that day; you know that better than anyone. It must be about a year ago now, I suppose. You make it feel so much longer.

Later that night—after the police and the doctor and the undertakers—we returned to my flat.

I was very aware as we rode up in the elevator and stepped into the corridor that my building wasn't in any way luxurious. There were none of those symbols of success here: no polished floors or spotless mirrored walls. But I had known this woman as an eleven-year-old girl, and she had never been impressed by wealth or success then. And I knew that she was still that same person. Those were the proclivities of her late husband; he liked money and indulgences and extravagance. But we both knew—had always known—that they were simply façades, trimmings that decorated but didn't change the substance of a thing.

Marnie had never spent much time in my flat and it was nice to have her there with me. I offered her a pair of my pajamas—my favorite pair—and she had a long bath and I made her a cup of milky, sugared tea.

I lay in bed and waited for her and I heard the plug being pulled and the gurgle of water as it descended through the pipes. I heard the bathroom door opening as she stepped into the corridor to collect the pajamas from the radiator. The light was off, but I heard her enter my room and then she climbed into bed beside me. The sun was beginning to rise, peeping over the horizon and brightening the edges of my blinds.

I couldn't sleep knowing that she was there. She was on her side, facing away from me, toward the window, and her breathing was calm and steady, and I wondered if perhaps she was so exhausted that she'd fallen quickly asleep.

I lay on my back with my hands clasped over my stomach and I felt very much in control. This wasn't what I'd planned—remember that, yes—but I wasn't dissatisfied with the outcome.

"Jane?" Her voice broke in her throat.

I didn't reply.

"Did you hear anything?" she whispered into her pillow. "Anything at all?"

Still I didn't reply.

"Jane?" she said again, a little louder this time.

"What?" I said sluggishly, as though already half asleep.

"Did you hear him? Did you hear when he fell? Or anything afterwards?" she asked. "You were there, weren't you? Perhaps there was—"

"There was nothing," I said, propping myself up on my elbows, peering into the darkness to where I thought she was lying.

"Nothing at all?" she asked. "All that time. And nothing at all?"

"No," I replied. "I didn't know . . . I didn't hear a thing. I guess he—"

"Was gone," she interrupted. "Yes, I suppose he must have already gone."

That was the fourth lie I told Marnie.

I didn't have a choice, did I? How could I answer those questions honestly? I couldn't. I knew it then and I know it now. And yet, curiously, it was my denial, my self-proclaimed innocence, that nudged us back onto our path.

The truth would have been far more damaging for her.

Because then she'd have had no one.

Chapter Twenty

A life doesn't end when a person dies. Wouldn't it be wonderful if it did? If you died and all the memories in which you existed simply evaporated from the minds of their hosts, disappearing into the ether. If you were erased—at that very moment—from everywhere and everyone.

I wouldn't remember Jonathan. I wouldn't remember loving him or marrying him. I wouldn't remember his freckles or his strong thighs or the veins that ran along the backs of his hands. I would be sad to lose those memories, certainly. But I wouldn't know that they'd been lost, so I wouldn't know to miss them. I would have no grief.

I wouldn't remember Charles. I wouldn't remember hating him or killing him. I wouldn't remember his firm jaw or the narrow bridge of his nose or the way he pinched his chin when he was thinking. I wouldn't remember him begging for help.

Marnie would never have met him. She would never have moved into that apartment, she would never have loved him, never have married him. He would have disappeared entirely.

But that isn't how the world works. There are no blank slates, no fresh starts, no clean cuts. There is only the messy aftermath of every decision you ever make. Because—and this is one of my greatest frustrations—life moves in only one direction. Every decision that you ever make will be written in stone, permanent, never to be undone. They are all entirely irrevocable. Even if you find a way to unwind a specific decision, to unpick those threads, that decision will always have been made.

You chose your first job. You will never have another first job. You picked an apartment in a part of a city, and you will always have lived in that part of that city, whatever comes next, whatever else you choose. It never stops. The decisions are always binding. You pick a partner. Perhaps you marry him. Perhaps he becomes the father of your children. He will always be the father of your children, regardless of every decision you make from that point onward; whatever you might do next, that choice will always stand.

It is overwhelming. I cannot escape from the endless suffocation of my own decisions.

I would like it better if life were like a spiderweb, with a labyrinth of options, sprawling out from a single, central point. We would have all manner of choices, and not one would be irreversible, because there would always be another path back to the beginning. But instead we have only one straight thread, no choices at all, a relentless momentum and only one direction.

Jonathan has gone. Charles has gone. And yet they haven't really left us at all.

Whenever I am working through a crossword, I think of Charles. I wonder what he might say, if he would know how to unravel the final clue, if he would know the answer that eludes me. Whenever I see a man whose toenails are slightly too long, I think of Charles. I think of his ugly feet and the way he insisted on wearing sandals around their apartment in the summer. Whenever I see a tie tied too tight, I think of Charles. When a man asks for the wine menu and then peruses it at length, inevitably settling on the most expensive option, I think of Charles. There are so many facets of his being that are still embedded in my memory and so he is never as far away as I would like.

By contrast, Jonathan is never quite close enough. I cannot watch the London marathon. I cannot stand to see the joggers in their bright Lycra, their numbers pinned to their chests, their headphones and their sweatbands and their tightly laced trainers. I cannot stand to see the charity runners in their fancy dress, their madcap contraptions, the smiles across their faces and the laughter they provoke. Because it all makes me think of Jonathan, and not of Jonathan as I knew and loved him, but of Jonathan as he died.

There are things that remind me of him in a more positive way, too. When I watch groups of men speed past on bicycles on weekends, heading out of the city and toward the suburbs, to charge up hills and fly back down, to clock the miles, and to stop for a pint and a sandwich in a pub on a country lane. That was something Jonathan loved to do. I think of him whenever I'm at Angel tube station, because that was where we parted each morning, after toasted bagels and bananas and the panicked hunt through the piles of shoes in the understair cupboard and the rush to the platform, because we were always running just a few minutes late. I think of him whenever I pour myself the dregs from an orange juice carton, because I never shake it and that last glass is always thick with pulp.

This is what it means to have been alive. This is what it means to have ghosts.

Marnie and I are stuck on the same single thread, living with death, never able to recover the versions of us that existed before it.

Are you feeling sorry for me?

Do you see a woman warped by guilt?

Well, if so, then you shouldn't.

I don't regret what I've done; I don't regret any of my decisions. I just wish that they were more malleable, that I could see my life both with and without them at the very same time. I would like, for example, to see what this life might look like with Jonathan and without Charles. What would my relationship with Marnie look like under those terms? Is there a world in which women have best friends and husbands? Or is it always one at the expense of the other? I would like to manipulate my timeline to find the best possible version of my life, rather than existing within what I can only assume is the very worst of them all.

I wish that my life had ended when Jonathan died. But it didn't. Because that is not how grief works. You are stuck with your life for as long as you live it, even when you will it away, unless you are willing to take it away. And, unwilling as I was, I had no choice but to live without Jonathan.

And now, Marnie had no choice but to live without Charles.

All of which is simply to say that the story continued. I hope you don't mind me going on; we do have the time, after all. And you wouldn't want to be here on your own.

The important thing to recognize is that in the days after that death I knew that I had made an irreversible decision. And I was content to live with the consequences. I felt sadness regularly, yes, when I saw Marnie's swollen eyelids, her chapped lips, the heartbreak written there on her face. But I didn't feel guilt. And in fact, I felt rather optimistic. I thought I had found a way to create a spiderweb. And I felt a little safer, a little steadier, too.

I'm getting carried away.

What you need to know is this: I wanted my best friend back. And it worked.

But only for a while.

The
Fifth Lie

Chapter Twenty-One

T he funeral was well attended. Charles's colleagues—mostly men with chiseled jaws and sharp, dark suits—brought their wives, all pretty and blond in tight black dresses and patent stilettos. They were accompanied by Charles's secretary, Debbie, the only woman in the group over 130 pounds and under five foot five. She was in her sixties, small and stout, with cropped gray hair and a smart jacket straining slightly at the buttons. I had met her once before: a couple of years earlier she had come to the flat on a Friday evening to drop off some paperwork.

Charles's school and university friends arrived at the same time, dark glasses propped on their foreheads and thin black ties hanging around their necks. They hovered at the gates of the church, finishing their cigarettes, stubbing them out on the railings and grinding the butts into the paving slabs beneath their feet. A couple of them were accompanied by children, hip-height boys in black trousers and white shirts, three of them playing together and laughing inappropriately loudly. I wondered if Charles, in his casket, was wearing a tie, too, tightened around his crooked neck.

Charles's sister, Louise, had returned from New York. Her husband had stayed behind and was taking care of their younger twins and older daughter single-handedly for the very first time. Louise veered between panicking about their welfare—would they have been fed, washed, changed?—and trying to prove that she was suffering the most, far more than anybody else. I imagined that this was probably not the case. Nonetheless, she was gallantly performing a strange exaggerated grief. She seemed to have an endless supply of tissues and was indulging in regular mascara top-ups and was constantly hiccuping tears. Charles's mother had been planning to attend. She'd been doing a little better, Louise had said, until suddenly she wasn't doing better at all and was too frail, too weak for the long journey. Marnie's parents were there. We'd expected her brother would come, too, but work was chaotic, he'd said, and he couldn't get away at such short notice and flights from New Zealand were so expensive, and he'd come over soon, he promised, when things were calmer.

Marnie didn't seem to mind. She had been quiet in the days before the funeral, gliding from my bedroom to the kitchen to the bathroom and occasionally sitting still like a statue on the sofa in front of box sets we'd originally watched when they'd first aired many years before. She had cried very little. But she had woken in the middle of the night a number of times, sitting upright and screaming and then waking and apologizing and lying immediately back down again. She was still in the eye of the hurricane, the reality of her situation spiraling around her while she stood trapped in the center, waiting to be whipped up and spat out.

For those first few weeks, she abandoned the internet entirely, muting her notifications and ignoring any messages that seeped through that barrier. She had tried to reply to everyone in the first day or two—to the heartbroken and the concerned and the suspicious—and it had all been too much. There were too many voices and not enough time. She disconnected not only from her work and from the world within her phone, but from the greater world around us. She simply sat and stared, as though waiting for instructions. She hadn't left the flat in two weeks; her first outing was the funeral.

I recognized most of the guests there from the wedding, but there were a few who were unfamiliar. I found myself drawn to a woman, probably my age, in dark trousers and heeled boots and a smart navy jumper. She was tall and slim, like a mannequin, so still that she was almost invisible. She had very short hair, blue-black, and the sharpest green eyes. Her fingers were heaped with silver rings and she had a small symbol, like a musical note, tattooed at the top of her spine. She seemed to be there alone. She stood at the back during the ceremony and at the back throughout the burial and, again, at the back during the reception. She had a black leather bag hanging from a strap over her shoulder and I noticed her retrieving a small red notebook and scribbling in it at least twice.

"Do you know who that is?" I asked Marnie, pointing to the woman as she ducked back into the lobby. The reception was being held in a small room with large windows overlooking the river in what felt more like a conference center than a private members' club.

Marnie shook her head.

She was present only in body, swaying slightly in her too-high heels, her eyes glazed with tears. Her mind was trapped somewhere else: in the moments crouched over her husband's dead body, in the minutes that stretched and stretched as she pretended that there might still be hope. She was like a frightened child, with trembling limbs and pursed lips and damp cheeks.

I remember my husband's funeral as though through a fish-eye lens. The images are distorted in my mind, curved like a balloon, uncomfortably bulbous. I can see the mourners as they swam in and out of view—their head tilts, their weak smiles, their glassy eyes—standing far too close to my face, their warm breath, the way they all squeezed my hands and my shoulders. I wonder what they saw when they looked at me. Did I look as fragile then, so dazed and distracted?

The afternoon passed and Marnie and I sat together and watched as Charles's school friends opened the patio doors to smoke outside and his university friends ordered an honorary round of shots and Louise wept vigorously, her head buried against the shoulder of some distant relative. I had tried to be sociable, to rekindle conversations with those I'd met earlier in the year, to offer condolences and share memories, but I sensed that all of them would rather be talking to somebody else. I felt—I have always felt—as though I am someone to whom people say, "It's been lovely, but I must go and find my friend," or "It's been great to catch up, but I'm just going to pop to the bar for another drink," or "Oh, I've just spotted Rebecca. Will you excuse me?" So I was relieved when Marnie gripped my forearm and stood up and ushered me toward the entrance and begged me to please take her home.

We sat silent in the taxi. The sun was setting behind us, earlier now that autumn was drawing nearer, and there was something about the orange reflected in the side mirrors that felt profound. It was like a farewell scene in a film, and it made me feel reassured, as though the world was grateful for my intervention.

We arrived at my flat and Marnie went to change out of her dress and into my favorite pajamas.

"I didn't know," she said, coming back in and perching on a stool in front of the breakfast bar. "I didn't know how bad it was. I didn't know then, when you were feeling it, how bad it really is."

"You did everything you could," I said, pouring boiling water into two mugs. "And anyway—"

"I didn't," she said. "Thank you for saying that. But we both know that I didn't."

I placed a cup of milky tea on the counter in front of her. "Drink this," I said. "It'll help."

She nodded and wrapped her hands around the warm ceramic mug.

I wondered—before Jonathan died—if a person who suffers a great loss inevitably became more compassionate. Now that I have experienced my own great tragedy, I feel quite sure that—if this is possible— the answer is both *absolutely yes* and *definitely not*. I have a greater capacity for compassion, but I am less empathetic. I understood almost intimately the burden of Marnie's grief, but I felt very little sympathy toward Louise, with her pouting and her hysteria and her general nonsense.

And I suppose my sympathy slackened slightly for Marnie, too, when she compared our respective losses. I knew that she was experiencing a genuine, agonizing, devastating grief. But it is one thing to lose a husband who is good and kind and loving, and it is quite another to lose someone who was never good enough at all.

Chapter Twenty-Two

I want to tell you about the weeks after my husband died. They were without doubt the very worst of my life and the words to represent them feel achingly incompetent. There is no language sufficient for the tremors that shake through you in the aftermath of an incredible loss. There is the death itself, which is everywhere, all the time, in every memory and in every moment that you wish you were with them. But that is only one pillar of grief. In its entirety, it is much more than the loss of a person; it is the loss of a life.

In those first few months, I was grieving in a brutal, ruthless way for moments that hadn't happened, for things that now never would. If over one shoulder were my memories of the past—how we met, our wedding, our honeymoon—then over the other were the memories we hadn't yet made, the things we'd expected for our life together: the children we were going to have, and the houses we might live in, and the places we would travel. I was caught between a past that felt too full of feeling and a future that seemed bereft of it.

I was restless with the scale of it, unable to position myself within my own life, fighting within my own mind to find any kind of quiet. I couldn't sit and remember him and mourn him. I couldn't focus on any one moment, because there were too many things that felt insurmountable. I was flighty and erratic, and I struggle now to recount this in any accurate way, because I was barely there at all.

But those few weeks are important. In some ways, they are where this all began.

That night, just after he'd died, I went to the Vauxhall flat. I discovered things that weren't mine in my old room: clothing folded on the chair in the corner, jeans that clearly belonged to a man, and three shirts on hangers. I climbed into Marnie's bed instead.

I could taste salt on my cracked lips. My throat was dry, and my brain pulsed within my skull, the sockets of my eyes throbbing and pounding and jarring against my cheekbones. My face felt swollen, my skin too tight. I stared at the ceiling, the patterns of light cast by the blinds and the streetlamps outside, and I willed myself empty, my mind quiet, my body still. I tried to imagine myself somewhere else but there was nowhere to go, nowhere that he wasn't.

I woke to the sound of voices in the hallway, then the key in the lock, laughter and footsteps against the plastic wood-effect flooring. I recognized Marnie's giggle immediately, but the other voice belonged to a man, its pitch lower, resonating and vibrating within a broader chest.

They went into the kitchen. I could hear the steady hum of their conversation. Then the front door opened and closed again and the radio was turned on and I went into the kitchen and I saw Marnie bent over a cardboard box, folding bubble wrap around champagne flutes.

"That was quick," she said, standing and turning around. "Oh," she said. "What are you doing here? What's wrong? Hey. What is it? What's happened?"

Charles returned to the flat half an hour later. "I've got more boxes," he called from the hallway. "Another six. Do you think that'll be enough?

I could have got more, but I wasn't sure and I also wondered if—" He stopped in the doorway and simply said, "Oh."

Marnie and I were wrapped together on the sofa. I don't think I could have told you where one of us ended and the other began. My head was against her chest, her arm draped across my back, and our legs were tangled like tentacles.

That was the first time I saw him. He was smart and tall and handsome. He had broad shoulders and an ironed shirt, thin pink stripes against white, tucked into his jeans. His top button was undone and I could see the hairs of his chest reaching up toward the base of his neck. He had a strong jaw and a narrow nose and his eyebrows seemed almost black, his hair a very dark brown and salted at the sides by strands of gray.

"One minute," she whispered into my hair and then she was gone. There were murmurs in the hallway and then the front door opened and closed again and then she returned.

I didn't see him again for a while; I suppose I don't remember leaving the flat for several weeks. But Marnie was keen that I got out, that I didn't spend all day every day lying in the same filthy bedding, sweating and crying and torturing myself, and so she eventually started to send me on menial errands. She needed butter to bake a cake, more milk for her cereal, a notepad, please, from the corner shop just down the road.

I returned from the supermarket perhaps a month later and he was standing in the hallway of the flat, just about to leave. He was wearing a suit with a purple silk tie.

"Afternoon," he said, holding open the door. "You must be Jane, right? Well, I must be going. Nice to meet you. And sorry—you know—about everything."

He stepped around me and disappeared down the hallway.

I caught the front door seconds before it slammed shut.

He started appearing more regularly after that, popping by on weekday evenings, just to drop something off, a package that had been delivered to him, or to collect something—his stuff was everywhere: neat piles of jumpers and rows of his shoes and his watches lined up on the windowsill. Sometimes he stayed over. She had mentioned—a couple of months earlier, I think, when I was still living in Islington— that she was seeing somebody. But back then Marnie was always seeing somebody. She was always going on dates and sending me messages about new men and becoming instantly infatuated and then very quickly indifferent.

But soon he was with us more often than he wasn't and one night I heard him and Marnie arguing in shouted whispers because they had their new apartment, dammit, he said, and when she'd suggested they buy somewhere together, he hadn't envisaged living there alone and how long was this going to last, really, what was the plan?

That was the first time I felt anything other than indifference toward Charles.

His presence up until that point had barely registered. I had noticed him in the apartment, of course, but I was broadly oblivious to everything other than my grief.

But that moment changed things; it changed everything. It lit a fire within me. Suddenly, I had a hatred that overwhelmed my grief. The anger felt fresh and exciting: I felt powerful and charged in a way that I hadn't for weeks. I couldn't believe that a man—an adult man—could be so terribly insensitive. I couldn't believe that he would make his living arrangements a priority over my grief, over my dead husband. I couldn't believe that I had existed on the periphery of such a horrible, desperate man for so many weeks and hadn't realized it.

I thought I knew what was going to happen. Marnie was going to say all the things that I was thinking: that he was selfish and egotistical and that unless he changed his attitude then they wouldn't be living together ever thank you very much and how could he possibly— seriously?—ask her to put him first when we had been friends for years— *years*—did he not realize what an impossible ask that was?

I pictured us laughing about it later that evening. My anger would have been quickly quashed, but the storm of it would have reignited something within me. It would have been refreshing, a palate cleanser, to experience something other than exhaustion and sadness and panic.

Except that wasn't how the conversation unfolded. I heard her murmuring, not shouting—not really angry at all—and quiet but not quite quiet enough.

"I know," she said. "I know. And I want to live with you, too. You know that I do. This isn't what I'd planned, either."

The following evening Marnie cooked me dinner. She explained that on the night my husband died she had been helping her new boyfriend pack up his flat. And the following morning, they'd started to sort out this one. She acknowledged they hadn't been together for long, but she had seen how happy Jonathan and I had been, and that had started quickly, hadn't it? They had put an offer in on a place on the other side of town. It had only been a few months but when you know you know; that's what she said. And it was on a whim; they'd seen the flat from the outside when they'd walked past and the real estate agent was there—he'd just shown another couple around the building—and so they went inside, and they didn't think their offer would be accepted—it was low; too low, really—but it was and everything happened so quickly after that. She'd been planning to call me to share the good news. She'd wanted to invite us to dinner, to be their very first guests. It was a lovely flat. Or at least it would be eventually. I'd like it, she said.

Things had been put on hold—of course they had; she wouldn't have had it any other way—because of everything that had happened. But it was time to start thinking about the next steps for both of us. She was struggling, she said, to pay both the rent on the flat and her share of the mortgage on the new place and, anyway, it was right for her to be thinking about moving in there; there was so much work to do and nothing was getting done. Perhaps I was interested in taking over the lease here? But maybe not—and that was fine, too—she'd help me find somewhere new if that was what I wanted instead.

I suppose I had known that she would fall in love at some point and want to leave the flat. But I felt shocked. I hadn't believed that it would happen so soon. And certainly not like that.

I left the flat that afternoon and I went to stay with Emma. But her strange world was too strange for me: the empty fridge, the odd rules. And so I rented my own flat: my first time living alone. The building had been constructed a decade earlier, and each flat was a perfect square: a bedroom, bathroom, and living space Tetrised into position. The previous occupant had been permitted to paint the walls: a dark blue in the bedroom, orange in the bathroom, and a yellow wall behind the sofa. The flat was in a good location and it was affordable and it was entirely inoffensive. But I hated being there. I wanted to be with Marnie. And so I cursed Charles constantly. I blamed him for everything—my loneliness, my sadness, my grief—partly because I could and partly because, frankly, I thought then and still think now that he was really, truly guilty of a great wrongdoing.

If I had known then what I know now—that very soon my life would exist again without him in it—would I have hated him quite so much? Would I have found comfort in the knowledge that the scales do balance themselves eventually?

I might have found things to thank him for. It is true, I suppose, that he forced me to find my feet again. I hadn't worked for nearly two months and his selfishness pushed me to find a strength that I thought I'd lost. I hadn't spent a night on my own in years—most of my life, in fact—and yet he took my companion and forced me out. My champions, my cheerleaders, my counselors were gone. There was no one to look after me, no one whose love was absolute and unreserved, no one to whom I was central. Not without Jonathan. And certainly not without Marnie.

Chapter Twenty-Three

I would later learn that the mysterious woman from the funeral was called Valerie Sands. She was thirty-two years old, divorced, and a journalist. She had been working for the local paper for a decade while simultaneously running her own, often libelous, website and she was determined to find a real story, something powerful, something true—something that could change her reputation.

LESBIAN LOVERS KILL THEIR HUSBANDS

That was the headline she chose. She used capital letters and dark red type, like blood inked against the white background of her blog. We didn't know it was happening—that it was going to be published online, that she was even investigating us—until it had already happened. We discovered the post about two weeks after the funeral, when "fine" was finally feeling like something that one day, someday, might again be possible for Marnie. Things had been easing, the weight of the grief spreading, yes, but thinning, too, like syrup diluted, and we had laughed once or twice. I had been flitting between absolute calm, because there was no way to identify my involvement, and palpating panic, because what if there was? And yet, as the first weeks became the funeral week, and the subsequent weeks elapsed, I felt more measured in general and the panic peaked only intermittently.

There hadn't been many questions—a few at first, but nothing significant—and everyone had accepted the most obvious version of events as synonymous with the truth. Charles had been suffering with a migraine and, dizzy and confused, had tumbled down the stairs, breaking his neck as he landed and dying almost immediately. And Charles did have a migraine that morning; Marnie had confirmed it in the presence of the paramedics. And Charles's migraines were often characterized by light-headedness, fuzzy vision, and occasionally vertigo, too.

The questions that everyone was asking—her friends and family, acquaintances, those who didn't know us at all but were simply shocked— were more questions of faith than questions of fact. How could a young man fall to his death in such a violent way? What did he feel as he fell? What were the chances? Weren't there many other ways in which he might have fallen, a million other stumbles that he might have survived?

But I knew that the questions of fact were inevitable, and the initial answers that came from the autopsy thankfully supported all the theories. The postmortem revealed that he'd eaten very little that day: some coffee and a few tablets—in quantities slightly higher than prescribed— for his recurring vertiginous migraines. He was obviously badly injured— the broken ankle, the dislocated shoulder—but it was the peg fracture at the back of his neck that proved fatal. He was very bruised, too, and it transpired that his cheekbone was fractured, they assumed from a knock on the way down. But they found nothing suspicious, so they stitched him up and ferried him to the funeral home and they all concluded that it was just a very unfortunate accident and very sad indeed.

If anything, I became less afraid. I wasn't thinking about the police or a prison or the truth. Because none of the authorities—not the paramedics or the pathologist—were in any way imaginative. Isn't that curious? I mean, I shouldn't argue. But it wasn't until later, after the funeral, after that article, that the fear began to simmer within me again. Because here was someone who seemed determined to interrogate the facts, who asked questions, who saw something darker blossoming in the account of this death.

Valerie had been looking for a story to alter the trajectory of her career. I don't imagine she disliked writing for the local newspaper initially, but she had been working there too long, a decade, and she was always assigned menial community events—dog shows and charity bake sales and occasionally stints tracking down celebrities at fancy waiting-list restaurants. I suppose she wanted something more. She must have been delighted when her story walked through the front door one evening and sat down on the sofa beside her.

Valerie had been living with her roommate, Joanna, for three years. She'd left her husband at a train station after years of not unhappiness exactly but simply emptiness. She'd found a room to rent and the two women had quickly become friends. Joanna was training to be a paramedic and Valerie loved to be regaled with stories of life and death and gore: the most extreme moments of a human life.

Joanna might have said that she'd spent the day with a crew of two men, one who was older and rather overweight, and another who was younger. They'd been to an accident at a posh block of flats—I imagine this was how she described it; it's what I'd have said—in which a young man had fallen down the stairs and his wife and her best friend had arrived to a twisted body sprawled in the hallway. And there was something strange, she might have said, about these two young women.

Valerie was intrigued.

She took her curiosity and tried to convert her suspicions into a story. Because she knew that if this was going to transform her career, then she needed to find some answers, to ask the right questions of the right people, and unearth all the nasty details and the gritty truths.

At first, she found nothing. She attended the funeral and noticed nothing untoward. She initiated a conversation with Charles's secretary and Debbie unwittingly confirmed that he did indeed suffer with migraines. She loitered at the front of Marnie's building—Jeremy spotted her on the CCTV—but Marnie wasn't living there then and there was nothing much for her to find. The most obvious truth was still the most probable truth.

I suppose it was when she had finished examining Marnie that she started to look a little more closely at me. I saw her once at the front desk of my office building, chatting with the security guard manning the reception area. He was an older man, balding with a paunch, and she was so much younger and taller with her short hair and sharp cheekbones. I remember her leaning over the countertop, her low-cut sweater gaping as she laughed excessively. Her mouth was stretched wide to reveal straight white teeth, and I recall wondering what it was that she wanted from him.

Other than that, I didn't notice her prying into my life, but that's not to say that she didn't. There was so much online that she could have found had she looked in the right places—which she probably did. There were articles I'd written for the university magazine and several pieces about Jonathan: on his death, on his marathon run, and the footage recorded afterward was still available. And there were one or two articles on my company's website that used my name and discussed improvements in customer service.

She must have found something in all of that to inspire her. Perhaps she really thought she'd solved a mystery. But the piece on her website put forth yet another lie. It said that I had murdered Jonathan, pushing him into the path of an oncoming vehicle. I had then sold his apartment, making a substantial profit, and scooped up his life insurance policy. I had made a fortune—her words, not mine—by murdering my husband.

But that wasn't all. Her piece continued, espousing bullshit backed by no evidence and no sources whatsoever. She claimed that Marnie and I—malicious vixens and secret lovers—had found our strategy so successful that we had promptly repeated our plan a second time.

MARRIAGE. MURDER. MONEY.

That was emblazoned at the very bottom of the page. She wrote that we were now living in utter bliss, reveling in our wealth, the fortunes extracted from the fists of our dead husbands.

Chapter Twenty-Four

We might never have heard of Valerie, might never have read her article, if it hadn't been picked up by a national tabloid newspaper. Her website had a few thousand followers—mainly young Londoners—and perhaps we'd have stumbled across it eventually or maybe it would have been flagged by one of Marnie's fans. But it was equally possible that our lives would have continued uninterrupted.

Unfortunately, it ended up on the front page of a paper distributed across the country in a piece that heralded the nation's growing fascination with true crime. Apparently, there were thousands of blogs, hundreds of podcasts. It used our story as an example.

They said that the blog post had gone viral. It had been shared on Facebook and Twitter more than one hundred thousand times, which while not exceptional was certainly remarkable. Maybe they were telling the truth; perhaps people really were interested in the story of two young women who'd murdered their husbands. I suppose I can't blame them; I'd have been, too. But the cynic in me wonders if that feature was simply a disguise, a clever way to publish defamatory stories and to cash in on the noise and the excitement without real legal risk. They quoted from Valerie's website several times, but they referred to an "alleged" murder and didn't directly accuse us of anything.

The piece was published a few pages in, but there was a small, incendiary headline on the front, and Marnie and I were immediately inundated by messages from our friends and families. They were horrified not by our supposed behavior but instead on our behalf. They didn't believe a word of it, they said. Have you ever heard such rubbish? And what was the world coming to; was fact-checking still a thing in this day and age? They eagerly reassured us that no one who mattered would pay any attention whatsoever to that sort of *drivel*.

We hadn't seen the article at that point—we didn't know there was a website—and so I rushed to the corner shop to pick up a copy, still in my flannel pajamas, the garish pattern hidden beneath a long black raincoat. I brought it back to the flat and laid it open on the breakfast bar. Marnie and I read it together, our eyes sliding left and right as we skimmed each line in tandem and our faces contorting at similar moments, identical frowns for the same terrible lies.

There was a line from Valerie at the end. It said, I absolutely understand the fascination with these stories, but I think it's wrong to focus specifically on the bloodshed and assume that death in itself is the cause of the allure. For me—and for many of my regular readers—it's more about the truth than it is about melodrama or scandal. There was a link to her website.

I pulled my laptop from beneath the sofa and opened it up on the countertop. The website was slow to load—I suppose we weren't the only ones looking for the original piece—but eventually that red headline appeared on the screen.

The truth is that Valerie's article didn't make much sense. The facts didn't support her proposed version of events at all. I didn't kill Jonathan. He was killed by a taxi driver, a man in his late fifties who was serving a prison sentence, having been arrested for inadvertently causing a death while driving drunk. And, after the mortgage had been repaid, there was very little profit from the sale of his flat, mainly thanks to the recession and the subsequent property crisis. And I hadn't spent a penny of his life insurance payout.

Valerie was suggesting that we were so inspired by this overwhelming success—again, her words—that we then waited a not insignificant four years to reenact our plan once more.

How did they do it the second time? she wrote. I have to confess that I was tempted to finish the story here today. I considered keeping you waiting until next week for an update. But I just couldn't do it, not with a story this tantalizing. Even so, I'll leave a space below and do take a moment or two to think about this: What did they do the second time?

I scrolled down.

The drugs, she wrote. Is that what you were thinking? If you had something more grisly in mind, then I think you're underestimating these two women. Jane Black wasn't directly responsible for the death of her husband: she wasn't driving the car that killed him. She simply manipulated the situation to achieve her desired result. The same is true of Marnie Gregory-Smith. She didn't push her husband down the stairs—we know that she was at the library when he died—but she might have smuggled a few extra tablets into his coffee that morning.

It was nonsense.

But the truth didn't matter. Because, as I've said before, even the strangest fiction can feel entirely true. And believable lies are no great feat. It was a brilliant story. And that was what mattered most.

I should say now that I didn't respond this calmly at the time. I wasn't pragmatic at all. I was really fucking angry. It burned in my stomach, like that acidic ache when you know you've eaten something rotten, and I felt a strange adrenalized excitement spasming in my limbs. I was alive with rage, much as I had been when I first hated Charles. I assumed that Marnie would feel the same, but when I looked over at her she was crying.

"How could she . . ." she whispered, so quiet and airy that her voice sounded almost like a hiss. "How could she write something like . . . It's not true. How can she lie? She's said that—oh, God—how can she say this stuff? Who is this woman?"

She pointed to a line in the middle of the screen. Her index finger was trembling. A few words were there in bold, isolated from the rest of the text.

"They've always been close," says a friend of the two young women. "Always very insular. Intimate, I'd say."

"Who the fuck is that?" She slammed her empty mug down on the worktop. "Who the fuck has said that? What sort of— Both our husbands are fucking dead. And some little bitch is— Who the fuck, Jane? Who is that?"

"Marnie," I said, and I was a little frightened by her, because I'd never once, not in twenty years, seen her lose her temper—she was always so contained—and yet here she was, angrier than I'd ever seen anyone. "Let's just take a minute."

"A minute? We don't have a fucking minute. Jane, this will be everywhere already. This bloody piece is on doormats across the country, waiting to be read with a cup of coffee and a slice of fucking toast, there in supermarkets and newsstands and at fucking airports, and then they'll all pick up their laptops—we did, didn't we? It's there in people's tablets already, all black and white and shining on a screen."

"Marnie. Let's just—" It was sort of thrilling to see her so wild.

"Do you think my parents have seen it?" she said. "Oh, God. My parents have read it. Oh, fucking hell. And if they haven't, then how long will it be—not very long, I can tell you that right now—until they receive a knock on the door from a neighbor or a polite little text from a golf club chum that says, 'Oh, I'm so sorry that your family are featuring in the fucking tabloids, what an imposition,' and snicker snicker, then they'll fucking know. It's on the internet, for fuck's sake. They're going to be livid. Their colleagues will read it. Oh, Jesus, Jane. What do we do?"

And then, as quickly as she'd appeared, she was gone, and Marnie was crying again, her head in her hands and her body shaking and all of that strength and power dissipating into the space around her.

That was the moment my fear reappeared. It built in me like a fever. It started with her anger. I could see the shape of it; I could feel its vibrations. I knew that it might one day come for me. And then the realization that there was someone somewhere who was unconvinced by the most obvious answers, the facts as they'd been confirmed.

There was something in the way Valerie wrote, in the shape of her sentences, that was so much more sinister than the words themselves. I had this inkling then that we were only at the very beginning. I had a suspicion tightly tied to my fear that the worst was still to come.

Chapter Twenty-Five

A few hours later, we began to receive calls from other media outlets. I'd installed a landline phone when I'd first moved in because it made my internet substantially cheaper, but I soon regretted that decision. The messages were never-ending, long and descriptive or short and punchy, but vast in number and arriving quicker than we could possibly delete them. And soon they were emailing and texting us, too. The story had captured the imaginations of their readers, or listeners, or audiences. And what did we have to say about it? Did we want to add our comments? They promised us—all of them—that they were different from the other reporters, or radio hosts, or broadcasters. The others simply cared about numbers, about the drama, about being part of the hype. But us? No, that's not us at all. We really care. And this was the moment—"this is *your* moment," they all said—to put the record straight.

Don't laugh. It's not funny. What are you laughing at? "Put the record straight"? Well, yes, I suppose that is a little funny. I certainly wasn't going to be doing that.

Anyway, Marnie and I knew that the lie—the fantastical tale of two lesbian murderesses—was more tantalizing than the truth. Or, at least, than the assumed truth. Who didn't want to read about the two Machiavellian widows living in sin?

And so we said nothing. We unplugged the landline and turned off our mobiles and redirected every email that wasn't from a recognized sender to our junk and spam folders. Then we locked the front door and didn't leave the flat for two weeks, ordering food online every few days and illegally streaming new movies. I didn't call my boss, but I assume someone in the office had seen the article because I received a very simple message to be in touch as and when I felt able to return.

Marnie and I were confident that the drama would ease eventually. There is always a more interesting story waiting to be told. And, thankfully, the photograph used in the newspaper was horribly pixelated. It had been taken in our first summer home from university and our fancy-dress costumes, while undeniably sexy, made us rather hard to identify. There were others of Marnie—on her website, on social media—and I know that there was one of me hidden somewhere on my company's website, but that must have been the only one of us both. We simply had to be patient.

Even so, I wanted to know more about the strange woman who had so disturbingly inserted herself into our lives and so I scoured the internet for information. I found out about her marriage: her ex-husband, his new wife, their wedding website. I scrolled downward, backward, until I found the wedding venue, the endorsement they'd given the caterers. I found photographs of her home on Instagram: they showed the shared flat she now lived in; her roommate, recognizable immediately; the balcony where they'd sat in the summer drinking wine. I could see the name of the café opposite and it was easy then to find it online, to know where she lived. In the last few weeks, she'd started attending tap dancing classes and she'd uploaded several videos of a troupe of six all spinning and clacking and moving with frenzied feet as though their limbs were elastic. Her work was perhaps the easiest of all: the previous entries on her website, none of them nearly as tantalizing as the one she'd written about us.

I didn't think then to retrace her steps through the previous decades—that came later—but I was still astonished by the volume of data available literally at my fingertips, with just a few clicks. It frightened me to know that I was just as visible, that my life could be so easily penetrated. I watched her in the intervening weeks, as she uploaded images of her whereabouts with the locations tagged and posted about her plans and wrote a roundup of upcoming events in the area.

I felt sure that she was watching me, too.

Maybe the furor would have quieted if we'd waited a few more weeks. But Marnie didn't. She couldn't. The fiction written online was intensifying within her: the murder, the drugs, his death. It seemed more likely every day. She slept with it at night as it staged itself in her dreams. She was by turns listless then restless, only ever sleeping briefly before the nightmare began again. She could remember dropping the tablets into his coffee. She could picture herself standing on her tiptoes, reaching for the packet in the cupboard above the sink and popping the pills from their blister packs and poisoning her husband. And then, when she hadn't slept in days, she started experiencing strange hallucinations and wondering if maybe she'd pushed him after all. Had she been there all along? Had she stood behind him at the top of the stairs? She could see it: the prints hanging framed on the wall and the carpet beneath her feet and she knew what it felt like to touch him, to run her fingers between his shoulder blades, to lay her palm flat against his spine. She wasn't eating; although she was drinking. She wasn't sleeping; she was frantic and feverish. She needed to state the truth as she knew it before the lie consumed her.

"It wasn't for me," she said afterward. "I didn't do it for me. I could have lived with it. But Charles? He would never have married the woman they said that I was. They've all made him seem so naive and so stupid and he was never those things. I couldn't let that become the story that defined him."

And so she met with Valerie just two weeks after that first piece was published. She exhumed the newspaper from the recycling bin and she searched for the journalist's name and she went back to the website and she sent an email. And received an offer of a breakfast the following morning at the café on the ground floor of my building.

If I had known, I could have stopped her. But by the time I woke up, her spot beside me was cold.

Valerie was, I imagine, rather disappointed by Marnie. I suppose she had been hoping for sordid details and revelations and something that confirmed her version of events. Marnie might have confessed to doling out the tablets that morning, to not checking the instructions quite carefully enough, or perhaps not at all, to being overwrought and overworked and overestimating the quantities in her haste. But, of course, she didn't.

I can only guess that the story was unexpectedly dull. Marnie would have gone on and on about Charles's migraines. She would have said—at least twice—that she'd been worried that he might have a brain tumor. But the doctor—and he was a nice man, a good doctor, they trusted him—had always been insistent: just migraines. And when they came they were pretty severe; they always had been. She should have stayed at home. She could have looked after him. She'd have brought him a glass of water, or a sandwich, or whatever it was that he'd wanted. She could have saved him.

Valerie would have looked at Marnie—slight and fair, her hair unbrushed, the dark circles pooling beneath her eyes, the almost imperceptible trembling—and would have known that her piece, as entertaining as it was, simply couldn't be true. This woman—sniveling into her coffee, so bloody frail and broken—was incapable of murder.

I wonder if Valerie felt frustrated. She had hoped, I'm sure, for something else. She wanted Part 2 to build on Part 1: more detail and drama and excitement. And instead she had a contradiction, an accusation that wouldn't survive scrutiny.

She must have been livid. But she was also smart. And so she worked with what she had. She manipulated their conversation—the little revelations, the snippets that she'd wrung from a grieving widow—to expose a more interesting update.

Marnie returned to the flat with fresh croissants—they'd been our weekend treat in the Vauxhall flat—and I assumed that this marked a change in her outlook, the beginning again of striving for a new normal. I didn't suspect anything until the following morning when I received a call from Emma. She had registered for updates from Valerie's website and had received an email in the early hours informing her that a new post had been uploaded. The email said that Valerie had revised her earlier piece as a result of some "new evidence." She had—this time—uncovered the real truth, a much darker truth and one that revealed not only the relationships that these two women had with their late husbands, but also more detail about their relationship with each other.

I opened the page on my laptop.

Valerie had written that I was jealous. She said that Marnie had been happy—unexpectedly so—and that I couldn't stand to see her so content with somebody else. I had committed a murder for her—apparently—and I was horrified when she then wouldn't do the same for me. The piece was long and convoluted, and almost all of it was nonsense. But the main point she wanted to make, it seemed, was that the blame rested solely with me. Marnie had been unable to kill Charles, because "perhaps she really loved him," Valerie had written. And so I had taken the necessary steps to ensure that she couldn't renege on the original deal. I was the puppeteer of the entire dastardly scheme. I was the true antagonist. I had killed him.

And while Marnie Gregory-Smith has an alibi, the same cannot be said for best friend Jane Black. I'll let you draw your own conclusions, Valerie had written. But it seems to me that the clouds are beginning to part over this mystery.

Do you know how it feels to be accused of a murder you've committed? It's incredibly frightening.

What?

Why are you looking at me like that?

Oh, I see. You want me to acknowledge that she's far closer to the truth than any of the others: the police, the pathologist, our friends and families. And you're wondering if she was right. Had she found a small piece of the truth? You want to know if I was jealous of Marnie.

No. I can confidently say that I was never jealous, not of her life, not of the trinkets that decorated her day-to-day. I was occasionally envious of her self-confidence, her warmth, her kindness, but those are very different things. Does that answer your question?

But the one that you should have been asking is whether I was jealous of Charles. And I suppose that I was. It sounds childish, and perhaps I don't mean it as it sounds, but he had something that belonged to me, a love that had once been mine, a love that had chosen me.

She didn't specify that she'd spoken to Marnie. But somewhere between the new evidence and her description of a teary widow clasping her cold coffee to her chest and unable to balance her breathing sufficiently to actually take a sip, I realized what had happened.

I went into the living room and found Marnie sobbing on my sofa, her laptop open in front of her, apologizing in heavy, breathy gasps.

"I've made it worse," she said. "I've made her turn on you. It's all my fault. She's written that you did it. Have you read it? I'm so sorry, Jane. I'm so, so sorry." She closed the lid of her laptop and lowered it onto the coffee table. "I thought she'd see that I was telling the truth. I wanted her to see that she'd been wrong, and—I'm so bloody stupid—I thought she'd publish a retraction or something and that it would all go away. She dropped her head into her hands. "I thought she might say sorry," she said, her voice muffled by her palms.

"This isn't your fault," I replied, although I should admit now—in the spirit of honesty—that I was a little frustrated. I'd told her what we needed to do, and she'd blatantly ignored my instructions. But her intentions had been good; she'd thought she could unwind the web. "You weren't to know," I said.

I tried to stay calm. I looked at her flannel pajamas turned up at the ankles, her legs crossed on the sofa. The buttons of her shirt were undone at her neck and her chest, and red hives were flourishing across her skin. She needed me to be strong, to look after her.

The truth is that I hadn't expected repercussions. And with the autopsy and the funeral, this assumption had begun to feel more concrete. The police and the coroner had no reason to look beyond the facts as they first found them. But I knew that there were other pieces of the truth still hidden elsewhere. And this strange woman—who had appeared in our lives unexpectedly—seemed determined to dig and pick and claw until she found something that felt more authentic.

I had hoped that Valerie's version of events would quickly be overtaken by gossip and news and other lies. But after the second article? I couldn't be so sure. I didn't know how far she might go in pursuit of the truth.

I wanted to send her a message, confronting her, arguing that her behavior was simply unacceptable. But I knew that if I provoked her, there was a reasonable risk that she would grow more determined rather than less.

I took a deep breath. I knew what we needed to do. We needed to trust in the absence; to let it widen over the next few weeks, until it was the only thing still standing, until mine was the last possible truth, until an accidental fall down the stairs was the only thing left.

And, in that moment, I was so focused on fixing the situation with Valerie that I failed to notice another problem expanding.

Marnie has always been one of the brightest, most intelligent, most dynamic people, and the tears and the grief and the chaos changed none of that. She has always had a marvelous ability—it's something creative, I think—to unite vague ideas into something more solid, to build a jigsaw from the disconnected pieces. And I could suddenly see that she was doing just that.

"I should never have approached her," Marnie continued, the pitch of her voice shifting with each word. "I should have known that she couldn't be trusted. I don't know why I expect better from people. Why is that?"

"Stop it," I said, sitting down beside her and taking her hands in mine. "You're only making yourself feel worse and it's done now; there's no point."

"And it doesn't even make sense," Marnie continued. Her cheeks were lined with tears. "How exactly does she propose that you murdered Charles? At least her first post was theoretically possible. I could have drugged him. I mean, I didn't, but I could have. But you weren't even in the building when he died. You didn't hear anything. It's just nonsense."

"Marnie, stop it," I said. "Let it go."

"What did you do? Push him down the stairs and then go home? And then what? Return to the flat later that evening? You didn't even know that he was sick. You'd have thought that he was at work."

"Exactly," I said, although my heart was beginning to beat a little faster and I was finding it difficult to swallow. At the back of my mouth, my tonsils felt swollen and dry; they were obstructing my throat and restricting the air to my chest. I could feel my hands growing clammy around hers.

"And why would you bother? I mean, I know you weren't exactly the best of friends—maybe that's a slight understatement—and I know that things had been particularly bad—that big misunderstanding—but even so, it's just not feasible."

Her voice was getting louder, starting to shake and stretching into shrill. Her gestures were manic, her hands waving wildly. Her cheeks were flushed, rosy and enraged.

"You left him dead in my hallway. Is that what she's saying? Turned up, killed him, and then left? And then what? Popped back a few hours later just to watch me find him? There is something seriously wrong with that woman."

She couldn't stop herself and I couldn't stop her, either. She went on and on, listing the many ways in which it didn't make sense, couldn't be true, was utterly impossible, and I listened as she reeled off examples of how I could have—but also couldn't have—murdered her husband. The articles had opened these questions within her, and I didn't know how to close them. I tried to steer her in other directions, but she kept falling back into her interrogation, and I felt as though my ribs were too small for my lungs—the flesh pressing into the bone—and I wondered if I could keep my face static if she reached the right conclusion.

"We were madly in love. That's what she says, isn't it? You and me? And so we killed your husband. Of course. Because that makes sense. And then I fell in love with Charles." A small sob broke through her anger. "And then you killed him so as to keep me for yourself? Is that it? Is that what happened?"

I expected her to keep going, to keep ranting, to continue trying to unravel her confusion aloud. And that would have been alarming enough. But she didn't. She stopped. She stared at me.

"Is that what happened?" she repeated, her eyes wide and her chin jutted forward, her lips trembling. "That's what she says, isn't it?"

I shook my head—feigning bemusement, horror, repugnance—and she stayed quiet and so I reached into the conversation and I tried desperately to end it.

"Imagine," I said, and I raised my eyebrows and I tried to laugh. "Just imagine."

I wondered what she could see: if my cheeks were pink, my eyes frightened, my breath frozen; if the truth was written there on my face, as eager as her tears.

"Imagine," she repeated, quietly.

"I know," I said. "It's impossible. As if I could do something like that. I would never do something like that."

That was the fifth lie I told Marnie. I told her that I could never do something that I'd already done. I told her that I could never hurt her when I already had. And as I sat there deceiving her with my entire body, I trusted that she would continue to believe me. And she did. She shook her head slowly and sighed, leaning back against the cushions and scraping her fingers through her hair.

I don't think that she was really interrogating me. She wasn't asking a question and expecting an answer. But the sound of her doubt—however vague—was unnerving. I felt the truth like a small bone in my throat, aching to be released. It brought a small part of me to the fore that wanted to be acknowledged, that was tempted to say, *Yes. That's what happened*, to say, *Yes. And I did it for you*.

But I knew, too, that I would lie again and again to protect what we had.

"We need to decide what we're going to do," I said eventually.

She wiped beneath her eyes and dried her fingers on her pajamas. Her top had curled around her waist and she pulled it back down. "There's nothing we can do," she said, standing and moving into the kitchen, calmer now, contained. "It's published. And trust me, Jane," she continued. "You don't want to have this out with her. She'll just publish more crap online and we know the truth, and our friends and family do, too, and really, isn't that what matters most? I'm not saying it's fair. Because I'm cross, too, Jane. Really, I am. And I hate that she's going to get away with just saying whatever the hell she wants without a thought for the people at the end of her lies. But I need this to go away."

"Okay," I replied. "Then let's just wait it out."

The adrenaline slowly started to dissolve, and I finally exhaled in full and I thought I might faint because she'd been—hadn't she been?—so very, very close.

Do you want to know something? That fifth lie scared me. I realized then the risk that I'd taken—inadvertently, yes, but taken all the same—and how that decision would affect my life going forward. I needed to be careful, to stay in control.

I read the newspapers in the days that followed. They were full of it again: opinion pieces and pretend news and anonymous sources. But it did ease eventually—another political scandal stole the headlines and rolled on and on into months of coverage.

I kept the pages about us in a shoe box beneath my bed. They reminded me that I wasn't invincible. They reminded me to keep looking over my shoulder. They reminded me to keep lying.

Chapter Twenty-Six

I think that some women are made for motherhood and others simply aren't. That's controversial, I know. And something I probably shouldn't be saying to you, of all people. But I think it deserves a
mention.

I always dreamed of being a mother. As a child, I cradled my plastic
dolls and I bathed them, and I pushed them around in a pastel pram
with a thin pink fabric seat that turned in on itself like a hammock. And
I lined them up in rows and changed their nappies one by one and
dressed them in patterned cotton onesies, pinching the snaps between
their legs. They were all much the same—hard round bellies and rosy
pink paint on their cheeks and bright blue eyes that blinked—but my
favorite was Abigail. She was bald and her limbs were fixed. One of her
eyes blinked open and closed, but the other was sticky, its plastic lashes
glued together. It opened and then refused to shut, staring straight ahead
while the other one winked threateningly. I loved her nonetheless.

I eventually grew out of dolls and into babies. I peered into prams as
I passed them on the streets, leaning over to look inside in cafés and
making the obligatory cooing noises and asking the requisite questions—
how sweet and how old and how lovely. I participated in this rhythm of
adulthood quite willingly and I saw a version of my life in which I

would one day push the pram and another woman's coos would cascade over me.

And then, at some point—in the aftermath of Jonathan's death—I began to question that imaginary future. Did I want a pram? Did I want the clucking and questions and judgments and a bit of my heart to forever live outside of my body? To do what parents do and feed and heal and nurture?

No. I didn't. Not without him.

If you wanted me to, I could write a list of all the women in my life and I could draw a straight line across that piece of paper dividing those who were made for motherhood and those who simply weren't. Emma and I would be on one side. Marnie would be on the other.

The promise of peace had a positive impact on Marnie's overall outlook. She was less angry, less flighty, less afraid of the something and nothing that exists in the aftermath of loss. We found a way to coexist that felt comfortable and peaceful. She cried—often—but she also laughed and cooked and even wrote a few short pieces for her favorite editors. She redirected her mail to my flat, which was oddly comforting; I liked seeing her name beside mine in our postbox every day. And when her main sponsor sent her a pink ceramic gift set, part of their most recent cookware collection, she even managed to film a few videos.

Occasionally she would turn to me—normally over breakfast or while we sat on the sofa in our pajamas late in the evening avoiding sleep—and say:

"Death really lasts a long time, doesn't it?"

"Oh, yes," I would say. "The longest."

"Because it's been a month"—or six weeks, or two months, she would say—"and I just can't quite fathom that this is my life now. I can't bring myself to believe that no matter how many more months I live, no matter how many years, or decades even, he will be dead in every single one."

I felt like an expert. And for a while my tutelage seemed to be working. It was such a delight to have her back in my life. And we were good together, really good. We knew each other intricately, intimately, all of the history, all of the detail. We bemoaned our parents—who left, and fell sick, and ignored us. We laughed at our siblings—one of whom was entirely dependent and the other entirely absent. We reminisced about the adventures that had defined our teenage years—the firsts, and the lasts, and the never agains. We were two people who had shared so much that we were almost only one again.

I watched as she recovered; not entirely, of course, not at all, but in small, significant ways. It was a thrill to see her cooking again. She painted her nails and complained when they chipped the following morning. She looked at her hair in the mirror one afternoon and lifted some strands in her hands and then frowned. That evening, she returned with the ends neatly trimmed. She listened to music. She watched the news. She cried regularly—all the time—but the moments of overwhelming sadness were set against something better.

And then things changed. Marnie regressed, reverting to the chaos of the very first weeks. She stopped sleeping. She was exhausted. She fell ill. She stopped eating. When she did manage something—even just the smallest of meals; some toast, some fruit—she was overcome by such violent spells of vomiting that I stopped buying food to keep in the flat simply to save us both the horror. The hunger was intense. The fatigue was far worse. And with neither nourishment nor rest, she was entirely unable to shake her strange sickness.

Or so we thought at the time.

It was early in the evening—we'd just opened the blinds again; there were fireworks outside and we wanted to watch them—and Marnie and I were sitting together at the breakfast bar. We were eating plain rice— a sachet of boil in the bag each; quick and easy—and our silence was effortless. We were once again used to dining together, our worlds entwined, no longer intermittent guests in each other's lives but a curious sort of couple.

"I haven't had a period," she said, laying her fork down beside her bowl. "I thought it was just stress, you know, with everything. But it's been three months."

"Well, of course it's the stress," I said. "And the bug. You're losing weight—look at you—and with all the vomiting— Oh."

"I need to take a test," she said.

I cleared my throat, dislodging the clump of grains that had congealed there, and stood up from the table. I went into the hallway and collected my handbag from the peg. I walked from the front door, into the elevator, and out into the street. I walked along the road—cold without my coat—to the corner shop.

I returned with the test less than ten minutes later.

Marnie was sitting exactly as I'd left her, her elbows on either side of her bowl, her head supported between them.

"Here," I said. "Do it now."

She silently took it and went into the bathroom, the plastic bag hanging limply from her wrist.

I don't need to tell you that it was positive.

I got drunk. I drank tequila straight from the bottle and lined up shots of rum from a bottle so old that the liquid inside tasted of nothing but stickiness. Marnie—already a mother in so many ways—poured apple juice into plastic shot glasses and drowned her fear and panic in a more abstemious way. At two in the morning we climbed into the bathtub, wearing our swimsuits in the steaming water in a strange and unnecessary display of modesty. We smeared honey onto toast at three and worked our way through an entire loaf. And then we lost ourselves somewhere between grief and shock and hysteria, and sobbed and laughed until we fell asleep, which didn't last long, and then we both spent the best part of the following morning with our faces resting against the cool porcelain of a toilet seat.

You see, no one expects their lives to pan out as ours were. I was widowed and in a dead-end job and never far from misery. Marnie was widowed and pregnant and in the midst of a great fall from a charmed life.

"I need to move home," Marnie said the following evening. "I need to sort my life out. I need to see a doctor and start working again and I need to move home."

She called her cleaner right there at the table. She wanted the place spotless, she said. And she wanted Charles's stuff boxed up and put into storage—his toothbrush, his clothes, anything that was obviously his.

We visited the flat a couple of days later. We were both shocked to find that the cleaner had left a thick white rug with black detailing stretched across the floor of the hallway. I wondered what lay beneath—a dark bloodstain, or scratches on the varnished flooring, or just the scent of death—but I resisted the urge to lift the edge and peer underneath. Some of Charles's things were gone—his coat from the back of the door and his shoes, which had been lined up neatly along the wall—but he was still everywhere. He was in the books on the shelves and the prints on the walls and his tall black umbrella was still propped beside hers in the hallway.

"Are you sure?" I said, trying to catch up with Marnie as she flitted between the rooms.

She frowned and then began to climb the stairs.

"That you want to live here," I said. "Are you sure? We could find you somewhere—"

"No," she said, standing on the top step and turning to face me. "It should be here. It's right that it's here. I want this little one"—and she held her hand to her stomach—"to know at least a little of their father. And this was once our home. It makes sense. It has to be here."

She looked past me. "This is the spot," she said. "Probably right here, where my feet are standing now. This is where he took his last breath. That's something his child should know, don't you think?"

What do you think? Is it something you'd want to know? I know I'd be devastated if I received a call informing me that my father had died. Not because I would miss the man he is today: a cheat and a deserter. But because I would miss the man that he once was.

For my first decade, he was constant and unwavering and honest and true. He was always there and always encouraging and, despite everything that happened when he stopped being a good father, he was never selfish before that. Instead, he was broken and flawed and determined that he wouldn't be defined by the very worst parts of who he was. And then something changed. Those difficulties that had bubbled beneath his skin for decades—the impatience and the uncertainty and the volatility—started to seep through his pores.

Will I want to visit the place where he dies? I don't think so. For me, he died at the front door, suitcase in hand, smiling as he left us behind.

"Maybe a fresh start—" I began.

"I want to be back in by Christmas," Marnie said.

"That's only a few weeks—"

"I'm going to host it," she said. "I'm going to decorate and cook—I'll need a tree and a turkey—and I'm going to make it count."

"This is a lot," I said. "Marnie, it's a lot for me to take in and it's a lot for you to take on."

"I've decided," she said. "And you're coming. And so is Emma. I'm going to make this happen."

"We'll be with—"

"Your mum. Yes, that makes sense. That's the morning, isn't it? Well, after that, then."

"I—"

"This isn't optional," she said, her face suddenly stiff and her eyes wide. "I'm inviting you to join me for Christmas. Whether you accept that invitation or not is your decision. But I am going to be living here by then and I am going to do this."

Marnie and I have very few shared traits. She is open and warm and loving and unafraid. I am closed and cold and angry and fearful. She is light and I am dark. But we are both notoriously stubborn. I know without doubt that on some things she cannot be moved; she cannot be bought or bribed or won.

"Then, yes," I said. "I'd love to come."

"And will you help me move back in?"

"Of course."

"Right, then. Let's get started. I want to measure up for a new bed."

So that was what we did. We wrote down the measurements for a new bed because, although she could sleep in her dead husband's flat, she couldn't possibly imagine sleeping in his bed. She ordered a replacement that afternoon. A small double—"it'll only be for me," she said—with a blush pink button-backed headboard—"he'd never have gone for pink"—and storage underneath—"for muslins and nappies and all the other things that babies seem to need."

She moved back in two weeks later, the day the bed arrived, and I tried to be pragmatic but I felt like something was being taken from me all over again. I packed up her suitcases and the kitchenware that had overtaken my cupboards and boxed up her shoes from behind the front door. We piled everything into a taxi early in the morning, bags at our feet and on our laps, and then she proceeded to leave me.

I'm being dramatic, I know. I felt sad that she was going but I could rationalize my grief because I was also pleased to see her so focused and satisfied. I had enjoyed nursing her and caring for her and being her strength, but it's not a sustainable way to live.

The world is full of vulnerable people. They lean on others, relying always on that additional support, that additional strength. Emma, for example, is incredibly vulnerable. But Marnie is not. She'd started working again a few days earlier—turning on her phone and uploading her videos and sharing updates and engaging with the world she had built around her. She seemed stronger, somehow, with that platform beneath her.

"You can go now," she said, after we'd carried everything into the lobby and carted it up to the flat, load by load in the elevator. "I think I have it from here."

"But the unpacking," I said. "Don't you want some help with that?"

"No, thanks," she said. She was standing in the doorway—her doorway—with her hand against the frame and her feet squarely on the wooden floor and I was in the hallway, on the other side of the entrance. "I'm good now," she continued. "But thanks."

"But—"

"I'll call you tomorrow," she said, and then she closed the door.

I felt sort of angry and sort of proud.

And sort of embarrassed, too. I looked left and right, but there was no one else, no one there who had witnessed my eviction. I stared at the spot where I'd sat nearly three months earlier. That felt like another person, another time, another world. And then I went home.

Here's the thing. Marnie had a family—as we all have families—but it had never felt much like a family to me. As a child, I believed that a family was unshakable, unbreakable, something fixed and immovable. I had a sister, and she would always be my sister, and parents, who would always be my parents. It wasn't until much later—when my father left and my mother disowned me—that I realized I'd been wrong. It wasn't fixed at all. But it had been throughout my formative years. I didn't realize that I'd need to build my own unit until much, much later. I didn't realize that I'd need to become someone who others wanted to love.

But it was a lesson that Marnie learned at a far younger age. Her family had come in waves—sometimes in, sometimes out—and was entirely unpredictable. She wanted this family—her new family—to be different. She had the power to craft this thread of the web, to build this unit as she wanted, and this was what she wanted.

Chapter Twenty-Seven

I have always loved autumn. I like that sense of something ending but not quite over. I like open fires and curtains drawn and thick woolen jumpers and boots that encase your feet and cushion your toes. I like winds that nip and clouds that soften the sky and that feeling of stepping out of the cold and into the warmth. The summer is too much, too full of expectation, with so much pressure to be joyful and buoyant and bright. And the winter is too dark, even for me.

But December has always been a strange month in this city, an anomaly that doesn't quite follow the pattern of the calendar. For that month only, the fabric of the place feels different. There is something unusual in the appearance, the atmosphere, the people who filter through as the darkest days approach.

Some of the changes happen slowly, over the course of several weeks. Strings of lights are hung between buildings, sparkling against the black of a night that draws in earlier each evening. Shop windows are overhauled, decorated in festive tones with ornaments and pine trees and sleighs and snow. There are fewer people on the streets. As the last weeks of the month draw nearer, the workers—who spend the entire year on the trains and pacing the streets and flowing in and out of rotating office doors, people like me—tack annual leave onto the bank holidays and stay curled on their sofas instead. The tourists—

wearing red hats with white bobbles and carrying shopping bags and cameras and children strapped to their chests—are present in their droves, filtering in and out of toy shops and ice skating on makeshift rinks in otherwise underexploited venues and standing on the wrong side of the escalator. But, even then, there are not enough of them to balance the absences, to counteract a city half emptied, its occupants stationed instead in their homes.

Other changes are almost instantaneous—suddenly we are smiling at our fellow commuters, and then we are making polite conversation with our colleagues in the kitchen, about their plans for the break, who will be cooking, and gosh, that's an awful lot of children for two whole days and aren't you all outnumbered. And then, almost without noticing, we are suddenly wishing a merry Christmas to everyone we pass— the man at reception who always seems so curmudgeonly but is now wearing a festive light-up pin on his suit jacket, the director in the elevator grinning in a rather unnerving way, the barista at the café where you buy your morning coffee, the garbagemen, the cleaner, the woman who washes up mugs in the kitchen sink. The structure of the city shifts and suddenly we are all better people than we were before: kinder, happier, optimistic—the very best versions of ourselves.

We do not register the colleague who has no partner anymore, whose children will be elsewhere, whose parents are long dead. We still ignore the homeless woman sitting at the side of the road, her worn sleeping bag beneath her, a blanket draped over her shoulders and the cold seeping into the whites of her eyes. We cannot bring ourselves to acknowledge the sadness that still exists in this festive joy.

At that time in my life, I could be both. I could bring the sadness and the joy. I had a best friend who was hosting lunch and a beautiful sister, but an absent father and a dead husband and a mother plagued by dementia.

I suppose this year I will bring little joy; only sadness. I can't shake it, you know. It has been getting worse. It is still getting worse.

I suppose, now that I think about it, that was my last joyful year. I called Emma just after midnight on Christmas Eve. We had agreed to visit my mother first thing in the morning the following day. We hadn't admitted it aloud, but I knew that we both wanted to go in as early as possible, so that it was done and so that we didn't need to think about it for the rest of the afternoon. I knew that Emma didn't want to visit, that she was dreading it, and I was expecting her to grasp at excuses, to find a way to exempt herself from the trip. I called her and listened to the phone ringing and I wondered if she might ignore it, if she might ignore me to avoid my mother.

"What's the plan, then?" I asked when Emma finally answered. "Shall we meet at the station? Walk over from there?"

"Is she better, do you know? Have they said?" replied Emma.

"They say she's still flu-ey, but I reckon an hour or so'll be fine."

"Oh, but if she's—"

"Emma," I replied. "Come on."

"I don't know, Jane," she said, her voice exaggerated in an overstated performance of concern. "If she's not well . . . and then we turn up, bringing in all these bugs . . . Should we hold off? Go next week, maybe, instead?"

"Em, she's our mother. And it's Christmas."

"I think I'm going to give it a miss, if it's okay with you," Emma said. "Shall I meet you at Marnie's? Around twoish, threeish? Will you text me the address?"

"Em—"

"Thanks, Jane. Love you. Merry Christmas."

And then she hung up.

I looked at the phone. I was angry but this conversation had happened in many different guises over very many years and so I wasn't surprised.

Emma was—rightly, I felt—angry with my mother, who had provided very little support in the very worst years of her life. But I was angry, too. And I was just as entitled to that anger, if not more so. I had not only been briefly disowned, entirely abandoned, but also ignored for the majority of my childhood. Emma had always been the favorite. But she never thought about that; she never even tried to see it from my perspective. Emma was always anxious, always on edge, always distracted by her own issues and fixated on her own feelings and that made her selfish. She could refuse to visit because she knew that I wouldn't do that. I couldn't do it and I never did. Because that would have been cruel.

But what if I had opened that conversation by saying that I couldn't find the courage to go, couldn't silence my anger for an hour, and that this time it was all on her? What if I had done as she always did? What if I had stopped being her strength and asked her instead to be mine?

I still don't know the answers to these questions. Can someone who has spent her whole life leaning on others ever support someone else? I'm not convinced that they can. I think that when you willingly take on that role in someone else's life, you have to accept that they will always put themselves first and that the structure of that relationship cannot be reversed. They will let you fall before they sacrifice themselves to support you.

I arrived early, because the taxi driver—who was charging triple for a bank holiday journey—had exceeded the speed limit at every opportunity. I had hated it: the momentum, the vibrations, that feeling of being completely contained, so completely surrendered to somebody else.

I walked into my mother's room and she was sitting up in bed wearing an orange T-shirt and a bright blue cardigan that was slipping from her left shoulder. It had a frilly collar and pinned to one of the scallops was a festive badge, a tree decorated with multicolored baubles, flashing small pinks and yellows.

"Morning," I said, and I grinned as I stepped through her doorway and underneath the mistletoe pinned to its frame. "How are things?"

"Good," she said. "I'm good."

I pulled the armchair from the corner toward her bed and sat down beside her. When she first moved into this facility, I hired a man with a van—I found his card pinned up in the post office window—to transport some of her things from the house. The armchair was the most substantial addition. And although there were a few raised eyebrows from the nurses, I insisted that it was absolutely essential. I also included four of the cushions that had decorated her king-size bed at home, some framed prints, a tasseled lampshade, a pile of books, and her jewelry box. I eventually introduced some other small improvements: a nonslip coaster stamped with a childhood photograph for her water beaker, for example. A speckled gray vase for flowers—I had bought a festive bunch from the florist at the train station the day before—and a tablet so that she could watch films and scroll through old home videos and sometimes, when she was feeling able, send me an email. I was receiving them less and less by then.

I look back now at the version of me that spent so much time caring for and—maybe this isn't the right word but—mothering her. And I'm surprised by my own dedication. I fought as a child to be recognized: I did incredibly well academically, winning prizes and accolades from my teachers; I was helpful, almost obsequiously, around the house—laying the table and emptying the dishwasher and changing the bedding; I tried to be lively and entertaining, a positive influence within our home. Those things—the ornaments and the weekly visits—were simply more recent examples of the many ways in which I'd danced for her attention.

I lifted her cardigan back over her shoulder and she glared at me, her pupils wide. I could tell that she'd been given something—perhaps for her cold, perhaps simply to keep her calm—and thankfully the drugs seemed to be obscuring Emma's absence. It slipped past entirely unnoticed. And yet, despite the medication, she was astute in many ways that day, grilling me for details of my journey and demanding to know my plans for the afternoon.

"You'll be with Marnie and Charles?" she asked.

"Just Marnie," I replied.

"Not Charles?" she asked, and her brows furrowed at the center of her forehead.

"No," I said, and I dropped my head to one side and her face shifted from confusion to concern because that movement has only ever preceded bad news. "I've told you this before. Do you remember?" I sighed. "Charles is dead."

"He died?" She was horrified, her voice high and her face ugly with disbelief, as she was every time she received this information. "When?"

"A few months ago."

"How?"

"He fell down the stairs. You know this already. You just don't want to remember it."

"Well, no," she said. "I wouldn't. It's awful."

"I know," I said. "I was there." And I don't know why I did this because I hadn't shared any of these details with her before, but I think I wanted her to acknowledge that this grief wasn't hers to appropriate. "Marnie and I found him sprawled at the foot of the stairs. We saw him."

"Dead?" she said.

"Yes," I said.

"He died alone." She looked sad as she said it, as though this in particular was something unbearable. I realized then that we had never discussed death, not in any depth, never further than its simple fact, a simple loss. "What a thing," she said.

"I'm afraid," I said, "that I might have been outside their apartment when it happened. I was waiting for Marnie to come home. She was at the library. And I was there for an hour, just sitting there, reading and waiting."

"Afraid that you might have been able to do something," she said, and it was part question, part statement.

"Perhaps," I said. "If I'd heard something. If I'd had a key."

I don't know why I did this. Except, at the same time, I think I do. I wanted her to protect me, to look inside me and see that something was broken, and I wanted her to mend it. Isn't that what a mother does? And if she couldn't do that, if she couldn't see or fix the fractures, then I wanted her to think that I was the sort of person who could save a life and not the sort of person who could take one. I wanted her to think that if I could have done something, I would have, that if I could be a better version of myself, then I would be.

"A key," she said.

"I used to have one," I said. "I watered their plants when they went on holiday. But I don't have it now, not anymore. I returned it."

She nodded.

"Do you remember David?" I asked. "He lived next door. He used to water yours when we went away."

I arrived at Marnie's just after two o'clock. Her flat was full of far too many people and it exuded an unlikely medley of cheer and sorrow and pretense. There was a tree in the hallway adorned with silver ornaments, a glittering angel sitting at the top. There were decorations scattered artfully up the stairs and a plate piled high with tiny mince pies. Merry jingles were filtering through the speakers and Marnie was wearing a ribbon of tinsel around her neck.

I sort of wanted to strangle her with it.

"Jane!" Marnie called when she saw me hovering by the open front door. "You're earlier than I expected. How was your mother? Come in. Come in. What can I get you? A drink? Wine? A sherry, perhaps?"

I handed over a small gift bag. I'd struggled to find a present that was both sentimental and yet understated, too; respectful, I suppose. I'd opted eventually for a set of cookie cutters—they seemed ridiculously expensive to me—that she'd pointed out years earlier in a shop just a few minutes from our first flat. "Wouldn't they be perfect?"

she'd said. They were pairs of breasts, all shapes and sizes, with separate cutters for all manner of nipples. I hadn't quite understood the
appeal.

"Thank you," she said, leaving it wrapped on the floor by the radiator beside a few other gift and bottle bags. "Come on through. Emma's
here already. I think she's in the kitchen. She's a bit . . . When did you
last see her? Wine, did you say?"

"Who are all these people?" I asked. I didn't recognize anyone although there were at least twenty—maybe thirty—others crammed
into the flat.

"It's lovely, isn't it?" Marnie replied. "They're a fascinating bunch.
That's Derek." She pointed at a middle-aged man wearing a checked
shirt and a reindeer tie. "He lives three doors down. Wife died earlier
this year. Cancer. So we've a lot in common. And that's Mary and Ian."
She pointed at a couple who were both at least ninety. He was trying to
eat a mince pie, but most of the pastry was crumbled down his jacket.
She had the most exquisite gray hair pinned beautifully so that it fell
down one side of her neck. "They live on the ground floor. I met them
in the lobby yesterday and invited them along. Over there is Jenna.
She does my nails. And that's Isobel. She cleans the flat. You've probably met her before. She's separated from her husband and she was going
to spend the day alone and I just thought, no, that's not right at all, and
so I told her to pop in. Isn't it lovely?"

"It is, Marnie. Absolutely. But are you sure . . . How are you feeling?
What can I do?"

"Everything's under control. I have two turkeys in the oven. Can
you smell them? It's good, right? And lots of nibbles out already. Have
you got your phone? Maybe take some photos? I'm going to do a big
post on how to host an 'everyone welcome' Christmas."

"And the baby? Are you resting enough?"

"I'm really starting to show now, can you see"—she turned to one
side—"can you believe it?"

"Jane!" Emma grabbed hold of my arm and then enveloped me in a hug. "Merry Christmas! How are you?"

She pulled back and I held on a moment longer, just to be sure that I really could reach both arms around her waist and touch my palms to my opposite elbows. She was so much worse than she'd been in years. I stepped back and glanced at her face. Her cheeks were hollow, so sunken that I could almost see the shape of her teeth through her skin. Her spindly wrists poked from an oversized jumper and her tight jeans were loose around her thighs.

"That man," she continued. "Do you see? In the salmon pink shirt? He's been talking to me for about twenty minutes and I've only just managed to escape. No offense, Marn, I'm sure he's a great friend or whatever, but—"

"In the red cords?" Marnie asked.

Emma nodded. "And the paper cracker hat."

"I've no idea who he is. Did he say anything about— Give me a minute," she said, and she waded across the kitchen to introduce herself.

"Mince pie?" I held out the plate.

"I've had a few already," Emma said, rubbing her stomach as if to indicate that she was already far too full. "And there's still the turkey to come."

We locked eyes and several conversations passed unsaid between us.

You're not eating.

I am.

You're lying.

I'm not.

Don't lie to me.

How dare you accuse me of lying?

Or:

You're not eating.

I'm not hungry.

You must be hungry. Eat something.

Stop telling me what to do.

Or:

You look terrible.

Well, fuck you.

I'm serious. When did you last eat?

It's none of your business.

None of it needed saying.

"Don't," she said instead.

I nodded. "Can I do anything?" I asked.

"No," she replied. "How was Mum?"

"She was okay," I said. "Tired, but much better."

"Was she cross? With me. For not coming?"

I wanted to say that she had been cross, that she'd felt let down, abandoned even, so that I could be the better daughter. And I wanted to reveal that she hadn't noticed, so that Emma could be the forgotten one, relegated to the pits of dementia. But we both knew that I was never the best-loved, most memorable daughter.

"No," I said. "She was fine."

Emma nodded, relieved. "Well, that's something, I suppose. I'm sorry. For not coming. I just . . . I couldn't."

"Let's talk about something else," I said, and I wondered if other families had so many lines drawn in the sand, so many words that couldn't be spoken. "Is that one of her jumpers?" I asked.

"Yes!" Emma grinned. "Do you remember it? It always makes me think of that Christmas when Dad dressed up as Santa Claus on Christmas Eve to sneak into our rooms and then fell over the toy chest and made such a fucking racket that he woke us both up and we all ended up in the emergency room."

"I remember," I replied.

"We were in our pajamas and Mum was in this jumper and the rest of the waiting room was drunk and merry and injured, too. Do you remember? And that man who'd sliced his hand open on a tape dispenser?"

"And the nurse who gave us sweets at midnight."

"She had pink hair."

"Yes!"

"I always planned to have pink hair after that."

"Do it, then," I said.

"Maybe I will," Emma replied.

"It's okay," said Marnie, stepping back into the conversation. "I do know him after all. He works in the post room at Charles's office, and, anyway, crisis averted. Let me check these turkeys. I thought you were going to take some photos?"

There was sadness that day. It emanated from the two framed photographs on the mantelpiece, side by side, snapshots from their honeymoon. It was there in the wooden bauble hanging from the tree and engraved with *Our First Married Christmas*. I suppose they must have received it as a wedding present. How was anyone to know then that the marriage wouldn't last the year? There was sadness in the ghosts that sat beside us all: beside Marnie and me and beside the other guests—drifters and strays—all of whom brought their lost loved ones with them, too.

But there was joy that day as well. And plenty of it. So I did as instructed and ignored all the things that couldn't be addressed and focused instead on the food and the conversation and the games that we played in the late afternoon, all manner of strangers shouting out answers and high-fiving our teammates. I won at charades, if it's possible to win. And I lost at Scrabble. Ian placed three eight-letter words and scored well over five hundred points. Emma and I beat Jenna and Isobel at canasta.

By seven o'clock most of the guests had left, and Marnie had abandoned her apron and was sitting on the sofa, her arm draped over her small bump.

"Shall I—"

"Just a quick one?" said Marnie.

Our friendship had been built on "just a quick tidy-up." In our first year at secondary school—the first year of our friendship—our teacher Mrs. Carlisle was fanatical about neatness and cleanliness. With hindsight, it's clear that she suffered from fairly extreme obsessive-compulsive disorder. At the time, we thought she was simply a neat freak, but, as always, the truth is never evident in the moment.

Most mornings—sometimes more than once—she would insist that the entire class engage in "just a quick tidy-up." This meant hanging coats and jumpers on the pegs at the back of the room, squaring rucksacks beneath our seats, textbooks in desks, ponytails retied if loose, no hair ties on wrists, no squiffy collars, no laces undone, no rolled shirtsleeves, and an endless list of small demands.

We always complied but it became a stock phrase, a joke that defined our friendship, one of the first things we shared that others—our parents, our siblings, other students in different tutor groups, and those at other schools—failed to understand at all.

Marnie and Emma watched two festive films—back to back—as comfortable together as they had been when we were children, while I flitted around the flat, stacking the dishwasher, clearing plates and glasses and wiping down the counters, until order was restored and I could settle beneath their blanket, too. I remember that the flat felt loud despite the silence. There was the whir of the dishwasher and a dripping somewhere within the walls. It ran along the skirting board and up the stairs and I turned up the volume on the television to drown it all out.

As the opening sequence of the third film illuminated the walls of the room, I felt my phone vibrating against my thigh. I pulled it out— I'm not sure what I was expecting, but I think I wondered if it might be an unexpected message from my father—and found instead an email from Valerie Sands.

The subject line read **PLEASE READ: DON'T DELETE**.

I felt suspicious, but intrigued, too. We hadn't heard anything from Valerie: not a word since she'd published the second of her two articles. My initial anxiety had diminished in the intervening period. I had taken her silence and assumed that she was finished. And yet, here she was, on the evening of the most intimate day of the year, a day for family and friends, for home and for happiness, sending an email to someone she barely knew.

I'd stopped following her online as regularly, only occasionally tracing her footsteps and mentally mapping her days. I had seen that she'd attended but not performed in a show organized by the dance studio where she now had lessons at least twice each week. And that she'd written a few festive pieces for the newspaper: when the pop-up ice rink flooded, when the high street Christmas lights were switched on by an entirely forgettable celebrity, and something rather profound about homelessness and loneliness. But I wasn't tracking her route through the city each day or researching every tagged location anymore. But it seemed that despite my indolence she'd remained just as committed to us.

I opened the email, hiding the brightness of the screen beneath the blanket. She said that she knew that her first story wasn't entirely accurate, that as soon as she met Marnie, it became painfully apparent and very quickly, too, that she'd misinterpreted her suspicions. She said that she wouldn't make the same mistake again and wished me a merry Christmas. "But"—she said—"I don't think your story, your version of events, is entirely accurate, either." She said that her jigsaw had missing pieces, certainly, but that she'd uncovered enough of them to know that there was more here, more hidden, more that still needed saying. She encouraged me to respond, to fill in the blanks, to finally tell my truth. Because, she said, and she promised this, she would find the answers eventually.

I squeezed my phone into the gap between two sofa cushions. I was feeling it again, the burgeoning fear, a panic reigniting within me.

But then Marnie jolted, the blanket slipping from her shoulders and her hand darting toward her stomach. "I just felt something," she said. "I think I felt something."

"Felt what?" said Emma. "What did you feel?"

"I don't know. The baby? Like a butterfly. Like a butterfly in my stomach."

"Let me," said Emma, shifting Marnie's hand away and folding hers into that space. "I can't feel it. I can't feel anything."

"Well, it's stopped now."

"Oh," said Emma, disappointed, withdrawing her hand. "Well, let me know quicker next time," she said. "So that I can feel it, too."

I would watch over the next few months as that bump grew and grew, swelling and stretching underneath Marnie's skin, until it sat in front of her like a ball tucked beneath her shirt. I saw her changing in the flicker of a flip book, inch by inch, week by week, as we fell back into our old routine, dinners at the end of each week. It was sort of beautiful and definitely strange to watch this woman—who I'd first known as a girl—evolving into a mother. At every stage of that evolution, I had protected her. At first, it was from her parents, and then from her boyfriends, and then from her boss. And later from a contemptible husband.

And always, even now, from the truth.

Emma and I stayed over that night. We shared a bed and I felt like we were children tucked into a coastal caravan all over again. Over breakfast, Emma asked about Valerie, and Marnie explained that they'd met just that once and that she had inadvertently prompted the second article, that it had been all her fault, and that I'd been right: we'd simply needed to be patient. I excused myself under the pretense of going to strip the bed because I couldn't navigate that conversation with a hangover. And then, as we left, Emma looked down at the rug at the foot of the stairs and she said, "Oh, look. This is where she left your husband to die," and she rolled her eyes. Her humor was uncomfortably dark, wicked, and uninhibited, but Marnie laughed, liberated by the bluntness. And I tried to smile, too, to be part of the joke.

But I knew then that it might still fall apart, that the truth might still find me. It was close, always nearby, never fully in the past.

Chapter Twenty-Eight

The mornings were dark and the evenings were dark and the nights were darker still. It was cold enough for snow with the sky set in dirty white. The trees were bare, just twigs, threatening to snap, and the air was crisp and biting. My skin was so dry that it itched constantly, flaking into my bedding and towels and there in my clothes when I undressed at the end of each day.

I had been working long hours since the beginning of the month, covering the holidays, the parents who couldn't come back until the middle of January, when their children returned to school. And the most senior members of the staff, who wouldn't be back until the end of the month, because the beginning of the year was the perfect time for the Caribbean and much of East Asia.

Every morning when I arrived at my desk, I reread Valerie's email and I tried to concoct a reply in my mind. I played with the words, preparing a polite version that encouraged her to please step back and find another story, and a vicious, angry one that challenged her, and, sometimes, in only the quietest whisper, one that confessed. But then the workday would begin, and I would deliberately distract myself with issues that were easier to fix.

It sounds ridiculous, I know, but I had this sense that she was watching me. I sometimes saw her, or at least I thought I did: outside my flat;

in my office; sometimes through the plastic windows of the tube, or on the platform or in the next carriage. I saw women with cropped hair everywhere, and I was always squinting to see a tattoo there in black at the back of the neck.

I found myself replaying his death in my mind. I wasn't lingering on feelings—the adrenaline, the anticipation, the relief—but instead, rather pragmatically, on the clues that she might someday find. There were no fingerprints. There were no witnesses. There were no suspicions from anywhere else. There wasn't even a body anymore, just a skeleton decomposing six feet beneath the earth.

I careered between absolute confidence—there was nothing to uncover; she'd give up eventually—and the most extraordinary panic. But I should admit that my fear was escalating. I became convinced that she'd find the one loose thread that would reveal my involvement.

I replied to her email at the end of the month. It was a Friday. I should have been visiting Marnie, but she'd called me on the Monday to say that she'd been invited to the launch of a new restaurant, and could we please pause our plans for just one week. I stayed late at my desk and when the work was finished—all of it; even the tasks that had been on my to-do list for months—I responded to her email.

I'm sorry that it's taken me so long to reply. But thank you for the apology.

What do you think? Was it too sycophantic? I wanted her to like me.

I'm concerned that you've become obsessed with us, and really we're not worth your time.

It was obvious that her fascination was more than academic.

There's nothing further to find. My husband died in a tragic accident. The same is true of Charles, who—as you already know—was my best friend's husband. It's devastating, and a horrible coincidence, but really that's all this is. I expect that this email is redundant by now.

I didn't.

I'm sure your investigations have led you to this conclusion. So it's probably not even worth me saying this, but I'd be really grateful if you would stop investigating us, and stop writing about us, because we really need to find a way to move on with our lives.

She replied seconds after I pressed send.

Let's meet.

I replied: No, thank you.

She wrote I have something you'll want to see.

I think that's unlikely. I replied. But tell me what it is, and I'll let you know.

I looked around the empty office. It was nearly nine o'clock and everyone else had left hours earlier. I gave my phone a small shake, as though that might knock loose the next message. But my inbox was still empty. I ran my thumb down the screen of my phone, refreshing my emails again and again. I kept it lit up on the office kitchen counter as I washed my mug in the sink. I kept it in my hand as I switched off my computer. I turned it off and on again after pulling on my coat, as though something might have happened in my sleeve. I kept it held in front of me as I walked out of the building and toward the station.

I lay in bed that night with it beside me on my pillow, the volume turned right up. I was shocked by every single message: the automated complaints update that arrived late in the evening, emails from retailers that had gathered my details without my consent, a generic travel update with information for the following day.

But there was nothing from Valerie.

I waited and waited, but I must have fallen asleep eventually because just moments later the alarm on my phone was ringing; it was time to get up and visit my mother. I did as I always did: going into the bathroom, having a shower, getting ready. Which, of course, was when the message then arrived.

I found it when I returned to my bedroom ten minutes later, one towel fastened around my chest and another like a bandage shrouding my hair. I tried to keep my head steady as I read.

Something happened the week before, she had written. **I don't know what. But your neighbors (they seem like fun girls) were leaving after midnight to go out and they saw you return. They said that you were dripping wet and that it looked as though you were crying. It's no secret that you went to visit Marnie and Charles every Friday. They said you normally returned around eleven. So what happened that week?**

"Nothing," I said aloud. And then: "Shit."

I knew that I had to reply, because my silence could be misinterpreted. But I didn't know what to write. Because I couldn't confess the argument without giving myself a motive. And it wasn't just the content of her message that had startled me, but her means of acquiring that information, her so-called evidence. She had been in my building. She had been right outside my flat. She had been speaking to my neighbors.

I sat on my bed and the towel wrapped around my head fell loose and my hair dripped cold down my back.

Crying? No. But I was certainly drenched, so it might have looked that way. I walked home from their flat that evening. Which is why I was so much later and so much wetter than normal. But there's nothing more to it than that.

I pressed send.

You shouldn't stare, you know. It's rude. And don't you know that some people really do enjoy walking in the rain? They find it refreshing. It's bracing, in a way, to be so close to nature.

She didn't reply.

I reread her messages from the previous day and clicked the link in the signature block at the bottom of one of them. It took me straight to her website. And there—again, in red type and in block capitals—were the following words:

BE PATIENT. THERE'S MORE TO COME.

Chapter Twenty-Nine

F ebruary came and went and I didn't hear from Valerie again, and there were no updates on her website. I was still working all the sunlight hours and, even when the clocks shifted forward, I didn't see daytime. I saw nearly no one that month, other than Marnie. She cooked for me, as she always had, and she talked about her pregnancy: how it felt physically—the stretching and aching and straining—and emotionally, too—the weight of being responsible for another life.

"It's so strange to be here without him," she said every time we saw each other. "I can feel him in this building. I can smell him sometimes: his aftershave, and a very masculine, slightly musky smell that always makes me think of him."

"But it's important," she would say, "to focus on the future." She would tell me about new opportunities: she'd been sent baby bowls with suction bases that stuck to tables and was considering dedicating a space on her website to recipes for children. "I can't simply marinate in my grief," she said more than once. "I have to build a life for me and for the baby."

She often talked about the years ahead, and what came next, and how her life might look without him in it. And sometimes it seemed that she forgot to mention me. I felt as though it was my responsibility to reinsert myself into the story.

"I could come and live here for a little bit," I said.

"Oh, that's kind," she replied. "But I don't think it'll be necessary."

"I can come around all the time," I said. "I'll help however I can."

"Absolutely," she said. "Although I reckon we might need peace and quiet in the first few weeks."

I felt sure that she'd change her mind. I had once looked ahead to a life with children and I had known that she would still be central in every single way. I saw us together in coffee shops, and on walks in the park with a pram, and passing a baby between us. I felt sure that she would need me. Because everyone says how exhausting it can be, caring for a newborn, and that it takes a village, and how essential it is to have friends and family nearby.

It didn't occur to me that I might not be the right sort of friend for this next stage of her life.

I was busy at work. I recruited five new people, two women and three men. The business was growing exponentially—more and more orders each week, new retailers adopting our platform, a permanent sense of panic as our systems, our staff, our setup all proved too immature to handle such a step up.

I sat at the head of a table in the Customer Services Unit. My table was called "Zadie." Apparently, women's names made people more comfortable, more at ease, and so every workstation in the building— from the loading bays to the offices on the eighth floor—shared equally ladylike titles. Curiously, there was no Jane. I think the CEO preferred girly, feminine options, names that ended in "-y" or "-ie."

My new employees sat on the benches on either side of Zadie. The two women were in their fifties, both recently divorced and desperately in need of a regular wage. There were two young men, new graduates hoping to earn a quick income to bolster their wallets so that they might travel the world: surfing and diving and skiing and seducing naive eighteen-year-olds on gap years. The oldest man was in his early forties. His name was Peter. He'd worked in a bank for over a decade, receiving a six-figure salary and a matching bonus. Until two years before. He had been sitting at his desk in a spacious corner office in a redbrick building in the city when his heart began to accelerate faster and faster, until he felt like it would explode within his chest. He had felt his lungs fill with water, his heart pulsing and pounding and thundering against his ribs, his eyes swelling in their sockets. He had clutched at his chest and his breathing had grown shallower and shallower until eventually he'd lost consciousness.

After a series of tests and checks and scans, he was told that he was fine, nothing medically wrong, all good on all counts. He went back to work the following day and, that afternoon, his heart exploded again. And then the next day, the same thing happened. And then the day after that. Until eventually Peter stopped going to work and simply stayed at home. His doctor diagnosed stress—"as though it were an illness," he said in his interview, "as well as a state of mind"—and signed him off. Which put an end to the panic attacks. But contributed to the onset of a deep and sticky depression.

He was so honest. He said that the months had stretched into a year, until he'd finally found the courage to attend twelve sessions of counseling in a poky room in a small terraced house in the suburbs. He'd tried to focus on the garish wallpaper and the hand-drawn bluebirds frozen in a moment, or the squelch of the leather chair beneath him, or the thin gray hairs on his therapist's upper lip, her dangling earrings that skimmed the tops of her shoulders. But she'd outsmarted him and, somewhat unwillingly, he'd found himself revealing his truth: the secrets he'd tucked deep within himself decades ago and the way he really felt about things and people and life (even when his thoughts weren't thoughts one ought to have about things and people and life).

I was drawn to him immediately, instinctively. He had all the right skills—talking to customers and inputting data—and he said he wanted to start at the bottom rung again, to work his way up the corporate ladder in a more measured way. He owned his every failing in a way that felt completely alien. And not only was he honest with himself, but he was also honest with me, a stranger, yes, but his interviewer, too. I found it so impossible to comprehend. Why would he choose to tell the truth?

Back then, I couldn't have predicted this moment: me being honest, recounting my lies.

Peter was my favorite of the five new employees. He was also the most competent. He was a natural problem solver. The customers seemed to like him. And the computers liked him, too, which was often the most challenging part of the job. When he was around, I was happier, better at my job, more efficient and driven and confident. I was glad that I'd hired him.

On the last day of March—just six weeks after my new recruits had started—I arrived in the office just after eight o'clock and opened my inbox to find an email from my boss, sent at half past seven, asking me to come to his office immediately, because there was something we needed to discuss and it was important.

I turned around, back toward the elevators, and squeezed in with a dozen others, all on their way to the top floors in their neat skirt suits and pinstripe jackets. My trainers squeaked against the polished tiles. As they exited, at floors five and six and seven, I saw them looking at me, wondering what on earth I was doing heading toward the eighth floor. I suppose they, too, assumed that I was about to be fired.

My boss had an office that overlooked the city, a single-paned glass window stretching from one side of the room to the other. He was sitting at his desk. His tie was undone around his neck and he had shadows beneath his eyes, his dark skin sallow, as though the warmth had been siphoned from within him. The door was open, but I knocked beneath his nameplate regardless. Duncan Brin. Director of Customer Service.

He jolted and glanced up. "Jane," he said. "Come in. Sit down. Do you need anything? Coffee?"

I shook my head.

"You're early. Not that I'm surprised by that. I've been hearing lots of good things about you."

I felt my shoulders relax, my stomach unfurl, and I sank into the too-low armchair, which was actually an ordinary office chair disguised as something more elegant and which then spun unexpectedly on its axis. I drilled my feet into the floor to hold myself steady.

"In fact, I've not only been hearing good things, but seeing the result of those good things myself. Do you know what I'm talking about? I think you do. We're up on calls, you know that, but we're up on customers, too—good for us—so that's not much of a surprise. Not a lot to be done on that front. But what we can do—and what you are doing—is dropping the percentage of customers who call back to complain a second time because they aren't happy with our initial response. And, more than that, the processes you're putting in place based on data collected by your team are drastically reducing the number of customers who call at all. Against the overall number of orders, we got a third fewer calls in the first quarter of this year compared to the first quarter of last. That's quite something, right? And that's your team. Your work. Your recruits. And we wanted to recognize that. Don't look so frightened. This is good news. We'd like to promote you."

He reached into his drawer and slid an envelope across the desk. It had my name typed on the front in small black capitals.

"There's a lot more detail in there, but the gist of it is we'd like you to be our Senior Customer Service Manager. We want you on the strategy. Drilling into the numbers. We want you to keep doing what you're doing—train up that team!—and doing more of it. Can you do that?"

I nodded. There was barely the space for me to interject and I didn't know what I'd have said if I could.

"Well, take this, check you're happy, sign, and get it back to HR.

Effective immediately. Well done, Jane. Go-getters. That's what we're looking for. Now back to it. Lots more getting to be gotten downstairs."

I'm not going to pretend that this encounter felt anything other than ridiculous. Duncan Brin was a strange man at best. He spoke only in short sentences and he often shouted them, and he had a bizarre array of hand gestures that accompanied his every word. But odd as it was, it was rather nice, too.

Here was a place in which I mattered. Here was a place in which my efforts were recognized. I meant something to someone. I went back to my desk and I told my new team, and Peter went out at lunchtime and returned with a brown paper bag from the bakery.

"It's a celebratory muffin," he said. "For you. To say well done."

Chapter Thirty

I wish the day had ended there. It didn't.

Peter and I worked late. I had been developing a new software system for months, and we were going live in just a few weeks. The other four excused themselves between five and six, rushing back to their parents or to their children, to see friends in the pub or to watch the latest play at the National. But Peter had no one to go home to—his wife had left him somewhere in the midst of his depression—and there was no one waiting for me, either.

"You're a fool," said Peter, lifting his head above his monitor.

"Pardon?" I replied, thinking I'd misheard.

"You're a fool, Jane," he repeated.

I was shocked but not unpleasantly so. I didn't doubt that I was a fool and in a great many ways. And I felt sure that Peter was a wise man and I was eager to hear what he had to say. I wanted to be distracted.

He smiled and nodded his head in the direction of the large white clock that hung above the door. It had just gone midnight.

"Get it?" he said.

I shook my head.

"April Fools'." He grinned and I felt disappointed, and also stupid for feeling disappointed, and also somewhat charmed by his ridiculous humor.

"Oh, very good," I said. "Although the same can be said for you. We're both here far too late when there must be something else out there for us to be doing."

We stared at each other for a moment and it felt nice. In among all the shit that seemed to be floating to the surface, here was something good. I was—for the first time in a long time—being recognized for my contribution and, more than that, here was someone who liked me enough to tease me. I thought that maybe the summer wouldn't be so bad that year, that perhaps I'd be suitably joyful and buoyant and bright. But it didn't last long. Don't you know now that it never does?

Because then my phone rang and we both sat straight up in our seats, startled not only by the noise itself but by its alarming sound, the sharp tinkling tune, too cheery and high-pitched for the middle of the night.

"I better get this," I said, lifting the phone to my cheek. "Hello?"

"I've been trying to get through to a Mrs. Jane Black." The woman's voice was clipped, her accent posh and her tone formal. "But I've been . . . Well, I've spoken to a great number of people who are not Mrs. Jane Black. Have I . . . Are you . . . ?"

"I'm Jane," I said. I swiveled in my seat so that I was no longer facing Peter. "You're through to the right person now. Sorry," and then I added, in a voice similar to hers, "for the inconvenience."

"My name is Lillian Brown. I'm a nurse. I'm calling from St. Thomas' Hospital. We have you down as the next of kin for a . . ." The pause as she bent her head to check her notes felt eternal, the rustling of pages and the hiss of her finger against the paper, searching for the right name. "For a Ms. Emma Baxter. Is that right?"

I felt suddenly breathless. "Yes, I'm her sister. What's happened? Is she . . . ? What's happened?"

"She collapsed. She's doing well, considering the circumstances, but we do have some concerns. Perhaps you might be able to visit? She's just arrived. I'm afraid we aren't yet in a position to discharge her. But she's being quite insistent that she won't stay here."

"I'm on my way. I'll be half an hour. Tell her I'm coming?"

"Thank you, Mrs. Black. That's much appreciated."

The line went dead.

"I have to go," I said to Peter.

I was meant to be the last out, to turn off the lights, but I didn't have time to wait while he shut down his computer and went to the bathroom and washed his mug in the sink.

I gestured toward the ceiling. "Will you get them?" I asked. "When you leave?"

"Sure," he said. "I hope everything's okay."

I nodded and pulled my coat from the back of my chair.

"Thanks," I replied.

The hospital was quiet. The white walls and the tiled floors and that recognizable smell of disinfectant had a library-style effect and we all shuffled along the corridors in silence, just the smack of our shoes and the rustle of our coat sleeves against our bodies.

I asked at the front desk, almost whispering, and was directed to an assessment ward on the third floor. I followed the signs and distracted myself from the reality of my being there by focusing instead on the framed photographs of children with cancer smiling and elderly women waving and mothers clutching their newborns.

I had visited Emma in many different hospitals, but for five years she had been teetering in a space that could almost be defined as "well." I entered the ward and the nurse at the desk was on the phone, canceling a hospital transfer for the following morning because the patient had unexpectedly been rushed to surgery and wouldn't be leaving anytime soon.

I hovered, waiting for her to hang up and yet eager for her conversation to continue and to postpone what would inevitably come next.

"Your turn, love," she said eventually. "Who're you here for?"

"My sister," I said. "Emma Baxter."

"Bay two," she replied. "Just through those doors."

"Thank you," I said, but she had already turned back to her computer and to the stack of pages piled beside it.

There were six beds in bay two and five patients. There was a steady stream of noises: gentle snores and intermittent beeps and the quiet murmur of a television. There were two elderly women sleeping with their duvets pulled up to their chins and their bedding tucked beneath their frail bodies. There was a younger woman, perhaps in her thirties or forties, with her leg raised above the bed in a hoist and the pay-as-you-go screen positioned directly in front of her. One of the beds was empty, without sheets or spare chairs or gurneys. Another was hidden, soft wheezes seeping from behind a thin blue curtain, and diagonally opposite, nearest the window, was my little sister.

She didn't notice me straightaway. She was on her phone, the backlight casting a blue-white glow across her face. It highlighted her bone structure: her too-big eyes that sat in hollow pools, her sunken cheeks, the tendons that jutted from her neck. Her fingers, clasping her phone, looked too long, her knuckles bulbous, the bones of her wrists pressing up against the skin.

I exhaled slowly and my stomach groaned as the knot that had tightened there tried to untangle itself.

Emma looked up. She smiled. "You came," she said. She placed her phone on the table.

"Of course I did," I replied, pulling up a wooden dining chair to sit beside her bed. "What happened?"

"I fainted," she said, and I must have rolled my eyes or raised my brows because she frowned and then became defensive. "Really," she insisted. "It was nothing more than that. They're all just overreacting. And that nurse. Brown, I think—is she the one who called you?—she won't stop fussing."

"She's probably just good at her job."

"If she was, she'd have sent me home by now."

"Did someone call an ambulance?"

"Yes."

"So it must have been more than a faint. Or you'd have been fine by the time the paramedics arrived."

"Oh, Jane. Stop it. Please don't do this."

"They're clearly worried about you," I said. "Or you wouldn't still be here."

"They don't need to be," Emma replied.

I sighed and placed my hand over hers, willing her to confide in me, to share the truth and to be as confident and open as Peter had been just a few weeks before.

"What are they worried about?" I asked.

"My heart," she replied. She looked away from me, embarrassed, and I wanted to take her in my arms and promise her that everything would be okay and to tell her that she didn't need to hide from me because I understood that we didn't all become the people we wanted to be.

"It's okay," I whispered instead. "We'll find a way to fix this."

When she looked back at me, her eyes were wet with tears.

"I don't think so," she said. "I'm never going to be"—and she screwed up her face, almost disgusted—"healthy."

"But—"

"No," she continued. "That will never be me. I haven't been that person in over a decade." She shuffled down beneath her covers and turned her head toward the window. "This is going to kill me," she said. "You know it and I know it. That's the only way this will ever end."

"Now, Emma," I said. "Come on, now. That's just not true. There are ways to survive it. You know better than anyone. Look at you; it's what you've been doing all along." And even though I knew that it could be true, that it was for some, I knew that it would never be true for Emma. She was right: I knew and I had known for years.

Emma had always been invincible, and yet at some point it became very clear that she was broken, too, and that even the best of her would never be enough. She started to exist in a peripheral space inhabited only by the sick and inaccessible to everyone else. She lived with a countdown, ticking in the depths of her mind, measuring the fight left in her. And we all knew her fight was running thin.

"You can do this," I insisted. "You're strong."

"I am," she replied. "But I'm also sick. They aren't mutually exclusive. I'm not giving up and I'm no less brave for knowing that the end is a real place."

"I know," I said. "I know all of that. I just—"

"I'm getting worse," she said. "You can see it, can't you? I see it in your face when you look at me. I'm not in control of it anymore; it has me completely."

"We can find a new normal," I said, and I look back now and I know that I was sort of begging.

"You don't understand," she said. "And it's not your fault; I wouldn't wish that you could. But it owns me. It's all that I am."

"That's just not true," I said. "You are so much more than simply this."

And then tears flooded the corners of her eyes and I imagined then that she must have been terribly sad, but perhaps she was simply incredibly frustrated, exhausted by the myriad of people unable to understand her and a disease that she couldn't understand herself.

"No," she replied. "You wish that I was, but I'm not. Maybe once upon a time. Maybe. But not anymore. Remember what you were like when you first met Jonathan?"

"Emma—"

"No. Stop. Let me finish. Do you remember? Because I do. You were totally overwhelmed by him. He was in everything you said and did and probably your every thought too. That's what this is. It's like being in love. It is utterly consuming. It's unstoppable. It's all that I am."

"No," I said. "What you're describing is horrible, miserable. Love is wonderful, Em. You'll see. One day, you'll see."

She laughed and I wanted to cry. "I don't think so," she said. "I think I'm past the big things now. Just one more at the end of the road for me."

I wanted to shake her. I wanted to shake her from her stupidity and I wanted to reach deep inside her and pull that demon out. I knew I couldn't save her, but I also knew that I must have been able to at some point. I knew that there must have been a way to stop this before her bones became brittle and her muscles started to waste away and her heart began to stop. I must have failed her somewhere along the line for this to be her ending.

We heard footsteps approaching and fell silent. A nurse appeared at the end of the bed.

"Mrs. Black?" she said. "My name's Lillian. We spoke earlier. Now, Emma. The paperwork's complete, so you can go home whenever you're ready."

"But—" I began.

"I've discharged myself," said Emma. "There's nothing they can do for me here."

I tried to persuade her to stay in the hospital. She refused. I tried to persuade her to spend a few weeks in a rehabilitation facility. She refused. I tried to persuade her to live with me for a little, while she recuperated, while she recovered. She refused.

I took her home in a taxi and put her to bed.

I feared that it might be the last time I ever saw her, but I was exhausted and overreacting and, most important, wrong.

I wish the day had ended there but, still, it didn't.

My phone was beside me on my pillow, there in case she needed me in the night. I was almost asleep, my mind fogging with thoughts that weren't quite conscious, when it vibrated. My hand jumped immediately, drawn to it like the pull of a magnet.

It wasn't ringing—the vibrations ceased quickly—but there was a red circle suspended over the mail icon. I opened my inbox and there was her name: Valerie Sands.

You stayed in their flat for a whole week.

She hadn't written anything else, just that one sentence, and I sat up, pushing my pillow against the headboard, to work through her meaning.

She was right, of course. She was almost always right.

Charles had asked me to water their plants while they went on holiday, and I had done just that. Except I had also stayed over, without invitation, living in their home for nearly a week.

How much of that did she already know?

And what was she going to do with it?

Here was the thing that was slowly seeping through, that was starting to make sense. My fear manifested only when my friendship felt threatened. I was less perturbed by the possibility of police and prison because there was no body, no motive, no reason to doubt the reports already written. But I was becoming increasingly aware that the small threads protruding from my lies, if pulled, would devastate my friendship with Marnie. The problem, it seemed, was that those were the threads that most appealed to Valerie. She was determined to see us unraveled.

The
Sixth Lie

Chapter Thirty-One

Charles had been dead for more than six months and I was sleeping badly for the first time in several years. I had slept as a child—not easily, but comfortably, often after reading late into the night, a flashlight clasped beneath my covers—but I had struggled throughout my teenage years. I had spent long nights rotating my pillow and adjusting my position and refilling my water glass, which would quickly absorb the thickness of a warm bedroom and gather a filmic, stale taste. I know that I slept best with Jonathan beside me.

It was often difficult to believe that one simple action had been so effective, that he had died so easily, that death was so attainable. I found myself returning to it regularly, retelling that story, developing my role, but it never frightened me. In fact, I found it strangely comforting. It was reassuring to know that I had some agency in the course of my own life.

And I felt, again, like that might be necessary, that I needed to do something in order to maintain control. I couldn't have articulated this for you then, but I had a sense that I was losing my balance. There had been a temporary stability—just those few months—but things were beginning to feel uneven again.

It was mid-April the day that Marnie went into labor, a Friday, and I was exhausted. I had been interrupted by my neighbors going out the previous evening at half past eleven—their incessant giggling, the clinking wine bottles, the thunderous hum of voices trying to be quiet—and then returning to the flat just after three in the morning. I had hopped between dreams: of Emma, of Marnie, of Charles.

I hadn't dreamed about Emma's corpse since my years at university, almost a decade earlier, and yet that vision had returned and it felt more frightening, more graphic, than it ever had before. It would creep into an entirely unrelated narrative. I'd be in the middle of a work dream—hundreds of calls simultaneously and not enough staff to answer the phones, wait times reaching several hours, being summoned to that windowed office on the eighth floor—or one of those traditional anxiety dreams, in which I was standing naked in front of a crowd or my teeth were falling out. And then suddenly, in the stationery cupboard or at the dentist's office, I would discover her lifeless body, simply nudged into a corner, stiff limbs fixed and eyes clouded. And I would wake gasping for air and sweating and trembling in cold, damp sheets.

It wasn't unusual for Charles to appear unexpectedly in my dreams, too. He would be there, sitting at another desk in my office, or on the hygienist's stool, either in his suit and tie or in those striped pajamas and that university sweater. He rarely participated or addressed me directly; he was just there, present in the corner of a nightmare, watching as things unfolded. I wondered if I was haunted by my actions, if his presence in my dreams suggested the early symptoms of some deep-rooted guilt or shame. But the truth is that I never felt disturbed by his company. He was simply there, as in my real life he was simply not.

Marnie called me in the middle of a nightmare. I was stuck in the mirror of my wardrobe watching Emma's dead body rot between my blankets. I could hear a lawnmower rumbling somewhere outside, shaking against the earth, and it continued to reverberate, its engine growling, until I finally forced my eyes open.

My phone was vibrating on the bedside table beside me. It shivered off the lip and clattered to the ground, still attached to its charger. I slid my hand across the floor and finally found it still ringing.

"Hello?" I said. My voice caught in my throat and emerged in a croak. I coughed to clear the phlegm that had set there overnight.

"Jane?"

It was a woman's voice, but I didn't recognize it. There was something breathless about it, something desperate.

My heart began to beat a little faster.

I knew immediately that it wasn't Emma—I knew her too well; it wasn't her voice and she'd have filled this silence immediately—but it could have been a friend of hers, or another nurse, or someone from my mother's facility.

"Speaking," I said in response, and in an unnecessarily formal manner.

There was a sharp intake of breath. "Just . . . one moment." Then a loud sigh. "Okay—thank goodness—it's done. I—"

"Who is this?" I interrupted.

"Oh, it's me," said the voice. "Sorry—not helpful at all. It's Marnie. Jane, it's me."

Which didn't make sense. It was barely light outside.

"Marnie?" I asked. "What . . . ? Why are you calling? It's the middle of the night."

"It's not the middle of the night," she said. "It's nearly six. I thought you'd be up."

"What's happened?" I asked. "Is something wrong?"

"Now," she began, "there's no need to panic. I just . . . I think that maybe stuff is starting to happen. You know, with the baby. And I wondered if you might be able to come over. I wanted to catch you before you left for work, you see. There's still time, I'm sure. But I'm getting these quite overwhelming twinges. I've been up since around three.

They come and go, you know, as they're supposed to, but I just couldn't get back to sleep. And I've been waiting to call you and—as I said—I thought you might be up by now."

We had lived together for years, so embedded in the details of each other's days that there were no secrets, no missteps, no unknowns. I could easily have woken one morning and lived her day instead: drinking her tea, going to her gym and using her shower gel, speaking in her voice, using her words—simply being her. And she could have done the same for me. She knew my routines and habits. And she knew, too, that not once in my entire life had I left for work before six in the morning.

"When do you need me?"

There was a long silence.

"Shall I come over now?" I asked. "I can bring a few bits with me; I can shower at yours instead."

"Yes," replied Marnie. "Please. If that's okay."

She told me that she loved me, really loved me, which was very unusual and, truthfully, entirely out of character. We didn't have—have never had—that sort of friendship. We don't profess love in a heartfelt way or make promises of forever. Perhaps that has been our undoing. But, regardless, it revealed to me that she really was very frightened, that she really did need me.

I liked it, that feeling of being needed. And being needed by Marnie specifically. I felt that I was sliding backward along the thread of a spiderweb, toward the place we used to be, when it was just us, and we were friends, and there was nothing to complicate that simple fact.

I pulled on my jeans and a jumper, yanking my charger from the socket and throwing it into my leather holdall. I had bought it for Jonathan as a Christmas gift the year before he died. I took a few things from the pile of clean clothing on the chair in the corner of my room—underwear, a spare T-shirt, a small towel—and packed them as well. I grabbed my washbag from the bathroom. I tucked my toothbrush into the front pouch and found all manner of other products there, too—

shampoo samples and a comb with missing teeth and an array of tampons in colorful plastic packaging and mascara with black paste crusted around the seal—and I zipped it up and threw it all into the bag as well.

I darted down the stairs—two at a time, smelling my stale breath as my breathing came quicker—and I arrived at Marnie's in less than half an hour, shiny with sweat and pink-cheeked, but delighted to see relief spreading across her face as she opened the door.

A man walked past us in a suit and an animal-print tie, his hair still damp and a briefcase swinging from his fist. He must have seen me, marathon red and panting heavily, and Marnie, heavily pregnant and standing in the doorway in a calf-length peach nightdress. He turned his head away quickly. "Morning," he muttered.

"Morning," sang Marnie.

As he disappeared around the corner, Marnie's hands shot out to the side and grabbed the door frame.

"Oh, not again," she murmured.

She stepped backward, cradling her stomach in her arms.

The flat fell into chaos around her. I could see the TV screen dancing in the living room, and the radio in the kitchen was turned up and music was filtering down the stairs. The hallway was littered with clothing: cardigans over the banister and scarves piled in a corner and the pegs on the wall overflowing with jackets and coats. There were endless trails of things in all directions: tea-stained mugs and empty water glasses heading toward the kitchen, and half-eaten biscuits and sweet wrappers and unopened crisp packets through to the living room, and muslins and onesies and miniature socks scattered on the stairs.

I contorted my shock into a huge grin.

"It's happening," I said in a sort of singsong way and I did an awkward jig, shifting my weight between my two feet and clapping my hands together without ever really separating them.

Marnie groaned.

"Okay," I said. "Okay. You're having a contraction."

"No shit," she hissed, waddling back toward the lounge.

I watched her walk away, her feet turned outward, her hands pressed into her lower back, and I felt immediately overwhelmed. I tried to remind myself that this was all entirely normal and that women did this every day, all over the world and at all hours. But it felt far from ordinary. We had first known each other as children, and then as young women, and as wives, but with her as a mother? The magnitude of that felt impossible.

Marnie yelped.

I rushed after her.

She was lowering herself onto a gigantic blue inflatable ball.

"Right," I said. "Of course. Yes. Deep breathing. That's the way. In. Out. In. And then—"

"Are you joking?" she said. "Stop that. Shut up."

"Okay. Yes." I said. "I'll just wait here."

I perched on the edge of the sofa, holding my leather bag between my legs. She bounced vigorously, up and down, fiercely blowing air through her pursed lips. Eventually, she leaned backward, stretching her chest and stomach up and out, and then she sighed. She began gently bouncing, lifting and lowering her considerable weight.

"Should we be going to—"

"The hospital?" she said. "No, not yet. But they are getting longer. "How are you doing, anyway? Sorry about that. And for getting you up so early. Just"—she waved her arm at the surrounding madness— "everything's got a bit out of hand."

Marnie abhors mess; she categorically cannot stand it. This, curiously, is one of the very few things on which we absolutely agree. We work in very different ways. We are our bests in very different situations. I like silence or just the quiet murmur of voices. She likes the radio or music or the television, preferably all three. I am introverted: I need my own space and my own company and to be alone. And she is a textbook extrovert, confident and outgoing and thriving off other people's conversations and opinions and those interactions that drain me so quickly.

I've said it already, haven't I? She is light and I am dark. But untidiness made us both useless.

I think she could probably have handled the pain and the discomfort and the fear of labor itself—I wonder now if she really needed me there for those things—but she simply couldn't function amid that much disarray.

"I can see that," I said. "What happened?"

"I know," she said. "The place is a state. I was trying to go with the flow, eat what I needed, and focus only on the contraction, and then I thought I might just tidy up a bit, just to get ready, you know, and then everything got a bit intense, and, well"—she circled her hand over her head again—"it all looks like this now."

"Right," I said.

I knew what she wanted from me. I knew what she needed. I always had. And she had always known that I would deliver it, whatever it was that she wanted: without question, without complaint.

"How about you stay there," I said, "and I'll do just a quick tidy-up?"

Marnie smiled, and it felt nice that at this precipice, at the beginning of yet another stage of our lives, it was time again for "just a quick tidy-up." I think it reassured me—wrongly, as it happens—that things weren't going to change, that there was no reason to feel overwhelmed by the significance of this moment, that everything would be fine.

Marnie bounced on her ball and I flitted between the rooms, gathering and rehoming clothing, clearing litter into the bins, and folding the strangest, smallest, freshest-smelling blankets. I opened the windows. It was one of the first bright days of the year—I hadn't needed a coat—and the breeze through the flat felt refreshing. When the flat was spotless, I had a quick shower and then made us cups of tea—hers with plenty of milk, mine with just a thimbleful—and sat down on the sofa to watch the twenty-four-hour news channel and hold her hand.

"Will you call my mum?" she asked.

I hadn't expected that. "What?" I replied. "Why?"

"Perhaps she'll want to be there? She might at least want to know what's going on."

"Okay," I said. "Are you sure?"

She nodded.

"Well, all right, then." I went into the hallway and I hovered there, and I neatened the coats on the pegs and kicked a feather into a gap beneath the skirting board and I called her mother and I felt relieved when she didn't answer. I left a brief, mumbling message that probably wasn't particularly clear and returned to Marnie a few minutes later.

By the early afternoon, Marnie's contractions were three minutes apart and I called for a taxi to take us to the hospital. She changed into a light summer dress. She said that she was too hot and uncomfortable for anything else. We sat together in the back and she grunted as we went over the bumps, her eyes closed as though the darkness made the pain bearable.

We arrived at the hospital and she shuffled through the main reception to the elevator and I was surprised when we arrived at the maternity ward. It had all the trimmings of a normal hospital—the pale walls and a tiled floor and that smell of disinfectant—but something was different. Perhaps it was the lighting or the smiles on the faces of the staff or the pastel uniforms, but it didn't feel quite so threatening.

We'd passed so many sick people on our way through the corridors; ghoulish elderly women being transported along hallways in beds that made them look tiny. And yet here the patients were all swollen and sweating and bursting—literally—with life.

A smiling midwife in a blue and white tunic led us to a side room.

"Here you go, pet," she said. "Get yourself comfy and I'll be back to check on you in five."

Marnie held on to the bed frame and swayed from side to side, her cheeks puffed out, her eyes again closed.

"Will you stay?" she whispered. "For it all? Until the baby gets here?"

"Of course," I said. "Of course I'll stay."

Because where else would I have been?

Audrey Gregory-Smith was born at ten past seven in the evening on the twenty-fourth of April. She was small and angry and her face was red and her eyes were squeezed firmly shut, closed almost as tightly as her fists. She had thin tufts of fair hair on her scalp, wrinkles across her knees and elbows and knuckles, and pink pouting rosebud lips.

Marnie clutched her little girl to her chest, caught between joy and panic, insisting simultaneously that she might be sick and that she might drop the baby and then suddenly shouting, "Who's in charge here?" to a bustling room.

I reached over to place my hand on top of hers. "You." I didn't want to frighten her, but wasn't that the truth? "You're in charge now."

"Oh, fuck," she replied and then grinned manically. "Well, that's a worry, isn't it?" And then she began to sob.

I shushed her and stroked her hair away from her face.

"Where's my mum?" she asked. "Is she on her way?" She looked up at me.

"I don't know," I said. I didn't think that her mother deserved to be there for a moment that important.

"You did call her, didn't you?" she asked.

"Yes," I replied.

"Yes?" she repeated.

"Definitely," I said.

"And she said she'd come?"

"Not exactly," I said. "She didn't answer. I left a message. I guess she's probably listened to it by now. I didn't want to worry you. I thought that she'd come to the hospital. But I suppose . . . Shall I call her now? Let her know the good news?"

"No," said Marnie. "I don't think so."

Which was exactly what I'd hoped she would say. Because this was a moment for the most important people in that child's life.

Chapter Thirty-Two

Marnie was staying in the hospital overnight, and so I traveled home by myself. I was thinking, in the taxi, as we slipped through the backstreets of the city, how much had changed in the course of that one day. And how world-altering days must happen to different people each and every day. I was thinking that those days— the big days—are the junctures that define a life: when you gain someone, when you lose someone. I felt giddy at the new possibilities, the shape of my life in that moment, this new person who existed for me.

I had left home very early and hadn't opened the blinds, and so it was dark when I stepped into my flat. I immediately noticed the red button flashing on my phone, a message waiting. I felt along the wall for the light switch.

I had plugged the landline back into the socket a few weeks earlier and discovered every single one of the messages that had been lingering there. I'd listened to a few: voices that seemed to speak from another world, from months earlier, when our newborn wasn't yet born. But then the messages began to ask questions—about Jonathan, about Charles— and so I deleted them all.

I pressed my finger to the blinking triangle.

"One—new message," said an automated female voice. "Received— today—at ten—twenty-three—p.m."

"Hello," said another woman's voice, a human voice. It echoed through my hallway, ricocheting off the walls, a booming, elongated "Oh." "I thought you'd like to know," she said, and her voice was low and sort of husky, "that I've been looking into everything: everything you've said and everything that's happened. And I've been finding things, too. I knew there was a story—I know that there is—and I'm going to get there eventually. I'll find it, you know."

She was slurring, her consonants weak, her vowels long and drawled, letters rolling together, as though she'd been drinking heavily all day. I looked at my watch. It was nearly eleven o'clock.

"So, whatever," she said. "I know you were there for over an hour. I read the police report: waiting, you said. D'you know that the neighbor in the flat below reckons she might have heard someone shouting? Earlier in the day, she said, but shouting all the same. That's strange, I reckon. Because he died straightaway, right? Which doesn't leave a whole lot of time for screaming. And it's more than that, isn't it? That time you stayed there. Why spend such a long time in someone else's home? And the week before. Just a walk in the rain? I don't think so. There's something, isn't there? We both know that there is. There's no need to call back."

"You have—no—new messages," said the automated voice, robotic and monotonous.

The steady joy that had filled me throughout the afternoon turned instantly, curdling like milk.

What had the neighbor heard? I walked into the kitchen and I turned on the tap. It splashed cold against my hand.

Who lived in the flat below? I took off my coat and hung it on the back of the stool tucked beneath the breakfast bar.

Was he loud in the hours that came after his fall? I turned on the radio and twisted the dial to turn up the volume. The room was engulfed in some song, some tune that meant nothing to me.

That would undermine his time of death.

I turned on the television. I'd lost the remote control a few months earlier and so I used the buttons at the side of the screen to increase the sound.

I sat on the sofa. An urgent panic was inflating itself inside of me, and my chest and my breath felt tight. She was getting closer; I could almost feel her behind me, in the tickle of my hair against the back of my neck and the rub of my clothes on my shoulders. I felt jittery, my body protesting the jump from joy to terror. It felt like there was something submerged within me and, desperate to expel it, I roared into the cacophony: the water, the music, the voices.

And then I sat silent.

I felt a little better then: cleaner, fresher, lighter, too.

I stood up and I turned off the tap and I turned off the radio and I turned off the television, and then I sat back down.

I needed to focus.

I told myself to stay calm.

So someone had heard something.

It wasn't ideal.

But perhaps it wasn't a catastrophe.

Because everyone who's ever lived near others knows that people are loud, often very loud. And those few dozen apartments squeezed into a mansion house always felt very dense to me. We could all hear the babies crying, and the mothers shushing, and the music playing, and the dinner party laughter, and the washing machine vibrating wildly against the floor, and the doors slamming, and the stomping feet, and the ringing of an alarm clock or a telephone. We could all hear the insults creeping louder and louder, the generic grievances: the "you don't listens" and the "if you weren't always naggings" and the "why don't you at least try to see it from my perspectives."

It wasn't impossible that someone had heard him screaming. But it didn't matter. There was no tangible evidence that he didn't die instantly. The scream of a falling man could quite easily be the squeal of a child playing or the rage of a disgruntled teen. The roar of his frustration, those pangs of anger, could comfortably be the clash of an overwrought couple, married too young and too long.

None of it was new. None of it was noteworthy.

None of her small discoveries had the power to effect any sort of change. Her evidence was circumstantial at best and would probably be deemed irrelevant. And so I wound down the last of my panic, piece by piece, taking it apart and dismissing each section in turn.

But the bigger issue—and the one that clearly needed addressing, that couldn't be unpicked quite so easily—was her indomitable persistence. I needed to get rid of her, to find a way to silence her. I needed to ensure that she wouldn't—couldn't—find anything further, that she could never have anything that might threaten my friendship.

I rifled through my kitchen cupboards, looking for something to eat. It had been a very long day and I was feeling a little fraught and I had a headache that existed somewhere beyond my forehead, in the space in front of my face. I discovered a few slices of bread in the bottom of a bag. I picked off the mold and I toasted them—all four of them. I smeared them with butter, thick and yellow, and I watched as it melted translucent. I was in control; I could stay in control. I squeezed honey onto the top of each slice and I tilted the toast to spread it across the surface. Against the toast, speckled brown, the gold was rich and it made me think of Marnie.

I took my bread to bed and I ate it carefully, channeling Emma, cautious of crumbs. I sent a message to Peter, explaining my absence that day, and he replied congratulating me almost immediately. It made me excited, reignited a little of that joy that I, too, was deserving of congratulations.

I turned off the light and in the glow from my phone scrolled through some new photographs of Valerie. She'd uploaded a photograph of her and her flatmate holding lurid cocktails in a bustling restaurant, another of the sun setting beyond her balcony. There was an incredible video of her and five others dancing in a round. The caption beneath revealed that they were preparing for a performance later in the year, in the summer.

I set my alarm for the following morning and I told myself to be happy, to be brave, to be unafraid. Because I was going to find a way to end this.

Chapter Thirty-Three

I returned to the hospital early the following day, excited to see Marnie, excited to see Audrey. I asked for them at the entrance to the maternity wing and was directed to a ward at the other end of the corridor. I went toward bed seven, as instructed, and discovered that it was hidden behind a thin blue curtain. I found a break in the fabric and I opened it slightly and I spoke into the gap.

"Hello?" I said.

"Come on in," she replied.

Marnie was sitting up in bed, blankets twisted around her legs and her red hair gathered on the top of her head. She was wearing a pale blue hospital gown and she looked beautiful, her skin puffy and soft, her eyes fresh and bright.

"Morning," I said. I perched at the foot of the bed, the mattress deflating beneath me.

"Who is it's come to visit us?" Marnie sang, looking not at me but at the baby bent across her chest, her voice high-pitched and tinny. She twisted Audrey toward me, so that I could see the creases in her little cheeks, the folds from sleep, and her lips opening and closing. "Who's this?" Marnie squeaked.

"Morning, Audrey," I said.

"Hello, Auntie Jane," said Marnie, still shrill.

"How did you sleep?" I asked.

"Not much," she said. "But that's fine; it's all fine."

She smiled and folded the baby back against her body, nimbly, never releasing her head and yet rotating her gracefully.

"And how are you feeling?" I asked.

"So-so," she replied. "Sore, but that's to be expected. And I'm happy. I feel good."

"And this little one's doing well?" I asked, holding my hand out and letting my fingers hover a few inches away from the baby.

"She's perfect," Marnie replied.

"I know," I said.

"Oh," she said, "and I meant to tell you this—it's a bit odd—but before I forget: I had a message from that journalist. You know the one? The one from before? She left it last night."

I wonder what my face looked like in that moment. I know that my hand stayed frozen in front of me. I felt bile building at the back of my throat, and I inadvertently retched and had to turn it into a hiccup so as not to look suspicious.

"You heard from her?" I asked.

"She left me a message," Marnie replied.

"She left me one, too," I said.

The ward felt suddenly far too cold. The hairs on my arms stood erect beneath my cardigan. I clenched my teeth together to prevent them from chattering. But Marnie barely noticed the change in me. She was concentrating instead on Audrey, whose white cotton hat had slipped down over her eyes.

"What did she want?" I asked. I felt nauseated not only somewhere in my head and in my stomach, but in my bones and my muscles, too. It was like waves were swelling through every layer of tissue within my body.

"I don't know," she replied, still trying to press the hat onto Audrey's head.

"What do you mean?" I asked.

"You know," she said, "I don't really want to think about her. She isn't a nice woman, and I have plenty of nice things in my life now. I don't need to allow her that space in my brain."

"Did you call her back?" I asked.

She looked up at me. "I didn't even notice the message until this morning," she said. "I thought it was my mother actually. I don't think I'd have listened to it otherwise."

"And?" I insisted.

Marnie lifted the hat from Audrey's head and scrunched it inside her fist. "Her head's too small," she said.

"Marnie," I snapped. "Will you look at me? What did she say? In her message? Has she found anything? Is she still looking into us?"

"Jesus, Jane." She threw the cotton hat toward me, and it caught in the air and settled between us on the blue bedspread.

"What?" I asked. "Don't you want to know if she's going to be writing about us again? I don't want to be on that bloody website, not after last time. Do you? Doesn't that matter to you at all?"

"You need to calm down," she said. "This isn't the place. And why do you care so much about it anyway? What does it matter if a journalist investigates us? She can waste her own time all she wants. She's not going to find anything, so what's it to us how she spends her time?"

Audrey began to whimper.

"Oh, no, no, no," said Marnie. "Don't do that. Here we go." Audrey was lifted into the air, her body still so curled, and then finally it made sense.

Whatever was in that message was irrelevant. There had been no revelation, no evidence, no something undone. Because, if there had been, this conversation would have been a different thing from the very beginning. Because Marnie has never been someone who keeps secrets. She has never been someone who allows anger to build insistently within her, who lets it percolate and then erupt. If there was something that needed saying, she'd have said it.

But I had been too consumed by my own panic. I had inadvertently created a storm from still air and had carelessly revealed my own fear. I had assumed that it would be mirrored in Marnie. But she didn't know that there was a reason to be afraid of the articles, or the messages, or the constant meddling. I had foolishly assumed that we still knew everything together, still felt everything together, that any spaces that ever opened between us were quickly cemented, but of course that wasn't true anymore; it could never be true again.

I needed to de-escalate the conversation, to hide my anxiety, because she was right to be shocked by it.

"Is she okay?" I asked.

There was something distracting in the eerie contrast between what Valerie might have uncovered and the perfect serenity of that small, curtained cubicle.

"I think so," Marnie said, pulling Audrey close again. She fished another small hat from her rucksack, which was crammed with rolled-up onesies and frilled socks, and she slid this one over Audrey's forehead until it sat snug above her eyebrows.

"I'm sorry," I said. "And you're right. We should just ignore her. She'll stop eventually."

"Exactly," Marnie replied.

A midwife arrived, a different one, to assess Audrey, to test her hearing and to weigh her again and to formally discharge her into the world beyond these hospital walls. She was older, warm and smiling, with a very confident matronly stature. I was grateful for the interruption.

"And how are you getting home?" she asked, her eyes flickering between the three of us.

"I was going to book a taxi," I replied. "Shall I do that now?"

"Do you have a car seat?" she asked.

I nodded toward it, squared away at the back of the ward.

"Then perfect," she said. "You're all ready to go." She tickled Audrey's toes. "Aren't you a lucky little sausage to have such lovely mummies taking you home?"

I didn't correct her.

Jane," said Marnie, as we waited for our taxi outside the hospital. "Can I ask you something?" She was shivering in her summer dress despite the sunshine.

"Anything," I replied.

Audrey, already strapped into her seat, bundled beneath blankets, whimpered and then sneezed.

"You seem different," she said. "Has something upset you?"

"I'm fine," I said.

"Was it that journalist?" she asked. "That message?"

An ambulance stopped in front of the main entrance, its sirens still shrieking.

"Jane," she said, exasperated.

"What?" I asked. "What did you say?"

The sirens ceased. A gurney was lowered from the rear of the vehicle and rushed into the building, accompanied by two paramedics in green and a doctor in blue.

"Are you still bothered by that journalist?"

"Maybe," I said.

Marnie sighed. "I get that. But, if anything, it's worse in some ways for me. She tricked me. I thought she was nice, that time that we met. She seemed lovely, actually. And very beautiful, too. She seemed so kind and compassionate. I really thought that I could trust her. But it was all a performance, wasn't it? So there we go: lesson learned. I know it's miserable to have to absorb those accusations—I know what that's like, remember—but she's not important anymore."

I nodded as though I understood, as though this made sense, as though I, too, was unsettled by a false accusation.

"Or is that not it?" asked Marnie. "Was it something she said? In her message? Is that the problem?"

I shook my head.

"What did she say to you?" Marnie insisted.

I paused, searching for a safe answer. "I expect she said the same thing to me that she said to you," I replied.

"I only listened to the beginning of it," she said. "I deleted it as soon as I realized who it was from. But what was it? What did she say?"

I felt a shiver of relief shake through me. I had been right not to panic. She knew nothing more than she had known before. And then that brief release was overwhelmed by a subtler fear. Because it wasn't that Valerie had left an irrelevant message, stating nothing of note. Which is where my hope had led me. But simply that I had been lucky. If Marnie hadn't deleted that message, who knew what she might now know?

"Jane?" she asked.

"She was calling to apologize," I said.

The truth—and I'm almost ashamed to say it—is that I fabricated the rest of this made-up message spontaneously, without really thinking about it, embellishing this lie as easily as I had the others.

"She said that she'd been having a bad time, that her ex-husband had recently remarried, and that she had thrown herself too forcefully into her work. She said that she was sorry for the hurt that she'd caused, and that she hoped we could forgive her."

That was the sixth lie.

I told it for the same reason that I told the others. But it felt different, this lie, because it was a pause, not a stop, to a problem. Valerie had come for Marnie. She would come again.

The pressure to do something was building, and I needed to address it.

"Oh," said Marnie, staring at me. "That's strange. I thought she sounded quite distressed at the beginning of the message. What were the words—"

"It's not important—" I began.

"No, I know," she said. "But it's bugging me now. She said something that immediately made me bristle, you know? And I knew straightaway that it was her and that I didn't want to listen to it. Because I was sure it was going to be antagonistic and full of ridiculous lies all over again, and I just wasn't in the mood quite frankly. But . . . Oh, I can't remember."

"I think she'd been drinking," I replied.

"Perhaps," she said. "Although I'm sure there was something more."

Did she know? Did she doubt me? I couldn't tell. But I didn't think it likely. Because this journalist was the unstable presence—who stalked us and harassed us and published malicious lies on the internet. And I was her reliable friend: solid and stable and permanent. If it was the word of one against the word of the other, I know where I'd lay my faith. And yet I felt the smallest of doubts because I don't think she'd ever disagreed with me quite so easily before.

"Right," she said, as a taxi pulled up in front of us. "This must be it."

I traveled home with them, clipping Audrey's car seat into position and carrying her things—nappy bags, blankets, spare outfits—up to the flat. I hovered outside the front door as Marnie wrestled with the key, as it scraped and scratched its way into the lock. And then, eventually, it swung open.

The flat was just as we'd left it: tidy but for the blue ball anchored in the middle of the lounge, the hallway uncluttered and neat, the black and white rug squared against the bottom of the stairs.

I stood there with the bags hanging at my calves and then Marnie turned to me and she said: "We've got it from here."

And just like that, I was dismissed.

Again, I was dismissed.

Chapter Thirty-Four

The spring began to inch toward summer, and I felt frustrated. I wanted to be spending more time with Marnie.

We made plans, and she canceled them with very little notice. I visited her several times in those first few weeks, delivering supplies—new nappies, medicines, an ice tray—but I never stayed for very long. Because there was always something happening, someone interrupting, a phone call from the nurse or a visit from the midwife.

She was so determined to tackle this new stage of her life independently. She relied on other women, other new mothers who could provide advice that was alien to me. I felt inadequate. She trusted medical professionals who could prescribe ointments of all sorts that were apparently necessary in the first few weeks of an infant's life. I wanted to be there—I really did—and I promise you that I tried to be supportive. But I often felt like a hindrance, not knowing where all the new paraphernalia belonged or how to support a baby's head or which way around a nappy went.

I wanted so desperately to be part of their world, and it didn't make sense to me that they wouldn't want that, too. I wanted to learn along with Marnie, to discover the challenges standing beside her. I had a vision for how our lives should look, the way the three worlds would be woven into one, and at this distance it felt impossible.

We went for brunch once, when Audrey was maybe six weeks old. I was so excited to see them both, and I bought a jingling ring of plastic pieces as a present for Audrey. But she wasn't interested in the gift. She cried constantly, distressed by the new noises and smells and the bright lights of a café in the sunshine. She was livid, flustered—her little face red like a blister—and Marnie was bouncing her up and down, hushing and shushing and sweating herself.

"Fuck it," she said. "The fans. The fucking fans."

"What fans?" I replied. The waitress brought our plates to the table: scrambled eggs for Marnie and a bacon bap for me.

"I was meant to pick them up," she said. "It's too hot, the apartment. It's a nightmare, to be honest. She's not sleeping, and I have this little thermometer and it's bright red all the time because it's so damn hot—I've never known a spring like it—but there's not a lot I can do about the weather, is there? So I ordered three fans. That's probably a bit over the top—maybe I only needed one—but I was in a flap. Anyway, they've got to be picked up by noon and I'll never get there now, not with her like this. I'll just have to go tomorrow. Which is another night of screaming."

"I can go," I offered. "Where is it?"

She paused. "Are you sure?" she asked. "Do you mean it? You'd have to leave now."

"Of course," I replied. I wanted to help.

"Well, let me just—" She rifled through her handbag and pulled out a receipt. "It's probably only ten minutes if you walk fast?"

"Sure," I said, taking the thin piece of paper from her hand. "It's no problem."

"But your food—don't you—"

"I had some cereal earlier," I said. "I'm fine. Really."

"Well, take this," she said. And her right hand disappeared into her bag again. She pulled out a small gold key and I recognized it immediately. "I'll pay up and I'll meet you there, but I need to sort her out first, so you might get back before me. Are you sure about this? It's all paid for."

"Absolutely," I said, and I reached out to take the key. I felt the scratch along the flat circular top and I knew that it was the exact same one I'd held before. "I'll see you there."

I collected the fans, and I carried them back toward her flat; they were heavy and awkward. I let myself in. It felt different there then: inhabited, hectic, full. I opened the three boxes in the hallway, and I assembled the fans, and I plugged each into the socket beside the radiator, one by one, to check that they worked. There, crouched on the floor, I was drawn again to that black and white carpet. I lifted one of the corners to peer beneath. Nothing. I pulled it back a little farther, but there wasn't even a stain by the bottom step.

I left the fans at the foot of the stairs, and I sat on the sofa and waited for Marnie and Audrey to return home, and I didn't touch anything because I didn't want to further upset the sense of the place. They returned just after one o'clock, and Marnie said that she was tired and needed a rest and thanked me for the fans and said that we must try for brunch again soon, or maybe lunch, that she'd be in touch.

We haven't managed to see each other since.

I was meant to be seeing her for dinner last week, but then she called my office in the afternoon to say that she didn't feel much like cooking, she was exhausted, and could we please rearrange? I said not to worry, to come to me and I would cook, or I could cook at hers, or how about takeout. But she was insistent. Not today.

It has been over a month.

I have been using the time—this space—to concentrate instead on Valerie.

I wish I could say that it had proved a satisfying distraction, but that would be untrue. And I did promise you the truth. So here it is. I found myself contemplating things that would—how might you say it?—prevent her from interfering in a very permanent way. I knew where she lived. I knew where she worked. I might not have known her secrets in the way that she knew mine, but I was quietly confident that I could create a fatal situation.

But it wasn't that straightforward. I couldn't find a way to do it that didn't make me feel queasy. I liked the idea of pushing her in front of a car. It would have had a satisfying symmetry. I imagined ways to snaffle her pills—I'd seen her posting about hay fever tablets—and replace them with something more deadly. But I bristled every time my thoughts became more pragmatic and less fanciful. Which, in many ways, served to prove her wrong: I wasn't a murderer after all.

And so I needed a different plan.

That afternoon, I found myself scrolling again through her recent uploads—photographs, newspaper pieces, and tweets, too—and discovered a new image, posted only that morning. It showed a row of tap shoes, and the caption said: *Final rehearsal—here we go!* I went onto the website of the dance company and discovered that their show was taking place just a few hours later in a church hall in the city center. They weren't selling tickets in advance—first come, first served—and would instead be accepting donations for a mental health charity on arrival.

I decided to go. I wanted to see her.

I arrived promptly at seven o'clock. The woman holding the collection bucket at the door asked if I'd watched one of their shows before, and when I said no, she asked if I knew a member of the cast.

Without thinking, I responded, "Valerie."

"Sands?" she said. "Valerie Sands?"

I nodded.

"She's been such a wonderful addition to the team," said the woman. "We're so thrilled to have her. She hadn't danced since she was a teenager, but she's picked it all up again so quickly. She'll shine tonight, I'm sure. You'll be very proud."

I smiled and nodded again and gratefully accepted a bright pink program. Valerie was listed as one of six dancers performing in the opening sequence.

I stepped into the body of the church and was amazed by its size: the ceiling, so incredibly high and decorated so ornately; the thick wooden pews; the stage hidden behind thick green curtains. The benches were full—children sitting on laps and teenagers packed tightly together—and so I went to stand near the front beside a few other stragglers. A crowd began to form behind me: families and friends and loved ones.

Then the lights fell and the curtains opened, and I saw her step onto the stage. She was one of three women with three men behind, all of them in loose black trousers and tight black tops. They looked ordinary, boring, until the song started. The speaker beside me began to vibrate, and they became instantly magnificent. They were moving so fast— their bodies sharp, punctuating the music—and the sound from their feet was aggressive and bold. The energy made me feel more alive and I was completely absorbed until she looked toward the front of the stage. She was searching for someone. She found me instead.

She stumbled, just briefly, before righting herself. She caught up quickly, but it felt good to have upset her rhythm. I liked that, for once, she was surprised by me.

I snuck out at the end of the song, and I liked, too, that she knew what it felt like to be thrown off balance.

Chapter Thirty-Five

It was a Saturday morning and I was on my way to visit my mother. I had been tempted to stay in bed, but she knew to expect me—or, at least, she had known; she may well have forgotten.

The weather was warm, too rich and too humid for long lie-ins and cozy mornings. It had been over eighty degrees for the last three weeks with no rain in almost a month. The grass across the city had shriveled to yellow straw and even the early mornings felt sticky and oppressive. It was the sort of weather for ice cream in the park and sitting in the shade and visits to the lido and late alfresco dinners in the rolling heat of a long evening. It was not the sort of weather for train journeys and windowless nursing homes and the tight bonds of familial duty.

The train was busy. We were still at Waterloo and not due to leave for a few more minutes. I was sitting by the sliding doors on a row of four seats, all backed against the window. The seats opposite were occupied by a young family: a mother, a father, and their two young daughters. They had rucksacks on their laps, and I wondered if they were going to the seaside or to the countryside, where the temperature was a little cooler and the air a little less thick.

Behind them, another train was readying itself to depart. The guard leaned out, scanned the platform, and blew his whistle. The other train groaned and began to move and my stomach lurched, as though we, too, were moving. I sat back and closed my eyes.

I'd be back in the city by the afternoon and my role as the dutiful daughter would be complete for another week.

When I opened my eyes, we were at Vauxhall.

"You need to stop it," said a woman, standing on the lip of the train, facing outward, her hands stretched to the sides, holding the door frame and blocking the entrance. I couldn't see her face, but I could tell that she was near tears from the shake in her voice. "Do not get on this train."

"Ah, lady, come on now," said a man on the platform. "What's the matter with you?"

She inhaled and her chest rose, and I could see that she was frightened but trying hard not to show it. "Excuse me!" she shouted toward the guard on the platform. He was facing away from her, speaking into a walkie-talkie. "This man is stalking me. Excuse me?" He didn't turn around.

"I can get on whatever the fuck train I want to," the man continued.

"Not this one. You've been following me and shouting obscenities and I'm not having it anymore." She looped the strap of her handbag over her head so that it hung across her chest. Her sweater was bright pink—it made her look younger, more vulnerable—and her denim shorts revealed toned, tanned thighs.

I caught the eye of the woman sitting opposite. Her husband wrapped his arms around the shoulders of their two young daughters as we silently discussed whether we ought to get involved.

"Oh, fuck you!" shouted the man.

"Ah, that's enough, now," said the father opposite, his voice measured and calm. "Just give it two minutes, mate. There's a train right behind this one. No fuss, yeah?"

The man stood still on the platform, as though considering the request. "Fuck you all," he said eventually, and stormed down the platform.

I exhaled. Backing down to a small woman in denim shorts and a pink top? Well, that would be emasculating, a sign of weakness. Whereas walking away from another man—slightly older, slightly broader—was just common sense.

Charles had been intimidated by strong women. He would dismiss his female colleagues over dinner, labeling them overly emotional or, in the same breath, too good-natured. He felt threatened by the success of the female partners who had happy children and great marriages and impressive careers. Or maybe that's simply what I wanted to see. I added his every failing to a list and counted the many ways in which he didn't deserve a woman like Marnie.

The woman in pink pressed the button and the doors slid closed in front of her.

"Thank you," she said, turning to face the father with his young daughters. "Thank you for getting involved."

She turned and stepped toward the empty seat beside me.

I knew her.

I recognized her immediately.

I'd know that face anywhere.

Chapter Thirty-Six

S he was so familiar. I recognized her dark hair, slicked back, and the tattoos on her left wrist and thumb matched those in her photographs. She looked different up close: much sharper, more re- markable. I'd seen her stand that way before, too, her weight through one side, her hip jutting to the left, and she had the same black leather bag that she'd worn at the funeral. But it was more than that: more than just the way she looked and stood and the things that she owned. I felt as though I knew how her mind worked, the way she constructed a thought.

"I know you," I said.

"You do," she replied. "Although you weren't meant to see me. But then I couldn't have anticipated all that commotion with that weird man. I feel a little shaken, actually. He was awful, wasn't he? That's the second time he's followed me. And it's never nice being followed by a stranger, I suppose."

She raised an eyebrow and then she laughed.

I was astounded by her confidence; she was so self-assured, so un- afraid. I should have felt frightened. I know that. It should have been un- nerving to have her confirm that she'd been pursuing me—likely for months—with nothing but the worst intentions. And yet, in that mo- ment, I felt reassured. I had been correct. I had been followed. I was right.

"You weren't quite as subtle as you think," I replied. "I've seen you. More than once, in fact."

"Oh, really?" she replied. "Damn. That's so disappointing." I hadn't noticed it before, but there was something very pretty about her features, her face.

"What do you want?" I asked.

"I want to know where you go every Saturday," she replied. "Do you mind if I sit down?"

I shook my head, because I didn't want her there beside me, acting as though we were friends, as though this was anything other than the mess that it actually was.

"Yes," I replied. "I do mind."

"Oh, don't be like that," she said.

"You've just intimated that you've been following me and you want to sit down beside me and have—what, a chat? No. I'm not interested."

"You're so dramatic," she said. "I hadn't expected that. I thought you'd be very measured, sort of indifferent, but you're just leaking emotions, aren't you? Which is strange because it isn't really such a revelation, is it?" she continued. "If you knew that I was following you."

I hated that. I hated the implication that I was being hysterical when I desperately wanted to be the absolute opposite: calm, composed, controlled.

She sat down beside me regardless. Her arm nudged mine. I stayed still so that the bobbled fabric of her jumper nestled soft against my bare skin. I felt this anger prickling within me, and I knew that I needed to ignore it and be cautious, to be calculated rather than ruthless.

She sighed and ran her fingers through her hair.

I wanted to slap her even though I know that violence is never the answer, because everything about her—her smirk, her pink jumper, her mettle—was infuriating. She had accused me of murder, not once, but twice. She had accused me of killing my own husband. And when Marnie was finally beginning to find a path through her grief, it was this woman—sitting there beside me—who tore it away, suspending our way forward.

"You should get off at the next stop," I said.

"But then I won't know where you're going," she said, and she pulled one of her feet onto the cushioned seat to retie her laces.

"You could just ask me," I replied. "It isn't interesting. And frankly, if your investigation has led you here, then it's definitely time to stop. I'm on my way to visit my mother. I see her every weekend and I'm always on this train."

"Where does she live?"

"The end of the line."

"Can I have her address?" She smiled at me conspiratorially, as though we were in this together. She put her foot back onto the floor and then started to lift and lower her heel repeatedly, so that her leg bobbed up and down, the tanned flesh of her thigh trembling.

"She's in a residential home," I said. "Dementia."

I suppose I needed to seem honest, as though I had nothing to hide. I was willingly giving her the information that she wanted to make myself seem innocent.

"I'm so sorry," said Valerie. "That's a real shame."

"Why?" I asked bluntly. "Because she won't be able to tell you anything?"

She looked shocked. "No," she insisted. "What an awful thing to say. That isn't it at all."

"Right," I said. I didn't know if she was telling the truth. It didn't really matter.

She looked over her shoulder, out the windows, at the hedgerows sliding past, a blur of green. "You think I'm a monster," she said. "I'm not. I just know that there's something else here that still needs uncovering. So I have to keep going. It isn't going to get any better, I'm afraid."

I think my face must have contorted in some way—perhaps she saw the fear that was nestled inside me—because her eyes shifted quickly until they were almost sympathetic.

"Sorry," she said. "That sounds a little like a threat, doesn't it?"

"Isn't it?" I asked.

"No, you're right," she said. "It probably is. Do you feel like I'm getting closer?"

"There's nothing to get closer—"

"Stop that," she said. "You can see it as clearly as I can. There are these little cracks throughout your story. And, somewhere, there's a wrecking ball that will destroy it completely. I'm going to find it."

I shrugged. "You're wrong," I said. It didn't sound convincing.

"I don't think you killed your husband, though," she said. "If that's any consolation."

"It isn't."

"And I am sorry about that, I suppose. It's tough."

"You get used to it," I replied. "To the shit."

"Oh, I hear you," she said. "Sometimes I'm into my fourth vodka before the edges even begin to soften . . ." She started to twist at the silver ring sitting snug around her thumb. "I've just remembered that message," she said, and she grimaced. "I left you a message. On your answering machine. Anyway, I felt terrible the next morning; I'd drunk far too much. But I meant what I said."

"That you're still investigating us?" I asked. "I'm just glad Marnie deleted hers before listening to any of that nonsense."

Valerie tilted her head slightly to one side and her eyes widened, and I knew then that I'd made a mistake.

"What do you mean?" she asked. "She didn't listen to it?"

I shook my head.

"I thought she'd heard it but ignored it."

I didn't say anything. The family of four got off at Richmond. There was a last-minute kerfuffle—over hats and rucksacks and where was the sunblock—and the mother smiled at us uncomfortably as she hurried her family out of the carriage just before the doors beeped and closed and we pulled away from the platform.

The air-conditioning grunted and groaned and then whistled to a stop. The train suddenly felt quieter, without the whir of the fan and the hiss of cool air entering the carriage. The temperature began to increase. I stood to open the window, but it was sealed shut. They were all sealed shut.

"All right, princess," came a voice behind me, and I turned to see that the man had returned and was sitting opposite us, where the family had been sitting a few moments before.

I stayed standing but said nothing.

"What was it you said back there?" His voice was loud, and others in the carriage were stirring, staring, waiting to see how the situation would unfold. I wondered if they'd been listening all along, how much of our altercation they had overheard.

"Hey!" he shouted. Valerie was peering into her purse. "Weren't ignoring me earlier, were you?"

"There are some seats further down," I said. "Just over there."

"I'm not looking for a seat, am I, love? I'm wanting to speak to her."

Valerie refused to look up, fiddling instead with wads of old, faded, folded receipts, her empty water bottle, her phone. I should have walked away. I should have let her handle him herself, but there's this unwritten code between women, and it exists in public places, and more than ever on public transport, that you unite in the presence of threatening men, and so I inevitably—without really thinking about it—stayed there beside her.

"Look at me!" he shouted, and, instinctively, she did.

Valerie inhaled and then stood up. "Look," she said. "I'm just trying to have a nice day out with my girlfriend." I felt her fingers climbing along my wrist toward my hand. I let her take it. Was she still playing? Was she in control? Or was he? "And we really don't want any trouble, so what is it exactly that you want?"

"Well, doesn't that explain it," he said, standing up.

I tensed, but he didn't move any closer.

"You're a dyke." He laughed. "Why didn't you say? Suppose I should've guessed, what with all the rage and hating."

He walked past us, holding his middle finger up behind his head as he disappeared farther down the carriage.

We watched him go and then sat back down.

"He's been stalking me," she said, very quietly. "We went for a drink once. About a piece I wanted to write. And then I saw him at my show, a dance show. He was watching me from the front of the stage. It really threw me. Anyway, I hope that's the end of him."

"I want you to get off at the next stop," I said again.

"I won't follow you," she replied.

"I don't believe you."

She laughed. "I suppose that's fair."

"I want you to stop investigating us now."

"I'm not going to do that."

"You are," I replied. "There's nothing to find, and you're stalking me now, which is an offense in itself."

"I'll tell the police what I've found."

"You think they'll care? About a rainy walk and a noisy apartment? Those things aren't evidence, Valerie. They're nothing. You haven't found anything. You're wasting your time. There's something wrong with you."

"There's nothing wrong with me," she said, and I could see that I'd found something that unsettled her.

"This isn't normal." I was trying not to shout, but the anger inside me was bursting within each capillary, tiny explosions beyond my control, itching and pulsing and desperate to escape. "You're not normal."

"Says you." Her face was distorted: her jaw clenched, her eyes narrowed, her mouth scowling.

"What does that mean?" I said. "What are you saying?"

"That you murdered your best friend's husband. You want to talk about obsession? You want to talk about *not normal*? I'm coming for you. And you know it. You just can't quite believe it yet."

"You know what?" I said. "I think you're jealous."

It was a new thought. It hadn't occurred to me before that moment. But it must have been percolating somewhere, because it made such perfect sense.

She opened her mouth to speak, but she didn't say anything. Her cheeks sank slightly, indented between her teeth, and her forehead was instantly clear of its creases.

"I'm not," she said eventually.

I shrugged, as she had done earlier, in a deliberately flippant way.

The train pulled up at the platform. She reached into her handbag and held out a business card. It had an illustration of a fountain pen embossed in gold foil on one side.

"I'll go," she said. "But take this. And call me. I really want you to. I mean it."

"Not a chance," I replied.

Chapter Thirty-Seven

The door was open, as always, and I knocked lightly against the frame. My mother was sitting in the corner of the room in her armchair. It had a pale wooden frame and polished wooden legs. I hadn't noticed the pattern before—the cushioned body decorated with electric green swirls—but it was hypnotic set against the purple of her woolen jumper. She was wearing shoes instead of slippers, and I wondered if she'd been using the moisturizer I'd bought for her birthday, because her skin looked a little softer, a little suppler.

"Morning," I said.

She smiled at me and tapped her hand against the armrest of her chair. She still spoke—sometimes—but less and less, and instead used small gestures to convey her meaning. She had once described how it felt to lose words on the way to her lips. She said it was like shepherding children to school, each word a child, but they were unmanageable and arrived at the wrong time or, sometimes, they didn't arrive at all and stood on the path spinning in circles. Or, even worse, the children who arrived were the wrong children, somebody else's, and not the ones she'd wanted. The silence was a less frightening alternative.

She turned her head toward the bed, encouraging me to sit there. I did as instructed, even though the mattress was horribly uncomfortable.

"You," she said. And what she meant was: *Please tell me about your week, about your day, about your life, about everything that has happened to you since we were last together.*

"Not a lot to report," I said. Which was the truth. I had fallen back into a very familiar routine, a reliable combination of work and home and home and work. "But I'm going to call Emma later."

My mother's face twisted slightly as I said this, and I continued talking so that she didn't have the space in which to form a reply or to begin her manic gesticulations.

"I might even pop over to see her. She's doing much better since that last trip to the hospital, but it's probably a good idea to visit even so."

My mother frowned. She'd ignored Emma's suffering until the illness was thoroughly entrenched in her bones. She hadn't known me as a wife, only as a widow. But despite these crushing shortcomings, she knew us. And perhaps in a way that only a mother can know a daughter. She knew, for example, that I was manipulating the truth because I was weak. I couldn't admit that Emma was not doing much better, but in fact seemed to me to be a little worse. Her hair was thinning, and a small bald patch had erupted by her left temple. She shivered all the time, constantly cradled in layers of jumpers and blankets and socks. She had a cough that she couldn't shake.

But I couldn't admit any of this because I couldn't stand to confront that reality. And my mother knew that. She knew, too, that Emma didn't have the strength to be much better and that, at best, she was suffering.

My mother danced her nails across the wooden armrest and then said: "John?"

"Jonathan?" I asked.

"Tomorrow," she replied.

She pointed toward the calendar hanging on her wall. I had bought it for her a few Christmases earlier, a generic calendar with dates but no days, with photographs of flowers, a different image for each month.

She had been frustrated by her inability to remember significant events—our birthdays, for example—and so we sat and filled in the most important ones. Jonathan had been dead for a couple of years and yet his dates were still my dates and I had written them in as though they were my own.

I stood up and approached the calendar. Each morning, my mother's carer moved a small yellow sticker onto the day's date. There was little use knowing when the important moments would fall if she had no idea where she stood.

The next day would have been Jonathan's birthday.

I had forgotten.

In another life, I would have been preparing for weeks, if not for months—with gifts and a cake and a card and balloons. I might have booked a table at a nice restaurant or organized a surprise party. I might have looked for wrapping paper that matched his personality—decorated with bicycles or cricket bats or animals—or collected croissants from the bakery.

And—even a couple of years ago—I would have been approaching this day with lungs about to burst from the most insurmountable grief. I would have been anxious and panicking, watching the days roll forward, thinking of all the things I'd be doing if he were alive and the things that I wasn't because he was dead.

"Yes," I said, wanting her to think that I'd remembered, that I already knew, because what sort of wife forgets her husband's birthday. "I'll probably visit him. At the cemetery. First thing. Before I see Emma. I'll take some flowers, I think. Maybe a balloon. No, not a balloon."

She nodded. "Dad?" she asked.

She sometimes—more often than not—forgot that he was no longer a part of her life. She thought that he came to see her and, occasionally, she told me about his visits. She told me that he brought flowers, although there were never any in her room that hadn't been brought by me, and that he had put up the shelves at home, although she had asked him to for years and he never had. He was well, she said, and I knew that he was, but that he was well some many miles away with some other woman who was not my mother.

Once, when we'd been squabbling about our shared responsibility, Emma suggested that I visited so regularly, not because this was my mother and not because of some sense of familial duty, but because I envied my mother's ability to forget. She didn't know that the person she loved most was no longer around.

I tended to avoid having this conversation with my mother where possible: I either ignored her questions or replied with something terribly vague, something that suggested that he might visit sometime soon without actually making a promise to pass on a message or to pop in and see him myself.

Perhaps she had never tried to remember my father's absence. Perhaps she was happy to forget.

"Marnie?" she asked instead, with a smile.

"She's doing really well," I said. "Audrey's doing great, too. She had a checkup a few weeks ago. She's putting on plenty of weight. Although I haven't seen much of her these last few weeks. They seem to be so busy."

"Motherhood," said my mother, and then she yawned, as though that, too, was part of our conversation.

"I know," I replied. "But friendships are important as well. I've been thinking that I should surprise her."

My mother nodded her approval enthusiastically.

There was a clatter from next door and then a frustrated groan as my mother's neighbor dropped something onto the floor. We heard the fast slap of shoes on tiles and then two nurses rushed past the door to assist.

"I thought I might make her dinner," I continued. "Do you remember that we used to have dinner together once a week? I'm thinking I should reinstate that. It would be nice to have a way to stay in touch. What do you think?"

In other places, with other people, the absences were filled by other, louder voices. But here mine was the only one.

"I'm thinking of leaving work early next Friday," I said. "It's fine, really. Everyone seems to be sneaking off after lunch, what with the weather and them all wanting to get away for the weekend. We have fewer people to answer the phones, but—so what? The phones are ringing less because everyone everywhere has buggered off on holiday. Anyway, I know that Marnie meets up with some other mothers at three o'clock on Fridays—she makes time for *that* weekly commitment—so I know that she won't be home. I'm planning to let myself in and cook something incredible, something that even she will be impressed by."

My mother frowned.

"I have a key," I said. "So, no, don't get the wrong idea. I wouldn't be breaking in." I laughed and it felt awkward.

My mother began to shake her head.

"She gave it to me," I said. "What's the matter with you?"

"No," she said, and her head shaking became more vigorous. "No."

"Don't be like that," I said. "It's a good idea. It'll be a nice surprise."

"A key," she insisted.

"Yes, a key," I said. My mother stopped shaking her head and stared right at me.

I was the responsible adult in my family and yet she still occupied this traditional omniscient mothering role with eyes that sharpened in the way that only a mother's can and a head tilt that demanded answers. It took her weeks to accept that my father had really left—we were sure he was bluffing—and when she finally did, she fell apart. He sent us a postcard from a Thai beach explaining that he had a new number now and that he wouldn't be sharing it with us but that he thought we ought to know that he was no longer ignoring our calls and messages but simply not receiving them. She cried and drank too much and shut herself in her bedroom, and I went in regularly to leave water bottles on her bedside table and load microwave meals in the fridge. She hadn't been much of a mother then.

"It's fine," I said. "Don't get all worked up."

She slapped her hand against her wooden armrest, hard, and she flinched, snapping it back against her chest, trying to shake out the pain.

"Stop that," I said. "Stop that right now. What are you doing?"

She slapped her other hand against her face and then knocked her beaker of water onto the floor from the standing tray beside her.

I jumped up and rushed over. "What's wrong with you? Stop making such a mess."

"Key," she hissed.

"I've only just been given it," I said. Which was the truth. "This isn't about— This hasn't got anything to do with—"

A nurse paused in the doorway. My mother and I turned to stare.

"Morning, Jane," she said to me. "Morning, Helen," she said to my mother. "What's all this about?"

My mother slapped her hand against her thigh again. She stared at me, wanting to say something but unable to, incapable of finding the right words to express that want.

"What's the matter now? Your daughter's here to visit you. It's a lovely treat." The nurse knelt on the floor in front of my mother and took her hands, holding them together so that the slapping ceased.

"Key," groaned my mother. "Key."

The nurse looked at me and I shrugged.

"I'm afraid I've no idea what's set her off," I said.

"Oh, dear," said the nurse, assuming responsibility for the chaos. "Well, I'm afraid I'm not sure either. What on earth's got her so upset? Why don't you take a few deep breaths, sweetie?" Her voice was soothing. "There you go. We'll work this all out in just a minute, but let's get you all sorted first. Because we've had a lovely week, haven't we? The hairdresser's been in and this is looking glorious now, isn't it?" She gestured toward my mother's hair with a wild sweep. "Did you tell Jane all about that, did you? We're all ready for visitors, aren't we, so we are?"

"Key," my mother insisted, still glowering at me.

"Right, all right, then," said the nurse, sitting back on her heels. "What do you need? You want a key? Do you want me to open the window, is that it?"

She was thinking the worst of me: that I'd had the key all along, that I was lying to her now.

My mother slammed her hand against the tray and the whole contraption toppled to the floor, sending her tissues, her water jug, and her framed picture spinning across the room.

The nurse looked at me. "Perhaps we should—"

"That's fine," I said, standing up. "Not to worry. I'll be back next week. Perhaps a bad night's sleep or something."

I was losing it, losing control, making mistakes.

I had told her before that I didn't have a key. And—worse than that—I'd said that if I did have a key, I'd have used it to save his life. Which was nonsense. I'd used that key to take his life, and she now knew it.

I wasn't lying now, but I'd lied before, and she'd caught me in my own web.

"Dad?" said my mother, and I turned to face her. She was asking for him because she needed him. She wanted him to step in, to be my father. She knew not to trust me, and she knew that she was too weak, too frail, to put this right.

"You know he's not coming," I said in my most sympathetic voice. "We've talked about this. He doesn't live here anymore. Do you remember? He hasn't been part of our family for years."

And then I left.

It was only afterward, on my way home, that I found myself wondering if she wasn't reprimanding me at all, if she wasn't trying to punish me, if she wasn't angry but afraid. Was she protecting me instead? Was she warning me, telling me to be more careful, to watch myself, to not get caught?

Because isn't that what a mother would do?

She was frightened for me. She had looked inside me and seen that something was broken, noticed my fractures, and acknowledged that I might not be the very best version of myself. And, despite that, she still wanted to protect me.

Chapter Thirty-Eight

When I arrived home, I called Emma, but she didn't answer and so I watched three movies and ordered takeout and then went to bed. I called her again the following morning and there was still no answer, and I thought nothing of it because she was probably asleep—she was so weak and often exhausted—and because she often isolated herself when things felt overwhelming.

I called her again on Monday after work and she still didn't answer, and I decided to head over to her flat with some fruit—she'd occasionally eat a few slices of apple, even in her very worst weeks—and to remind her that I loved her and that I wanted to help.

At no point over those three days did I for a moment consider that she was in trouble, in danger, that something was wrong.

I arrived and knocked on her door. There was no response.

The police later asked me if I could smell anything at this point and, although I'll never forget that repugnant stench, I didn't notice it then.

But I did begin to feel afraid. I knew in that moment that something bad had happened.

I went back downstairs and found the security guard. He'd been hired to patrol the area after a young man had been stabbed in the nearby car park. He was perched on a low brick wall and I interrupted the film he was watching indiscreetly on his phone to ask for help. He sighed loudly and said that there was nothing he could do, that I needed to come back with the police.

I called them immediately and spoke loudly, explaining that my sister was vulnerable, hospitalized only a few months earlier, virtually housebound, and that I couldn't get through to her at all. I stood there in front of the security guard, pacing, interrupting him further, while waiting for the police to arrive.

I felt sort of ridiculous, because while I was absolutely sure that something was terribly wrong, I couldn't shake the fear—the hope, too—that I was unnecessarily making a fuss.

The police arrived and I think that they knew, too, that she was dead.

At their insistence, the security guard contacted the maintenance man, who accompanied us up to the flat.

"You want to wait here?" asked the policewoman. "We can go in first."

I shook my head. "It's fine," I said. "I want to be there."

I knew that my little floret of hope was wrong, that she was dead, and I didn't want to be a coward this time, to look away because I was afraid.

They opened the door and I stepped inside and then I smelled it, and I walked in and she was lying on the sofa, swollen thicker than she'd ever been before, her skin mottled and gray, her eyes wide open, flies swarming and one sitting just above her eyelid.

I stood and stared, and the policewoman rushed past me to feel for a pulse but we all knew then that there wasn't one. The maintenance man retched behind me and I heard him rush back onto the balcony.

I had known for years that she was going to die.

That sounds morbid, and perhaps it is, but she was terminally ill. She had a disease from which she would never recover. There was only one outcome.

The policewoman stood up and shook her head and then walked toward me and put her arm around my waist and turned me around and led me back toward the staircase.

I wasn't afraid. I knew what to expect. I had experienced grief and I was ready.

"Is there anyone I can call for you?" she asked me.

This time there was no one at all.

Here are some of the things that you have when you have others, things that I no longer have: the steady, reassuring, harmonious hum of someone somewhere who cares; the reflex that reaches toward the story, the retelling, when something goes laughably wrong; the someone you'd call from the side of the road, the hospital, the back of a police car; the knowledge that you'll never lie dead in your bed unfound for long because someone somewhere is searching.

What is it to live without these things? Without love and laughter and friendship and hope?

I don't want to know.

I don't want to live that life.

I'm making a choice—that sounds bold; it feels bold—to recapture those things, whatever it takes, to make this life something worth living.

I won't live like this anymore.

Which means that things are going to have to change.

The
Seventh Lie

Chapter Thirty-Nine

Emma died less than a week ago.

That's not very long, is it?

I'm still in shock. I must be.

And yet, at the same time, I think that I've already reached that theoretical final stage of grief. I know that she has gone; I can accept that she has gone.

I had always known, I suppose, that she would never grow old. I never assumed that she would become one of those ghoulish women with crepe-paper skin lying on a hospital gurney. It just never felt likely. Perhaps because she was already, in so many ways, like those old women tucked down hospital corridors.

She spent so much time alone. I had never before seen her as weak as she'd been in those last few weeks. Her bones seemed so frail. Her back ached and her knuckles were swollen and arthritic. She struggled to climb the stairs to her flat. It was her hips, she said. She suffered from such a complex menagerie of ailments that most of her adult life was spent balancing precariously at the boundary between life and death.

And so I had known for a very long time that this was coming. I could see it there in the stars every night, shining the truth, a moment waiting to be decreed. It is not the worst way to lose a loved one.

Those deaths that appear unexpectedly—the bolts of light against a dark night sky—are far worse. You glance out the window and suddenly it's there in front of you, brighter than any of the other stars and falling fast. There's no time to prepare or to ground yourself before the earth shifts beneath your feet.

Those are the deaths that you cannot accept. They are the fiercest and they land the hardest, destroying other lives and other futures and trailing devastation. Because you feel it all at once, in just one moment, as a life glides through the cracks in the earth like liquid through clasped fingers.

I returned home immediately after discovering her. I cried, but only a little. And then I fell asleep.

I woke up early—too early—and I felt horribly imbalanced, as though all the pieces that had made up my life before that moment had shifted position overnight. I pulled on my jeans and a jumper and went out into the street to remind myself that the trees were not shaking and that their roots weren't quivering underground and that the pavement wasn't being slowly peeled away from the surface of the earth. I wanted to remind myself that this was not the worst, that I had already survived far worse.

I saw that the sky was black, lit only by the moon shining overhead and the sharp, warm glow of streetlamps. I marched through the city, into the small squares of suburb hidden within. Parked cars were lined up along the curb, their wheels snug against the lip of the sidewalk. I walked past the curry house with its neon sign sparking fiercely against the night, the supermarket, its door chained closed and a single fluorescent bulb flickering within. I passed two real estate agents, three hairdressers, and saw that the city was unchanged.

I returned to my flat and I saw flecks of dust floating in my bedroom and in the kitchen and I started to clean. Because life doesn't recognize small, individual losses. The dust still gathers. I had a shower and put on my favorite pajamas and I sat on the sofa and I didn't move except to use the bathroom and to refill my wineglass and to make a few slices of toast. I told myself to be patient, to persevere, that this, too, would pass.

The following evening, I dragged a dining chair into my bedroom and stood it against my open wardrobe and clambered up, looking for the old photograph albums created by my mother decades earlier, when we were still a family. I found them there: thick and dusty and bound in red leather.

I sat on my bed and leafed through the pages, trying to find photographs of Emma and me together. There were dozens. There was one of me in denim dungarees and pink sandals nestled into the corner of an armchair, holding her in my arms and across my thighs. She must have been only a few weeks old, because there were still tubes bent into her nose and curled across her cheeks.

One was taken against a brick wall, the two of us hand in hand in matching school uniforms. She was standing beside me, her head at my chest. There was a lovely one of us sitting in a field, sausage rolls and sandwiches and biscuits laid out between us on a tartan blanket, a Frisbee in her fist, and cows standing sturdy in the background. There was one of us in matching orange swimsuits at a waterpark with monstrous slides twisting behind us. Then, her little body was a miniature replica of mine: the same straight thighs, the same square shoulders. There were two festive photographs toward the back of the album. In the first we were sitting side by side in our pajamas, presents piled around us in colored paper, the tree glittering behind us, and these bright, excited grins on our faces. In the second we were in matching duffel coats and Wellington boots beside a snowman with a carrot for a nose and twigs for arms. And, at the very end of the last album, one of us in front of our final family home, on the day we moved in, standing between our parents.

I knew that I needed to tell my mother.

It was a Wednesday. I had never visited her on a Wednesday before, but I knew that I shouldn't wait until Saturday. I went to the station and I boarded the train, and I saw my own face in the window and that my eyes were red and swollen and my skin puffy and gray. I rubbed at my cheeks to revive them. I tried not to cry on the journey in the hope that they might look a little better by the time I arrived.

I pressed the buzzer at the desk, and the receptionist approached me and sighed loudly when I said that I needed to speak to my mother and that it was an urgent matter.

"We weren't expecting you today," she said.

"As I said," I repeated, "it's urgent."

"She might be in the dayroom—"

"She won't be."

"We have allocated visiting hours . . ."

She trailed off as I turned and walked down the corridor toward my mother's room.

She didn't seem surprised to see me. She smiled as I sat down at the end of her bed; she probably thought it was the weekend. She was wearing that blue cardigan again, the sleeves rolled up around her elbows, and it seemed as though she still had her pajamas on underneath.

"I need to talk to you," I said.

She nodded.

"It's not good news," I said.

She nodded again.

"Mum," I said, "it's really bad news—the worst."

I hadn't called her "Mum" in years. The word always felt unnatural in my mouth, as though it didn't belong to the woman in front of me.

She tilted her head to the left. She nodded again, more vigorously this time, urging me to say it, to tell her, to stop this unnecessary stalling.

"It's about Emma."

She stared at me. I continued.

"I went to see her," I said. "Like I said I would, to check that she was okay. She hadn't been answering her phone. And when I turned up, she didn't answer her door. I had to call the police eventually because no one would let me into the flat, and then they arrived. They opened the door."

I wanted her to say something, but she sat silent, and so I continued to tell her what had happened, reeling through the moments that happened next, my thoughts, my fears, all the ways this might have ended differently. I knew that she was bewildered, but I couldn't slow down. I told her that her daughter was dead in words I'd never used before, words that were waiting within me but that I'd hoped would stay there always.

"Mum," I said, "she's gone. They think it was her heart."

I think that then she finally understood, because she gasped and her eyes took on this wild, startled stare. She opened and closed her mouth, and then she turned away from me.

I tried to hold her hand, but she snatched it away.

I tried to speak to her, but she began to hum very quietly, and I knew that she wasn't listening.

She wouldn't look at me again after that. I stepped toward her, bent my head to see into her eyes, but she gazed, unfocused, as though looking right through me.

I knew that this was it, that the fungus she'd been fighting for the last few years was going to sprawl unimpeded across her brain. Holding on to herself had been such a battle; it required so much effort, every single day. And it wasn't going to be worth it anymore.

And so I left.

Chapter Forty

I have been my mother's only family for so many years. I have been her husband, her elder daughter, and her younger daughter, too. And yes, I begrudged it sometimes. And yes, it was unfathomably boring going to see her every weekend. And yes, it was frustrating that no one else felt guilty enough to do it.

They were all so selfish. They didn't give a shit. They did not give a shit.

I shouldn't have given a shit, either. I shouldn't have fucking bothered; it was a waste of my time and my patience and my life, spending it with her and thinking I was doing something good and being something better and sacrificing for her and then the fucking cheek of her being unable to be there for me.

Oh.

I'm sorry.

Did I frighten you?

Please don't cry.

I discovered my sister dead at the beginning of the week. And my mother retreated into her dementia two days ago. So if anyone should be crying right now, I really think it should be me.

She couldn't exist without her younger daughter. She couldn't exist for me.

It has been a very bad week.

This morning I received a message from Marnie. She said that she was very sorry but that she needed to cancel our dinner this evening, which seems to be the norm nowadays. Her excuse—and there's always a good one, something that's hard to challenge—is that Audrey has been unwell and was awake all of last night with a temperature over one hundred degrees.

I replied saying not to worry at all about me and sent love and get-well wishes.

But I didn't feel sympathetic. I simply felt sad. Because we weren't children with paper cups and a ball of string stretched between our bedroom windows anymore. We were so far apart, so disconnected, so far removed from each other's lives.

Valerie had talked about a wrecking ball, as though there was something somewhere that would be the death of this friendship. I wanted to make our walls strong, sturdy, so safe that nothing—even something substantial—could shatter those bricks. I needed to reinforce our friendship, to underpin it and make it something that could withstand the force of the truth.

I was going to weave Valerie's various findings into our conversations in a very nonchalant way, mentioning some noisy neighbors, that the walls and floors of her building were desperately thin, that sounds seemed to proliferate between the apartments. I planned to refer very casually to my week in the flat—to refer to my stay in some way: the creaking of the pipes at night or the ticking of the clock in her bedroom—and to be shocked by her inevitable surprise.

"Charles never told you?" I'd say. "It was his suggestion."

I would tell her about the encounter on the train. I would reveal—and this bit at least would be true—that I had been followed, stalked even, by that menacing journalist and ask if she thought I ought to call the police. *Valerie.* I would say her name and I wouldn't be afraid. Because this time her story would belong to me. And I'd be building her into something else, into someone unreliable, into a liar.

But I needed to spend time with Marnie in order to do these things.

While I was disappointed that she had canceled, I felt sure that she'd have time for me once she knew about my sister, about my mother. Because while death is the ultimate divider, it also unifies. You never know how loved you are until you're at the epicenter of a grief so tall and wide that you cannot see beyond its edges. Because then, very quickly, faces begin to appear at the tops of those walls, passing down cards and letters and flowers and food. And those people are your people and they find a way to pull you out.

Marnie found a way to pull me out the first time.

I knew that she could save me again.

A friendship like that matters. You don't give up on a love like that.

Valerie, too, seemed entirely unable to give up on a love like ours.

I discovered her waiting in the lobby of my building earlier today. I'd been to the supermarket and I didn't notice her at first, but she called out to me after I'd collected my mail. She was perched on an old office chair that was awaiting collection, spinning in circles and leaving grubby footprints on the freshly painted walls. She had a new tattoo—a small illustration of a flower—beneath her left earlobe. Her jeans were loose, ripped at the knees, and she was wearing a tight black jumper.

She stopped spinning and smiled. "Fancy seeing you here," she said, pulling her legs up to sit cross-legged on the seat. "I wanted to talk to you," she said, "about last week."

"This isn't a good time," I replied, standing by the doors to the elevator, my mail gripped in front of my chest. I wasn't surprised to see her. I should have been, really, in a space that felt so completely my own, but something had shifted between us. I knew her a little better now— her doggedness—and so she couldn't shock me in quite the same way.

"It's important," she said. "You upset me."

I laughed; I couldn't help it. It felt lovely, a burst of relief, although the grief and the guilt quickly followed. "I upset you?" I said. "Really?"

"On the train," she replied. "When you said all that about me being jealous."

"Aren't you?" I asked.

"No, I am," she replied. "But that isn't the point."

There was something childlike in her sincerity, in her presence there, in the simplicity of what she was saying. In the preceding weeks, I'd tracked her through the internet, following her from her school days— she'd written a piece on pond life at sixteen that featured on the school's website—and to university, where she'd edited the campus newspaper. I found her early social media platforms: her top friends and her interests and the list of people she'd like to meet. I traced her change in hobbies and homes and habits. She had taken up outdoor swimming in her twenty-ninth year. She went at least once a week. She had moved to Elephant and Castle at thirty after her marriage had ended. She'd had a new tattoo inked on her skin every birthday since; the one at the back of her neck had been her first.

But what was perhaps most striking—it's something that didn't register until that moment—was that every single one of her top-ranked friends, recorded as such at seventeen, had been absent ever since. They didn't feature on Instagram. They weren't following her on Twitter.

"Just answer me this and then I'll let myself out," she continued. "How are you still such good friends?"

I didn't reply.

"Come on," she said. "This is it. The last question I'll ask you. Because it doesn't make sense to me. To have a best friend. At our age. It's a bit infantile, isn't it?"

"I think it's quite special," I said.

"That isn't what I think," she began. "Because it isn't real, it—"

"Don't you have any old friends?" I asked. "Who are so much a part of you that you can't remember your life without them in it?"

"No," she said. "I don't."

"That sounds very lonely," I replied.

She shrugged and uncrossed her legs, dropping her feet back onto the floor.

"I think," she tried to continue, "that—"

"Not even one?" I asked.

"I want to talk about you," she said. "I'm interested in you."

"But I'm not interested in you," I replied, holding my mail out in front of me, trying to seem indifferent. There was a letter from the bank, another from my university. There was a scrawled note from a resident who lived on the ground floor of the building insisting that we all take more care to close the front door *properly*.

I looked back at her and she was grinning. "And yet you're asking me plenty of questions," she said. "I know you, Jane. You wish that I didn't."

"You don't know me at all," I said, but I could feel the balance of the conversation slipping, she taking control, pulling at my strings.

She shrugged. "You're lonely. Has she canceled your plans for this evening? I wonder if she knows how upset it makes you. I don't expect she does. She doesn't know you like I do, you see. And—"

"I need to go," I said. I turned toward the elevator and I pressed the button.

She laughed. "If you say so. But if I know you—and I think that I do—then there's nowhere that you need to be."

"Are you done?" I asked, as one of the elevators creaked down through the shaft, inching toward us.

"Not yet," she said. "I came here to tell you something else. Don't you want to know what it is?"

"No." I pressed the button again.

"That's a lie. I know that you do."

"Go on, then," I said.

I could pretend to myself—and to you—that this was a ploy. I could say that I encouraged her purely to accelerate the conversation, simply to give her the space to say her bit in the hope that she might then leave. But she was right, of course; I wanted to know.

"I'm done following you." She paused and looked at me. "That doesn't even get a smile?"

"I don't care."

"You do. You're relieved. Well, that's it. What I wanted to say. It isn't that this investigation is finished. It isn't. I still want to make sure that Marnie discovers the truth. Because it's so much more than what was in my first message, isn't it? There's so much that she doesn't know. But I'm not in a rush anymore."

"Valerie—"

"You're going to tear this thing down all by yourself."

"Oh, for—"

"I'll write about it then."

The elevator juddered into position and the doors cranked open. I stepped inside.

"Call me when it's over," she whispered.

Chapter Forty-One

I haven't been to work the rest of this week. Duncan sent me an angry email about neglecting my responsibilities. I received a concerned text from Peter. I didn't reply to either.

I have, I suppose, been feeling very sorry for myself and today has been the worst, the culmination of so much bad news.

But then, unexpectedly, things started to look a little brighter. Just as I was beginning to feel hungry, starting to think about dinner, I received a phone call from Marnie. She was frantic, flustered, flapping, as she so often is, unable to hold a calm and measured conversation. She said that Audrey's temperature had shot up again, that they'd managed to get a last-minute appointment with their doctor—who was really very good, always willing to bend the rules for a baby—and that he'd diagnosed an ear infection and she had a printout of the prescription, but they'd also sent a copy to the pharmacy. Would I mind, she said, because it was a pharmacy between our flats, open for a little longer still, and would that be okay?

"Of course," I said. "I'll be with you as soon as I can."

I pulled on my old jeans and this sweater and my dark brown boots, and I walked to the tube station in the rain, and I sat in a carriage full of families in dripping anoraks and with condensation clouding the windows and I felt hopeful. Because this was good news, wasn't it? Here was the reunion, the remedy, a way to rebuild what felt so broken.

I knew exactly what was going to happen. I could picture her face when she discovered what had happened to Emma: her shock, her sadness. I could see her boiling the kettle and ordering takeout and then deciding that tea wasn't the right tonic, not for this wound, and opening a bottle of wine instead. Audrey would fall asleep quickly—the antibiotics, the painkillers—and then we'd unpack this sadness together.

But it wasn't quite so straightforward. Because I went to the pharmacy, as instructed, and discovered that it had closed an hour earlier than we'd expected. The sign on the door was accurate—*Fridays: 8 a.m.–7 p.m.*— but somehow the messages had been mixed, the information muddled. I called Marnie. I said that I'd continue to hers, collect the printed prescription, and find another pharmacy. She started to panic—because what if there was no other pharmacy, no way of finding the right medication tonight?—and I reassured her that everything would be fine, and I envisaged a moment, sometime later that evening, when she would instead be comforting me.

I boarded the next train and by the time I reached her station there was a sprawl of gray across the sky, the buildings, the tarmac. I followed my ordinary route to her apartment, through the passageway and past the small row of shops. And all of those steps, all of those moments, were positive. These were my places, the path to my people. I cried briefly—which isn't unusual for me at the moment—but it was in a strange, sort of cathartic way.

I met your neighbor in the lobby. Do you remember the man with the briefcase, rushing off to work the day you were born? He had just returned from the office and was standing in the doorway, pulsing his umbrella into the street to shake off the droplets. He acknowledged me with a small smile and an even smaller nod.

Jeremy greeted me with a quick wave.

I felt like I belonged.

I knocked on the door and she opened it and she seemed pleased to see me.

"You're here," she said, and she smiled.

She was wearing dark jeans and a cream T-shirt, slack at her hips but snugly cuffed around her upper arms. Her hair was scraped into a loose bun and, as always, the shorter strands had fallen loose at the front. She looked beautiful.

"I'm so sorry," she said. "They said eight o'clock. I'm sure they said eight o'clock."

The flat was impeccable: the floors were shining, and the surfaces were cleared of all debris, and I didn't recognize a single thing that had belonged to Charles.

"Is something the matter?" she asked, and she leaned in close toward me, as though to get a better look. "Have you been crying?"

I suppose I must have nodded.

"What is it?" she asked, ushering me into the living room.

Audrey was lying on a yellow mat on the floor, wearing only a nappy and with her cheeks flushed and pink.

"Here," Marnie insisted. "Sit down. What's going on?"

She stood in front of me and I looked at her black leather belt and its gold clasp and I tried to concentrate. I wasn't crying anymore, but my eyes were sore. I wondered if they were red or framed by black smudges.

I sat on the sofa and hugged a gray cushion to my chest.

"I've had a terrible week," I said. "Emma . . ."

I didn't know how to finish the sentence, but then I didn't need to say anything further.

"No," Marnie said, in a breath. "Oh, God. When? What happened? Why didn't you call me?"

"I found her."

"Jane!"

"On Monday."

Marnie paced her living room, running her fingers through her hair, circling the coffee table. It had wooden legs and a glass top, and when I looked closely, I could see that there were small smears—fingerprints and watermarks, white rings from mugs and glasses—spread across the surface.

"You should have called me," she said. "I'd have come straight over. I can't believe this. How did they . . . Have you told your mum?"

Marnie shut the doors to the balcony and then pulled the curtains over the glass. The room felt suddenly smaller, without the noise of car horns and voices on the sidewalk below.

It was just us.

"She's barely there," I replied. "It felt as though she disappeared instantly the moment I told her. She wouldn't look at me after that. She wouldn't listen to me. She was still sitting there, just as she'd been a few minutes before, but she was completely gone."

"Oh, Jane, I'm so sorry." Marnie sank down onto the sofa beside me.

"It makes sense," I replied.

"It doesn't make sense," Marnie said. "I mean . . . how does it make any sense at all?"

"She's always adored Emma, hasn't she? And whether it's the dementia or . . . What does it matter? She's never been there to support me before."

Marnie secreted a small squeak from the back of her throat. "What an awful thing to happen," she said. "This is terrible. I mean . . . You poor thing. This must have been such a shock. Have you been at work?"

I shook my head.

"You've been at home? All week? By yourself? Why didn't you . . . ?" She grabbed my hands and her fingernails were painted in pink polish and they were so long that they tickled at my skin as she warmed my knuckles between her palms. "I could have been there," she said. "I could have taken care of you. I hate thinking that you've been going through this on your own."

"It's not so bad," I said.

"Don't be ridiculous," she said, slapping me on the arm. "It's crazy to be on your own after such a . . . such a trauma. I'm always—I've always been—just at the end of the phone. You should have called. But that doesn't matter now. I'm here. I'm here. I'm always here. When is the funeral? Will your mother come? Do you need help organizing it? Or with her place? What can I do?"

"I've agreed to clear out her flat tomorrow," I said. "They have someone new moving in on Monday. I hoped it wouldn't be such a rush, but they're in such demand—they're so cheap, you know, and—"

Audrey began to whimper and within seconds she was screaming. Her little face was a painful red, her little fists clenched and pounding at the floor, her feet flailing in the air.

"Oh, I know, I know," said Marnie, rushing to pick her up. "I know you feel awful, my poor little darling." She bounced Audrey on her hip, spinning slowly, facing me and then turning away, but never looking my way. "I know, I know." She held the back of her hand against Audrey's forehead. "Oh, my little one, you're burning up again. What time is it?" She glanced at the clock hanging on the wall, its thick roman numerals, its thin metal hands. "Yes, let's take something to sort this fever. And Mummy will get that prescription for Auntie Jane and we'll have you back to your normal self in no time."

They disappeared toward the kitchen.

"Jane," she called, "will you look for one that's open?"

I told myself to stay calm, to be patient, not to read a truth that wasn't there into the sense of abandonment that was filling my lungs, the panic that was crackling through me. I forced myself to do as she'd asked, and I found only one pharmacist open nearby. It was just a few miles from the flat, but it wasn't close to a train station and there were no bus stops in that area, either. I could hear Audrey squalling, Marnie's incessant platitudes—"There, now. Don't cry. Mummy's here"—and I felt a rage building within me and I tried to suppress it.

"Well?" she said as she came back in, and she frowned as I explained the problem, that it would take me over an hour to get there—I'd have to walk most of it—and perhaps even longer to get back.

"Oh, this is ridiculous," she said. "We're in one of the biggest cities in the world and I can't find a fucking pharmacy that's in any way accessible. Okay. Right. I'm going to put her down and then I'll have to do it myself. I'll drive. That'll be quicker. And you'll stay here with Audrey? Is that okay?"

I nodded.

"Good," she said. "Give me a few minutes."

They went upstairs and I turned on the television and I tried to find something that I wanted to watch, and there were so many choices but nothing that felt even vaguely appealing. I went to the fridge and there was a bottle of white wine, so I opened it—I didn't think she'd mind— and poured myself a small glass. I looked through the cupboards, trying to find a DVD or a book that appealed, but I couldn't concentrate properly. Five minutes passed. And then ten. I stared into the black of the television screen, a dark void in the center of the fireplace.

"Okay," said Marnie, rushing back in. "She isn't asleep—I'm so tired that I can't quite believe either of us will ever sleep again; she's totally wired—but at least she's calmer now. The crying's stopped and that's a start." She rushed around, gathering her purse and her phone and the car keys and pressing them into her black leather handbag. "I think that's everything," she said. She dragged her trench coat from the wooden peg in the hallway and pulled it over her shoulders. She pointed up the stairs. "Will you check on her in a few minutes? Make sure that her temperature's dropping? There's a thermometer in there: one of those ones for the ears. If she gets too riled up, try feeding her. It's in the fridge if you need it. Her change bag is underneath the stairs, but I think there's everything in her room already. Right. I'm off. I'll be back in no time, half an hour at most. We'll talk properly when I'm back. I'm so sorry, Jane. I won't be long."

I didn't say anything. I couldn't think of anything to say. I felt the most incredible disappointment and I thought I might feel angry, but I didn't. I was simply sad.

So I came up here, to your bedroom.

And I started to tell you this story.

Because it's something that you deserve to hear.

This, after all, is the story of how you came to be, of your life, and the people that led us both to this moment. It was meant to be a story about your father, about his inadequacies, about his death. It was meant to be a story about your mother, about her brilliance, and all the little ways that our love has sustained us both. It was meant to reassure me, to remind me, to make this evening feel less unforgivable.

But it wasn't and it hasn't.

Chapter Forty-Two

There are plenty of things that make you feel worse when they ought to make you better. Takeout, for example. It feels wonderful in the moment: the sharp tomato base of a pizza, acidic mango chutney with a poppadum, crispy-duck pancakes. But it weighs heavy within you. It never feels quite as good afterward as you thought it would before you ate it. I had anticipated that my conversation with Marnie would follow a very different path. I didn't expect to feel so much worse afterward.

Because I thought I knew her. If you'd have asked me, I'd have said that I could accurately predict her response to just about any conversation. I could tell you, for example, that she'd like her burger cooked medium-well, extra cheese, and yes, please, to tomatoes. I could tell you that she'd roll her eyes if you asked about her parents, no matter who you were, no matter what your question. I could tell you that she'd deliver her copy after the deadline you'd set, but that it'd be no more than a few hours late. I could tell you that she wouldn't call you back, and not to bother leaving a message, because she was unlikely to ever listen to it. I could tell you that she couldn't—absolutely wouldn't—eat a pickle, and that she'd be much happier if you'd eat yours quickly so that she didn't have to see it sitting there on your plate.

All of these things are still true.

And yet that conversation was not at all what I'd expected. I had scripted it, both of our parts, perfectly—her concern, her support, the way her attention would be focused on me—and then without warning she had improvised.

I feel disappointed. I feel afraid. I suppose I am confused.

I know that you're unwell. And I'm not stupid. I understand that it's her responsibility to ensure that you have the correct medication, to care for you, to mother you. But to cut me off in the middle of a sentence, to move so seamlessly onto something else, to minimize my loss so overtly, so insensitively? I don't think these are things that a best friend should do. Do you?

She sent me a message, more than an hour ago, to say that the pharmacy was closed, that there was a sign on the door that said FAMILY EMERGENCY—OPEN ON MONDAY and that she was going to find another one, and then I turned off my phone because I wanted it to be just us and our story, and because I needed space to think, to unravel my anguish alone.

My father always said that when you fall in love with someone, you should do your very best to love them just a little bit less than they love you. It's the only way to protect yourself, he would have said.

But it's too late for that now. Could I walk out of this flat in a few hours' time and never look back, never call either of you again? I don't think so. It's too hard to unravel a love this big. I wouldn't know how to unwind the threads of it that are woven through my ribs and my joints and my muscles. And even if I could, I wouldn't want to.

Anyway, my father was wrong. I think that if you love someone too much, you should do whatever it takes to make them love you, too. And I do love her: her openness, her warmth, her confidence, and the brightness that emanates from within her. None of those things have changed. But they aren't enough anymore. She is open—but for you—warm—but for you—loving—but for you.

She shines no light for me anymore.

Am I allowed to say that I wish your mother loved me as much as she loves you?

Perhaps not.

But it's true.

Because she used to. It was together that we discovered friendship and realized that it was different, better than our relationships with those who were obliged to love us. We found that it anchored us in our own lives. And then, years later, we relinquished it. I wish I could tell you that you weren't going to make these same mistakes, but you will, because we all do. We all sacrifice the best loves in pursuit of something better.

Oh.

Oh, no.

That's it, isn't it?

I didn't know there was more. I couldn't see it.

But I'm right, aren't I?

It makes such perfect sense.

You extricate yourself from your family and then from your friends, limb by limb, bone by bone, memory from memory, as your one becomes part of a different two, part of a romantic love. I thought that was it: the final stage. I didn't see that the pattern repeats one last time. That it isn't a thread, but a circle, that one stage feeds into the next, until you end up standing in the spot where you started: that it returns, again, to family.

You craft new limbs and new bones and you are not one person anymore because, this time, you truly are two. Your skeleton houses another life. It exists within your own. And that can never be undone. Those limbs and bones—that new being—will exist beyond your body and a part of you will forever live outside yourself. Your heart is now two hearts and one of them is always somewhere else.

I hadn't seen it before.

But it is you.

You have unpicked this friendship, with your tiny legs and tiny arms and that tiny heart thundering in your chest. You have created this relentless, thankless, imbalanced love.

I thought it was me—something that I had done—but it isn't; it isn't at all.

Do you remember the two women at the beginning of this story? One tall and fair, one shrunken and dark, entirely comfortable in each other's company. Do you remember their strong branches, their long, tangled roots? I've been watching that tree wither. But I can revive it. I lost my romantic love and then I crushed hers. I created a way for us to fall back into friendship. I need us to be sturdier than we've ever been, and there's only one way to achieve that.

I need to do it again.

It seems excessive. Doesn't it seem excessive? But if I do nothing, then I am stuck here in this terrible, awful life in which people voluntarily leave me because I am simply not enough to live for and that is just not the life that I want. There is only one path that will take me there, to a life worth having. And I'm so sorry, but you're not on it.

Call me if there are any problems," she'd shouted as she disappeared down the corridor, still slipping her other arm into her coat sleeve. She rounded the corner. "Take good care of my baby," I heard her sing.

"I will," I called, and the door slammed shut.

I guess that was my seventh lie.

Chapter Forty-Three

O nce upon a time, I almost had a baby of my own.

I remember the night he died. It's possible that he was a she, but he was always a he to me. I only really knew him for that one evening.

We had been out for dinner with some friends—just a few, not too many. I had invited Marnie. Jonathan had invited Daniel and Ben, whom he'd known since school, Lucy, Ben's wife, and Caro, who was the only woman in their cycling group. It had been nice. We'd gone to our local curry house and ordered far too much food, and bottle after bottle of beer, and finished the evening with tumblers of liqueur. We had hugged our goodbyes, and Marnie had said that she had exciting news, that we needed to catch up, that there was a man and that things were going well and when could we talk? Caro and her girlfriend were leaving the following morning to cycle through France and she promised to send us a postcard. Ben and Lucy were having dinner with both pairs of parents the following weekend and we all knew, although none of us said it, that he would propose to her in the next few weeks.

It was a normal evening: an enchanting, wonderful, normal evening. I really miss it, you know. When you look around a room or across a table and realize that you are surrounded by people who love you, who need you, who choose you. I miss that feeling of being wildly, unexpectedly lucky. I haven't felt that way in so long.

That night the bleeding wouldn't stop. I sat on the toilet in our small tiled bathroom and the cramps in my stomach were furious, pulsing relentlessly within me. I held my nightdress around my waist and my underwear was stretched between my ankles and flushed with a deep red stain.

I remember tears spilling onto my knees, trickling down my calves. I hadn't known that I was pregnant, so I don't suppose I was grieving, but I was frightened, trembling, my entire body quivering. And then suddenly I was angry. I remember this terrible noise, this terrible roar, from the depths of my stomach, a noise that thundered through my bones and filled that cold, sparse room.

"Jane?" I can remember him calling for me. I can remember how he sounded: I can hear him now as though he were still here. "What is it, Jane?"

I ignored him because there were no words with which to explain it.

"Jane. Please. Open the door."

I said nothing.

"Jane!" he shouted. "Unlock it. Now."

I didn't. A few seconds later he stumbled into the room accompanied by noise and chaos as the door shook on its hinges and the wood around the lock splintered and fell to the floor. I remember that he was wearing dark blue jeans. He wasn't wearing a belt and so they were loose around his waist, hanging on his hips. His gray T-shirt had a stain on the hem: yellow paint, I think. His jaw was clenched and his eyes were fixed and focused but his lips were small and scared.

"Okay," he said, as he knelt on the floor in front of me. "It's all going to be okay."

He leaned forward and kissed me on the top of my head. He was a

good man, the very best. I remember him offering me his hands and
then registering that mine were wet with blood and instinctively flinch-
ing but then forcing himself to hold his still. Because he wanted me to
know that, despite what was happening, he still had me and that ours
was still a bond—always a bond—that would never for a moment fail.

He stood and he lifted my nightdress over my head.

"I'm going to get you some new underwear," he said. "Is that okay?
Will you stay here?"

I nodded, and he smiled, the softest, smallest smile that told me not
to panic.

And then I heard him run over to my dresser. I guess he didn't want
to be away from me for very long. He returned with an old pair of
underwear—once white, now gray—and a thick cotton nightdress.

"Do you need something for . . . ?" He glanced at the clean underwear in his hand.

I nodded and pointed to the drawer beneath the sink.

"This?" He held up a sanitary pad packaged in purple plastic.

I nodded.

"Do you want to . . . ?" His eyes were begging, saying, *Please, you can
do this bit yourself*, and it makes me smile now to know that he would
have done it for me had I asked. He turned away and I wiped between
my legs, over and over again. I continued until I felt drier, but no cleaner.
I replaced my underwear and pulled my legs apart to hold the fabric
taut as I fastened the cotton pad in place. Jonathan held a flannel under
the tap. He wiped my hands, one after the other, in between my fingers, and gently around the ring he had given me. I stood up and he
eased the nightdress over my shoulders.

"I need bottoms," I said.

"As well?"

I nodded again.

"Okay," he said. "Get into bed and I'll find them."

I walked into the bedroom, my legs still sticky, the pad already damp. I pulled back the duvet and slid beneath, surprised by the sight of my hands, how clean they looked, how unaffected.

Jonathan handed me a pair of his own pajamas. They were red and green tartan with an elastic waistband. He wore them all the time: in the mornings as he drank coffee and read the newspaper, in the evenings when we lolled on the sofa watching films. I still have them.

"But they'll get—" I began.

He shook his head. "It doesn't matter," he said.

I hadn't known that I was pregnant. I thought back through our previous weekends—the places we'd been and the people we'd seen—and I realized that it had probably been a month or two but I'd been busy, happy, and the passing time hadn't registered at all.

I hadn't known—and I found this difficult to articulate at the time—but I felt as though that negated my experience. I was sad, but I couldn't justify that sadness, because how can you miss something that never was?

And yet, at the same time, it really was something: not something big, something small, but something all the same. I saw the person those few cells might one day have become. I saw a little boy who looked like Jonathan. I saw a little boy on a little bike with fair hair and a small pointed chin. I saw a little boy who wanted to hold my hand, who swung between us, who grew up beneath us, who was loved and knew it always.

A few weeks later, Jonathan returned from his final run, his last in preparation for the marathon. He was comfortable again around me; he had stopped pausing when I entered the room and glancing my way every few minutes. We ate dinner from our laps on the sofa and, because difficult conversations are often easier side by side, I told him what I wanted. That I wanted that little boy who looked like him.

And he smiled and he turned toward me and he said that he wanted that, too.

I think that Marnie would have loved that little boy. I think that she would have bought him gifts and planned adventures and taught him how to cook. I think she'd have been better for him than I am for you.

No.

I know that she'd have been better for him than I am for you.

I can't help but admit that I feel a little excited.

Because, after this, without either of you, we will be inseparable.

Chapter Forty-Four

You are lying in your crib. You are distracted by the mobile hanging from the ceiling, the gray and white felt stars dancing on twine. She made it beautiful, this room, and perfect for you. The cream roller blind with dainty birds etched in white. The shelves piled with books and toys and pictures of brightly colored animals in glossy white frames. You are very loved.

I see your mother in you, in everything about you. In the little pink lips that sit pouting on your face, matching your pink speckled onesie. In the bright blue of your eyes. In the impatient clasping and unclasping of your fists as you wait to be fed one final time before you go to sleep.

I see your father only in your long legs, your strong thighs. I remember watching as his propelled him forward through his life and into every avenue of success. He was a lucky man, you know. He had all the privilege and such great fortune, and a charm that seemed to inspire confidence. Everyone wanted to make him laugh, to smile, to be the one to provoke something good. It is an incredible advantage to be someone by whom others want to be liked. I suppose I'd have liked to have a little charm myself.

It is hard to believe that our time together is almost over.

I want you to know that I loved you first, before anyone else had seen you or even begun to know you. I saw you first. I loved you in that

space between life and not life, when you crossed the boundary between something that was not quite and something that would always
be. But I never really knew you after that, never really had a chance to
turn that initial love into something more substantial. I wanted to,
truly. I had a life planned for us.

You are falling asleep. I'm sorry; I know that it's late.

I'll be quick.

I'm not afraid of what might happen. If everything goes wrong—and
I know that it might—then I will be in the same position that I am now.
I will still be alone.

But will anyone even think to question it? Another tragedy on the
periphery of my life? I don't think so.

As I've said, I'm one of those people. I suppose Marnie is one of us
now, too.

This cushion was a gift. It once belonged to my sister. I gave it to her
when she went into the hospital, age thirteen. I made it. Ridiculous,
now, I know. Can you imagine me at a sewing machine? The embroidered cake on the front was a joke. She was amused, but our parents
were livid. They couldn't believe that I would be so insensitive when
she was so ill and it made us happy to see them so angry. She gave it to
you when you were born. Your mother had this rocking chair already,
shiny white wood, and she said that it needed something more, something human, something loved.

Right.

Stop fidgeting. Enough of that now.

It's time.

The
Truth

———————

Chapter Forty-Five

The pillow is in my hand—its scratchy fabric, its cushioned core—and I'm lowering it slowly, entirely in control, when the front door opens so frantically that it flies all the way back on its hinges. It crashes against the wall, the chain jingling as it swings, the clunk as it slams itself shut again. There is this moment then when the room is in freefall. And then it's her footsteps on the stairs and it's clear immediately that something is wrong because they are fast, pounding, and she isn't even careful to avoid the creaks, the ones with the weak wood, the ones that might wake the baby.

When she appears in the doorway, she is chaotic and her hair has fallen loose at the front, stuck against her skin. Her face is flushed and her eyes are wet, wild, bloodshot, blinking like a butterfly in flight, her lashes set by tears. She is trying to breathe, to steady herself, but she is failing and the sound she is making is weak, just a whimper.

She darts toward the crib and droplets of moisture from the surface of her coat seep into my sweater, bleeding through to my skin. "Jane!" She is shrieking. "What did you— Audrey?" She leans over the crib. "Sweetheart?" The belt of her raincoat is undone; it hangs around her calves, dripping water onto the carpet. Her hands curl around her daughter and, as they do, something falls from her pocket, tumbling onto the mattress. I step closer, to see more clearly, and there is this burst of surprise, a surge in my chest.

It is a phone.

And it is this room.

And it is me, in miniature, reflected on that screen. I move toward the crib, to balance myself on its frame, and the mirrored version of me goes, too, matching my movement.

"What is this?"

But I needn't have asked, because I am already scanning the room for the camera, the counterpart, and there it is: another phone perched on a shelf beside stuffed animals and books stacked in piles.

The shock is its own inimitable thing, like a virus stirring inside me, crawling up from my stomach like acid.

"I heard you, Jane," she says. "I heard what you said. I checked in at the pharmacy. I wanted to see that she was okay. I listened the whole way home. And if I'd not been going so fast . . ." She closes her eyes, squeezes them shut, and bites her lips together. "You were talking about Charles, and about the night he died, and then . . ." A tremor falls through her body and, in response, Audrey gurgles, kicking her legs, the flesh of her thighs jiggling, dimpling.

"It isn't what you think—" But there are no words with which to finish the sentence, no way to undo what had already been done.

"Don't," she hisses. "Another lie? Is that what you're looking for? I've been such a—"

"Marnie, I—"

"I heard everything, Jane. That you finished work early the day he died. I was so relieved that you were here, to hear your voice in this room. And then—what was it?—that you had a key. And I didn't think to question it at first; I have always assumed the best of you, never doubted you, not once in—what, twenty years?"

"I can explain—I—"

"Jane," she says.

I shudder at the sound that my own name makes, like the bark of a dog, the way it comes from the back of her throat. I see then that there is no way to disguise the truth: there are no more lies.

"I'd like you to put down the cushion," she says.

It is still hanging from my hand, soft against my thigh, and I let it fall to the floor.

She walks out of the nursery. It is so dark outside, just the streetlamps casting patterns against the sidewalk, and this room is so eerie without them in it. I feel the beginning of an almighty grief swelling within me and yet it is too soon to see it fully. I follow her.

She is at the top step, gazing down the stairs, and her coat sleeve is trembling, just slightly, almost imperceptibly, and I know that she feels it, too: this inexplicable fear.

We have held the strings and dictated the shape of each other's lives. It is a frightening thing to live with, and even more unnerving to lose. There is hope in me, then, in that moment.

Audrey gurgles—almost a giggle—and her little fist furls in an auburn curl. She tugs and Marnie turns back toward me. Her cheeks are rosy, lined by streaks of mascara. Her eyes are swollen, and the edges of her lips have blurred into the surrounding skin.

I know those features in perfect detail. But, somehow, she seems startlingly unfamiliar. There is something new here now, something more.

"Leave," she says, eventually. "Get out."

Afterward

Four Years Later

Chapter Forty-Six

J ane is sitting in her car—she has learned to drive in the intervening years—and she has stopped between the school playground
and the train tracks. She has been awake for hours—since three, almost
four—and it is still early now. The sun is there in her windshield, rising
slowly between the office blocks at the end of the road. She reclines her
seat and pulls the blanket from the backseat over her legs. A train thun-
ders past, rattling on its tracks: one of the very first of the day. The
empty windows blur together.

Jane remembers traveling by train—she used to do it all the time—
and she is relieved to live in the suburbs now, in a town three stops
from the end of the tracks, with little need to visit the city itself. She
owns a flat—her sister would have approved—in a redeveloped mansion house, carved into seven apartments, decorated in muted grays and
whites. She likes the sinister intermingling of old and new: the fireplace
with its perfect symmetry, the sleek white kitchen appliances, the in-
terlocking plastic floorboards. She hopes that there are stories hidden
in the walls, secrets silenced by a layer of plaster and a coat of fresh
paint.

Her own secrets are very quiet now. There was a moment that felt
daunting, just after things fell apart, but she'd held her nerve. She'd
told the police that she hadn't said anything of the sort—"A confession?

Certainly not!"—and that it was a shame that the baby monitoring app was nothing more than a live feed, that it hadn't recorded her words, because, if it had, it would have proved her right.

She had always been an excellent liar.

Marnie had been insistent for several months, pleading with the police to do more, to persevere, to officially investigate, but there was no evidence, they'd said, and it was the word of one woman against the word of another. But they had called Jane in a second time—probably simply to satisfy Marnie's complaints—and the officers had been almost apologetic as they went through their questions again. At the end of the interview, they talked about loss and heartbreak and how the mind was a powerful thing. And Jane had nodded, and she hadn't needed to contort her face into one of sorrow, because her grief was genuine.

There is tea in a thermos in the footwell, and she takes a sip. It is still warm. She watches as a man in a thick woolen coat drives past, signals, and stops at the gates to the school. He winds down his window, holds out a small fob, and the metal gates crank apart. After that, the roads become much busier. Commuters march past on their way to the station. Teachers park their cars and heave piles of paperwork from their passenger seats, scurrying inside to the warmth of their classrooms. It is the first day of school and there is a freshness to these proceedings.

Jane is always looking for auburn hair, twisted into spirals of red and gold, the curls that fall loose at the front. Jane is never looking for cropped black hair and yet she sees it everywhere, but never dark enough, and never that tattoo. She scans the crowd as the children begin to arrive, but they are all slightly older, accompanied by their parents, who wave rushed goodbyes at the gate. Jane sinks a little lower in her front seat, bending her legs, aware of people passing too close to her car: the children on scooters, the parents juggling bags and babies.

Jane looks up and there she is: Marnie approaching the school from the other side of the gates. She is wearing loose black trousers cropped at the ankles and bright white trainers. She is holding her blue coat closed at the collar and she walks as she has always walked: purposeful, confident, unafraid. She is talking, and Jane feels a sudden surge of envy, because she is so familiar with the movement of those lips, the rise and fall of those cheeks, the spirited shifting of that jaw.

Audrey is walking beside Marnie wearing a red duffel coat and shiny black shoes. Jane thinks that Audrey's hair, auburn, has been newly cut; it is cropped neatly around her chin. She has a small red satchel swinging from her hand and a red hat on her head.

Jane owns that hat, too. A few weeks earlier, she'd followed Marnie and Audrey to The School Shop on the high street. Marnie came out carrying bags of uniforms, and Audrey was skipping ahead excitedly wearing that hat. And so Jane went in and bought one, too, with a story of her daughter whose hat had gone missing the previous year. She had wanted to feel the fabric—a rough felt—between her fingers.

At the front gate, Marnie bends down and says something to Audrey. They look up at the teacher, who is smiling, welcoming the new students and reassuring the parents. Marnie is nervous. Jane recognizes her pursed lips, the way she is holding her hands on her hips. She wants to be standing beside her best friend, because she knows she is needed in moments like this.

Audrey doesn't seem worried at all. The teacher urges Marnie to leave—gesturing for her to go—so that Audrey will come inside, and reluctantly Marnie walks away. She turns and waves several times before she reaches the corner at the end of the road and disappears.

It is then that Audrey begins to look a little lost. She looks around.

Jane cannot remember her first day at primary school. She is fairly confident that Audrey won't remember this day in twenty years' time. But, if she does, it seems unlikely that she'll recall looking up and seeing a woman sitting in a red car watching her. She won't remember that this woman smiled and waved.

That she always smiles. That she always waves.

ACKNOWLEDGMENTS

There are many people without whom this story would not exist. The first is my husband, Malcolm Kay. You are owed so many thanks that it is impossible to represent your contribution in just a few words, but I shall try my best. Thank you for the many long walks in which you encouraged me to unravel and rebuild this narrative aloud; for your smart, insightful input; for taking care of our lives, and of me, as I lost myself in this story; for your endless confidence, your constant support, and for urging me to persevere.

Thank you to my parents, Anne and Bob Goudsmit. Mum: you have been my cheerleader, champion, and counselor. Thank you for my love of books, for reading and writing and stories. Dad: thank you for challenging me, for your never-ending generosity, and for encouraging me to find something I really loved and to pursue it relentlessly. To my sister, Kate Goudsmit, I am endlessly grateful for your fervent encouragement and honesty. There is no one else in my life who tells it as it is. To the Goudsmits, Dundases, and Kays, who have been so incredibly generous with their support.

This book is in many ways about female friendship, and I am fortunate enough to be surrounded by brilliant, intelligent, formidable women. Thank you to Eleanor Thomas and India Merrony, who mock me mercilessly but are the kindest, most loyal friends one could hope for. To Bethany Hadrill, Charlotte Piazza, Frances Johnson, Florence

Peterson, Freya Hadrill, Lois Parmenter, Lucy Gilham, and Sarah Cawthron.

I owe an incredible debt of gratitude to those who have worked tirelessly to turn this story into a book. Thank you to my agent, Madeline Milburn, who had faith in it long before I did. She is the very best an author could hope for and without her guidance, determination, and support this book would not exist. To her outstanding team: Alice Sutherland-Hawes, Anna Hogarty, Georgia McVeigh, Giles Milburn, Hayley Steed, Liane-Louise Smith, and Rachel Yeoh. To my UK editor, Lucy Malagoni, who is so wonderfully perceptive, patient, creative, and calm: I am so grateful to be working with you. And to the team at Little, Brown: Abby Parsons, Gemma Shelley, Stephanie-Elise Melrose, Rosanna Forte, all of whom have been instrumental in bringing this book to life. To my US editor, Pamela Dorman, whose wisdom, vision, and ability to identify the problem with a chapter and then—thankfully!—provide the solution are unparalleled. And to her team: Jeramie Orton, Brian Tart, Andrea Schulz, Lindsay Prevette, Kate Stark, Roseanne Serra, and the rest at Pamela Dorman Books and Penguin. A huge thank you, too, to the teams who are publishing this book in other countries across the world. I am so grateful to all of you.

Thank you to everyone at Transworld Publishers, where I wear my "editor" hat and where I have received the most incredible mentorship and made the most wonderful friends. A special mention must go to Sophie Christopher, who was a dear colleague and friend, and who, without having read a word of it, was one of this book's very first champions. You are so missed by us all.

And, finally, to the readers of this world. If you have picked up this book and reached the end, then thanks to you above all for spending your time in these pages. I hope you enjoyed it.